Never Seduce a Duke

The Mating Habits of Scoundrels

VIVIENNE LORRET

AVONBOOKS

An Imprint of HarperCollinsPublishers

NEVER SEDUCE A DUKE. Copyright © 2023 by Vivienne Lorret. All rights reserved. Printed in the United States of America. No part of this book may be used or reproduced in any manner whatsoever without written permission except in the case of brief quotations embodied in critical articles and reviews. For information, address HarperCollins Publishers, 195 Broadway, New York, NY 10007.

First Avon Books mass market printing: February 2023

Print Edition ISBN: 978-0-06-314308-1
Digital Edition ISBN: 978-0-06-314309-8

Cover design by Amy Halperin
Cover illustration by Judy York

Avon, Avon & logo, and Avon Books & logo are registered trademarks of HarperCollins Publishers in the United States of America and other countries.

HarperCollins is a registered trademark of HarperCollins Publishers in the United States of America and other countries.

FIRST EDITION

23 24 25 26 27 BVGM 10 9 8 7 6 5 4 3 2 1

Never Seduce a Duke

〰

It wasn't until then that she realized her hand had somehow found his chest. And this wasn't the first time.

She withdrew it at once. "I don't know why I am forever touching you."

He took that same hand and curled it around his telescope, the instrument substantial and weighty. Then he turned her by the shoulders and pointed toward the constellation. "I should think it quite obvious."

"Oh?" She lifted the eyepiece to search the heavens.

Then she felt him behind her, warm and solid as his arm slid along hers to guide her toward the occultation. "You are attempting to seduce me."

Seduce him? Her heart lurched, then beat faster as she abruptly remembered her role as Lady Avalon. Honestly, she had no idea how to behave like an adventuress. And yet, apparently, she must have been doing something right.

"Flirting. Only flirting," she clarified. "There will be no seduction from my quarter."

"No? So you're not trying to tempt me with every look and light caress?"

As he spoke, he adjusted her hold on the instrument, his large hand covering hers. His other settled on her waist as if to steady her. When she shook her head, the tip of his nose stirred the downy curls that dangled against the side of her neck, sending a frisson of excitement through her, and she wondered who was seducing whom.

By Vivienne Lorret

The Mating Habits of Scoundrels Series

The Misadventures in Matchmaking Series

The Season's Original Series

The Rakes of Fallow Hall Series

The Wallflower Wedding Series

For my boys, who filled the house with castles and knights
and who watched *The Sword in the Stone* until the VCR
ate the tape
and
for my brother-in-law, who generously shared his
encyclopedic knowledge of King Arthur and the knights of
the round table

Acknowledgments

This is my twentieth title with Avon and I feel so blessed to have had such a phenomenal team of remarkable individuals help me continue to make this dream happen every step of the way.

So to my editor, Nicole Fischer, and the entire team, I'd like to say thank you for everything that you do. And to Chelsey Emmelhainz for that first "call." You are all dream makers.

Thank you to Amy Halperin and the Avon art department for this stunning cover.

I'd also like to thank those responsible for my international titles and for the wonderful work you do. And thank you to the copyeditors who have painstakingly combed through every comma, word, and fact to ensure that each page is in tip-top shape.

A heartfelt thank you to my agent, Stefanie Lieberman, for keeping this dream alive.

And an immense thank you to my readers who have welcomed my stories into your hearts and homes. I am eternally grateful for your kindness and generosity, and for sharing your lives with me through your emails and posts. Sending hugs to each of you.

Warm wishes and happy reading,
Viv

"But tell me the truth, and I shall love you the better . . ."

—Thomas Malory

Never Seduce
a Duke

Chapter 1

A half-baked plan

Reclining on a bent elbow beneath the long-fringed shade of a willow tree, Margaret Stredwick eyed her travel companions with fond suspicion.

They were up to something. She was sure of it.

An outside observer would never suspect the two older women of any sort of mischief. The Parrish sisters were well-favored among the *ton*; Maeve for her refined, stately demeanor and Myrtle for her infectious, ebullient charm. And as the beloved aunts of Meg's sister-in-law, the Marchioness of Hullworth, they had quickly burrowed into her own heart as well.

But they were also meddlesome matchmakers.

It didn't escape her notice that this *supposedly* impromptu picnic had brought them to the picturesque grounds surrounding the reclusive Duke of Merleton's residence. The *bachelor* Duke of Merleton.

Not only that, but in the five hours since they'd left Wiltshire on holiday, the pair had been uncharacteristically quiet on their favorite subject—*1001 ways to procure a husband for Meg*. They had to be close to bursting by now.

"How fortuitous that our driver should happen to take a wrong turn that led us here," Meg said, pretending to be oblivious to their plot.

The aunts exchanged a decidedly guilty look.

Meg continued, absently twirling a blade of grass. "I was certain the groundskeeper would never permit us to picnic here. He spent twenty minutes complaining about the inconvenience of giving tours when there was genuine work to be done. But the two of you proved to be more determined."

Maeve, the elder sister, was perched with prim decorum on the flat surface of a sarsen stone as she smoothed a hand against the iron-gray hair that would never dare stray from her ever-impeccable coiffure. "It wasn't altogether difficult. Over the years, we've learned that there are three approaches to persuading a man: feed him, flatter him or flirt with him."

"Or all three at once," Myrtle said with a cheeky grin as she shined a green apple against the arm of her lavender day frock while a warm breeze stirred her silver-floss hair like dandelion fluff. "When the offer of sharing our picnic didn't seem to do the trick, I had to think of something. I merely opted for the small pretense of stumbling so that he would catch me. And I saw no harm in telling him how strong he was."

Meg laughed. "I believe you called him a *virile specimen of manliness*. You were positively brazen!"

"Indeed." Maeve pursed her lips and flicked a crumb from her Esterhazy skirts. "My sister could benefit from a spoonful of subtlety, to be sure."

"At our age? Pish tosh. Where would that have gotten us, hmm? Certainly, nowhere with such a promising vista." Her pointed gaze turned from her sister toward the little spired stone chapel on the grounds.

Promising vista, hmm? Most likely, the only view they were hoping to see was of Meg walking down the aisle toward a duke waiting at the altar. She'd never even met the man. And if it was up to her, she never would.

There would be no chapel in her future, and no man

waiting for her. Not any longer. Not since Daniel Prescott— her soul's counterpart—married another.

The reminder sent a sharp twinge to the center of her chest. She sighed, but more out of irritation at herself for allowing her thoughts to return to him again. After all, a broken heart wasn't something she cared to think about on holiday.

Standing, she shook out her striped skirts, then stepped over to the water's edge with a crust of leftover bread in hand. She shredded it, tossing the crumbs to a pair of pink swans and watched as they bent their graceful necks toward the lily-pad-dappled surface. "We should be on our way if we wish to make the next coaching inn by nightfall."

Their little detour had already cost them a half day, and Meg was eager for this summer of exploring the Continent to begin.

This trip would be her final foray as a debutante. One last hoorah before she put herself firmly on the shelf. Because when she returned to Wiltshire and her brother's house, she planned to devote the rest of her life to becoming a loveable— and perhaps even meddlesome—aunt to Brandon and Ellie's children.

"Oh! But we cannot leave," Myrtle interjected fretfully, lowering her unfinished apple to her lap. "We have yet to see . . . everything."

Every*thing* or every*one*? Meg wondered wryly as she brushed an errant raven curl from her forehead.

"I daresay the grounds here could rival even those on your brother's estate," Maeve supplied in her usual nononsense tone.

Well, that much was true. Meg had never seen gardens comparable to those at Crossmoor Abbey. In fact, she didn't think it possible. When the aunts had been all atwitter over the prospect of visiting a *keep*, she'd pictured a sparse, utilitarian military ruins hidden behind the ramparts. Hardly anything to stir one's excitement.

It wasn't until they'd driven over the drawbridge—*an actual working drawbridge, of all things*—then through the crenellated gatehouse that Meg had found herself awestruck.

Caliburn Keep was no medieval fortress. It was a palace of such splendor that it stole the breath from her lungs.

There was something altogether fanciful in her surroundings. The sprawling castle with Gothic arches and mullioned windows polished to mirror glass was straight out of a storybook. Set amidst a backdrop of ferns and tall sedges, lazy fronds of weeping willows that bent and swayed over the water, and flowers and trees blossoming in a myriad of vibrant colors, it was like entering a painting.

"It is quite lovely here," she reluctantly admitted, watching the swans float around the bend toward a low waterfall flanked by clusters of golden-tipped bulrushes.

"Then, it's settled," Myrtle said with relief. "After all, I'm sure it shouldn't take too much longer."

Meg turned her attention back to the aunts in time to see the older nudge the younger with her elbow. Her eyes narrowed. "*What* shouldn't take—"

"I believe Myrtle meant that it shouldn't take too long to apply to the housekeeper for a tour of the house."

"And whyever would we do that, hmm? Unless . . . the two of you are plotting something."

The elder sister sniffed. "I have no idea what you could mean by such an accusation."

"No? Well, what about the time you both dropped your handkerchiefs for that baron and then quickly darted behind me? Or when you *accidentally* nudged me into the path of that viscount in the village square?"

"I still attest that I saw a bee alight on your back," Maeve said, but she averted her gaze to the cuff of her tapered sleeve as she fidgeted with the silver button.

"Besides," Myrtle chirruped, "it isn't as though we've

given any thought to a chance encounter with the duke. Or imagined that His Grace would take one look at you in your becoming blue frock and fall madly in love with you. Or that he would be so overcome with passion that he would take your hand, drop on bended knee and . . ."

Her words trailed off when Meg huffed and put her hands on her hips. She'd known it wasn't the driver's mistake that had brought them here. This only confirmed it.

"I hate to spoil your matchmaking plot, but the grounds-keeper said that the duke wasn't even here."

"Actually, he said that His Grace was not *at home*," Maeve clarified. "Which simply means that the duke does not wish for company. I should expect no less from a man who rarely enters society."

"A hermit. How delightful," Meg said under her breath, picturing Merleton with a pallid complexion and a beard long enough to drag on the floor.

"But that is neither here nor there," Maeve continued. "Because we did not travel this way to encounter the duke at all."

"We didn't?" both Meg and Myrtle uttered in unison.

The elder Miss Parrish shook her head, her expression severe as a scholar's. "There are recipes we wish to collect. *Legendary* recipes, in fact. Nothing more. Isn't that right, sister?"

"You never told me of—"

"You've become quite forgetful in your old age, Myrtle. Why, it was just yesterday when we discussed the fables," Maeve reminded her through a tight smile.

"Ah, yes, *those* recipes."

Meg eyed the two of them. She wasn't buying it for a minute.

But that didn't stop Maeve from trying.

"You might have heard the tales of them as well, my dear," she said. "The book dates all the way back to King

Arthur's court. It is said that the pages are illuminated in gold and silver, the cover encrusted with precious gems. The recipes themselves were once touted as *divine creations that no man could resist*. They hold the power to imbue the person who sups on them with certain attributes. A knight's valiance and bravery in battle, for example, or even a maiden's steadfast love . . ."

The threads of a memory from long ago tickled the back of Meg's mind. And as she listened to Maeve speak with unmistakable reverence, gesturing with a sweep of her slender arm toward the grounds and castle walls, she felt her certainty of their plot waver.

After all, if there was one thing more important to the aunts than seeing every young person they knew advantageously married, it was finding the perfect recipe . . .

And then stealing it.

The aunts were positively unapologetic in their quest. Meg's sister-in-law, Ellie, had once revealed that the aunts had been pilfering the kitchens of fine houses for years in preparation of her long-awaited nuptials. And after Ellie and Brandon's wedding last year, the aunts had gained a level of notoriety for their selection of dishes and discerning palates.

Their success had been so great, in fact, that they'd received over a hundred requests for an invitation to the christening breakfast they'd hosted for Johnathon, the newest addition to the Stredwick family, this past spring. The unprecedented feast had been raved about in the society pages as well.

". . . and this illustrious book was the very reason that the duke's family first received their noble titles and lands," Maeve concluded.

In that instant, Meg realized that it wasn't too far-fetched to believe their reason for coming here was about a recipe. Perhaps it wasn't a matchmaking scheme, after all.

But just as the thought entered her mind, Myrtle burst forth with a clap of excitement.

"Oh, sister! We *must* have these recipes for hosting our next wed—" She stopped and cleared her throat, recovering awkwardly with "*Wed*-nesday breakfast."

Aha! Caught you!

They were likely itching to outdo themselves at their next fete. Clearly, their unexpected fame had gone straight to their heads.

But Meg was not about to be the sacrificial lamb on their altar!

Tapping the toe of her nankeen half boot on the grass, she crossed her arms. "I am not marrying the duke."

"Of course not, dear. You've never even been introduced," Maeve said with an unconcerned flit of her fingertips. "My sister and I are hardly the types to throw you into the arms of a stranger, no matter what his title and financial holdings might be."

"Oh? And what about that afternoon walk in Regent's Park with the visiting *vizconde* from Spain? I distinctly recall being driven into *his* path."

Myrtle blinked owlishly and lifted her rounded shoulders in a shrug. "Another bee?"

So, they were playing the innocents, were they?

Meg was not fooled one bit. If this detour was precisely what they declared, then she wanted them to prove it.

"Very well," she said, calling their bluff. "If we truly are here for the sole purpose of stealing a recipe, and there are no tours allowed inside Caliburn Keep, then how do you propose we do it? It isn't as though they will put up the bunting if we knock on the door."

The Parrish sisters smiled at each other.

"I do believe I just heard a challenge," Myrtle said, her cornflower blue eyes dancing with mischief as she tossed the core of her apple toward the water, then chafed her hands back and forth.

"As did I," Maeve answered with a cunning arch of her brows. "Mark my words, Miss Stredwick. We will not only gain entrance but we'll have the perfect recipe in our hands when we depart."

Meg swallowed down a sudden rise of apprehension. There was something a bit too determined in their gazes. And she wondered if it was wise to ever underestimate this pair.

Chapter 2

A recipe for disaster

After a short walk along a slender path, their skirts rustling against tussocks of striped grasses as a melody of birdsong cascaded down from the boughs of fragrant foxglove trees, they entered a manicured front garden of slate flagstone with a burbling fountain at its center.

Meg was thoroughly charmed. But this picturesque setting made the facade of Caliburn Keep even more imposing as they neared.

A high wall of ancient stones seemed to have risen from the earth in this very spot, like a mountain after an earthquake. The pale escarpment hosted a towering oaken door large enough to drive a carriage through, and lofty arches filled with mullioned windows that appeared to trap the blue sky and cottony clouds within the diamond panes.

She wasn't certain if the story the aunts had told her about the dukedom dating all the way back to the time of King Arthur was true, or even if there were actual legendary recipes. Yet she had to admit that, in such a place, it would be simple to confuse fancy for reality.

And against her better judgment, her curiosity was most definitely piqued.

Unfortunately, they didn't advance much farther than the dragon's head doorknocker before the stony-faced butler informed them that there were no tours inside the castle walls. He was brusque in his delivery. Then, without giving his audience a chance to utter a syllable of dismay, he began to close the door.

At least . . . until Maeve suddenly spoke.

"My good sir, you wouldn't be related to the famous actor Mr. Cooke by chance?"

He paused, his head tilted in speculation, either because he'd never been asked such a question or he didn't know whether or not to be insulted by it. "Nay, madam. Not as far as I am aware."

"Pray, forgive me," she continued. "It's only that, with the way the light graced your visage just now, I was certain that you were the same man I'd had a terrible girlhood fancy toward. I can remember seeing *Richard III* at the Theatre Royal a dozen times and sighing like a lovesick calf throughout the entirety."

The door opened a bit wider.

"I recall that play. Might have seen it myself a few times, back when I was a strapping young lad. But that was ages ago," he said, standing taller in his dark livery and giving a smart tug to the hem of his waistcoat.

"Then, the years have been most kind to you, sir." Maeve looked askance as if embarrassed by her boldness.

Was it Meg's imagination or had Maeve's voice taken on a breathy quality? She expected such behavior from Myrtle. Heaven knew *she* flirted shamelessly with every nut seller in Regent's Park. But this hidden side of Maeve was an absolute revelation. What an outlandish minx!

The butler cleared his throat, and there was a hint of ruddy color brushing the crests of his cheeks. "I don't suppose a brief tour of the Hall of Knights would be out of the realm of possibility."

Then the door opened.

When they were led inside, Maeve gave her a secret nod as if to say, *And that is how it is done, my dear.*

Meg had to bite the inner wall of her cheek to keep from laughing.

But the three *F*s of persuading a gentleman was a lesson lost on the likes of her.

She had not always been so cynical. At one time, she'd dreamed her London Seasons would have been filled with flirtations, dances, parties, and calls from gentlemen wishing to escort her to Gunter's for ices or on afternoon drives through the park. Her ivory dance card would have been forever full and Daniel Prescott would have been so jealous that he'd have begged to marry her without delay. She had even imagined putting on a coquettish display of needing time to consider his proposal, before finally giving her eager consent.

But that was not the reality she had encountered.

Even though she was an accomplished woman of two and twenty, she had a rounded face that made men treat her as if she were fresh out of the schoolroom. Even Daniel had told her that she was—

No. She stopped before she gave him another thought.

The entire purpose of this holiday was to cast him as firmly from her mind as she might a spider that had vanished from sight in her bedchamber. Since she wasn't the type to bury herself beneath the coverlet and let dread consume her, she'd decided to be strong and rationalize that a single spider bite—or broken heart, as the case may be—surely wouldn't kill her. Would it?

Meg shuddered. Perhaps that wasn't the best analogy. Because now, she couldn't help but imagine herself cocooned in a silken pod and waiting to become a hairy arachnid's midnight snack.

So much for casting *that* from her mind.

Realizing that her musings had gone a bit dark, she blinked and abruptly redirected her attention to the butler.

Mr. Gudgeon recounted the keep's history as he led them through a broad archway and into a vast tapestry-strewn hall where knights in armor stood at attention on either side. And Meg noticed that his tone had become theatrical as if to reach a great audience hiding somewhere in the minstrel's gallery at the far end.

Maeve batted her lashes up at him. "Positively riveting. And to think, all these knights had once protected a book."

"Not just a mere book, madam. No, indeed," he said with chest-puffing pride. "A treasure trove of recipes that once fed King Arthur himself as well as every knight at his round table. Not only that but the very stone that once held the sword is the same pedestal upon which the book sits."

"Gracious! Aren't you afraid that someone will come along and try to take them?"

He chuckled. "Many have tried. They're locked up tighter than the crown jewels. And the Tower of London has nothing on the family vault."

A frustrated sigh left Myrtle, and Meg wondered how the sisters planned to move forward after this revelation.

They were in the middle of the sixteenth-century armor—an era that she would forever think of as the *Age of the Codpiece*—when her attention was diverted from a rather alarmingly turgid specimen as Myrtle's question for the butler prickled at Meg's ears.

"Forgive the interruption, good sir, but my young charge has bid me to inquire about a repairing room where, perhaps, she might freshen up before the lengthy journey ahead," she said, not caring a whit that Meg's cheeks were quickly turning as red as the dragon standard hanging on the wall.

Mr. Gudgeon seemed hesitant at first. However, as it became clear that the two of them planned to leave Maeve behind with him, the butler was more than happy to direct them.

Through Myrtle's uncanny ability to divine a path through the winding corridors and down the stairs, they promptly found themselves standing at the humid mouth of the bustling kitchens.

The cook had her back to them, her attention divided between the fowl turning on the roasting spit, loading pies into a mezzaluna opening of the bake oven, stirring two copper pots atop the surface of a brick Rumford stove nestled into a flued alcove, and calling out instructions to a troop of harried sculleries over her shoulder. She was so occupied with a myriad of tasks that she never even looked toward the door to see Myrtle skirt inside.

As she snooped, Meg remained just outside and smiled at the din of culinary commotion. She didn't know what it was about the companionable chatter, the rattle of pots and pans, the hollow thwack of a cleaver against a wooden trestle table or the chiming of a whisk in a wide copper bowl, but the sounds had always appealed to her.

They reminded her of home, she supposed. Not Crossmoor Abbey but the quaint country cottage where she'd lived when her mother and father were still alive.

"This way," Myrtle whispered, drawing Meg out of her musings, then summarily towed her down the corridor. "Not a recipe in sight. Must have them all stored away."

Meg was about to suggest that they return to the Hall of Knights when she was ushered into a little cupboard of a room just beyond the larder.

Blinking to accustom her eyes to the dim light filtering in through the partially open door, she noticed a shelf of preserves, a flour-dusted pinafore hanging on a hook and a slender writing desk tucked into the corner. Above it hung a framed square of muslin embroidered with the words of the famous chef Marie-Antoine Carême: "The fine arts are five in number: Painting, Music, Poetry, Architecture and Sculpture—whereof the principal branch is Confectionery."

By all accounts, this was the cook's office. Meg emitted a gasp of wonder. "How in the world could you have known where to—"

Myrtle set a finger to her lips, silencing her as a pair of chatting maids passed by in the corridor. Meg nodded, somewhat dumbfounded, and more than a little impressed, at witnessing this *de cape et d'épée*—cloak-and-dagger—side of the elder woman.

Myrtle was crafty and quick in her search. She even slipped a hatpin free to manipulate the lock of a drawer and summarily withdrew an aged book. It was filled with pages that were yellowed and wavy at the edges, some hosting scrawled lists splattered with constellations of various sauce drippings and others written in a looping curlicue script and topped with full moons of teacup stains.

A recipe book!

She paused on a particularly well-used page with the words *The Duke's Favorite* scrawled across the top. Without delay, she slipped a folded scrap of foolscap from a hidden placket on the side of her lavender skirts. She smoothed it on the desk surface, then dipped a waiting quill into a bottle of ink and hastily jotted down the recipe.

But as she finished, and before she could turn another page, they heard voices in the hall again.

"Better not let Mrs. Gudgeon catch you dillydallying belowstairs or she'll put you to work scrubbing chamber pots. In a right solid snit, she is."

"Don't I know it. I've already had an earful about not having the proper tray for Lady Morgan. She said if I don't find the lemon curd with rosemary for her ladyship's crumpet, then I shouldn't bother coming back at all."

"Oh, don't take it to heart. I'm sure she's just mad at Mr. Gudgeon again. Wonder what the old flirt's done this time."

"I'm sure I'll hear her caterwauling about that later, too . . . if I still have my post."

"*Don't fret. If we can't find it in the larder, I'm sure Mrs. Philpot'll have a jar on her shelf.*"

Meg glanced over her shoulder to see that there was, indeed, a jar of lemon curd with rosemary on the shelf. Beside her, Myrtle tucked the book back into the drawer and tried to slide it closed. But it halted halfway, the wood issuing a high squeak of protest.

Just then, a pair of shadows paused directly outside the door.

"*Hang back. Did you hear something?*"

Meg held her breath. Her heart stuttered to a stop beneath her breast. Then, at the appearance of slender, chapped fingers curling around the edge of the door, the organ suddenly kicked into a full rushing gallop in her ears.

They were going to be caught!

"*Yes—my head on the chopping block if I don't find that curd. Come quick. Help me look in the larder before I'm sacked.*"

The hand fell away from the door, and the shadows moved. It wasn't until she heard the diminishing scuttle of hurried footsteps that Meg's shoulders dared to sag with relief.

That was a close call.

Truth be told, until a moment ago, she'd only felt as if she and Myrtle were having a lark. The consequences of her actions hadn't seemed too severe considering how easily Mr. Gudgeon had been for Maeve to handle. *Mrs.* Gudgeon, however, sounded like a veritable dragon—one less likely to be forgiving should she discover a pair of trespassers whose companion was flirting with her husband.

The distant thwack of the cleaver echoed down the hall, and Meg put a protective hand around her neck.

Unquestionably, it was time to leave.

After ensuring the hallway was clear, Meg and Myrtle made their escape, albeit with one minor complication. The virtually unpopulated route they'd taken down to this level was now chock-full of maids, either toting ash bins or baskets of linens, blocking their exit.

Quick as a compass, Myrtle turned on her heel and scurried down a set of narrow stairs. Meg followed close behind. And moments later, they were deeper inside the keep, sprinting on tiptoes through the windowless, winding—and thankfully vacant—corridors with a pilfered recipe in their possession.

Myrtle had just turned a corner when the slip of foolscap fell from her pocket. It drifted silently to the stone floor, its felonious owner oblivious.

In Meg's rush to scoop it up, she created a gust of air that sent the paper skittering like a sail in a tempest around the corner, the shadows eclipsing it from sight.

"Psst . . . Aunt Myrtle," she whispered from beside a low, rough-hewed arch. But her cohort in crime hurried ahead, heedless, the shuffle of her slippers already growing fainter.

It took another moment for Meg's eyes to adjust to the dim light enough to locate the recipe. Then, when she bent to pick it up, she heard brisk, heavy footfalls coming from the corridor behind her.

Drat! All she had time to do was to step on the fallen paper, press her back against the sloped stone wall, hold her breath and hope that whatever servant might be heading this way would pass by her without a blink.

A tall man approached, striding forth at an agitated pace. He appeared somewhat preoccupied, pushing a hank of dark hair carelessly back from his forehead and leaving it to fall to one side. And he was garbed in a blacksmith's apron, the heavy leather accentuating the leanness of his hips and breadth of his shoulders.

In this light it was difficult to determine his age, though he appeared to be beyond thirty. He had a sort of rawboned face, angular and chiseled—striking, though not necessarily handsome—with a prominent aquiline nose. And, sitting on the bridge of said nose, was a pair of round spectacles with brass frames.

She didn't know what his position in this household was—what with his apron, soot-smudged cravat and the cuffs of his shirtsleeves rolled up—but he possessed an air of superiority, as if he oversaw many people and kept them on task.

Definitely not one to trifle with, she thought. And she quickly banished the fleeting notion of attempting the three *F*s for the first time on him, should he continue on his course directly toward her.

But as he drew near, she caught sight of the dull cast over his noticeably smeared lenses and wondered if he might not spot her in the shadows at all.

When he walked right by, a silent sigh of relief escaped her. Luck was on her side.

Or at least, it was . . . until he stopped.

Like a hound catching the scent of his quarry, he lifted his head and stiffened, suddenly alert. Then he turned on his heel and stared directly toward her hiding place.

"What are you doing in this part of the keep? You know this is off-limits."

His voice was deep and commanding—a baritone so low that it was more like a growl. It tingled in her ears before traveling directly to the pit of her stomach in some sort of strange tumult. How odd. Especially considering that his expression was austerely disapproving in a way that she'd always disliked in men.

However, it was clear that this man assumed she was a servant. The dim light and dirty spectacles likely kept him from seeing the azure spencer, striped day dress and white kid gloves that would have revealed her for the interloper she was.

"Yes, sir," she said with a hint of contrition that she hoped would fool him. "I was just on my way out."

At once, his mouth turned down at the corners. He took a step toward her and tore off his glasses. "You're not one of the maids. Who are you?"

Meg couldn't answer. Her lips parted, but no sound came out.

She drew in a breath to start again but tasted the air instead. It was flavored with the char of creosote and something else. Something enthralling like a combination of sun-warmed spices and worn leather. Something that made her lungs cinch tight around it, refusing to release. Something that made her want to lean in for a deep inhale.

But she couldn't move. All she could do was stand there, *not* breathing, and stare fixedly into eyes that seemed to hold her own captive. They were intensely dark brown with flecks of gold, a color so rich and earthy that it reminded her of the smooth stones resting on the creek bed at Crossmoor Abbey. And she felt as though her body were filled with those very stones, stacked one on top of the other, rooting her in place.

"I'll ask once more before I call my servants. *Who* . . . are . . . you?"

His servants? No, it couldn't be.

"*You* are the Duke of Merleton?" Her voice was oddly hoarse, throat dry as biscuit crumbs.

"Who the devil else would I be?"

He seemed to grow larger before her eyes. But she, as a fully grown woman who didn't appreciate being talked to as if she were still in leading strings, was suddenly snapped from her peculiar trance.

Straightening to her full height—which put the top of her head nearly level with his chin—she replied with equal terseness. "I am sure I shouldn't know. From your attire, you might have been anyone from blacksmith to chimney sweep to dungeon-dwelling troll. I've heard of you, of course. A bachelor duke, but one who rarely enters society. And

clearly that is for everyone's benefit," she added beneath
her breath as she watched him attempt to clean his lenses
against the sleeve covered in a black sooty substance. "And
let us not forget the fanciful stories of your lineage's connection to the legend of King Arthur. Well, I half pictured
the Duke of Merleton as an old man with stooped shoulders
and a long white beard."

*And perhaps with several members of your family kept
in the attic.*

He paused his circular buffing motions of the lenses
against sleeve and squinted at her. "Are you accusing me of
having lunacy in the family?"

"If it's any consolation, I did not intend to say that last
part aloud."

His brows flattened. "Since you are refusing to answer my
questions, I'm left with no alternative than to escort you—"

His speech stopped abruptly as he thrust the now thoroughly blackened spectacles onto his nose, only to growl
"Merlin's teeth" under his breath, then rip them off again.

A giggle escaped Meg. She clapped a hand over her
mouth. That shouldn't have slipped out either. However,
seeing this censorious man struggle over such a rudimentary task struck her as humorous.

The duke cocked his head in curious assessment as if he
didn't know what to make of the sound. Perhaps no one had
dared laugh in his presence before.

Taking pity on the confounded and untidy duke, she
withdrew a clean handkerchief from her sleeve. Then she
reached for the spectacles.

He held fast. "What are you doing?"

"Allow me," she insisted, tightening her grip.

They engaged in a small tug-of-war, a give-and-take in
increments of inches. The ridiculous episode had the unforeseen result of drawing him a step nearer.

Those river-stone eyes stared down at her with wordless

intensity. She felt a jolt deep inside—a strange cinctured sensation that wrapped around her middle and made it difficult to breathe again.

"You called me a *bachelor duke*," he said, his accusatory tone penetrating the peculiar fog that kept enshrouding her. "*That's* why you're here. You're a husband-hunter."

She scoffed. "I am, most definitely, *not*. As a matter of fact, I have absolutely no interest in marriage at all and for reasons that are . . . well, none of your concern. But you can rest assured that, should I ever change my mind, yours would be the last threshold I'd cross."

"And yet, you've crossed it, nonetheless. But for what purpose?"

Only then did his long blunt fingers release the spectacles. Even so, he did not retreat to a more socially acceptable distance. Instead, he studied her ministrations carefully as if he thought she'd hidden something nefarious in the folds of her handkerchief.

It wouldn't have bothered her, if only he wasn't so terribly tall and dark. He made her feel as if she were on the verge of becoming eclipsed by his form. As if, were he to take one more step, she'd become absorbed in his shadow.

Though, more than likely, he was trying to intimidate her into revealing all her secrets.

"You have quite the suspicious nature. Did it ever occur to you that the answer of my being here could be as simple as happenstance?" she asked, issuing a sniff of haughty indignance as if she didn't have a pilfered slip of paper beneath the sole of her shoe.

"Happenstance does not exist," he said. "Men and women make choices. We are not automatons. We are not fitted with gears and springs but with a complex system of nerves and muscles that react to the brain's command to place one foot in front of the other and, in your case, venture into places where you do not belong."

Splendid. If there was one thing worse than a lunatic, it was an educated lunatic.

"I am not insane," he said evenly as her cheeks colored in embarrassment at another slip of the tongue. "If I were, I can assure you that I would not be exerting the utmost patience toward a trespasser who has stolen into my house for purposes yet to be determined. Were I a madman, madam, I would have already dragged you through the halls, tossed you outside and bolted the door.

"Then again," he added, taking a half step closer, his eyes darker still, "perhaps, I would have locked you in the attic with all the others."

She caught that underlying fragrance again. This time, instead of merely making her lungs cinch, her skin seemed to draw tighter over her frame, too. Not unpleasant, but disconcerting, all the same.

"Fine," she said relenting, pressing her shoulder blades against the wall. "My party and I merely came to tour the grounds. Which are lovely, by the way. It isn't often one encounters pink swans and a moat. Or a drawbridge or gated portcullis for that matter. And in such a setting, it was only natural that one would stop for a picnic, a perfectly harmless endeavor . . ."

She realized she was rambling when she heard him expel an impatient hiss through his teeth. Yes, she was stalling. And not because she was so high in her morals that she couldn't tell a lie. No, indeed. After all, she had an overprotective elder brother and, as long as dire consequences weren't involved, she saw no harm in telling a small fib or two. But, for some unknown reason, lying to this man was proving unaccountably difficult.

And besides, it made her nose itch.

She wiggled it in an effort to alleviate the discomfort, then cleared her throat to continue. "So I'm certain you could imagine that my party expressed an interest in touring inside your grand estate."

"There are no tours *inside* the walls of Caliburn Keep. Ever."

"As we were informed after we rapped on your gargantuan door."

"You should be grateful you were allowed to tour the grounds at all. I'd only recently reopened the gates. Much to my current regret."

In that instant, she decided that this man wasn't a lunatic. He was just rude and arrogant. And suddenly it wasn't all that difficult to lie to him. In fact, she wished she had stolen *all* his recipes.

"Since my traveling companions and I have a lengthy journey ahead of us, we inquired if we might be directed to a repairing chamber."

The tip of her nose prickled. Ignoring it, she stripped off her glove and applied her thumbnail to a particularly stubborn speck of dirt on his lenses, all the while wishing he could feel the abrasion.

"Which is also not in this older portion of the keep."

"Well, obviously, I became turned around at some point and found myself here, subject to your delightful company."

Finished with her task, she looked up to see that one of his brows was arched higher than the other as if he expected her to apologize for her sarcasm. *Not likely, Duke of Disdain.*

With an unconcerned shrug, she offered up his glasses. However, seeing that his hands were still covered in soot, she tsked wearily. "Better allow me. You'll only smear them all over again. Now bend forward a bit. You're far too tall."

He obliged, those brows drawing together, puckering over the bridge of his nose in a fan of three vertical furrows.

"You still haven't told me who you are," he said, and with

his face so close to hers, she felt the brush of his breath across her lips. It sent a shiver through her.

Meg's gaze collided with his once more, and there it was again . . . that peculiar cinching sensation around her middle. It was accompanied by a strange tug in the pit of her stomach as if there were an invisible rope through her navel and someone behind him had gathered the end of it in their fist. And in the back of her mind, she envisioned the thick braiding coiled around the two of them, pulling their bodies flush . . .

Feeling herself teeter forward on the balls of her feet, she released the frames at once and dropped back on her heels.

She'd only managed to secure one side, leaving the spectacles to dangle crookedly from his right ear. But she didn't dare try to correct them now. She was too light-headed and her heart was racing at a most peculiar gallop.

"I must go," she rasped, laying a hand against her midriff.

She realized that her glove had fallen at some point. Her gaze drifted down to it, pausing along the way to study his corded forearms, strong and dusted with dark hair, the skin swarthy and tanned. And she found herself wondering if he spent time out of doors with his sleeves rolled up or, perhaps, with no shirt at all . . .

The errant thought took her completely off guard. Especially when her mind flashed to an image of this man standing bare-chested in the sunlight and brandishing a long, gleaming sword like one of Arthur's knights during the age of myths and legends.

She became oddly short of breath. Winded, even. Clearly, there was something amiss with the air down here.

Lifting her gaze, she saw him staring back at her most curiously, his black pupils eclipsing all those golden flecks. His nostrils flared. Then she heard the scuff of his boot against the stones. Felt the slight crush of her skirts against her stocking-clad shins. Saw his gaze fall to her mouth. And then his hand lifted, hovering for a fraction of a second . . .

just before she felt the touch of his thumb and forefinger against her chin.

Her lips parted on a gasp.

The sound cut through the stillness of the shadowy corridor and seemed to bring them both to attention.

He released her at once. Then, retreating a step, he stared down at his hand with marked confusion as if he'd never seen it before.

"Were you going to"—she splayed a hand over the buttons of her spencer, the garment impossibly tight—"kiss me?"

He flinched as if she'd dashed a glass of cold water in his face. Looking down the ridge of his nose at her, he crisply enunciated, "Of course not."

She didn't believe him. And her racing heart didn't believe him either. "Was that your method of intimidation, then?"

"Of course not."

"Is that all you have to say, *of course not*? You won't even bother to explain yourself?"

"I—" He looked at his hand again and then over his shoulder, toward the corridor. And, when he spoke again, his tone was distracted, faraway, his attention clearly diverted. "I'll leave you now. I trust you know the way out."

Then, before she could make heads or tails of anything at all, he turned and strode back in the direction from which he'd come. The intense focus he'd given her an instant ago had apparently shifted to something else.

In other words, he was a typical man.

Dipping low for the fallen glove, she stole beneath her hem to take hold of the recipe as well. Just in case the Duke of Distraction should turn back around, she tucked the folded foolscap against her palm beneath the kid leather and stood.

As she watched him go, she nodded to herself and expelled a breath. "Most definitely lunacy in the family."

Chapter 3

The secret ingredient

Lucien Ambrose, the seventh Duke of Merleton, dismissed the intruder from his thoughts. He had more pressing matters to attend to, rather than dealing with the machinations of a wayward husband-hunter. And time was of the essence.

This was about his life's work, after all. He could already feel the effects of this latest experiment dissipating. Therefore, he focused on ensuring that the length and speed of his gait was adequate enough to reach the buttery before his research was altered by any further delay.

For the past eleven years, he'd been studying his family's ancient book of recipes, searching for the truth behind the myth. And for eleven years, his efforts had offered nothing except frustration.

At least, until today.

There had been something distinctly different in this afternoon's sample. Named the Recipe of Glatisant, it was a meat pie said to have suffused the knights with the attributes of the questing beast, making them feel powerful and virile, and heightening each of their senses—all the symptoms that he had experienced moments ago.

Which meant that there might be some truth to the old tales passed down for centuries in his family.

His pulse leapt with excitement as his stride continued

to eat up the flagstones beneath his feet. Though, to be honest, he'd never expected his experiments to render a demonstrable result.

He'd always been pragmatic. Logical to a fault, some would say. Fancy was not in his nature.

Even as a boy of six walking in the garden with his mother, he could recall when she'd pointed to a rainbow and told him that it was a *wonder of creation*. He had disagreed, explaining that it was a prismatic effect of bending light and even showed her the triangular prism he'd kept in his pocket. Mother had laughed, then had taken both his hands and spun him around in a circle, telling him that he was a wonder of creation, too.

He'd never really known precisely what she'd meant by that, because there was no question of the manner in which he had appeared in this world. It was a simple matter of procreation. At the time, however, and because he adored his mother, he'd accepted those nonsensical comments as the idioms of her lexicon.

His mother had often spoken of wonders and miracles, of chance and fate, and his father of knights and legends, of improbable romantic tales.

Given time, Lucien may have begun to understand and, perhaps, even believe their delusions. But they had died when he was seven, and he'd been raised by his grandfather instead.

The sixth Duke of Merleton had been shattered by the death of his only son. The once-enigmatic duke, who'd enjoyed sharing ancient stories about noble quests with anyone who cared to listen, had become closed off and grim. He'd taught Lucien that what mattered most was keeping the book locked away, safe and secure, so that no one—not even the family—would ever clap eyes on it again.

Then Lucien had been sent away to school, his key to the vault confiscated.

Even though he had obeyed his grandfather's orders, it had been difficult. After all, he'd barely been introduced to the book before he was barred from it. And he'd had so many questions that required answers.

So when Lucien had succeeded the title and reclaimed the key to the vault, that was precisely what he'd set about to find: answers. Proof.

A less determined man might have given up after a year or two of constant failure. Most definitely after five. But his own nature forced him to exhaust every single possibility before he surrendered.

And it might have all been leading him to this very moment.

His footsteps echoed around him as he traversed the ancient halls of the original keep built in the fifth century. The motte-and-bailey fortress had eroded over time, sinking into a devouring earth that wished to reclaim it. Then, around the sixteenth century, his ancestors had simply built new over the old.

Their actions had the unforeseen consequences of preserving, entombing, these corridors. The sloping walls, the adze-notched timbers, the great hall with the inglenook fireplace and hexafoils carved into the mantel were the same as they had been when a round table sat at its center.

As he lifted a torch from an iron wall-bracket and lit it in what was left of the dying embers, he gave the carving of a circled daisy a passing glance. He'd always been curious about the people who had believed that these apotropaic symbols held any power in their lives, as if they had no control of their own.

But that was a question for another day.

Turning on his heel, he continued onward through the screens passage. At the end of a short and constricted corridor, he turned the key in the lock, ducked his head beneath the warped lintel and stepped into the old buttery.

The narrow barrel-shaped room was no longer used to

store ale, wine and spirits. Those were conveniently located for the butler's access in the more recent addition overhead. Yet, the shelves remained, lining the bowed stone walls.

Even though the ceiling was too low for him to stand upright unless he kept to the center, and the air was stale and three degrees shy of being uncomfortably cold, he didn't care. This was his laboratory where no one would bother him. Here, he could devote all of his considerable concentration to every recipe in the book to test their validity.

It was his life's mission to understand them.

Crossing the room in three strides, he turned the wick of the oil lamp on the ancient and scarred trestle table that served as his desk. Light flickered over the meticulous lines of the code written in his ledger.

His notes never revealed the actual recipes. Those were still kept in the vault, and he possessed the only key. So instead, he had developed a mathematical cipher he used. A code. And with it, he could calculate with absolute precision the exact alteration from yesterday's sample to today's.

"The metheglin," he hypothesized aloud, tapping the page over his concise script.

Standing, he moved to the shelves and withdrew a dark bottle. The recipe had called for the organ meat to be soaked in mead, which he had always done before. This time, however, he had used metheglin—a spiced mead that would have been more common during Arthur's time.

Lucien had even made his own honey. Caliburn Keep's apiary was surrounded by the very herbs that gave metheglin a medicinal flavor—agrimonia, angelica, lemon balm and mead wort.

Removing the cork, he sniffed. The rich, syrupy and redolent brew contained a sharp, astringent undertone that caused the glands at the back of his mouth to contract.

Was this the secret ingredient? The answer he'd been searching for since his parents had died?

He wasn't certain. And he needed certainty *per centum*. In other words, he had to be one hundred percent sure.

Lucien moved to the shelves lining the opposite wall, ducking his head along the way. This was where he kept the finished samples to study them further. Neat rows of identical earthenware jars were tagged by date and a corresponding code for the ledger entry. He left nothing to chance.

Taking down today's jar, he returned to his desk and removed the lid. Retrieving the remaining half of the pie, he held up the semilunar wedge to the light and admired the layers of various cuts of meat and organs, fats and spices. An exultant exhale left him as he studied the pastry with a mixture of fascination and triumph.

But no, not triumph. Not yet. He was not one to rush to judgment.

And yet, his heart was thrumming again as he recalled that brief moment in the corridor when he'd felt the effects.

Something had been different about this one. There had been a distinct alteration in his own physiology.

It had been distracting, to say the least. Especially when the symptoms had begun while he was standing with that directionally challenged woman who liked to speak in circles.

The first thing he'd noticed was the peculiar levitation of the hair on his nape as he'd walked down the passage. This had caused him to stop. Catching an unfamiliar sweet scent in the dank and musty air, he'd turned. That was when he'd initially located the trespasser in the shadows. Through his grimy lenses, he'd surmised that the figure was female but soon established that she was not from his serving staff.

Thusly identifying her as an intruder, he'd stepped closer. And that was when the recipe truly began to take hold.

He had felt predatory. Strong. Virile. There was no way around it. And those were precisely the effects that the recipe was reputed to have imbued in the warriors who'd supped on it centuries ago.

Nevertheless, Lucien couldn't consider this actual proof without expanding his test to other subjects. And he knew who would be the perfect guinea pig.

🦋

"WHAT MAKES you think I'd want to try your weird little pie?" Without lifting his blond head from the corner of the camel-backed drawing room sofa, Viscount Pellinore Holladay eyed the offered wedge with dismissive interest. His cousin spent most of his evenings in that exact spot, lounging with utter insouciance, his trouser-clad legs crossed at the ankles and a glass of whisky dangling from his fingertips.

"Because I once watched you consume the larva of a dung beetle. You'll eat anything."

"That hardly signifies. I was only four years old at the—" Pell stopped when Lucien nudged the sample against his lips. On a grunt of resignation, he took a bite and chewed.

Lucien waited for him to finish and checked the time on the ormolu mantel clock. "How do you feel?"

"Rather put upon, if I'm to be honest," he said as he took the remainder of the wedge and finished it off. "Dare I ask what's in it?"

"Primarily pig snout and ears, calf tongue and brain, goose neck and tongue, frog legs—"

"Forget I asked." Pell held up a hand in surrender. "Whenever one of your experiments begins with pig snout as the pièce de résistance, just pretend you didn't hear me ask."

Lucien turned a deaf ear to the complaints and studied his subject with keen interest. By his calculations, it had taken approximately seventy-six seconds for him to walk from the buttery to where he'd encountered the trespasser and first noticed the effects of the sample.

With a glance to the clock, he knew it was time.

Sliding his index finger up the bridge of his nose, he anchored the saddle of his spectacles in place as he bent over the sofa and looked for any pupil dilation or flesh discoloration. "Do you feel anything now?"

"Other than you breathing down my neck and manhandling my collar—*Ow!* Those are still attached."

Lucien shrugged. "I had to see if the hairs on your nape were standing on end."

"Well, they are now. They're in full revolt," Pell groused, scrubbing a hand over the back of his neck.

"Perhaps you should stand up. Move about. Get your blood flowing." Without waiting for agreement, he took his cousin's hand and hefted him upward. Then linking arms with him, he began to pace quickly around the rectangular perimeter of the rifle green room. "And now? Anything?"

Just then, Lucien's half sister walked through the double arched doors. Her brows lifted toward a widow's peak of auburn hair, and her lips curled in a wry grin. "Taking a turn about the room, boys? I hear it's excellent for the constitution."

"Well, something ought to be after what your brother just made me eat, or else this may be the last you'll ever see of me."

"Then, wishes really do come true," Morgan said as she clutched her hands to her bosom and sighed.

"You wound me, madam."

She blew him a kiss. "Daggers of fondness, cousin."

"If the two of you are finished, I should like to continue my study," Lucien said. "Now, Pell, tell me if you feel the slightest difference in your physiology. Elevated heartbeat? Sharpened sense of smell?"

"I do believe I sense something rather pungent. It smells like a dying bloom and disdain for mankind." He made a point of sniffing in Morgan's direction and curling his nose. "Oh, wait. Never mind."

"I'm surprised you can smell anything at all over the odor of the bay rum you've apparently bathed in. I'm sure half the finches in the aviary died as you walked by." She squinted at him and walked over to the red lacquered sideboard to pour herself a claret. "So tell me, Lucien. I was under the impression that you refused to try your experiments on us. I seem to recall a rather magnanimous speech about taking all the risks yourself. Has that changed, or is this just your way of trying to exterminate our cousin once and for all? Just so you know, I'll be happy to help you dig the grave."

"Such a generous soul, your sister."

Lucien ignored their banter. "There was something different with this one, and I required a control subject. Of course, it would be better if we could simulate the entire experience as it transpired . . ." And for him a female had been present. But that gave him an idea.

Stopping near his sister, he situated his cousin directly in front of her and asked, "Is there anything you feel now?"

As Morgan's green gaze gleamed like a cat who'd spotted a canary with clipped wings, Pell shifted until his hands were cupped in front of his groin. "Other than a need to protect the family jewels?"

Lucien expelled a defeated breath and turned toward the clock.

It was well beyond the time it had taken him to notice the effects. Why wasn't it working? What could have been different?

He stalked to the window without paying attention to the lush gardens or the sun on its decline over the verdant rolling hills beyond the ramparts. Instead, he was mentally calculating the possibility of a temperature fluctuation of the pie and wondering if he should drag Pell down to the old buttery while he prepared a fresh sample and have him taste it after a precise allotment of time.

"Perhaps it was just your imagination, cousin."

"Lucien doesn't have an imagination. It must have been a fluke."

"And I don't believe in flukes. Everything has an explanation." He raked a hand through his hair. "Damn it all, if I hadn't been distracted by that woman, I might have been able to pinpoint the changes precisely as they'd occurred."

"What's this?" Pell asked, his tone dripping with intrigue. "You let a woman into the old fortress? Ah, so that's what you've really been up to for all those lengthy hours. You've finally found someone to polish your sword."

"Hardly," he growled as a fresh wave of irritation crashed over him. "She was merely an unwanted distraction. Apparently, Mr. Gudgeon allowed her and her companions to refresh themselves after touring the gardens. I've already spoken to him about that, and it won't happen again."

"Well, was she pretty? Is that what's put you in this state?"

Lucien leveled a glare at his cousin. "You know I hold little stock in such things. All I know is that she—whoever she may have been—was a nuisance."

Pell laughed and plopped down onto the sofa. "Don't tell me that the master of detail didn't even get her name? That's too rich. And it would be my guess that she was incomparably pretty. So much so that she scrambled your wits."

"Oh, leave Lucien be. Can you not see that he's frustrated? He's been waiting years for a shred of proof, and today was the closest he's ever come," Morgan said with surprising understanding.

Since his older sister had never been accused of being sympathetic or tenderhearted, Lucien anticipated the delivery of her usual salt into the wound. Like, for example, reminding him that there would have been no trespasser if he hadn't decided to open the gates to the public for a few hours each week. She'd been harping on him for that decision for the past month, warning him that he was only asking for trouble. In response, he'd told her that they hardly need worry about families with small children touring the garden. Though, clearly, he hadn't predicted how troublesome one trespasser could be.

He was surprised, however, that Morgan refrained from doling out a smug rebuke.

"Besides," she continued blandly, "I have it under good authority that her appearance was merely a contrivance to meet you, dear brother."

"What *authority*?"

She shrugged. "My maid overheard Mrs. Gudgeon arguing with her husband and calling him a flirt. He defended himself by saying that the only topic of conversation had been in regard to the women and their travels. Apparently, they were on their way to Dover to begin their tour of the Continent. Which may have been true. However . . . they came from Wiltshire. Somerset is a bit out of the way, wouldn't you agree?" Morgan issued a laugh as Lucien frowned. "Haven't I always told you, brother? There's nothing a woman wouldn't do to seize what she wants. To claim what, she believes, rightfully belongs to her."

"Cheer up, cousin." Pell crossed the room to pour another whisky. "I can think of many things worse than having a comely woman steal into my house just to make my acquaintance. At least you know the interloper wasn't up to anything nefarious."

As the statement hung in the air, Lucien felt an icy shiver crawl down his spine.

Nefarious. Why hadn't he thought of that before?

Because he hadn't been thinking clearly. At least, not until now.

Without a word, he stalked out of the drawing room.

Suspicions on alert, he recalled every minute detail of the day. With each measured footfall through the keep, he composed a comprehensive list of his actions and those of the persons he'd encountered.

His pace quickened. A breeze swept an errant hank of hair from his forehead as he strode through winding corridors that gradually took him to the secret family vault.

He shouldn't have been worried. After all, only he possessed the key forged to fit the lock. The very key that was hidden inside the dagger he kept in his boot.

And yet . . .

There had been a brief moment when he had unknowingly mislaid it.

He'd been in the buttery and had reached inside his boot to cut off a slice of the meat pie for Pell to sample. But the dirk had not been in his boot. Instead, he'd found it resting beneath the ledger. At the time, however, he'd convinced himself that his eagerness to finally have proof had merely made him forgetful and that he'd removed the blade an instant before.

But had he? As he felt the icy prick of pins and needles along his shoulders and all the way to his fingertips, he wasn't sure at all.

The air turned colder as he navigated the maze of underground chambers that were familiar to him now. But he remembered the day he'd first walked them at his father's side.

He could still smell the scent of his father's pipe tobacco and hear the clipped percussive beat of his riding boots on the stones. Lucien had been about as tall as the keyhole then, and slight enough to have been crushed by the heavy vault door if he'd gotten in the way.

"Are they real, Father? The stories? The recipes?" he'd asked with wide-eyed wonder as he saw the book for the first time.

The skepticism of his seven-year-old self wavered at the sight of the jewels on the cover. A starburst of cabochon

*rubies, sapphires, emeralds and yellow diamonds glowed
in the lamplight. They were smooth beneath the tentative
touch of his fingertips. The gilded pages rasped quietly
against each other as his father allowed him to explore,
knowing that Lucien was always careful with books. To
him, those were the true treasures of the earth.*

*"They are, for those who believe in them. So real, in
fact, that some men have done despicable things to possess
the power promised within the pages."*

"Even . . . murder?"

*Somehow, he'd known the answer even before his father
had laid a hand on his shoulder and nodded solemnly.*

*"That is the reason we must keep the book locked away.
We are the faithful stewards who ensure that it doesn't fall
into the wrong hands. Some of our ancestors have perished
for the sake of this ancient relic. We must honor their sacrifice by doing all we can to shield and protect what we hold
most dear. And now," he said, handing him the key, "you
are part of that legacy, my son."*

Lucien blinked away the memory as his hand curled
around the hilt of the dagger. Then, with a twist of the
bronze pommel, he removed the key hidden inside and set
it into the lock.

When the heavy vault door swung open on a groan, he
went still. The place where the legendary bejeweled book of
recipes usually sat on the scarred old stone was empty. Barren.

The book was gone.

His heart stopped beating. *This cannot be happening*,
he thought. Securing the book was his sole responsibility.
There had to have been a mistake.

Dread filled him as he staggered into the vault. The
chamberstick flame wavered, spilling a ripple of watery
light on the rough stone walls. He felt the shadows closing
around him as he went deeper into the tomb-like chamber,
hefting the candle higher. *It has to be here.*

His eyes searched wildly, frantically. Perhaps it had slipped, he reasoned. A strong gust of air from when he'd opened the door might have toppled it to the other side.

But no. The book wasn't on the floor.

Something else was there instead—a torn scrap of yellowed vellum.

Lucien knew, even before he bent to pick it up, and his hand shook as he read the taunting words left for him.

To the Duke of Merleton,

You've finally met your match.

Lady Avalon

Chapter 4

Shaken, not stirred

The shores of Calais were just off the port bow, the harbor filled with sailing vessels of every kind, from paddle steamers to packet ships, cutters to schooners, ferries to merchant ships as imposing as frigates, and each were vying for position in the slender strait.

After the fourth hour of their journey, the deck of their packet steamer was becoming quite the crush. Passengers who weren't driven aloft by curiosity were doing so due to the ripe stench of the hull below from the many who'd suffered bouts of seasickness on the journey.

Meg, who'd always possessed an iron constitution, hadn't felt the least bit queasy. However, when the aunts' maid had cast up her accounts into a makeshift bowl of her apron—the contents of her breakfast of coddled eggs, kippers, porridge and sausages looking as though they were strained through a fine mesh sieve—even Meg had needed to escape or become the next victim of the retching epidemic.

For that reason, she had been content to stay on deck for the duration and sketch in her book.

Even though she wore an ivory veil to protect her face from the sun and spray, her bonnet ribbons were whipped to a shred from the salty sea air. But she didn't mind. She was eager to put England and heartbreak far behind her.

She knew that on foreign soil she would be less likely to think about Daniel Prescott. Less likely to feel the hurt and sense of inadequacy she'd carried with her ever since he'd told her she was too young to know her own mind. And less likely to recall that, even then, she'd been determined to wait for him . . . only to have her heart shatter when she'd read his letter.

Dear Miss Stredwick,

I have married . . .

Meg reached beneath the veil to wipe the sea spray from her cheek just before the aunts joined her at the railing.

"Would you look at that sight, sister?" Myrtle said on a gasp of delight. "From this distance, Calais looks rather like a table set for a grand party, with towering puddings, sculpted pies and steaming tureens all just waiting to be tasted."

The younger Parrish sister was wholly unconcerned with the wind that toyed with her coiffure, the stray locks of silver floss escaping from beneath her bonnet, and the hems of her Saxon blue pelisse and worsted wool skirts being buffeted against her legs.

Maeve, on the other hand, was buttoned up to the chin, her hat ribbons secured into the high collar of her slate gray traveling costume. "You're looking through the eyes of your appetite again."

"Well, it has been over four hours since we left that Dover inn and the positively sumptuous buffet. I've never seen such a mountain of food."

"Indeed, and we had the pleasure of seeing it again in Mrs. Pendergast's lap," Maeve said with a shiver. "I'm surprised you can even think of food after the carnage we witnessed."

"I have pushed it from my mind as cleanly as an unsightly fishbone from the edge of my plate. After all, we have a grand purpose for our trip—to collect as many of the Continent's finest recipes that we can carry—and we certainly shall not allow a little bilious *reckoning* to stand in our way. No. We must forge onward for the greater good."

"That was actually quite a sensible argument," Maeve said with a surprised lift of her brows.

Myrtle cupped her hand to the side of her mouth and said to Meg in a stage whisper, "Besides, I do my best flirting when I'm hungry."

"Oh, sister. Whatever shall I do with you?"

Unrepentant to the core, Myrtle grinned. "Just imagine . . . for every muffin man and nut seller in England, there are likely croissant and macaron sellers here. Can I help it if I want to sample as much as I can without spending a single franc? And do not give me that put-upon expression, Maeve Parrish, for I recall how much you batted your eyes when we were last here, whenever our brother was looking away."

"I was six and twenty. That was over"—she cleared her throat—"well, a handful of years ago, at any rate. It hardly signifies."

"I daresay you broke a heart or two."

Maeve shook her head, but there was a hint of a wistful smile on her lips. "It was rather thrilling. And I suppose the most exciting part about traveling abroad is that one can be whoever she wishes to be for that one moment in time."

"And you were a flirt. Admit it," Myrtle said with a laugh.

"Hush, you."

They were both flirts as far as Meg was concerned. Between Maeve's sly flattery, honed to an art form, and Myrtle's cheeky grins and audaciousness, there hadn't been a single baker or confectioner from Somerset to Dover who'd stood a chance of resisting their charms. And with every new recipe conquest, they appeared to enjoy themselves immensely.

Over the course of their journey, they'd also shared the stories of their long-ago *grand flirtations*—the ones that their thoughts always returned to with fondness.

Meg didn't have any fond reminiscences like theirs. Instead, she had Daniel Prescott's letter, along with the knowledge that her soul's counterpart was now married to someone else.

She sighed as her gaze swept over the shoreline. Strangely enough, it actually did resemble a buffet table set with a feast of spired puddings, squat pies and square layered cakes with thatched roofs, she mused distractedly as her thoughts drifted toward the future.

What romantic moments would she have to look back on when she was in her dotage?

The answer was rather dismal. And she realized with surprise that she wanted to have stories like theirs. Or at least one.

One grand flirtation.

Yes, she thought, feeling the notion plant itself inside her heart and take root in all the broken places.

Why shouldn't she flirt a bit? Or a lot? This was her holiday, after all. And when she returned to Wiltshire to spend the rest of her life as a spinster, she might have a memory to look back on with a smile.

The only problem was, in her two Seasons, there hadn't been a single gentleman who'd seen her as a woman. Instead, most had treated her like a girl, practically dismissing her with a pat on the head. In fact, the only man who hadn't done the same had been the duke.

When he'd caught her wandering through his halls, he'd assumed that she was a husband-hunter. Not a girl but a woman. A woman capable of conspiring and scheming in order to seize what she wanted.

Of course, that hadn't stopped him from walking away. But there had been a moment, when he'd looked at her, when something dark and altogether thrilling flared in his gaze . . .

"Aha!" Myrtle said, peering over Meg's shoulder and giving her a start. "Now I realize why each of the handsome gentlemen that Maeve and I have pointed out on this trip have failed to spark your interest. None of them wore spectacles."

"Whyever would you—" Meg broke off when she saw the aunts looking down at her sketchbook. There, plain for all to see were a pair of spectacles, perched on the nose of a familiar brooding face. She quickly closed the book. "Merely scribbling."

She hadn't mentioned her encounter with the duke. If she had done, she was certain they'd never have let her leave without securing a wedding date.

Of course, that wasn't to say that they'd have had any luck in that regard. Even if they had managed the unlikely feat of bringing the unduly pedantic duke up to scratch, she would have refused. She believed in love and fate and would never consider marrying out of mere obligation.

Even so, for the past two days, they'd spoken of little else than their disappointment at not meeting him, making it impossible for Meg to scrape him cleanly from her mind. And with so much talk of him, was it any wonder that she'd inadvertently drawn his likeness?

"I had a music tutor who wore a monocle," Myrtle said dreamily. "He had silver streaks at his temples and once told me that I had exceptional breath control."

Maeve pursed her lips. "That tutor resembled a one-eyed owl, if you ask me. And the instant our brother saw him admiring your . . . *breath control*, he sacked him on the spot."

"Hmm . . . I'd forgotten that part." Myrtle's brow furrowed for a moment before it cleared, then she shrugged offhandedly. "Oh, well. It never hurts to be admired. And speaking of . . . I've heard that the Duke of Merleton wears a pair of eyeglasses and looks rather handsome in them."

Meg felt the collective weight of their bright, wedding-breakfast gazes drop pointedly to the newly closed sketch-book. She was half tempted to hurl it into the sea.

Shifting from one foot to the other, she cleared her throat. "Does he? I'm sure I shouldn't know."

"A pity we did not happen upon him at his estate."

Myrtle sighed forlornly. "And we so wanted you to meet him."

"I thought you said you were only after the recipes," Meg accused. "Though, it seems to me, you had an ulterior motive all along."

Maeve nudged her sister with a sharp elbow. "What Myrtle meant to say is that we thought you might have charmed more recipes out of him, if you had met."

"Yes, indeed. That is precisely what I meant."

Right. And I was born yesterday, Meg thought wryly.

However, this exchange only made her feel justified in keeping her brief encounter with the duke a secret. And she was inordinately glad that she would never cross paths with the spectacle-wearing bachelor Duke of Merleton again.

All she wanted was to find a man to flirt with on her holiday. And *not* one who would incite the aunts' matrimonial expectations. Surely, that shouldn't be too difficult. Should it?

🦋

AN HOUR later, they were officially on French soil, the air briny and charred and full of promise.

The port of Calais was bustling with activity and industry. Passenger ships crowded the docks, and freight was being unloaded by surly crews and stacked in crates on the damp cobblestones. Hawkers milled about, shouting the prices of their goods. And anxious family members waited for the passengers disembarking on wobbly sea legs.

Standing in line for the customs agent to check their bags, Maeve shook her head with sympathy as her gaze drifted to the seawall where her maid stood, shoulders hunched and a hand clamped to her mouth. "I fear Mrs. Pendergast is still a bit green around the gills. Though, I daresay there isn't much left in her accounts to cast up."

Holding her steady was Meg's own maid, Bryony Cooper. The fresh-faced girl offered assistance to her fellow abigail by mopping her brow with a handkerchief. The two of them had traveled in a separate carriage with the trunks, and it was not until earlier that morning in Dover that Mrs. Pendergast revealed that she had never sailed before. And as the apron that had been given a burial at sea could attest, the now sallow and raddled woman did not take well to the tidal surges.

"Oh, how I wish we were not trapped forever in this line. I'm sure she would be much improved if we were already at our hotel. I've heard that seasickness can linger for an entire day," Myrtle added with sympathy.

Maeve frowned as she looked toward the conveyances, where scores of passengers were crowding into a filthy three-rowed coach. Ushering them inside with impatient gestures were two surly outriders and an unkempt driver who wore a stained red kerchief tied around his neck.

"They look more like highwaymen than respectable drivers," she said and summarily shook her head. "We cannot allow her to travel in that vile *diligence*, else she will be ill for a week. Or worse."

Hearing this, their porter dashed off to hail two of the waiting cabs—one for their trunks and the other for them. Even so, it would be a while before they could leave, especially since they were still waiting for the customs agent.

"I do not see a reason for Mrs. Pendergast to linger," Meg said. "If you would permit me, I will take both maids to our cabriolet. Then the three of us shall follow in the one that will bear our trunks."

"Splendid notion, my dear." Myrtle beamed on a sigh of relief.

Maeve nodded but with hesitation as she reached for Meg's satchel. "Here. We'll take charge of this. But be careful. There's no telling what you may encounter."

"I shall be within forty paces of you. What trouble could I possibly run into?" Meg laughed. But seeing their hesitation as they mulled over the possibilities, she quickly issued a jaunty salute and left before they could change their minds.

But after seeing the maids to the carriage and sending them on to the hotel, Meg realized that trouble came in many different guises.

Turning back to rejoin the aunts, she discovered that a wall of crates had been unloaded directly behind her. And there were more coming.

A veritable stream of burly sailors hefted an assortment of imported goods down a springboard gangplank. Without paying heed to any obstacle that dared stand in their path, they loaded baskets and barrels and trunks of all sizes onto waiting horse carts.

Skirting out of the way, lest she become bowled over and flattened like a crepe, she caught sight of the tall figure of a man out of the corner of her eye. He was walking slowly with his head bent, apparently unaware that he was in the direct path of the cargo being unloaded.

"Sir! Sir!" she called out, but he paid no attention.

It was then that she noticed a half dozen casks of either wine or ale perched on the very top of the gangplank. A dire sense of warning prickled up the back of her neck.

Then, suddenly, one of the casks broke free.

A sailor shouted, "Ho, there!"

But the man, with merely a glance, continued at his methodical pace.

Meg couldn't watch. And yet, how could she look away

and simply leave him to his fate? He was about to be crushed! She had to do something.

Picking up her skirts, she rushed forward, full charge. Then she shoved him out of the way. Or tried to. But it was like a kitten hurling itself at an ox.

The man merely staggered forward a single step, then instantly whipped around.

"What the devil do you—"

She didn't give him time to finish, because now they were both in the path of danger.

So she launched herself at him again. Putting her shoulder into it, she slammed into his form. Hard.

A low grunt left the man's lips. Meg heard something crunch. Then they stumbled together in a disorderly confusion of limbs, like marionettes abruptly cut from their strings.

Oof! Her teeth clacked together as her back collided with a wall of burlap grain sacks. An instant later, he landed against her front and drove the remaining wind from her lungs. And as she lay dying, she dimly heard the wayward cask whoosh by in a gravelly rumble.

Now that the immediate threat was over, she expected the man to remove himself. When he didn't, she looked up, ready to scold this stranger. But her diatribe fell short as her gaze fixed on a pair of familiar, intensely dark eyes . . . sans spectacles.

"You!" she gasped, saw the same shock and dismay mirrored in his expression.

But the Duke of Merleton recovered quickly. A single brow inched toward his hairline as he said, "I should have known."

Chapter 5

Don't upset the apple cart

Meg tried to catch her breath. But since she was still held tightly against the duke and acutely aware of everything at once—like his long-fingered hand splayed against her lower back, the pressure of his fingertips, the warmth of his palm, the tangle of their legs, the press of their hips, their stomachs and chests laboring against each other—she could hardly think, let alone remember how respiration worked.

Was it in, then out? Or out, then in? Her lungs didn't seem to know what to do at all.

Thankfully, he righted the two of them and set her apart before she ended up swooning in his arms like a silly twit in a Gothic novel who fainted if a gentleman penetrated her with his gaze.

And yet, she was feeling a bit dazed, nonetheless. The collision had only lasted a few seconds, but beneath her breast, her heart struggled to catch up with its own beats. In fact, she was so stunned to find herself staring up at his face again that she repeated an incredulous "You?"

"Clearly," he intoned with that disapproving frown as he looked down to his hand.

She did the same, observing the spatter of mud on his cravat and coat along the way before spying the pair of brass-rimmed spectacles in his hand. Like the first time they'd met, he was dirty and so were his glasses.

Honestly, she was surprised the man was capable of making it out of bed in the morning.

Unaccountably irritated, Meg whipped a handkerchief from her sleeve, then reached out and took hold of the object. "If you'd have been wearing these, you likely would have seen that you'd been about to become flat as a flounder."

"I was aptly aware of the barrel's trajectory and had already calculated the seconds it would take to walk three paces out of the way without suffering an injury or fatality. Had I increased the speed of my gait, then the dray that merely splashed me when its fore wheel hit a puddle would have struck me instead. Of course, I did not factor in the possibility of a reckless woman charging at me while I was in the middle of polishing the mud from my lenses."

"A simple *thank you for saving my life* would suffice." She rolled her eyes in exasperation and stepped closer to put the glasses on his face where they belonged. "Now, bend down, if you please."

When her arms lifted, he shook his head. "I am afraid your efforts—"

"I haven't all day, Your Grace, and you are still far too tall."

He expelled a taut breath through his nostrils, but obliged and lowered his head.

And that was when she noticed the problem.

As she unfolded the hinged bronze arms to set the earpieces in place, she became aware of a certain twist in the frame that forced the glasses to sit rather cockeyed. The left side drooped. The right was tilted back to reflect the sky.

Hmm. In an effort to straighten them, she nudged the saddle over the bridge of his nose with the tip of her gloved finger.

"There," she said . . . just before a lens popped out.

The disk dropped neatly into his waiting palm as if he'd anticipated the calamity. "As I was saying, your efforts to *save* my life caused irreparable damage to my spectacles."

Ah. So that was the crunching sound she'd heard.

"Well, I'm certain someone could repair them." As she spoke, a hook-shaped portion of the frame snapped off. The glasses swung in a low-sweeping arc, dangling from one ear a moment before the remaining pieces fell to . . . well . . . pieces. "Or not."

Straightening his posture, he tucked the detritus into the inner breast pocket of his gray wool coat. "I find it curious that you have not commented on the happenstance that we should both meet again."

"You don't believe in happenstance."

"And you have quite the keen memory," he said with a knowing lift of his brows. "I have a sense that little escapes your notice."

That was a rather odd thing to say. Then again, he was a rather peculiar man. Even so, she was curious about why they should encounter each other again, and here of all places. "Very well, I shall ask. What brings you to Calais?"

"It has to do with a recent theft on my property."

"How interesting. I hope you enjoy your—" She broke off as she registered what he'd just said. Her throat went dry and she rasped, "Theft?"

Surely, he couldn't mean . . .

"Of certain recipes."

She gulped audibly. Somehow, he'd found out and had come all the way to France in order to . . . to . . . what? Confiscate the scrap of foolscap? Take her into custody? Have her clapped in irons? Exported? Hanged?

Well, that seemed a bit excessive for a single pilfered recipe, even if it was *the duke's favorite*.

"Have you heard of them?" he asked with a cool glance over her blanched complexion.

She tried to compose herself and not look guilty. It was just a little recipe, after all. Hardly valuable.

"A . . . a brief mention, perhaps."

He nodded as if in understanding. "It is true that they are not spoken of at such length as they once were. Then again, I imagine there are few who could hear of a bejeweled book, illuminated in gold and silver, and not remember it."

Ohhh! A breath of relief left Meg in a rush.

He was talking about the book. *The* recipe book. Not the stained collection that the cook had in the cupboard.

So then, this meeting of theirs could only have been a strange coincidence.

Huh. And to think, right around the time that she was there with the aunts, a diabolical stranger was plotting to take that ancient book. Such a shame. And, clearly, Mr. Gudgeon had a lot to answer for if he was allowing just anyone inside the keep.

Unless, of course, the aunts had managed to take it . . . No, that wasn't possible. They were determined, but not steal-into-a-family-vault determined. Besides, they'd only been separated for a moment.

Absolving herself and the aunts of any guilt, she tsked and patted his sleeve with sympathy. "I cannot believe someone stole something so precious right out from under your nose. The absolute gall. I hope you recover the book quickly."

"I fully intend to. In fact, I've managed to track the thief to France," he said darkly.

"Here?" What were the odds of that? Why, she might have traveled on the packet steamer with the thief in question. A truly uncanny coincidence. "Why do you suppose the culprit would travel to France?"

"I could ask the same of you, for I cannot reason it out."

"You're asking me?"

His mouth curled slightly at one corner. "I can think of no one more qualified to answer the question."

Meg was taken aback. *Flabbergasted*, to be honest.

Men never asked for her opinion. They typically took one look at her youthful, rounded face and observed her with a condescending air as if she were a green goose with nothing to offer of consequence. Even Daniel had done so.

But not this man. And she had no idea that she'd made such a favorable impression on him in those scant few minutes they'd spent in the shadowy corridor.

Flattered by this, she studied him from a fresh perspective.

He was still a brooding sort of fellow with an inordinately intense gaze. But in this light, she could see that his ears were nicely shaped and not flared in the least. His nose wasn't excessively large but fit the proportions of his chiseled countenance. His jaw was sharply angled, his chin strong but not overly mulish by any means. In truth, he wasn't terrible to look upon. He had a nice head of dark hair, too, even if it was a bit long on top and fell carelessly to one side. A quick trim could remedy that. His shoulders were quite broad and . . . well . . . what woman wouldn't find those appealing? And, if memory served, his forearms were finely honed.

All things considered, the duke wasn't half-bad.

However, the best part of all was that he didn't look remotely like Daniel Prescott.

Giving careful consideration to Merleton's query, Meg straightened her shoulders and tapped her finger to the side of her mouth. "Perhaps there are ingredients that can only be found in France. I know that the aunts have mentioned that the truffles residing in the soil here are the best in the world."

"Ah. Then the culprit wants to recreate the dishes as they were first made."

"Well, I do recall mention of the Broceliande Forest—Arthur's forest—located in Brittany. That might be a connection, as well."

His brows lifted in surprise. "You know your history."

She grinned abashedly and shook her head. "I know stories. My father loved to tell them, especially those of the knights of the round table. They were his favorites."

"Were they, indeed?"

This must have pleased the duke, for something glimmered in those alert river-stone eyes. Something that made her pulse quicken. And she discovered with surprise that being the sole recipient of his rapt attention was . . . well . . . rather appealing.

As soon as the thought entered her mind, she nearly rolled her eyes and was glad that a certain pair of meddlesome matchmakers would never know—

Oh, no! *The aunts!* She'd completely forgotten that they were waiting for her. Drat!

If they discovered her in the duke's company, they would likely start planning a wedding breakfast without delay. Then Meg could kiss the idea of having any fun or small flirtation—let alone a grand one—fare thee well.

"That is all the insight I can offer, I'm afraid," she said in haste, backing away as if he were a leper.

Frowning, he took a step toward her. "But we haven't concluded our discussion."

"I must return to my party before they become alarmed by my absence. But I wish you the best of luck in sorting this out, Your Grace." She turned to leave but couldn't stop herself from adding, "Then again, I don't imagine you believe in luck."

"No. I believe in facts, tangible proof and the knowledge that I will have my property in my hands quite soon."

"After you repair your spectacles, of course." With a hapless shrug, she grinned and noticed that he stopped his pursuit at once. As he stood there, staring after her, she offered a merry wave and walked away, bidding adieu to the duke for the last time.

SHE WAS taunting him, Lucien thought as he watched the thief from the confines of his carriage.

He couldn't believe how boldly she played her game. First, in manhandling him and catching him off guard, then in manipulating the conversation. From complaining of his height to mentioning the truffles, the Broceliande Forest and her father, Lucien could hardly fathom what she might have said next. It was enough to make his head spin like the wheels of a carriage, careening off course.

Not only that, but her reaction when he'd mentioned the theft—the widening of her eyes, the way she'd blanched, her throat constricting on a swallow—almost had him believing that she was innocent, caught up in a scheme of another's design.

The glimpse of her frailty surprised him exceedingly. But that was when he realized it was merely another ruse, a performance to gain his sympathy.

Therefore, he'd quickly adjusted his own tactics. He'd surmised that by pretending to require her assistance in solving the riddle, he would deceive her into thinking that he didn't suspect her, thereby filling her with a sense of complacency that would cause her to reveal her true nature.

He'd been right.

She'd given herself away by admitting a deep knowledge of Arthurian legend. He'd almost had her in his snare. Though, she must have sensed her own slip because her manner altered again. She had become agitated by degree, casting a nervous glance over her shoulder, just before she announced the need to depart without delay.

Lucien wasn't about to let her go. He wanted answers. And he had every intention of escorting her back to her party, even if only to cement the point that she couldn't hide from him.

But then, casual as you please, she'd flashed a grin. And he hated to admit that he had been disarmed by it. His brain had neglected to send the required information to his organs and limbs, leaving him momentarily arrested. Long enough for her to escape before he learned anything of much value.

"She is too clever by half," he said, his mood in a knot.

"That girl with the old biddies? I think you're barking up the wrong tree, cousin," Pell said from the adjacent bench. "She's far too young to be Lady Avalon. We were hearing rumors of her exploits when you visited London last year. And the infamous adventuress had been seducing men for their fortunes and secrets even before then."

"Do not be fooled by the careful application of creams and powders. If you'll recall from the list my investigator provided, the secret formula of a youth serum was among the items she has stolen."

The report stated that Mr. Sudworth, of the eponymously named Sudworth's Cosmetics, had been forced to apologize to the ladies of the *ton*—who'd paid handsomely in advance for the serum—stating that a woman who went by the moniker Lady Avalon had taken him unawares and had stolen the only copy from his safe.

A similar tale had been told by a certain Lord Hunnicutt, who'd discovered that his wife's diamond tiara had been purloined after a night at the opera with the lady in question. Then there was a banker in Brussels, a shipping magnate in America, a count in Cologne, a marquis in Marseille . . . and the list went on.

Thirteen pages in all. A myriad of treasures and secrets stolen, and none of them with any apparent connection. At least, not yet.

"Perhaps, but we still don't know to what end."

Pell's statement mirrored Lucien's own frustrated thoughts. "She must be working for someone. A collector of some sort."

Aye, that must be it, he mused. This villain knew about the legends, too. Lucien wondered about the extent of that knowledge and whether it might aid him in his own quest. He would have to meet him to discover the answer. And in order to do that, he would have to get closer to her. Much closer.

"And the old biddies?"

Distracted by his thoughts, Lucien answered, "It is obvious that Lady Avalon recruited them to act as her shield. Oh, she is quite cunning, to be sure, and not one to be underestimated. Mark my words, behind those crystalline blue eyes lies a wolf in sheep's clothing."

"Crystalline?" Pell puffed out a laugh. "Is that a word you've just made up?"

"It is from the Greek *krustallos*, meaning *crystal*, and dating back to the fifteenth century." And there was no more apt word to describe the startlingly clear, pale blue color.

"I thought you said she broke your spectacles. So how do you even know the color of her eyes?"

"Because I remember them from when we first met and my spectacles were still intact," Lucien growled beneath his breath. He detested being bothered by pointless questions.

Thankfully, his vision impairment was only with objects that were near. He could see quite clearly from a distance, like the way she'd just glanced surreptitiously over her shoulder as if to ensure she wasn't being followed before climbing into her carriage.

But damn, he wished he'd had his corrective lenses in place when they'd stood together a few moments ago. He wanted to catalog every look that crossed her face, note every subtle shift and twitch so that he would be armed with all the information he needed to discover the man she worked for. Given time, he knew she would give something away.

For now, however, they were engaged in a subtle dance of accusation and subterfuge.

So she claimed that he'd met *his* match? Well, he would soon prove that she had met hers.

"By the by, what color are my eyes?"

"They are—" Lucien stopped. "I refuse to respond to such an inane and insufferably provoking question when you and I are both aware of the answer."

"Do you know what I think?"

"That it still boggles your mind when two plus two equals four?"

"My cousin, the wit," Pell said dryly. "But you cannot hide behind your droll humor, because I think Lady Avalon has sparked your interest."

"You are delusional. All I want are those recipes and the name of the man she's working for. Nothing more."

And yet, he was surprised to recall the initial response he'd had when she'd hurled herself against him. Shock, of course. And then . . . something else.

The moment played through his senses with perfect precision—the feel of her body against his, the precise dimensions of the dip in her lower back as he'd pulled her close to keep her from falling, the warmth and softness of her breasts as she crushed the fist that held his glasses, the rush of breath escaping her lips as she looked up and saw him—

He shook his head. It was ridiculous to ponder over it or wonder why it felt as though her form had left an indelible stamp upon his own. He was the Duke of Merleton. His sole focus was to secure these pieces of his family heritage.

He refused to let a woman distract him with her charms.

No, indeed, for he knew her coy game. And if she thought for a minute that a pair of broken spectacles would keep him from following her, then she had underestimated her latest adversary.

"Suit yourself," Pell said offhandedly, easing back against the squabs. "All we need to do is follow her and her luggage, and then we'll soon have possession of the book."

Lucien shook his head. "It will not be that simple. I could send a man to search their trunks, but he won't find anything. She would not be that careless. No, indeed. Otherwise, she wouldn't have such an illustrious career as a master thief. We will need to keep a close eye on her and take careful note of everyone she encounters. And I'm beginning to wonder if the objects she has stolen were chosen at random or if there is a pattern," he said, sensing that he was on the cusp of unearthing something that would alter the course of his life. "A little more time with her is all I'll need."

Pell was silent for a moment, scrutinizing Lucien's profile. "Are you certain this isn't merely an excuse to bump into her again?"

He ignored the comment. "Whoever hired her could simply be a fanatic of the old legend, but I don't think so. It seems more like the plot of a military man, one with a particular appetite for power."

"Well, if your plan is to meet her again and learn her secrets, you might want to tame that prickly and obdurate nature of yours. At least pretend to be affable. More flies with honey, and all that."

That old adage might be true. But Lucien wasn't interested in flies. He wanted to lure a wolf into the open. And as the carriage set off in pursuit, he began to formulate a plan.

Chapter 6

Food for thought

The days that followed were so filled with traveling from Calais to Paris, with pilfering recipes from every boulangerie and patisserie along the way, and with the aunts displaying the art of the three *F*s, there wasn't a spare moment for Meg to think about the Duke of Merleton.

And yet . . . she did, nonetheless.

It was intolerably frustrating. She couldn't seem to shake the tumult still teeming inside her after their collision on the docks. At random moments throughout her day, her thoughts would return to those brief seconds of being crushed against him, his hold so strong and sure that it was as if he'd known precisely how her body should fit against his.

In his arms, she'd felt that tug again. Though, at the time, she'd been too perturbed at his recklessness to pay much attention to it.

But lately, she was becoming all too aware of its absence. It felt like a rope remained tied through her middle, only now she was just dragging it around, waiting for someone to pick up the other end. Someone *other* than the duke, of course. Someone that would keep the aunts thinking about grand flirtations and not—absolutely not—about wedding breakfasts.

Meg sighed, fogging up the glass of the carriage window.

She hadn't felt this way with Daniel. He'd given her butterflies that took flight whenever she'd thought of seeing him again. Every feeling had centered in her heart. Which was likely the reason it had shattered when she'd received his letter announcing his marriage.

With the duke, on the other hand, the sensations were lower, deeper. Infinitely more intriguing.

Even so, it took her by surprise that she should find her thoughts frequently on that irascible man, wondering if she would see him again. Which was particularly discombobulating considering she would rather eat celeries—her least favorite vegetable—than endure another encounter with him.

Thankfully, as they left the countryside and approached Paris in their hired coaches, Meg began to feel more like herself.

The city unfolded in a dazzling display of color and light, and she was eager to take it all in. There was a vibrancy in the atmosphere that instantly filled her with effervescence, a light buoyancy that had been absent in her for the past year. And she welcomed it, hoping to keep it with her all the while.

It wasn't long before they arrived at their predetermined coaching inn but were soon informed by a man at the door that there were no rooms available. This was surprising considering that it was so late in the spring when many began journeying to the country. Nevertheless, after a brief exchange, he recommended a rather lavish hotel, and they decided to indulge themselves. This was a holiday, after all.

Upon reaching the grand facade, they were welcomed with pomp and circumstance by a gray mustachioed concierge whose eyes widened at the mention of their names.

"Ah. C'est bon. Zee three Misses Parrish have arrived at last," he said with a grin and clapped his hands for a flurry of attendants to see to their trunks. "You shall have zee finest apartment of rooms."

"*Merci, monsieur,*" Maeve said, her pencil-thin brows drawn together in perplexity. "Were you expecting us?"

He winked as if she should know the answer. "But of course, *mademoiselle.*"

They were left to wonder how that could be as he scuttled through a side door to attend to other business, leaving them in the hands of the porter. On the way to their rooms, the aunts agreed that Meg's brother must have arranged it all, sending a letter ahead of them to ensure that they received the best accommodations.

And yet, if it had been Brandon, then wouldn't the concierge have known that she was a Miss Stredwick instead of one-third of *zee three Misses Parrish*?

The mystery, if it even was a mystery, quickly fell off the list of importance when they entered the corner suite that stole their collective breaths.

The vast room was furnished with impeccable refinement, all cream and soft golden hues. A flood of warm sunlight streamed in through two tall windows that were swathed in ivory drapes and parted to reveal an awe-inspiring view of the city.

And if that wasn't enough, no sooner had they and their maids begun to unpack than a knock fell on the door with an attendant bringing them a tea tray brimming with flaky, buttery pastries.

"I want to stay in this place forever," Myrtle said later as she lounged against the tufted jonquil chair and casually nibbled one last crumb that she'd plucked from the folds of her fichu.

Maeve stood at the window and winced slightly as she stiffly turned her neck. Pressing a hand to her nape, she said, "The coaches and roadways certainly leave something to be desired. I don't know if I've ever been so enervated in all my life."

"It's because we're old, sister."

"Speak for yourself," Maeve answered, a small smile on her lips.

But Meg was of an opinion that the pair would never grow old. Not truly. Age was a mere number for the likes of them.

Nevertheless, that did not stop them from deciding to take a restorative nap an hour later. And while they were dreaming of *mille-feuille* and *viennoiserie*, Meg stole out of the room to explore the hotel.

It wasn't long before she spotted a familiar face that took her quite by surprise.

"Honoria Hartley," Meg said with a pleased smile as the young woman in question ascended the stairs. "Surely this cannot be you, in Paris of all places."

"Meg!" Honoria blinked with recognition, then instantly rushed forward for a quick embrace.

Her smile was radiant as always, her hair a lustrous gold, and her complexion a flawless peaches and cream. In truth, she was the most stunning woman of Meg's acquaintance.

In fact, every one of the Hartley sisters were renowned beauties. Meg had known the family for years, even before Honoria and she had debuted together. They kept an estate to the north, near where Meg had lived when her parents were still alive.

"I haven't seen you since last Season," Honoria said. "I thought, perhaps, that you'd married and flitted off into the country in wedded bliss."

"No," Meg answered simply, not wanting to think about the past year . . . or Daniel. "But my brother is married now. I am traveling with my sister-in-law's aunts on a small tour of the Continent for the summer."

"What fun! And I'm positively jade green with envy. I'm here with my cousin Daphne and her husband, Colonel Whittingham, but we must set off for home at week's end. In fact, I was just on an errand for her at the apothecary," she said, pausing briefly to remove a brown bottle from her reticule, then handed it to a waiting abigail who left them with a bobbed curtsy.

"Oh, dear. I hope your cousin isn't unwell."

"Nothing that will not remedy itself in a few months, I should think. The nature of the illness has been the topic of whispered conversations between Daphne and the colonel that abruptly break off when I enter the room. However, after a visit from a local physician and the subsequent smiles and happy sighs, I've surmised the rest."

It took Meg a moment to understand, but as Honoria made a discreet gesture with her hand hovering over her midriff, she nodded. "Ah. My brother has recently become a proud father and has subsequently become impossible to live with. Even more so than usual."

"I don't believe it. Compared to my brother, yours is practically perfect."

"Oh, it's true. Brandon grins. All. The. Time. I've even caught him whistling off-key as he walks down the hallway. Positively dreadful." Meg rolled her eyes, but in truth, she couldn't have been happier for him.

Honoria laughed. "I still cannot believe that someone finally snagged *London's most elusive bachelor*." Linking arms, they sauntered along the corridor, the runner muffling the sound of their unhurried footfalls. "It's your turn up the aisle next, *mon amie*."

A sharp twinge pierced Meg's heart. She hated that losing Daniel still hurt. Not always, but still . . . It was as if the shattered pieces of her hopes and dreams hadn't been put back together in the right location, leaving jagged fissures behind.

"I think not," she said, attempting an air of nonchalance. "The notion has lost its appeal."

Honoria issued a groan of commiseration. "I know precisely what you mean. After all, why should we end our carefree lives of parties and flirting to settle for the drudgery of matrimony? I enjoy the chase far too much to give it up."

"Shameless!" Meg teased. "Though, being pursued by scores of men is not something I've ever had to worry about."

"Then, there is no time like the present. After all, you're on holiday. When better to practice your wiles than on random—exceedingly handsome—unsuspecting gentlemen?"

A rueful laugh escaped Meg. "I'm not certain I have wiles. If I do, I was never able to practice them with my brother always hovering over me like a hawk to his nestling."

Perhaps if she'd had wiles, Daniel wouldn't have . . .

No, she told herself firmly. *You will not finish that thought.*

"Nonsense. That was the old Miss Margaret Stredwick of Wiltshire, disappointed debutante, dutiful younger sister and prisoner of the home island," Honoria said with a cheeky grin. Stopping at a large window, she gestured with a dramatic sweep of her arm toward the cityscape. "Now you are here. In France. *Without* your brother. You can be anyone you want—woman of many wiles, lady of intrigue, adventuress, or even visiting royalty from a foreign land."

Meg shook her head. "*You* could surely do all those things, but I couldn't."

"Of course you can. I once invented an entire country and named myself its princess. Just a bit of fun for an evening."

"Fun for you, because you've always been brilliant at those sorts of things."

She remembered all the times they'd put on plays and how superbly Honoria embodied her characters. Not only that, but men found her intriguing and beguiling in a way that Meg had never been.

"Well, I do come by it honestly, or rather, *dis*honestly," Honoria said with an unrepentant glint in her tip-tilted eyes.

"Either way, it runs in the family. The Hartley clan is a veritable liars' club."

"Then, I wish we could travel together, so you could teach me everything you know." Meg wasn't wholly serious when she said the words, and yet, as they hung in the air she was suddenly compelled to seek her friend's counsel. "Might I ask you a question?"

"I would pinch you if you didn't."

Meg grinned, her teeth sinking into her bottom lip as she looked around to ensure that there was no one close by who might overhear. "What would you do if you'd met a man whom you'd rather not know—while doing something you ought not to have done—only to realize that, days later, you could not push him from your mind?"

"Mmm . . . I'm quite intrigued by the *something you ought not to have done*," she said with a sly lift of her finely arched brows. "I shall let you tell me all about that later. In the meantime, however, it seems to me that you require a distraction from these plaguing thoughts. And the only truly effective way to rid your mind of one man is to surround yourself with scores of others, upon whom you can practice your wiles."

"And if I do not possess any, as I highly suspect?"

Honoria issued an unconcerned shrug. "Then, you'll play the part of a woman who does. And it just so happens I know of the perfect place to start." She held up a finger, her expression bright with something between mischief and excitement. "There is a party at the home of the Count and Countess Andret tomorrow evening to showcase the new acquisitions to his collection of . . . well . . . whatever it is that he collects. The point is, his wife knows everyone in society *and* is known for being a bit of a flirt herself. So there are bound to be all sorts of gentlemen in attendance. And since my cousin will likely not attend due to her condition, perhaps you and your companions could join the colonel and me?"

Her friend made it all sound so simple that Meg felt an unexpected thrill at the prospect. "I shall speak with the aunts straightaway."

❦

THE AUNTS sent their regrets. As much as they wished to attend the soiree—if only to sample the menu and pilfer a recipe or two—their days of travel from Calais had caught up with them. And after spending the afternoon touring the gravel paths of the Jardin des Tuileries, they were more than content to rest their feet and lounge in their glorious rooms. In fact, they shooed Meg away, ordering her to expend her *youthful exuberance somewhere else*.

Honestly, it was a relief. She planned to practice flirting and didn't want to get their hopes up. Not only that but telling them the truth—that she was doing so to rid her thoughts of a certain duke who should not be named—was absolutely out of the question. So she simply bussed their cheeks with a kiss and left with Honoria and Colonel Whittingham.

Meg had never anticipated such a lavish affair.

When they arrived, a queue of carriages already lined the driveway, offering a view of a torchlit arcade, flanked by column arches swathed in garlands of sweet wisteria and tall spiral topiaries on either side.

The count and countess lived just beyond the city. Their sprawling manor house sat at the far end of a vast, pristinely manicured lawn, and hosted a pair of twin stone staircases leading up from the gardens to a grand terrace.

Ascending the steps, Meg lifted the hems of her icy-blue satin skirts so that she didn't trip and make a complete cake of herself. She cast a sideways glance to Honoria and saw that they were both stunned into speechlessness, attempting to hide their utter astonishment at their surroundings. Meg had to bite her lip to keep from laughing.

"Do not look at me again," Honoria chided playfully,

"for I will surely lose my carefully crafted facade and appear every bit the country bumpkin that I am."

Meg shook her head. "No one would believe it. In that seafoam gown and with your hair swept up in pearl-encrusted combs, you look like you belong in such a palace. You're a veritable siren, calling the men to fling themselves at your feet and crash against your hems."

"As well they should," she said with a laugh devoid of any self-modesty. If there was one thing that Honoria Hartley had always made perfectly apparent, it was that she knew what she deserved and she wouldn't settle for anything less. "And what about you, hmm? All set to practice your wiles and lure men to *your* shores and rid your thoughts of that pesky duke once and for all?"

Earlier, Meg had confessed everything about the duke, the pilfered recipe, and the uncanny coincidence of encountering him in Calais. She knew that, if anyone could understand her desire to forget all about him, it would be her friend.

Before she could answer the question, however, the breeze shifted, swirling around her gown and lifting the hair from her nape. She caught a familiar scent, something pleasing but unrecognizable . . .

Until she looked up to the terrace.

Waiting at the top were two men in tailored black wool. One was classically handsome with wavy blond hair and an easy grin. The other was striking—surprising, even—with dark hair swept back from his forehead in neat layers. There was a hint of a smile tucked into the corner of his mouth and a glint of torchlight on the lenses of his repaired spectacles.

A shock stole a soundless gasp from her parted lips. She nearly stumbled on the step and would have done if Honoria hadn't linked arms with her.

"You goose. That'll teach you to wear slippers that weigh ten stone each," Honoria teased. But then her gaze followed Meg's. "Do you know those men?"

"Only the one on the right. That's the Duke of Merleton."

"Is it, indeed? My goodness. And it appears as though he is waiting for you. Well, that certainly adds a bit of intrigue to our night of flirting. Your pesky duke isn't playing fair at all."

"I don't think he's aware that there is a game commencing," Meg said, numbly resuming the climb and grimly wondering how she was ever going to put him from her mind if he kept popping up out of nowhere.

"Nonsense," Honoria said. "Where men and women are concerned, everything is a game. And it is up to us to ensure that we always win."

Chapter 7

Piece of cake

When Lady Avalon stepped onto the terrace—her unswerving eyes round in disbelief, her gloved hands still gripping her skirts to hold them aloft even though there were no more steps to climb—Lucien felt an unquantifiable degree of smugness tug at the corner of his mouth.

So, she thought she could outmatch him, did she? Well, she could just think again.

With a bow of greeting, he leaned in to murmur for her ears alone, "Surprised to see me?"

Her mouth opened and closed three times without a single syllable falling from her lips.

Making her utterly speechless from shock sent a distinct thrill through him. He had gained the upper hand.

"What are *you* doing here?" she finally rasped.

"I should think it obvious."

He stared down at her, his brow arching in challenge. In response, a slow saturation of pink rose to the crests of her cheeks.

He wondered what she would do in retaliation. Just what *were* all the devices in this seductress's arsenal?

Truth be told, he was eager to discover the answer. To learn what she might use to regain a semblance of control and befuddle his wits. Or attempt to, rather. He had never been befuddled a day in his life. *Distracted?* Now, that was something else altogether.

But whatever he'd experienced while standing with her in the corridor of Caliburn Keep was a momentary condition which would never be repeated.

He knew better now. And it was clear in the way she visibly recovered her composure—her spine straightening as she released her skirts and smoothed them with a roll of her hands—that she was aware their game had changed as well.

She darted a glance to the others in their party, likely calculating her options.

They were not alone, which meant that she couldn't attempt to distract him with her nearness and casual touches, under the guise of assisting him with his spectacles. No, indeed. There would be witnesses to such bold behavior. Members of society might start to talk. And being noticed was likely the last thing that Lady Avalon wanted. Especially when she was currently disguising herself as a debutante on holiday with her aging aunts.

Ah, yes, he had uncovered quite a bit about her in recent days.

It had been a straightforward matter of paying the concierge at the hotel handsomely to report any news to him at once. The same had been true with the innkeepers from Calais to Paris. A bit of silver transferred from palm to palm, and he had all the information he needed.

Except for whom she was working.

But he was certain that would soon be revealed as well. After all, it could be no coincidence that a woman in possession of a book reputed to hold the promise of imbuing soldiers with prowess on the battlefield should find herself in the company of a colonel, in addition to attending a party at the house of a renowned collector of antiquities.

Foiling her plot was going to be almost too simple.

He watched as her throat worked on a tight swallow. But

it wasn't until he heard the soft rustling of her gown and pet-
ticoats as she took a step back that he realized he'd moved
closer to her without thinking.

Hmm . . . When had he done that?

She hastily gestured to her companion. "An unexpected
pleasure, Your Grace. May I introduce my friend, Miss
Honoria Hartley?"

He inclined his head, only briefly glancing at the companion before returning his attention to the woman he'd
crossed the sea to track down. There were questions still yet
to be answered and a surge of impatience teeming through
his blood.

"Enchanté, mademoiselle," Pell cut in, interrupting
Lucien's musings by taking possession of Miss Hartley's
hand and bowing over her fingertips. "You must pardon my
cousin for not doing his part of the introduction. He has the
politesse of an organ grinder's monkey. I am Viscount Holladay. *Pell* to my friends and *Pellinore Beauregard* when
I'm being scolded. But I vow never to give you reason to
scold me."

Miss Hartley smiled. "We'll have to see about that,
my lord."

"As for you, my lady," he said, turning his charm to the
woman who'd brought about this entire ordeal, "I have been
quite eager to make your acquaintance. And now I can see
precisely why your crystalline blue eyes have snared my
cousin's notice. Quite captivating, indeed."

She issued a curtsy. "Your cousin is most kind, Lord Holladay."

Pell chuckled. "*Kind* is not usually a word used to describe Lucien. *Blunt*, perhaps. *Analytical*, most definitely.
But kindness is a social nicety he would not waste his time
in developing when he has so many other dull pursuits. Nevertheless, it is clear that you've made an impression on him."

Those extraordinary eyes swerved back to Lucien. She

blushed anew, and her brow furrowed with delicate lines of perplexity as if she were not used to hearing such things.

Highly improbable.

This show of modest confusion was likely part of a carefully crafted ploy to lure unsuspecting men into her traps. To compel them to remark that even the stars winking above through the firmament of the night sky held no greater allure than her irises, fringed by those thick inky lashes.

But he was not fool enough to speak such words aloud. Given that there were four in their current tête-à-tête, a remark of that nature—a mere logical observation—had a seventy-five percent chance of being misconstrued as something other than it was, thereby forcing him to elucidate the matter. The effort would only put him at a disadvantage. And he was not about to give up any measure of the ground he'd gained.

No, he was wiser now and would not underestimate her a third time.

"I'm sure that I have done nothing of the sort," she replied with a skillful display of guilelessness. "In fact, after our previous encounters, I can attest that I have the opposite—"

"My apologies, Your Grace, my lord," Miss Hartley interjected. "But I see our escort hailing me from inside. If you would excuse us."

Without further ado, she curled her arm into Lady Avalon's, then set off toward the broad French doors. However, Lucien was almost certain that he heard Miss Hartley whisper to her friend, "Always leave them wanting more."

Confused, he frowned as they disappeared inside.

Out of the thirty-nine possibilities he'd formulated on her progression up the staircase, that was not one of the scenarios he had anticipated.

Damn it all! Her abrupt departure kept him from learning anything noteworthy about her plot or methods. And he needed more information to set his own plan in motion. He must retrieve that book.

Beside him, Pell made an indistinct utterance of frustration. "You're supposed to be affable, remember?"

"I was."

"No. You looked rather like you were about to toss her over your shoulder and carry her off for interrogation . . . or whatever else you had in mind."

"Preposterous. She is wearing layers of satin. There was a sixty percent chance that she would have slipped off my shoulder before I traversed the stairs." Realizing what he'd just admitted, he shifted from one foot to the other, ignoring his cousin's smirk. "It should not signify that I prefer a more direct approach. And besides, I'm not one for idle party prattle."

"Well, you're going to have to be for a time. She isn't likely to warm to you otherwise, and I doubt you'll ever see that book again unless you can gain her trust. If she is working for a military man, as you say, then she must have a great deal at stake. Find out what that is by learning more about her."

"By being affable," he grumbled, shoving a hand through his hair as he tracked her progress through the receiving line.

"Aye. Make her believe you're interested in her, which shouldn't be too difficult for you."

Lucien whipped a glare at him. "My sole interest is the book."

"As you've said. Many times. All I'm suggesting is that you charm her."

"There are no finite rules or procedures for exhibiting charm." He scoffed. "You might as well be asking me to turn myself into an owl."

Pell cuffed him on the shoulder, a pitying look in his eyes. "I'm afraid you're going to have to do this without rules or procedures, old chap. Just pretend you're a man who is looking forward to getting better acquainted with an attractive woman."

"In other words, behave as you would . . . *if* you were capable of cognitive reasoning?" Lucien turned toward the open doors and left his bewildered cousin to puzzle that out.

🦋

ALL THROUGHOUT dinner, Lucien inwardly practiced a series of *charming* invitations to tour the grounds with Lady Avalon. Periodically, he flicked a glance down to the opposite end of the table, where she was sitting in between Colonel Whittingham and a young lord whose attention more often than not was diverted by Miss Hartley. This seemed odd to Lucien because he'd hardly noticed her at all.

His gaze always found Lady Avalon. Which was likely due to the way she seemed to position herself precisely where the glow of candlelight best complemented her porcelain skin and those bright, clear eyes. It was impossible not to notice her. And the color and cut of her gown this evening could only have meant to entice. Quite cunning, indeed.

He wondered what she was saying to the colonel. Was he the man she was working for? Or was it Count Andret?

Lucien didn't know. But he intended to find out.

Ignoring the inane utterances of the woman seated to his left, who hadn't drawn a single breath since the first course of turtle soup, he finally settled on a method of procedure to get Lady Avalon alone. It was both direct and affable and should set matters into motion with utmost expedience.

Therefore, as soon as the gentlemen finished their port and cheroots and joined the ladies in the parlor, he crossed the room and stopped directly in front of her and the countess.

Standing at a display of canopic jars in the count's

collection—the gilded vessels containing the organs of mummified felines which, strangely enough, were the reason for this entire fete—her gaze lifted in question.

Lucien waited two full seconds for their conversation to pause before he bowed brusquely to Lady Avalon. "Would you allow me the honor of escorting you along the arcade?"

This approach seemed to set her off-balance, for he took note of the color that swept to her cheeks as her gaze darted to their hostess.

Beneath a lofty configuration of graying copper curls, the mien of the willowy Countess Andret spread in a rather vixenish grin as she looked between the two of them. *"J'aime l'homme qui va droit au but."*

Understanding that she liked a man who came straight to the point, he inclined his head and proffered his arm to his quarry. He was aware of certain societal niceties. Some had their place, he supposed. Being a duke, however, he was not governed by them. But he knew full well that Lady Avalon's current disguise demanded that she was.

Left with no alternative, she set her fingertips on his sleeve. Then, for his ears alone, she scolded, "You make it quite impossible to refuse."

"Which is something you would do well to remember, my lady."

He felt her gaze on his profile and anticipated a sharp retort. Yet, as he led them onto the terrace, where the gray of twilight was interrupted by the light of four torches, their orange flames sputtering and undulating in the cool breeze, she issued no challenge to his warning. They descended the stairs in silence, breaking through a veil of sweetly charred smoke before stepping down onto the path toward the garden.

With every step, he wondered if she was formulating a plan, devising new methods of distraction to extricate herself from his company and close scrutiny.

Or perhaps her attention was merely diverted by the pair of boys in servant's livery who dashed by, toting a large Catherine wheel between them with gunpowder-filled cylinders mounted on each of the spokes.

Lucien remembered a time when he'd been such a lad, fashioning his own rockets with various compounds for colors. Those were simpler days. He did not yet know of the horrors he would witness or the treachery that awaited him.

Absently, he watched as the boys trampled toward the pond, their eager footsteps crunching on the gravel. He drew in a deep breath, the dew-scented air cool and clear of smoke. Then he focused on the path ahead.

The crepuscular rays from the waxing crescent moon created delineated angles that fell on the path beside the columns lining the arcade. Every step took them from darkness to light and back again, reminding him that there was still too much he did not know.

"Are you looking forward to the fireworks?" his companion asked, drawing his attention to her upturned face.

The moonlight was also bright enough to create some intriguing shadows on her countenance. There were inverted arches beneath the thick fan of her lashes, an obtuse trapezoid beside the delicate shape of her nose, and two parallel scalene triangles along the philtrum above the crimson bow of her lips.

His gaze lingered on that philtrum a moment longer. It was a part of the anatomy that had never claimed his attention before. At least not that he could recall. And yet, he could declare with some authority that an illustration of hers—in a medical journal for example—would make for a particularly interesting study.

"Your Grace?"

"Hmm?" His eyes lifted to meet hers, and then he nodded. "Ah, yes, the fireworks. I enjoy a pyrotechnic display as much as anyone. Although nothing is quite so satisfying as combining the components together oneself and watching the cylinders spin and explode in a shower of sparks."

Distractedly, he mused that the use of copper salts would create a firework that would burst in a blue color to match her irises.

The arches of her fine dark brows rose three-eighths of an inch in a subtle query. "Do you often make your own?"

"Not since I was young, when we used to hold festivals at Caliburn Keep," he said and noticed a subtle curve of her lips in response. "Have I amused you with that information?"

"I was merely imagining you as a boy with smeared lenses, a hank of hair falling over your forehead and a propensity to blow things up."

He studied his adversary, trying to decipher the purpose of such a remark. Was this part of her process—the flirtatious smile? The playful tilt of her lashes? The softness in her expression? It must have been. And yet, he didn't know why he felt somewhat discomposed by it.

He shoved a negligent hand through his hair, then reached into his pocket for a handkerchief, only to realize that, as usual, he'd forgotten it.

"Here," she said and took the spectacles from his grasp.

Standing in semi-seclusion between a pair of tall conical cypress trees, she proceeded to polish them with a dainty square of lace-edged linen, hidden inside her glove. She even lifted them to her mouth, her lips parting on a soft *huuhh* of air that formed a steamy vapor on the lens.

Lucien did not know why he should feel as though she had breathed directly on him. Or why the flesh beneath his collar became unduly warm. After all, he was aware of her maneuvers—the semblance of ease and familiarity she deployed when they were separated from others—and he would no longer allow it to distract him.

"Your imagined portrait is not quite accurate," he said

after he took the frames and settled them in place again. "I have only worn corrective glasses for the past seven years and three months. Not as a child. But yes, I did have a propensity to *blow things up*, as you say."

Her attention returned once more toward the path, where a number of guests were milling along the arcade waiting for the fireworks spectacle, and they resumed their strolling pace.

"You certainly like to be precise," she said, her hands clasped casually behind her back. "And yet, it seems to have escaped your notice that we have not been formally introduced. You address me as *my lady*, but that is not a station which I have earned."

"Perhaps you remind me of a certain lady I know by reputation. A Lady Avalon. Have you heard of her?"

He waited for her complexion to pale at being called out. Or even for her to flash a boastful grin. But she did neither.

"I do not believe I have," she said, her head tilted to one side, her lips pursed. "Though, perhaps she is the one you would rather have in your company."

"I only wish to be with the woman beside me in this very moment—whoever she claims to be."

"Then who I am in truth matters little to you?"

At the slightly brittle edge in her tone, he had the sense of the conversation beginning to turn. Not wanting to light the fuse that would send him spinning in a Catherine wheel of his own demise, he eased away from his desire to have her reveal herself.

He wanted that book more than anything. However, as with any desired outcome, it would only be found if one adhered to the steps of proper procedure. And the only way he would learn what she'd done with it was if she were comfortable enough to lower her guard. Therefore, if she needed to play coy in order to believe that she was in control, then so be it. "If you prefer, I will address you as Miss Parrish."

Her brows lifted—he calculated one-sixteenth inch higher than before—in an indication of some surprise but not complete shock. Clearly, she had been expecting something. "You've been inquiring about me and my companions."

"Nothing more than rudimentary research."

"Then, I should probably tell you that I am not Miss Parrish either."

She was challenging him again. He could see it in the glint in her eyes, provoking him into disclosing all he knew about her. Regrettably, it wasn't much. Certainly not enough. At least, not yet.

"No?" he asked casually. "So, you are neither Lady Avalon nor Miss Parrish. Then, what shall I call you—*ma louve déguisée en agneau*?"

She laughed, flashing two rows of straight white teeth, the evenness only interrupted by the pointed elongation of her upper and lower canines. *"A wolf in sheep's clothing?"*

"That is what you are, is it not?"

She hummed thoughtfully, pressing her lips together to hide her smile. "Perhaps. Or, at least, I shall endeavor to be tonight."

He followed her gaze across the sward to where Miss Hartley was batting her lashes at his cousin. Pell, in turn, was puffing out his chest as if he were a hunter who'd just captured her with his net. He had no shame.

His cousin shouldn't even be wasting his time with the woman. If Miss Hartley was a friend to an infamous adventuress, it stood to reason that they were cut from the same cloth. She was likely toying with him to suit her own purpose.

Just as Lady Avalon was doing with Lucien.

From the start, he never imagined that she or her companions were traveling under their own names. *Parrish* was just as likely to be a nom de plume as *Lady Avalon*. He'd already hired an investigator in England to look into it when his butler first mentioned their names.

"Would you answer a question, Your Grace?"

"As long as I am permitted one in return."

She nodded in agreement. "A fair trade, then."

But before she could pose her query, a footman toting a silver tray of glasses filled with a pale liquid stopped by them. Lucien handed one to her then waved the servant along. He didn't want the interruption. Not when he was so close to drawing her out.

As the footman strolled away, she studied Lucien over the rim of her glass and took her time speaking the words lingering behind those keenly perceptive eyes. "You said you know *of* Lady Avalon. Am I correct in assuming that you've never met?"

"I've never met her *before*," Lucien clarified, wondering where this turn would take them. But he sensed that she was enjoying herself, practically daring him to outmatch her. "As I said, I know her reputation. She is infamous in certain circles."

"Oh? For what reason?"

"Seducing men—"

His companion suddenly coughed and sputtered, nearly spilling her lemonade.

"—in order to steal their secrets," he concluded.

Taking the glass from her, he set it aside on a pointlessly ornamental sundial. This was an interesting development. She appeared flustered at the mention of her conquests. But why? Shame? Guilt?

"Too close to the mark?" he asked.

She blotted her lips with her handkerchief and averted her face, taking inordinate care to tuck the lacy square back inside her glove. "Far afield, I'm afraid. I find it hard to believe that you would confuse me with someone . . . like her."

"Come, now. It requires no stretch of mental capacity."

Her gaze lifted. Her brows briefly knitted in perplexity as she studied him in return. Then her lips curved into a radiant smile. "Really?"

Apparently, the comment pleased her. And now he was thoroughly baffled.

Therefore, he studied this seasoned seductress more closely. It was important, after all, to note every subtle alteration and shift to gain a better understanding of his adversary.

However, when the tip of her cherry red tongue appeared as she briefly wet her lips, his mind went blank.

Well . . . not entirely blank. There were thoughts running rampant inside his head, just none related to his current objective.

He attempted to redirect his attention, but then a warm breeze stirred the glossy curls resting against her cheek and nape. His olfactory sense picked up a pleasing scent, his nostrils flaring to draw it deeper into his lungs. He'd caught this sweet fragrance before on their previous encounters, and even then, it had reminded him of something that he couldn't quite place.

But now his memory sparked to life—of summertime and warm Corinth grapes plucked fresh off the vine, the tiny fruits bursting with sweetness on his tongue; of autumn in the evenings by the fire in the great hall with a mug of mulled wine, spiced with cinnamon and clove, as his feet dangled from his father's chair; winters in the morning room with snowflakes collecting on the diamond-paned windows, his mother humming a tune as she sliced soft bread and warmed the pieces on the toasting fork; and of springtime when the kitchens were filled with clouds of sugar sieved off the cone. And all his favorite scents combined in the iced buns the cooks made for the festivals at Caliburn Keep many, many years ago.

Lucien's pulse quickened at this realization. And now he

was wondering if his little wolf in sheep's clothing would taste just as sweet.

He cleared his throat and gave himself a mental shake. Wondering such things served no purpose. The knowledge gained would not bring him any closer to reclaiming his legacy. Therefore, he dismissed the thought at once. Or tried to.

"But if you had never met this Lady Avalon before, then how did she manage to"—she pressed her lips together, then whispered—"seduce you?"

"By distraction," he growled.

Even he—a man led more by his mind than by baser urges—could not discount her allure. In fact, he was surprised to find himself plagued again by that primitive sense of a hunter after his prey.

Though, unlike before, he'd consumed no experiment that he might attribute the effects to. Which brought him to two initial conclusions: one, that he never had been suffering the effects of the recipe; and two, that his physiology was strangely attuned to her, as though he were an automaton and she held the winding key.

Either way, Lucien was forced to admit that he was strongly and undeniably attracted to her.

A rather inconvenient realization, truth be told.

His sole focus needed to remain on methods to retrieve the book, not on errant speculations about the taste of her lips and tongue, the warmth and softness of her skin, or the likelihood that her high, firm breasts would fit perfectly into his hands. He'd already made the mental calculations and had no doubts about his findings whatsoever.

"I'm not certain I understand," she said, looking up at him through her lashes. "If I remind you of this Lady Avalon, then why are you frowning down at me?"

His palms tingled, and he closed his hands into fists. "I do not like the distraction you pose. In fact, I would much rather be done with all this."

"This?"

"Pointless tête-à-tête, flirting, what have you," he added with a begrudging exhale. "However, my cousin told me to try to be affable in order to procure what I want."

"Your cousin told you to—" She stopped.

At once, he became fascinated by the alteration in her eyes, the beguiling blue turning so cold and yet flaring hot with torchlight as if she were on fire from within. He was so fascinated, in fact, that he was surprised by her next words.

"And I actually thought you meant all those things you said. How foolish of me! Well, if this is all so *pointless*, then I will save you the effort of taxing yourself further."

Then she turned and stormed off.

Merlin's teeth, he thought as she marched across the sward to collect her friend. This was not going to plan at all.

A moment later, his cousin strode across the lawn, his mood decidedly no better than the little wolf's. "What in the blazes did you say? I told you to act the gentleman, be suave and affable."

"Indeed," Lucien said, scrubbing the obtrusive night whiskers along his jaw thoughtfully. "I was. I even explained to her that I believed all of this was senseless, but that I was willing to talk to her regardless."

"You didn't say that aloud, did you?"

"Not those exact words but . . . aye, for the most part."

Pell slapped a palm to his forehead. "For a genius, you can be such an idiot. And now the loveliest creature in the world is mad at me because of what you said to her friend."

"I do not see that such an occurrence should matter to you. After all, Miss Hartley likely holds little information regarding the book. And you weren't courting her with the intention of marriage."

"So what if I wasn't? Sometimes a man simply likes the pleasure of a beautiful woman's company. The art of flirting takes a good deal of skill, I'll have you know. You should try it sometime. Perhaps you would have better luck."

"There is no such thing—"

"As luck. I know. I know. Bloody hell, I know," Pell interrupted sourly. "But whatever you want to call it, your efforts might have proven propitious if you had deployed one iota of charm."

A frustrated growl rumbled in Lucien's throat. Charm was not something he possessed in any measurable quantity. And it pained him immensely to think that he would have to solicit his cousin's tutelage in the matter. But he would do what must be done.

Standing on the gravel path as the first of the night's fireworks burst overhead, he finally understood the statement he'd overheard from Miss Hartley earlier. Because, as he watched Lady Avalon flounce away with her friend, he realized that she'd left him wanting more. Which would serve him well, considering that he wasn't about to let her get away.

The stakes were too high for him. And, when he surprised Lady Avalon tomorrow, he would be far better armed.

Chapter 8

Frankly, my dear, I don't give a fig

The aunts and Meg spent their final day in Paris on the Champs-Élysées, perusing the finest shops and cafés until the soles of their shoes were worn thin.

On their return to the hotel, Meg tugged on the knot of her ribbons and looked for a place to lay her hat, but there was hardly any room left in the carriage. The padded leather interior was filled with parcels of all shapes and sizes. Fortunately for their purses, only some were items they'd purchased. Most were gifts from merchants and bakers, florists and confectioners who had been flattered and praised until their cheeks were ruddy and eyes twinkling as they readily offered up their wares.

She settled on perching her hat atop the precarious mountain of string-tied boxes beside her, placing the smallest one at the peak on her lap. Peering inside, she found a tempting selection of macarons the color of toasted cream and chose one before passing them along.

The confection was delightfully crunchy on the outside, the inside melting on her tongue in a delicious pool of almond-sugar sweetness. "Positively scrumptious."

"I couldn't agree more," Maeve said, choosing one for herself. "Though, it's entirely possible that I never would have sampled one if the nuns during the revolution had kept the original name of Priests' Belly Buttons. *Macaron* sounds much more appetizing."

Myrtle nodded as she peered into the box as well. Then she lifted a pair of them for closer inspection. "So true. Although, I cannot help but think they could be improved with a little jam sandwiched between two. I said as much to the *boulanger*. In the next instant, the baker's eyes lit up like lanterns as he took my face in his hands and pressed a kiss to both cheeks. Further proof that food brings out our inner passions like nothing else." She popped one in her mouth and sighed contentedly before issuing an offhand shrug. "Then again, I might have said something else entirely. You know how I occasionally bungle my French."

"You do well enough when you want to flirt," Maeve said, and her sister waggled her brows at Meg.

"When did the two of you become so good at it? Flirting, I mean."

"Myrtle was born into it, without a doubt. Already batting her lashes at the postman at five years old."

"And Maeve was a late bloomer," Myrtle said, plucking the confection from her sister's hand.

"Well, some of us are not so easily impressed and prefer a man with a certain air of distinction."

"In other words, she likes tired old fussbudgets."

Maeve snatched back her macaron and gobbled the entire thing with relish, challenging her sister with a glare all the while.

Meg giggled, but the jesting made her miss Ellie. She loved her brother, but she'd become terribly fond of having a sister. Someone to talk to and tease good-naturedly. Someone who knew the thoughts pressing on her heart without even needing to utter a syllable.

She would have liked to talk to Ellie about the duke and the confusing feelings she had when she was with him. Honoria was a good friend, but she didn't understand. For her, flirting was all about the chase. And she was used to men vying for her attention.

Meg was not. It had never bothered her in the past because she'd always thought she would marry Daniel. So why should she care if gentlemen chose not to flirt with her?

After last night, however, she realized she did care.

In fact, learning that the duke's sole reason for speaking with her was because she reminded him of another woman incensed her to no end.

She growled down at the half-eaten macaron in her hand. "What if the gentleman you try to flirt with is an utter dunderhead?"

"Oh? Did you meet someone last night, my dear?"

"A gentleman who caught your fancy, perhaps?"

Meg knew her mistake the instant she saw Maeve and Myrtle smile at her, their bright gazes brimming with wedding-breakfast expectations. And when they exchanged a look, she could almost hear their unspoken conversation.

Do you think seven courses, sister?

No, indeed. Eight at the very least.

"Merely curious," Meg offered blandly. "In case I happen to meet someone worth flirting with. But I still have no intention of marrying anyone."

"Of course not, dear," Myrtle agreed with a nod, while her eyes were still dancing with thoughts of cakes, pastries and pies.

Maeve was likely estimating the number of guests they could fit in the ballroom at Crossmoor Abbey. But at least she was able to school her features. "You are quite right. This is a holiday. One should always be prepared."

"And by sheer happenstance, there is a rather illustrious guest staying at our hotel. Perhaps you could practice on him, hmm?"

Maeve nudged her sister and discreetly shook her head. Then she returned her attention to Meg. "It's best to remember that men believe they are the center of the universe. Of course, we know better."

"And keep the three *F*s in mind. If you cannot offer him food, then feed him flattery."

"Indeed. Men always want to be regarded as clever, as though they were the first creatures to string syllables together to form a language. So be sure to hold his gaze and nod thoughtfully. It will make him think you are hanging on every word."

"And keep a laugh at the ready in case he offers a quip."

Meg frowned. "But what if he isn't amusing?"

"A light laugh serves two purposes," Maeve added. "It will either knock him down from his perch of condescension or make him believe that the two of you are of like mind in all things, including your sense of humor."

"But shouldn't it feel more natural and less . . . oh, I don't know . . . calculated?"

Glumly nibbling on the chewy outer edge of the confection, it suddenly occurred to Meg that there might have been another reason she'd had little success with gentlemen during her Seasons. She'd never thought to try so hard to become someone she wasn't. If a man made a banal remark, she wouldn't praise him for it. And she certainly wouldn't laugh if he was behaving like an utter nodcock either.

All in all, these rules of engagement seemed like something the duke might study in order to *attempt to be affable*. At the memory of his confession, she grumbled in irritation.

"Fear not, flirting will be effortless when you are with a gentleman you regard fondly," Myrtle said.

Maeve nodded. "Quite true. And we were under the impression that you asked for the purpose of indulging in a mere holiday flirtation. However, if you are interested in a deeper attachment that might lead to an offer of marriage, then—"

"No," Meg interrupted with a quick shake of her head. "You have provided the perfect advice for what I want."

She was thankful that the carriage slowed to a stop in front of the hotel at that moment and for the distraction of the porters scurrying out to unload the packages. The only thing that interested her was a simple, uncomplicated holiday flirtation.

Maeve looked through the window and turned back to Meg with a small smile on her lips. "Nevertheless, we wish for you to know that you can always change your mind."

"I won't."

"Well, then, hold these"—Myrtle suddenly thrust the box of macarons at her—"just in case, dear."

"And what will I do with nearly a dozen macarons?"

Myrtle blinked. "Why, the same you would do with one, of course."

Confused, Meg stuffed the remainder of her own macaron into her mouth. And it wasn't until the hotel hostler opened the door and handed her down that she saw the reason for the aunts' sudden excitement.

Drat it all, the duke was standing on the pavement!

She nearly choked. In fact, if the confection wasn't primarily comprised of sugar and egg whites that were slowly melting, she surely would have done. Her eyes watered, nonetheless, as the sticky sweet clump congealed at the back of her throat.

"My gracious. Why, if it isn't the Duke of Merleton! What a complete and utter surprise," Myrtle said with a feigned gasp, the sound a bit too practiced for one who was actually in shock.

Maeve stood on the other side of her. "So good to see you again, Your Grace."

"And you, Miss Parrish," he said to each of them in turn, leaving Meg for last.

She nodded, trying not to wince when the remains of

the macaron slowly plodded down her esophagus as if she'd swallowed an elephant.

"Isn't this serendipitous?" Myrtle asked with a pleased-as-punch grin. "We were just at his estate a handful of days ago, only to leave without an introduction, and now here we are."

Maeve, apparently taking Meg's discomfiture for confusion, explained. "You see, we met earlier this morning when we returned from breakfasting. You were still bidding farewell to Miss Hartley, and His Grace just happened to be walking down the same hall of our apartments. He'd mentioned that you and he were recently introduced at the Count and Countess of Andret's soiree."

"How kind of him to make the *attempt* to remember me," she said tightly, the irritated growl in her voice not entirely the fault of the confection.

The corner of his mouth twitched. "You would be impossible to forget."

And suddenly he was the duke of charm? *Ha!* "Well, we've had a very long day and—"

"Do you like macarons, Your Grace?" Myrtle nudged Meg's arm forward. "It just so happens that we have a box right here. Perhaps we might, all of us, sit down and share them."

Maeve cleared her throat. "Unfortunately, my sister and I are quite fatigued. And it is such a pity, too, because our Meg was just talking about wanting to stroll through the hotel and gaze upon all the fascinating landscapes hanging in the upper gallery. She is an absolute marvel with her sketches. Although, if I've said it once, I've said it a dozen times—the best way to gain an understanding of any art form is to see something that sparks your interest and then to *practice*. Isn't that right, sister?"

"Oh, yes, indeed. Practice is most important."

As Meg felt a little push in the center of her back, she

began to wonder what level of stupidity caused her to utter aloud to these two the notion of having a holiday flirtation. But little did they know that, if she were going to practice on any man, it certainly wouldn't be the duke. At least, not again. As far as she was concerned, their time together the previous evening had been nothing more than a mammoth mistake.

But before she could make her excuses to join the little meddlers and retire early, he inclined his head.

"I would be more than happy to be her escort."

"Splendid!" the aunts said in unison, then bustled off in a flurry as if needing to outrun the arguments ready on Meg's lips.

Disappearing between the porters who were still unloading parcels from the carriage, they left her alone on the pavement with the duke. And a box of macarons.

She slid him a steely glare. "You cannot be a guest of this hotel."

"I assure you that I can, and I am. In fact, my cousin and I arrived shortly before you and your party."

How did he know when she'd arrived? *Hmm.* Could that have been the reason the concierge had been waiting for the *three* Misses Parrish? Had Merleton inquired about her and her party?

No. Impossible. Those would have been the actions of a man in pursuit, one who actually wanted to see her. Well, unless . . . he'd been attempting to gain enough information to avoid her instead. Now, *that* seemed far more likely.

But just to be certain, she asked, "So you just happened to be staying in the same hotel, the same way you *happened* to be at the party last night and at the docks in Calais? At the risk of using a word that likely doesn't exist in your lexicon, this all seems a bit too coincidental."

"Rather like the fact that you just happened to be lurking in the corridors of my estate?"

"Lurking, indeed," she muttered and knew that she had her answer. He'd been trying to avoid her. "Then, I'll just be on my way."

He stepped in front of her. "Wait. I should like to escort you to the gallery."

Highly doubtful, she thought, ready to walk off in a huff.

But then, one look into his eyes, and that damnable tugging sensation hit her! It compelled her to linger a moment longer. And worse, she had a terrible urge to smooth an errant dark lock from his forehead.

Such an action would put her person perilously close to his own and, at the mere thought, tingles traversed through her body, up from her fingertips and down to her toes.

Why didn't anyone else make her feel this way?

Because no other man has ever pursued you, a voice whispered in the back of her mind.

She instantly shushed it, discounting the thought as mere fancy. And yet, it was rather odd that they should have met so often.

Still holding his gaze, she said, "Tell me one thing. Are you only paying attendance on me because I remind you of that other woman—the one you mentioned last night— Lady Avalon?"

"No. There are other reasons," he answered. She waited for him to elaborate, but instead he asked, "What do you say to a temporary truce and a tour? If I make you cross again, you can throw macarons at me."

Her mouth twitched. Drat the man! Why did he have to be so unexpectedly amusing? And why did he have to entice her with the unanswered mystery of the *other reasons*?

She sighed and resigned herself to spending a few more minutes in his company. It shouldn't take too long before he said something awful that would drive her away again.

When she handed the box of macarons to one of the porters, the duke proffered his arm. "Shall we, Miss Parrish?"

Apparently, during his *chance* meeting with the aunts, they had not revealed her actual surname. She was surprised that they hadn't gone so far as to invite him to Crossmoor Abbey. To stay. Forever.

But perhaps they truly were only interested in ensuring that Meg enjoyed her holiday and were respecting her wishes to merely practice a bit of flirting. This was their last day in Paris, after all. And they likely understood that nothing would come of her acquaintance with the duke in such a short time. So she took his arm and didn't bother to correct him.

"Perhaps I can pretend for a few moments that you don't vex me exceedingly, and you could simply call me Meg."

He nodded. "And I am perfectly capable of being vexed by you exceedingly *while* allowing you to address me as Lucien."

She grinned despite her determination to hold on to her pique.

Inside, they climbed the grand staircase. When they gained the upper landing and passed by a colorful bouquet atop a white-glazed demilune table, he surprised her once more by plucking a stem of blue delphinium free and presenting it to her. He was very unlike the duke she'd met before.

Lifting the cluster to her nose, she inhaled the sweet fragrance. "Still attempting to be affable?"

"How am I doing so far?"

"Hmm," she murmured, tapping the velvety buds against her lips. "I'm not certain. Are you going to tell me that these blossoms remind you of my eyes?"

His brows drew together, creating a fan of vertical furrows between them. This was the same look he'd worn last night before he'd spoken and ruined everything.

So when they stepped into the empty gallery and lingered just beyond the doorway, Meg steeled herself against whatever he might say. Magnanimously, she decided to wait for his response before she left him without another word.

"No," he said, bending ever so slightly to study her eyes. "Your irises are much paler and clear. Like a beaker of water with only a single drop of indigo dye. The surrounding penumbra of darker blue is much closer to the hue of this flower. However, the best match would likely be the stripes on that frock you wore the day we met."

Her breath caught. That sensation of being tugged through the middle was stronger now. It felt like being high on a swing and that instant of weightless suspension . . . just before gravity took hold, propelling her in an exhilarating downward arc.

She felt herself teeter forward, losing herself in those dark, beseeching eyes. And did he just dart a glance to her mouth? Oh, yes. Yes, he did, indeed.

Her pulse quickened, her voice no louder than a whisper because she didn't want to break this spell. "You remember what I was wearing?"

"Of course." His gaze dipped once more as she wet her lips. Then he adjusted his spectacles. "I've replayed the event countless times, calculating the methods you might have employed to gain access to the inner sanctum of my house."

Then again, sometimes gravity made you fall flat on your face.

She growled. "Is that all you ever think about? My trespassing?"

Rocking back on her heels, she turned and marched down the white wainscoted gallery, paying no attention to the art on the celadon green walls. Of course, a man of his height had a long-legged stride and easily kept pace beside her. And for each curtain-swathed alcove she passed, she eyed the silver-fringed tiebacks with a passing thought to murder by strangulation. Then again, she'd likely need a ladder in order to wrap the cording around his throat.

"I think of a great number of things in each moment. In fact . . ." He hesitated when she whipped around to face him, her hands on her hips. "Your lashes are bunching together as you narrow them in my direction. Ah. Apparently, I've said something displeasing?"

"It doesn't matter."

"But it does. Clearly, you expected me to say something else."

"Not exactly."

"Then, what? Please," he said, his expression clearly confused. "I will never know unless you tell me."

She had a feeling that such a scholarly and fastidious man wasn't likely to let any matter drop. Besides, it wasn't until then that she realized this gallery had no other egress. She was trapped at a dead end.

She huffed. "Very well. You were standing close while gazing into my eyes and noticing things that no other man has noticed before, and I thought . . ."

"And you thought . . . ?"

"I thought you might kiss me."

And that was when the Duke of Merleton went utterly still.

He didn't blink. Didn't draw a breath. And for a moment, she wondered if she'd broken him.

"I do not think that would be a wise course of action. Considering the fact that you"—he cleared his throat and carefully adjusted his spectacles—"remind me of a woman who has seduced dozens of men, you are not one that I should underestimate."

Dozens? But what would a woman possibly do with dozens of men?

Why, the same you would do with one, of course, a voice whispered in the back of her mind.

Meg's cheeks heated, even though she had no idea what seduction might entail. All she knew about the relations between men and women was that Ellie had once compared nuptial bliss to *dying in the best possible way.* Then she'd gone on to add that Brandon was rather passionate. Meg had immediately changed the subject. There were certain things one never wanted to know about one's brother.

Then, when she'd asked her very sensible Aunt Sylvia, she'd been told to watch the animals in the spring. But when Brandon had caught her staring agape at the rearing horses in the paddock—*good heavens!*—he'd covered her eyes and sent her on an errand.

"But that is neither here nor there," Lucien offered, misinterpreting her blush. "Because I shall never allow myself to be taken in by your charms, no matter how alluring you are."

He'd done it again, startling the breath out of her body. And this time, when she felt the tug, she didn't resist it.

She stepped closer. Her hand splayed over the center of his waistcoat, the cashmere warm beneath her palm. "You think I'm alluring?"

"I doubt there is a man alive who would not." He glanced down at her hand, and Meg watched with fascination as a faint ruddy color stole over the crests of his cheeks, brushing the bridge of his nose.

"You'd be surprised."

"Ah, so a few of my sex have managed to resist you? I shall draw strength from that knowledge."

A sense of inner feminine power surged through her. Was this what flirting felt like? No wonder Honoria and the aunts enjoyed it so much.

Meg boldly pressed closer, her skirts crinkling in a hushed whisper against the legs of his trousers. "Surely, you'd allow yourself one small kiss."

His eyes turned black as onyx as he shook his head, and she felt the heavy thud of his heart beneath her palm. "I believe Shakespeare said it best in *Henry V,* 'You have witchcraft in your lips.'"

"'Nay, I will give thee a kiss: now pray thee, love, stay.'"

Feeling more emboldened than before, she slid her hand higher, fingers slipping beneath his lapel. She could feel the heat rising from his body.

His gaze dipped to her mouth once more, and a breath left him, brushing against her lips. "That quote is from a different play."

"I know. *The Taming of the Shrew*. I was trying to be clever," she whispered, not wanting to break this spell as she lifted herself to the balls of her feet.

"And you were. Quite clever." But he drew her hand away and took a step back. Then he swallowed. "Too clever. I should do well to remember that. For the moment, however, I should escort you to your chaperones."

So much for being alluring, she thought and sank back on her heels.

"No need. I can manage on my own, thank you," she said tartly and walked away. Her first practice session of flirting was officially and abysmally at an end.

When they neared the doorway, he reached out as if to stay her. However, he must have thought better of it when she stopped to scowl at him. "I've vexed you again, haven't I?"

"What was your first indication?"

He looked as though he was about to formulate a list, but then he raked a hand through his hair. "Would it please you to know that I was thinking about kissing you?"

She shrugged.

"As I mentioned earlier," he continued, stepping close enough to bring the crisp folds of his cravat into focus, "there are several thoughts in my mind during every moment. Since the day we met, you have been one of them."

"Yes, I know," she muttered on an exhausted exhale. "Because I was *lurking*."

"That, *and* you have a certain fragrance which has burrowed into my olfactory sense. It took several days before

I realized why." He lifted his hand, his fingers settling beneath the delicate contour of her jaw. "Your scent reminds me of iced buns."

"Buns?"

Ugh. Now she knew what was worse than being dismissed with a pat on the head.

"And I've been wondering if you would taste like icing." He held her gaze and the deep murmur of his voice sent tingles on a swift descent through her body. "All sweet and dissolving on my tongue."

Oh. Oh, my. That wasn't as awful as she'd thought.

Everything altered at once. Her blood changed seasons from frosty winter to molten summer, swimming in her veins and pooling low. Her limbs went from stiff to suddenly boneless. In fact, the only substantial part of her was where he touched her face, his thumb lightly stroking the sensitive valley between her mouth and chin. Her lips became plump, ripe and aching. And when he leaned in, she was sure they might combust from anticipation.

"But I cannot risk giving in to temptation," he whispered.

Then he released her, turned and left.

She sagged against the doorframe, too overcome by the tumult inside her to be cross with him. Besides, that was, quite possibly, the best kiss she'd never had in her entire life.

It was a shame, too. This was her last day in Paris, and she would never see him again. Well, not unless happenstance brought him to Germany, which was where she and the aunts were headed to in the morning. But the likelihood of that was next to impossible.

Nevertheless, she had enjoyed the practice of flirting with that irritating man.

Chapter 9

The Good, the Bad and the Cherry

Orchestrating Lady Avalon's residency at the hotel where Lucien stayed had taken careful maneuvering—not to mention, a good deal of coin—but it had served him well in the end.

The concierge had been exceptionally helpful, informing him of every coming and going of *zee three Misses Parrish*, including precisely when they were departing to continue their supposed holiday. And the moment their hired coach had driven away, Lucien and Pell had set off in pursuit.

Leaving France, they traveled over hills and dales, through vineyards and the forests that brought them into Germany. The land was green and abundant with cherry trees, laden with the red stone fruit, lining the narrow roads.

It had been days since his last encounter with Meg in Paris. Ten days to be exact, and Lucien was still no closer to discovering the whereabouts of his book than before.

All he knew was that, after a brief surveillance, neither Count Andret nor Colonel Whittingham proved capable of being the mastermind behind this plot. Erring on the side of caution, however, Lucien hired a man to follow Andret and report anything more interesting than mummified cats. He also sent word to his investigator to keep an eye on the colonel when he returned to England with his young bride, along with her cousin, Miss Hartley, whose close connection with Lady Avalon was still under suspicion.

He hated not having answers. It was taking far too long to unearth the name of the man that Lady Avalon was working for. Though, whoever he might be, he apparently did not live in France.

The Parrish women had been on a peculiar zigzag course into Germany. But they visited no jewelers, officers, heads of state or anyone he would consider the architect of this charade.

They'd paused for a brief stay in Trier to admire the Moselle from a hired boat for a few hours. Then they continued onward, making a point to stop at nearly every *Gasthaus* along the way, as if for the sole purpose of sampling the local cuisine.

It confused him exceedingly. Normally, he enjoyed a good puzzle, but he disliked when the pieces failed to fall in place.

What did these excursions have to do with the book she'd stolen from him? Or any of the other pilfered goods she'd taken over the years, for that matter?

He glowered through the window of his carriage, where it sat on an overlook shielded by bramble and coniferous shrubs. In the valley below, his quarry had been loitering in a quaint village square market for two hours and seventeen—*eighteen*—minutes.

"For a master of espionage, Lady Avalon certainly leaves loaves' worth of breadcrumbs behind," Pell said with a yawn from the opposite bench. "We've tracked her every step of the way through France and now Germany with minimal effort. At least on my part. I don't know the lengths you've gone to with all your calculations and deductions. Then again, I'm not interested. Just wake me when they leave."

As Pell eased into the corner of the carriage, arms crossed and hat tilted over his face, Lucien returned his gaze to the figure in the pink-striped dress as she idly twirled a frilly parasol and sauntered among the crowds with a basket on her arm. "Clearly, she is working with the older women. I hadn't thought so at first. But after seeing the elder two steal away into the kitchens of coaching inns and through back doors of market shops, I'm sure they are part of it."

"While Lady Avalon serves as a distraction," Pell murmured groggily. "You've mentioned that before. You always repeat yourself when something doesn't make sense to you. So they must be quite the clever team of cohorts."

"But to what end?"

Lucien scrubbed a hand along his shaven jaw. Thinking back to a previous conversation with Lady Avalon, he recalled her mentioning that certain ingredients could only be found in specific parts of Europe.

So perhaps she was delivering the ingredients and the recipes at the same time. Which meant that the man she was working for was interested in complete authenticity. Hence, he could very well be a scholar of the ancient texts. And hadn't his little wolf already confessed that her own father had known *all* the stories?

Perhaps the person he was looking for was in her own family, whoever that may be. He hoped his investigator in England would be able to unearth something more concrete than a list of thefts connected to her alias.

Lucien wanted to know more about her—who she was, where she came from, how she fell into this line of work and why she felt it necessary to seduce so many men.

Not that the last mattered to him. Not in the least. Her amorous escapades were none of his concern. Although, why she found it necessary to linger so long at the market stall with the burly chap in the lederhosen, he didn't know. But when her parasol tilted enough to expose her beaming smile as she drank from an offered cup, a seething hot breath fogged up the window.

"You know," Pell said as Lucien wiped his sleeve in a circle over the pane, "it is entirely possible that we have the wrong woman altogether."

He shook his head in instant denial. Then remembering that his cousin had his eyes closed, he said, "No. If you'd spent any time alone with her, then you would know just how cunning she can be. It almost makes me feel sorry for all those other men she has duped."

Even he had nearly been drawn into her trap. He'd thought that touring the hotel gallery while engaging in pleasant conversation would allow her to trust him and feel at ease. He should have known better. Instead, she'd beguiled him with those eyes and spoke of kissing, purposely drawing his attention to her all too tantalizing lips.

She was a master of her craft, subtly spinning a web around him. Before he knew it, he'd found himself ensnared and admitting things he'd never planned to confess. And when her lashes had descended over her eyes in a sultry, slumberous blink and her mouth parted on a sweet breath, it was only by sheer force of will that he'd been able to pull himself free.

When he'd walked away, he'd intended to leave temptation behind. It was a simple matter of mental fortitude, after all. He'd exercised those muscles often enough that he had no doubt of his success. And yet . . .

Because he was in pursuit of the book, and she was the holder of said book, it proved impossible.

She was all he could think about. And every night he was plagued with dreams of those candied-cherry-colored lips, of wanting to feel them beneath his own, opening, surrendering, of tasting her sigh and exploring every facet of her mouth until he became a scholar of the subject.

"Don't tell me the great monk of Caliburn Keep was seduced." Pell tilted up his hat and peered across the carriage with intrigue.

Lucien quickly schooled his features and scoffed. "I'm hardly a monk, but no."

"It has to have been ages."

"Unlike you, I do not keep a tally on my bedpost. I have my studies, and they are important to me. Lust only clouds the mind."

"Always clears up my thinking. You might want to give it a try. And besides, you're going to need to get closer to her if you want that book. Much closer."

"If you'll recall, that was my intention at Andret's party, to lure her into a false sense of security by being affable."

"And that went over like a lead balloon," Pell muttered.

Technically, osmium would have been a better example as it was the denser element, but Lucien kept the information to himself. "She is more likely to reveal the location of the book if she is at ease with me."

"Which is precisely what I'm saying." His cousin heaved out a great sigh as if exhausted from his efforts. "Honestly, haven't you figured her out yet? She's in her element when she's seducing men. That's when she feels most at ease, because she's in control. Therefore, if you want the chance of finding that book any time in this century, you should let her seduce you."

"Let her . . . seduce . . . *me*?" Lucien barely forced the words out, his throat suddenly tight, his pulse thick.

"Unless, of course, you cannot trust yourself around her."

He sent a glare to Pell, but his cousin had already lowered his hat again, a smug grin curving his lips beneath the brown beaver brim.

Regrettably, Lucien had to admit that his cousin was at least twenty-five percent correct. He'd like to think that he was strong enough but, more often than not, he was a slave to his own curiosity. All those questions that needed answers were simply impossible to resist. And now he was wondering about all the tantalizingly provocative things she might do to him if he let her . . .

He swallowed and slid a finger between his collar and his throat. Had it grown exceedingly warm inside the carriage just then?

Turning back to the window, he found her still twirling her parasol. She'd left Herr Lederhosen with the hairy thighs to stare after her as she continued to peruse the market. Lucien sent a warning glare to the man to stay at his stall.

But where were her chaperones? His gaze swept the square, searching the windowed shopfronts of quaint broad-roofed buildings and the rows of shingled huts and straw-strewn horse carts there to sell their wares. But the elder Parrish women were nowhere in sight.

Damn it all! He'd missed which way they'd gone. But why would they dare leave her alone in a foreign land? And there she was, drinking from another cup at a different vendor's hut, seemingly without a care in the world.

"Is that your stomach growling like a beast?" Pell mumbled. "If you're thinking of stepping over to the market, bring one of those wursts back for me."

"And risk having her observe me, spoiling ten days of careful surveillance? I think not. I have absolutely no intention of revealing our—"

Lucien stopped when he saw the way her head tilted back on a laugh and the heads of several men turned her way.

"Actually," he said darkly, "perhaps a surreptitious sojourn isn't a bad notion, after all."

Chapter 10

Cherry-picking

Meg ducked beneath the garland draped along the eaves of the hut to inhale the aroma of the scrumptious lebkuchen. The aunts had already slipped away to ferret out the best recipe at the bakery—or rather, the *Konditorei*—around the corner.

Smiling to the shopkeeper in a yellow kerchief and apron, Meg nodded in agreement to the price. After paying a few groschen, the paper-wrapped cake was handed to her. Then she was invited to partake in a small cup of delicious water that tasted like cherries. And this was not the first cup.

In fact, with every purchase she had in her overladen basket, she had been invited to partake. And she had partaken with much delight.

"Danke schön," she said with a wiggle of her fingertips before she continued to stroll along.

The market served as a lovely distraction to leaven the somber mood she'd been in these past few days, ever since departing from Paris.

It was silly, she supposed, to have imagined that the duke would show up at their coaching inn. And if not that one, then the one after that. Surely, a man didn't say such knee-melting things to a woman—like *I've been wondering if you would taste like icing . . . all sweet and dissolving on my tongue*—and never intend to see her again.

For the first few days, Meg even told herself that if he did appear, she would choose him to be the object of her grand flirtation. And she had been determined to employ every single *F* to ensure that it was unforgettable.

But he never came.

Therefore, she decided to put him from her mind, and this lovely water was certainly helping.

Yet, somewhere between the lebkuchen and the stollen, she thought she saw a tall and dark figure out of the corner of her eye. The downy hairs on the back of her nape lifted and her stomach swooped in anticipation. She turned quickly . . . but he wasn't there.

And he isn't going to be, she told herself. Dukes didn't pursue almost-on-the-shelf debutantes. They didn't leave their homes, sail to France and traipse through Germany for the chance of meeting one in a village market, no matter how exceptionally pleasant the market was.

She sighed. It was all true. But at least the vendors were friendly—and far more than the duke had been—always inviting her to sample the fruits and even more of their signature water. And underneath the lovely blanket of warm sunlight, the air smelled sweet and fresh and made her feel giddy.

Then again, the dizzy sensation might have occurred because she heard a familiar voice just then.

"*Nein, danke*," the voice said, the words curt, low and gruff, and her heart quickened.

She darted a glance over her shoulder. Searching just beneath the ruffled edge of her parasol, she happened to spot the golden glint of light bouncing off a pair of spectacles just before the owner of that voice retreated into the shadows between two stalls.

She gasped. Could it be? Was the Duke of Merleton actually here?

She faced forward again, her head spinning. It couldn't have been her imagination. Could it?

Whatever the answer, she could do nothing to control the excited flurry of her pulse, her blood fizzing through her veins like bubbles rising up along the inside of a glass.

Across from her, a vendor hailed her with a friendly "Fair *Fräulein*" and proceeded to tell her about his drinking horns for sale. They were attached to a leather strap that one wore slung over the shoulder and across the body. Distractedly, she told him they were very fine, but she could not see herself wearing such an adornment. He gave a hearty laugh and a wink and offered her a taste of the local beverage with good-natured hospitality. And since it would have been quite rude not to partake . . . she partook without spilling a drop.

Under the fuddling influence of a potential duke sighting and countless sips of this miraculous water, she decided that Brandon needed one of these and handed over a fistful of groschen to the agreeable man. As she did, she risked another sly peek over her shoulder.

This time, there was no mistaking it. He *was* here! And he was glowering at the vendor for some unknown reason, but that was neither here nor there. All that mattered was that her plans to have a grand flirtation with Lucien were still possible.

She bit into the cushion of her bottom lip to keep from smiling too broadly. For the moment, she played coy and pretended that she hadn't noticed him.

After collecting her brother's horn, she stopped to consider the porcelain dolls dressed in lederhosen as a gift for her nephew. It wasn't long before she felt the prickling of gooseflesh over her skin and caught a familiar masculine scent on the breeze as she heard the scuff of a boot sole on the pavement behind her.

"Are you following me, Herr Merleton?" she asked without turning around.

A second passed before she heard an impatient exhale. Then he stepped beside her.

"That would be Herzog Merleton. But addressing me by my surname would be Herr Ambrose."

"Very well, Herzog." She giggled and turned on her heel to walk away. But that made her muzzy-headed and she faltered . . . just before she felt his hand at the small of her back.

"What have you been drinking?" he asked in that severe tone of his, and she just knew his mouth was turned in that delightfully disapproving frown.

"Just a little water. Cherry water. They make it here, you know."

"Do you mean *Kirschwasser*?"

"That's it. Cherry water." She pointed at him. "You, *mein Freund*, are exceedingly clever to have guessed it. And according to that nice bearded man in the feathered Tyrolean hat, it fills one with vitality. What do you think, Herzog?" She grinned up at him. "Am I full of vitality?"

He continued to frown, and she was ever so tempted to put her fingertips to either side of his mouth and nudge a smile into place.

"You are certainly full of something. Where are your chaperones?"

"Shh . . . I cannot tell you. It's a secret," she said and wondered why her whisper sounded vaguely slurred. Perhaps there was something on her tongue. Perhaps she needed more water to wash it down.

Just as she was about to turn around and walk back to the hut with the drinking horns, Lucien liberated her basket and took her hand, tucking it into the crook of his arm.

"They should be here, watching over you."

Pfft. "I do a better job watching over them. They are terrible flirts."

"And you are not?"

"I'm only a terrible flirt with you, though little good it has done me. I haven't seen you for over a senny . . . a sennai"—she shook her head, wondering why her tongue couldn't say *sennight*—"for over a week."

"I think you should get out of the sun and beneath the shade," he said walking toward the vacant stall at the far end of the market row.

"Oh, look! Two butterflies," Meg said, tottering to the left as she pointed to the buttery yellow wings flitting from flower to flower among the posies piled up on the back of a cart.

"Moths, actually," he corrected at a glance and secured her to his side.

"Oh, how can you even tell? Your lenses are likely smudged again." When he looked down at her with another taut sigh of impatience, she saw that they were, for once, perfectly clean. She shrugged. "Besides, it makes no difference whether they are moths or butterflies."

"I should think it would matter to the moths."

He stepped beneath the shingled overhang and removed his hat, absently passing a hand through his hair as he turned to face her.

"What matters is that they found each other. In all of this," she interjected, gesturing with a wide sweep of her parasol, "they found each other. And just look at how happy they are."

"Their random flying patterns do not indicate any emotion but rather—"

His speech abruptly halted when, in midspin, her parasol suddenly caught on the corner of the roof. Meg lost her grip. She stumbled forward at a tilt, arms windmilling and she fell. Directly against him.

He caught her easily by the shoulders, his stern expression indicating she was in for a lecture. But then, every grim syllable he might have uttered seemed to have dried up, because she saw him wet his lips as he looked at her mouth. And for some reason, she wet hers, too, just enough to dampen the sudden tingling ache that made them feel plump and ripe as the cherries in her basket.

She wasn't certain what happened next.

All at once, her hands were curled around his lapels, and she was tugging him down as she rose up on her toes. And then her mouth was pressed to his. Right there. In the market. Underneath a clapboard roof with the scent of flowers and cherries in the air.

His eyes widened the instant before she closed her own.

It was little more than a brief meeting of lips. Enough time for her hands to slide to his shoulders, to feel their breadth and strength beneath her palms. For his hands, warm and strong, to meet her waist, then to rise an inch or two higher to frame the bottom of her rib cage.

Then he shifted. A nudge, an ever so slight tilt of the head. And somehow found the perfect angle to send tingles sparking through her body, all the way to her toes.

A hum of pleasure escaped her. A breath left him. It fanned hotly from his nostrils. She felt the responding pressure of his fingertips as he gripped her, drawing her imperceptibly closer. And there was that deep tug again, stronger than before.

She was starting to crave this sensation. In fact, she never wanted it to—

"Well, *hullo* there, cousin," Viscount Holladay said from behind her.

Meg startled, rocking back on her heels. The kiss disconnected with an audible smooch.

Lucien's head was still bent, his hands lingering on her ribs for the barest moment until he suddenly jolted to awareness. He straightened with a snap, shoulders back. But his lenses were foggy around the edges.

Tearing off his spectacles, he stared down at them as if he couldn't comprehend how they'd come to be in such a state. Meg understood perfectly. She felt a bit foggy around the edges herself.

"Imagine my dismay when you did not return to the

carriage with my food," Holladay continued with a nudge of his boot against a spill of cherries. "Then imagine my surprise to find you ensnared by our favorite agent provocateur." He touched the brim of his hat and smiled. "A pleasure to see you again, my lady."

She nodded distractedly, her lips damp, plump and tingling. Looking down at her fallen basket, she saw that the contents were strewn over the cobblestones. They seemed to represent her wits in this moment: completely and utterly scattered.

She moved to pick them up, but the gentlemen did it for her. As she watched them, the giddiness that she had felt a moment ago evaporated on the sobering realization of what she'd just done.

She had kissed a man in the market! In the full light of day. Barely concealed by the shade provided by the roof. Only a woman who had no care for her reputation would have done such a thing. Only a woman like . . . Lady Avalon.

But wait, she thought as another realization struck her.

Viscount Holladay had just addressed her as *my lady* and referred to her as *our favorite agent provocateur*.

Lucien had also said that Meg reminded him of her, even though he had never met the lady in question. And then there was that encounter in Calais when he'd told her about the theft of his family's legendary book . . .

"Why do you suppose the culprit would travel to France?"

"I could ask the same of you, for I cannot reason it out."

"You're asking me?"

"I can think of no one more qualified to answer the question."

As all the pieces of the puzzle clicked into place, Meg felt as if a weight had suddenly dropped in the pit of her stomach.

When Lucien stood, she jerked her basket from his grasp. "You think I'm Lady Avalon, don't you? That's the reason you followed me, isn't it?"

He stared back at her with an inscrutable expression but gave no response.

Even so, it was all the answer she needed. And suddenly, she was rather annoyed at knowing that every chance meeting from Calais to Germany wasn't because he found her irresistible but because he thought her a thief!

Though, to be fair, she had stolen one recipe. But not *all* of them! Someone else was to blame for that.

Her chin jutted forward. "And what if I told you that I am not she?"

If he hadn't been so busy *attempting* to be affable—which she now realized was likely for the sole purpose of extracting information—then he would have known that already. He would have seen her for who she really was. A woman who, according to almost every other man she'd ever met, was too young to know her own mind.

But no. Not the duke. Instead, he thought she was capable of stealing and of . . . seducing men. Dozens of them.

She swallowed. Her eyes met his in time to see his smoldering glance drop down to her lips. Her very *kissed* lips.

"Such a declaration would be rather unconvincing at this point," he said, and she felt a rush of prickling heat sweep over her.

Someone really ought to have warned her about the hazards of imbibing cherry water.

The viscount chuckled. "Shame on you, old chap. You've made her blush. And that pink color makes her look quite the innocent lamb, too, certainly not the portrait of a wolf you've painted. I think I'm inclined to believe her."

"Pell," Lucien growled, breaking his momentary silence.

"All I'm saying is," he continued, ignoring the glare he was given, "what if you're wrong?"

The question hovered between them, buzzing like a bumblebee that didn't know where to land.

Meg saw the way Lucien's eyes changed, unfocused as if he were running various possibilities through his mind. He was a puzzle-solver, and it was likely impossible for him to let a question go without considering all the answers.

But as Meg watched him, her own scenarios formed.

If Lucien kept to his current thinking, then he would continue to pursue her, all the while suspecting her of stealing from him. But if he was swayed by his cousin's—and her own—claim that she was not an adventuress, agent provocateur or seductress, then they would leave to search elsewhere for the real Lady Avalon.

Meg would likely never see him again. And any hope she might have of engaging in a holiday flirtation before she ended up on the shelf for the rest of her life would be crushed underfoot like a cherry pit.

She didn't know why but every part of her, every single burning drop of blood in her body, rejected that possibility. If he stopped believing she was Lady Avalon, that would bring an end to all of this. No more tugs. No more kisses. No more Lucien. And he was the only one who made her feel this way.

The flutter of interest, the stirring of butterflies in her stomach when she had been with Daniel Prescott were nothing compared to this. With Lucien, she was forever feeling as though she might collide with him. Or no, that she *needed* to collide with him.

Whatever it was, she knew she couldn't let this end.

So Meg had a decision to make.

You should tell him the truth, said the angel on her shoulder, poking at her conscience with a rather pointy pair of wings.

Or—whispered a figure from the other side, casually twirling a forked tail in the air—*you could tell him the truth in a manner that made it impossible to believe.*

It wouldn't be an outright fib, after all. Just a reason for the duke to continue his pursuit. And she would tell him eventually. Just not yet.

"I'm curious as well, Your Grace. What *if* you are wrong about me?" Meg batted her lashes up at him as she splayed a scandalized hand above her breasts. "Why then, you and I were both just caught in a rather compromising position. I believe my chaperones would expect reparations of some sort. Perhaps even a proposal of marriage." She shrugged as if the matter were out of her hands and issued an exhausted sigh. "Of course, we couldn't possibly marry this summer because, well, I'm on holiday, and I intend to enjoy myself."

The viscount snickered. "I believe that was a direct shot to your manhood, old chap."

The duke leveled him with another glare, then turned to Meg. The way those river-stone eyes held hers made her pulse quicken.

Her mouth went dry as well. It seemed that he was peering into her soul . . . all the way to the truth. Even though she still felt the burning pressure of his lips against hers, she was far from a seasoned seductress. And she worried that he saw through her facade.

Nervous, she plucked one of the cherries out of the basket and popped it into her mouth. Every bit of it. Which was unfortunate because the stem was still sticking out between her lips part of the way, like a lost worm.

Not wanting to reveal how much of an idiot she was, she took hold of the stem and withdrew it until the fruit was caught between her teeth. Then she plucked it free and swallowed the cherry—stone and all—in a single gulp before dampening her lips.

His gaze missed nothing. And she didn't know why, but his eyes seemed particularly dark as he growled, "I'm not wrong."

That low timbre spiraled deep inside her. He sounded so certain that even *she* believed it.

"Such a shame." Holladay tsked. "I was so looking forward to seeing you as a bridegroom, cousin. Waiting at the altar. Impatiently calculating the number of footsteps she would take up the aisle.

"As for you," he said to Meg, his hands clasped beseechingly, "it behooves me to mention that Lucien has an agonizingly determined nature. Once set on a task, he never stops until it is finished. So I beg of you, from the bottom of my heart, please travel somewhere exciting. I mean, after all, this is my holiday, too."

She laughed. "Then, I shall do my utmost to give you"—she glanced to Lucien—"both of you, an adventure you'll never forget."

LUCIEN WATCHED her walk away. Without a doubt, she was the most audacious woman he'd ever met. And she had just thrown down a gauntlet at his feet.

"Is that an actual grin on your countenance, cousin?" Pell scoffed. "And here I thought your mouth had been permanently etched into a frown since the age of five."

Ignoring the jibe, he allowed his admiring gaze to slip from the revolving parasol to the subtle sway of her hips. It took supreme effort not to follow.

He was a rational man, always in complete control of his responses. Yet, for reasons that defied logic, her unexpected kiss had done something to him.

Shaken him. Rattled him. Or perhaps even rearranged every cell in his body.

Of course, he knew that part of this hot surge thrumming through him was basic lust. He was no stranger to matters of sexual congress. As with the majority of pursuits throughout his life, he'd studied every aspect in depth, learned every facet in order to excel. Once those were mastered, he continued for the dual purposes of mutual pleasure and exercise.

But he was never controlled by his baser urges. Never caught off guard by attraction . . . until he'd felt her lips on his.

In that brief moment, he'd been reduced to a six-foot pile of blood, bone and tissue with the mental capacity of a hungry ape, face-to-face with a five-foot-four stack of irresistibly delicious bananas. His lexicon had been diminished to two words—*mine* and *want*—along with a primitive grunt.

Indeed, she was an alluring female with inky black hair, laughing eyes and a come-hither smile. All of her lovely attributes were perfectly situated, at least as far as he could tell without a thorough, in-depth examination. And he'd already identified the reason her scent appealed to him.

Aside from that, it was important to note that he had known an ample number of women with similar qualities with varying degrees of appeal. So what was it about this particular woman that continued to cause this undefinable reaction?

The obvious answer was that she was far more skilled than he'd anticipated.

However, now he knew what he was up against. Everything was out in the open. There would be no more games. No more surprise kisses to send him off-balance. And if his little wolf thought she could gain the upper hand by using her wiles on him, well, then he would be more than happy to show her all the things that he could do.

And he was willing to do anything to retrieve his book . . . even seduce the seductress.

"Come, cousin," he said, pushing his spectacles up the bridge of his nose. "Lady Avalon just issued a challenge. Far be it from me to refuse."

Chapter 11

A fine kettle of fish

The aunts were over the moon when they heard the whispers that the Duke of Merleton and his cousin were staying in the same hotel again. A thrill raced through Meg, as well. However, the feeling was combined with guilt, because she knew this would only fan their hopeful expectations. They didn't know that this all began as a misunderstanding.

She had to tell them the truth. It would be too heartbreaking for her if she allowed them to imagine that he was pursuing her for the purpose of marriage.

"The duke isn't here for me. At least, not in the way that you are imagining," Meg confessed that afternoon, once they were seated in the tiny parlor of their rooms. "You see, he thinks I stole something from him."

"His heart?" Myrtle asked with a hopeful chirrup. Even Maeve smiled.

Meg shook her head and distractedly plucked at a stray strand of yellow yarn dangling from the open mouth of their traveling valise that rested on the settee cushion beside her. "Do you remember telling me about his family's legendary book of recipes?" They both nodded. "Well, apparently, right around the time that we were pilfering the cook's cupboard, someone else was stealing that fabled book."

"No!" They both gasped.

"That book is ancient," Maeve said. "And from what I've heard about the jewels on the cover—"

"It would be a veritable treasure," Myrtle concluded with a thoughtful nod.

"And there's something else, too," Meg said, nervously winding the yarn into a ball as she considered how to explain the more difficult aspect. "A woman by the name of Lady Avalon, who is known for behaving rather boldly"— she cleared her throat—"has taken credit for this theft."

Myrtle let out a breath. "That is a relief."

"Well . . . not quite." Meg cringed. "He thinks that *I* am Lady Avalon, and I . . . sort of . . . let him."

Maeve shook her head in obvious bewilderment. "But whyever would you do such a thing?"

"I don't know." She shrugged. "All I can say is that it was so thrilling to have him look at me like I was a woman capable of . . . behaving boldly that I didn't want it to end. I cannot explain it, but I've never felt this way before."

The aunts exchanged a look. Meg hoped she hadn't disappointed them. Hoped they weren't about to tell her how silly she was being and then advise her to reveal the complete truth to the duke.

"We understand perfectly," Maeve said kindly, surprising her. "We've all been caught unawares by romantic feelings. That's what makes falling in love so—"

"Oh, I'm not in love. I only want to flirt with him," Meg clarified hastily, winding faster. "You know, have my one grand flirtation before I'm on the shelf."

Maeve smiled softly. "Of course, dear. We understand that, too."

"And we'll be glad to keep your secret," Myrtle said. "In fact, we'll even try to act suspicious so that he imagines we're conspiring together."

"I'm sure he already thinks that the three of us are the most conniving females he's ever met," Meg said. Then she looked down at the now giant ball of yarn, only to find a neat row of stitches trailing out of the valise. Realizing that she'd been unraveling a shawl the entire time, she said, "Oh, my apologies. I wasn't paying attention."

"Never mind all that. You've improved Maeve's work, I'm sure," Myrtle teased, her eyes dancing with delight as she narrowly missed her sister's pinch by slipping over to the settee. She took Meg's hand and squeezed it with affection. "As for our little conspiracy . . . I think I like being considered somewhat devious. It gives me an aura of mystique, wouldn't you agree?"

"It gives you an aura of something, to be sure," Maeve said dryly.

❦

THE DUKE and the viscount hadn't appeared in the dining room that evening, which disappointed many of the guests who'd hoped to invite him to their own table.

The aunts made no such complaint. They did, however, exchange looks that were usually accompanied by a secret smile that Meg knew all too well. Those were wedding-breakfast smiles. And she'd fought the urge to roll her eyes several times.

After dinner, they retired to their rooms. The aunts, worn out from travel, went to bed early. Meg, on the other hand, was far too restless to sleep.

Apparently, she was not alone in this, for when she peered out the window to the hotel garden below, she saw a dark figure walking just beyond the quadrangles of light falling on the manicured lawn.

She instantly recognized that purposeful stride and those impossibly broad shoulders.

Lucien.

She peered closer, forehead pressed to the cool glass, and saw that he was carrying something. But what?

As the sounds of snoring drifted out from the aunts' bedchamber, Meg decided to slip away and investigate for herself.

The night air was cool, a light breeze carrying the scents of water and damp earth. The river they would travel on in the morning was near enough that she could hear the occasional splash of waves against the hull of a boat.

She found Lucien beyond the garden border. He was standing behind a copse of trees, a long telescope held to his eye as he looked skyward.

He must have heard the rustle of her skirts because he said, "I had a sense that you would be out on a night like this, *ma petite louve*."

My little wolf.

She smiled at that. But because he had not lowered the telescope to see who approached, she asked, "How could you have known?"

"There's a full moon."

"Ah, of course." She almost laughed. He had such a dry sense of humor that she found strangely appealing. "Just so you know, I have no interest in howling at it this evening."

"A great relief for the other guests, I'm sure."

She stood beside him and followed his gaze, noting that his telescope was not aimed toward the moon. "What are you looking at?"

"An occultation."

"An occultation, as in an *eclipse*?"

"Precisely." He pointed. "The star is there. Tauri is located in—"

"The Taurus constellation," she interjected, squinting up at the sky.

When he didn't respond, she glanced over to see him gazing down at her, a grin etched into one side of his mouth. "You have a fascinating array of knowledge."

"And you have a dimple," she said inanely, the sight of

it kindling a peculiar glow inside her lungs that forced out all the air.

He shrugged. "It makes an occasional appearance, rather like our anomaly in the sky. Nothing at all like yours, with the pair winking into existence with every one of your frequent smiles."

"Are you saying that I smile too much? If you are, I shall become quite cross."

His grin lingered as he shook his head. Then his warm gaze left hers to skim over her cheeks where the dimples were hidden for the moment. "Although, it is important to note that the left is slightly deeper. I've estimated that it would hold a measurement of two minims of water, whereas the one on the right would hold a single drop."

Meg swallowed. He'd thought about her dimples? Evaluated them in depth?

There were likely some people who might think this odd or find his choice of words and acute attention to detail a bit off-putting. Or, perhaps, decide that he was too remote and analytical.

But not her.

Every time Lucien made a specific scientific observation, her pulse quickened, and a rush of heat bloomed over the surface of her skin. She wanted to hear his deep, rational voice tell her every thought he'd ever had, every calculation he'd ever made. She wanted to see the world through his eyes. She wanted . . .

"The stars?" he asked, a single dark brow arching above the rim of his spectacles as he glanced down to his waistcoat.

It wasn't until then that she realized her hand had somehow found his chest. And this wasn't the first time.

She withdrew it at once. "I don't know why I am forever touching you."

He took that same hand and curled it around his telescope, the instrument substantial and weighty. Then he turned her by the shoulders and pointed toward the constellation. "I should think it quite obvious."

"Oh?" She lifted the eyepiece to search the heavens.

Then she felt him behind her, warm and solid as his arm slid along hers to guide her toward the occultation. "You are attempting to seduce me."

Seduce him? Her heart lurched, then beat faster as she abruptly remembered her role as Lady Avalon. Honestly, she had no idea how to behave like an adventuress. And yet, apparently, she must have been doing something right.

"Flirting. Only flirting," she clarified. "There will be no seduction from my quarter."

"No? So you're not trying to tempt me with every look and light caress?"

As he spoke, he adjusted her hold on the instrument, his large hand covering hers. His other settled on her waist as if to steady her. When she shook her head, the tip of his nose stirred the downy curls that dangled against the side of her neck, sending a frisson of excitement through her, and she wondered who was seducing whom.

She gulped, caught off guard by this other side of him.

But that wasn't to say she didn't like it. Actually, it was rather nice, feeling the firm length of his body behind her. "I hardly give it a thought."

"Ah. Then you simply behave according to your nature."

"I am a firm believer that if something doesn't feel right, then one shouldn't—"

Her breath stuttered to a halt when he pressed his lips to her nape, just above her frilled collar.

"*So soft,*" he whispered, the syllables barely audible, as if he hadn't meant for her to hear them. Oh, but she had, and the words dropped heavily into the pit of her stomach, her body clenching around them.

As the pad of his thumb idly brushed the susceptible skin

of her inner wrist, Meg had to remind herself again that she was playing the part of a seasoned seductress, who would hardly deliquesce into a puddle at the first touch of a man. She was no Gothic-novel simpleton. Even so, it took effort not to melt back against him and to keep the telescope to her eye.

She cleared her throat, hoping to sound completely unaffected by his nearness. "Even when learning to ride a horse, I refused the sidesaddle. It just seemed unnatural, limbs to one side, twisting one's torso. I convinced my brother that it felt unsafe so he would permit me to ride astride. And I've done so for years."

"Scandalous," he teased, his breath warm against the shell of her ear.

"What is the point of doing anything if it doesn't feel natural?"

"And does this feel"—he pressed a kiss to the simmering pulse on the side of her throat—"natural?"

A mewl of surprise escaped her. As an untried debutante, she should likely be shying away by now. At the very least she ought to be wondering if she was in over her head. But being here with him felt like the most natural thing in the world.

She'd never been overly concerned with propriety. Losing her parents at a young age had taught her to live every moment of her life to the fullest. She'd spent the majority of it living by her heart, doing whatever felt right. Until she'd read Daniel's letter.

She'd lost part of herself then. It was sort of like when a foot falls asleep. You know that it's yours, but it feels like someone else's foot has been attached to your limb, and you're forced to walk around with the prickling deadweight of it as if everything were perfectly fine.

But only recently had she started to feel like herself again, vibrant and awakened. Alive.

"I think you might be trying to seduce me, Merleton."

His steadying hand moved from her waist to cover her midriff as he tucked her back against his solid form. Her body began to hum. "Turnabout is fair play. After all, I cannot have you thinking that you can run circles around me."

"In other words, do unto others as they might do unto you?"

"Something to that effect." His lips curved into a grin as they pressed into the sensitive valley where her neck met her shoulder, and she arched for him, allowing him access. "Are you still paying attention to the occultation?"

"I'm afraid I've lost interest in my study of this evening's sky."

He tsked against her skin. Taking the apparatus from her grasp, he set it aside. "Then, perhaps a new subject is in order."

She didn't know what he intended, but when he took her hand and turned her to face him, she didn't object. In fact, she was hoping he would kiss her.

"I want you to close your eyes but pay attention."

She squinted warily. "Why?"

"Because there will be an examination on this later," he teased in this new playful way that she was becoming quite fond of.

Humoring him, she did as he asked. And in the next instant she smiled when he pressed a kiss against her knuckles. It wasn't exactly what she'd hoped for, but the pressure was pleasant, his lips warm and enticingly firm.

"And now this." He turned her wrist and opened her hand.

The coolness of the night air swept over the exposed flesh, making her feel peculiarly vulnerable for such an insignificant act. Then she felt his breath on her skin, hot and humid in the center of her palm. Her lips parted on a gasp. She wanted to curl her fingers, but he kept her splayed as he blew a thin stream of cooler air along the edges, sending a wash of gooseflesh tingling over her limbs.

Again, he breathed hotly against the center. Again, he cooled the surrounding plumper flesh, until she became acutely aware of the pulse beating in the heart of her palm. It had the strangest effect, for she could feel that same heavy pulse in the core of her body, where she was overheated and liquid.

She shifted, sliding her slippers against each other, her knees touching as he exhaled a furnace blast that made perspiration bloom on her skin. And when he pressed his lips to her palm, something clenched deep inside her.

Her eyes flew open. She felt flushed from head to toe.

"There are so many unexpected regions of the body that are particularly susceptible to pleasure," he said in a whisper against that thrumming pulse. "Places where the skin is fine and delicate, where a breath is almost too much and a touch is just shy of tickling."

He blew that cool stream again, and this time allowed her to curl her fingers inward. Then he stepped closer. Brushing a tendril behind her ear, his gaze swept from her eyes to the crests of her flushed cheeks and to her plump, parted lips.

His pupils were large, his breathing just as shallow as hers. And she knew she wasn't the only one affected.

"Show me," she said—possibly begged—in a throaty rasp as she tilted up her face in eager anticipation.

He shook his head slowly. "I'm afraid tonight's lesson is over."

"But you didn't even kiss me." She tried not to whine, but any woman would in this situation.

"And I'm not going to either." Releasing her, he took a step back and adjusted his spectacles. "I intend to keep the upper hand—and I do believe that we can both agree that I just claimed it."

With her pulse still rioting, it took a moment for his statement to make sense. But when it did, Meg narrowed her eyes. The heat in her veins turned to ice. And she was fairly certain that, somewhere in the world, Lady Avalon would be furious.

"I wouldn't be too sure about that."

He shrugged. "I suppose it's a matter of opinion. But know this. Before we're through, I promise that I'll not only reclaim what's mine, I will know all your secrets."

That anomalous dimple of his appeared once more.

How dare he! And he looked so sure of himself that she desperately wanted to say something clever to put him in his place.

Unfortunately, Meg's ability to embody Lady Avalon fell short, and all she could do was huff and storm off in a flurry. Drat that man!

And yet, as she marched away, she realized something important from her so-called lesson.

Little did he know, he had just armed her with information. And she fully intended to use it against him.

Chapter 12

Hell hath no fury like a woman sconed

The following morning, Lucien didn't feel like he'd gained the upper hand as planned.

At first, his strategy to seduce the seductress had seemed foolproof. As with any experiment, he'd intended to act with remote efficiency, to be tactical and in complete control.

In hindsight, however, he might have underestimated her allurement and how her responses to his every touch would affect him.

Merlin's teeth!

His own plot had completely backfired.

He'd lain awake all night thinking of her: the shimmer of moonlight in her eyes, the warmth and softness of her skin beneath his lips, her sweet fragrance filling his every breath, the fit of her supple curves pressed back against him—and the way she stormed off in high dudgeon because of his refusal to kiss her.

The last thing he wanted was to vex her or make an enemy of the woman who possessed what belonged to him and potentially cause her to go into hiding.

But no, that wasn't entirely true.

What he actually wanted was to *stop* wanting to kiss her again.

Unfortunately, he craved her in ways that he hadn't experienced before. And he knew that if he'd given in, she would have had him wrapped around her finger . . . just like all the other men she'd duped.

He wasn't going to let that happen.

What he was going to do, however, was go back to his original plan—to diligently scrutinize her and learn all he needed to know. He would have to maintain close proximity. But he would do so in a carefully detached manner that wouldn't allow even a modicum of attraction to stand in the way of his main purpose.

Conveniently, the elder Parrish women invited his party to travel with theirs, and much to Meg's consternation, Lucien had accepted.

Today, he promised them a tour down the Rhine. The open-air seclusion would suit his purposes perfectly. At least, that's what he hoped.

However, the paddle steamer was only scheduled to run on Thursdays and Saturdays. This was Wednesday. Nevertheless, he quickly learned that, for the right price, the captain was willing to drive a private party down the Rhine on any other day of the week.

It was a boon, indeed, and fit perfectly into his plan. He didn't even mind the cold shoulder Meg had been giving him all morning as she kept to her end of the boat. A wolf caught in a snare was bound to snarl, after all.

His own mood was little better. Not only hadn't he slept a wink last night but he'd received an inauspicious missive when he left the hotel.

Standing at the rail, he read the correspondence and frowned. It was from the investigator he'd hired to look into the Parrish women. But it didn't contain the report he'd expected. Apparently, weeks of heavy rains had made the roads impassable and put him behind schedule. In other words, he had no useful information.

Lucien curled the missive in his fist, wondering if Mr. Richards was looking into every possible option to overcome this obstacle. There had to be *some* roads that weren't flooded. They were living in a modern age, after all. Surely man wasn't still limited by the laws of precipitation.

Irritated, he smoothed the missive and stuffed it into his breast pocket.

"The aunts have sent me on an errand, Your Grace," Meg said crisply, her posture stiff as she came up beside him, standing close enough that her damnably appealing scent teased his nostrils. "Scone?"

Upon her gloved hand rested a dainty handkerchief and, upon that, a golden black-currant scone.

His stomach growled. Though, he wasn't certain if he wanted the pastry or the delectable woman in sprigged muslin. Then again, as an errant breeze took that moment to sweep the gauzy fabric against her form, outlining every curve and valley with mouthwatering precision, he knew the answer.

But he settled for the scone and inclined his head. "Is this an olive branch, then?"

"Hardly." She sniffed, and there was an unmistakable flash of ire in the eyes shaded beneath the brim of her bonnet. But before she turned to walk away, she hesitated and gestured with the tip of her parasol toward the sky. "Were you growling at that cloud just now?"

"No. Merely a displeasing correspondence."

"Ah. Well, just so you know, if it does rain, I fully intend to blame you for ruining our outing."

The corner of his mouth twitched at her peevish response. "That is a cumulus cloud. Unless there is an atmospheric shift that causes it to grow vertically into a cumulonimbus, we'll have a suitably dry tour of the river."

Taking a bite of the scone, he glanced down the deck of the steamer where Pell was holding court beneath a striped awning with Maeve and Myrtle Parrish. Then his gaze returned to Meg, surprised by the flash of her dimples.

"Why are you smiling at me?" he asked, narrowing his eyes before he glanced at the half-eaten pastry in his hand. He swallowed thickly. "Is this poisoned?"

She pressed her lips together, considering. "Not this time. I'd prefer to make you suffer in other ways."

"Then, why the smile just now?"

"No reason." She shrugged and turned to face the water. "I just like hearing you talk."

Damn. He hated when she said things like that. It made it difficult to remember she was his adversary.

She's a wolf in sheep's clothing, he reminded himself. He would not be fooled into believing otherwise. And yet . . .

There were moments when he'd caught himself thinking of her as more—as a woman who kept him guessing. Who challenged him at every turn. Who intrigued him beyond reason. And who was simply *Meg*.

But he couldn't afford those thoughts. He needed to keep a distance between them. A separation. A necessary barrier. This was about his legacy, after all. It wasn't a game. Not for him.

Without glancing his way, she remarked, "You haven't taken another bite. Does that mean you suspect me of disguising my true purpose, the way you did last night when you pretended an interest in me?"

"I did calculate the likelihood of a sprinkling of arsenic. I'm sure there's some rat poison on this boat you might have procured."

She huffed and reached over to break off a piece. Around a mouthful, she said, "There. Satisfied?"

"Not necessarily. Such a small quantity of that poison would do little harm. Though, you likely know that already," he said merely to goad her. And when she moved as if to steal the rest, he stuffed the scone into his mouth.

A moment later, after he swallowed, he offered quietly, "There was no pretense on my part last evening. But I refuse to be led by my baser impulses."

She stared up at him for a moment, then issued a nod. Though, whether or not she was mollified or challenged by his confession remained to be seen.

Suspicious of her current objective, he frowned at the dainty lace-gloved hand on the rail beside his.

She lifted it to brush an errant tendril from her cheek, then set it back down, a fraction closer this time. "It must be difficult to be a man of reason when your family legacy demands faith in what cannot be quantified."

"You have no idea," he said darkly as her little finger slid against his as if by accident, before she moved seven-eighths of an inch away. But that did not stop the tingles left behind. "From the moment I was able to put thought to reason, I wanted to solve the riddle. To make sense of it."

"I understand completely." Her gaze followed the dubious lift of his brows. "No, it's true. You're not the only one who was brought up beneath a cloud of myth. I have been struggling to make sense of mine for a while now. You see, my family has a long history of love matches brought together by fate. Legend has it that we will know, beyond a shadow of a doubt, when we meet our soul's counterpart. It has been the same for generations with grandparents, parents, aunts and uncles, even with my brother."

He scoffed. "Fated love is a fanciful notion."

"Is that so? Well, it is my understanding that you are searching for a collection of recipes that hold legendary powers. And yet you think my family myth is fanciful?"

"Point taken," he conceded with a nod, albeit with extreme skepticism.

Noticing a wedge of sunlight fall just above her expertly fitted bodice, he realized her parasol was too insufficient to shield her pale skin in their current position. So he proffered his arm in a silent invitation to take a turn about the deck.

His intention was for her to be beneath the awning, which she was. He did not intend, however, for his awareness to shift to the supple warm curve of the side of her breast, the aimless back and forth stroke of her fingertips against his sleeve, and the escalation of his own pulse.

He swallowed. "And has the myth held true for you?"

"I'd thought so for a time, but . . ." She shook her head. "Perhaps I was too taken in by the stories my father would tell me and too eager for the rest of my life to begin."

At another mention of her father—the same man who'd studied the Arthurian legends—Lucien considered her closely and came straight to the point. "Is he the man you are working for?"

"My father?"

"Aye," he said. "You are far too clever and beautiful to have decided on this life you're leading. And I cannot imagine a father approving of it, unless *he* is the man you're working for."

She looked away as if to study the pair of chaises longues tucked in the shadows beneath the overhang. "My father was a country gentleman. A simple man who valued his family above all else. He often told stories. His favorites were of King Arthur, but mine were the ones he told about my mother. It made me feel as if I knew her."

Then both of her parents were gone, too, he thought.

"How old were you?" he asked, all the while knowing that it had nothing to do with his primary objective. But seeing her gaze turn distant, the blue of her eyes so somber that it created a peculiar stirring of panic inside him, he had to say something.

"Four," she answered and left it at that, which he understood.

Even though there had been no one to tell stories of his

mother after she died, he knew that some memories were better left alone. That was the reason he buried himself in his work.

"As for your other question," she continued, "I'm not certain if my father would have approved of my choices. He would have wanted me to marry and build a family of my own."

"Why didn't you?"

She exhaled resignedly. "Two words—or a name, rather. Daniel Prescott."

"Ah. So *he* is the man you're working for."

"Is that all you ever think about? No, don't answer," she said tightly, rolling her eyes. "He was the man I was going to marry. Until he . . . decided to marry someone else."

She slipped her arm from his and went to the railing again.

Lucien followed, a keen sense of irritation abrading his skin where she was no longer touching him. He wondered if it would cease with her hand on his arm again. But even as the thought traveled through his mind, he dismissed it. The irritation was nothing more than the concentration of heat reacting to the starch in the linen.

He tugged on the cuff of his sleeve. "And you believed this Daniel Prescott was your *soul's counterpart*?"

"I'd been certain of it," she said. "I remember, when I was young, climbing the wishing tree in the garden—"

"After years of dendrology, I can assure you that there is no such genus classification as *wishing tree*."

"And I can assure *you* that there are many throughout the world. Trees are mystical, after all. They outlive us by years, decades, generations. Who is to say what they are capable of?"

"Science," he said dourly.

She expelled an exasperated sigh and waved her hand as if to shoo logic from the conversation. "Nevertheless, when I was younger, I put a coin in the cradle of the highest branch and whispered my heart's fervent wish to have my future husband appear that very day. It just so happened that Daniel arrived as I was coming down. He teased me about how pretty girls weren't supposed to be up in trees. So I challenged him and said that I could climb faster than he could."

"And did you?"

She nodded, a wistful smile on her lips that bothered Lucien for some unfathomable reason. Absently, he scratched his arm.

"But then I fell," she said. "In more ways than one, I suppose. My heart was irrevocably lost that day."

Something niggled at the back of his mind, like a story that he'd heard once before. Unable to recall the origins, he brushed it aside and scratched again. He had more important things on his mind at the moment. Like where to find this Mr. Prescott.

"Until he married someone else," Lucien prodded. "And traveled to . . ."

"Upper Canada, of all places," she groused. Then she looked askance at him. "Why are you so interested?"

"Merely trying to understand why you decided to turn your hopes and dreams toward espionage."

"Perhaps I'm simply a woman who wants to have one grand flirtation before she puts herself on the shelf and dedicates the rest of her life to spoiling her brother's children."

Her gaze met his, and there was something imploring, beseeching in those crystalline depths. Something that made him . . .

No. He shook his head and chuckled wryly. "You spin a fine yarn, *ma petite louve.* But I'm not fooled. You don't believe in that romantic drivel any more than I do."

"You seem quite sure about that."

"I am, because men and women make their own decisions.

There is no such thing as happenstance, coincidence, fate, wishes—"

"Legendary recipes with the power to imbue a knight with valiance and a maiden with steadfast love?"

Her challenging taunt stopped him. Facing her, he straightened his shoulders. "Perhaps not."

She blinked, her face scrunched in confusion. "Wait just a moment. Are you saying that you don't believe in your own legend?"

"Any sensible person would harbor doubt," he said. "It reads like a storybook with the legendary powers attributed to recipes. One is the Recipe of the Beast. This is supposed to imbue the warrior knight with the frightening qualities of Glatisant, the barking beast. It is said that the warrior who eats this will have the cunning of a serpent, the strength of a lion, the patience of a leopard stalking his prey, and the speed of a rabbit. Another is the Recipe of the White Hart. Give this to your enemy, and it will cause his heart to falter, but a maiden who sups upon this will lose her heart forever," he said and watched her study him with fascination. Her total absorption made his breath quicken, and he felt himself moving closer.

Then he straightened and cleared his throat, continuing. "The most dangerous of all is the Recipe of Veritas. While it is said to imbue the noble knight with honor and truth, it is also a tool to use against the enemy. For anyone who tastes it is forced to confess their deepest, most hidden secrets. Now, tell me, does this sound like something that could be factual?"

"I cannot answer that. But I was taught to always be open to chance, to wonderment, to the Fates stepping in when you least"—she stopped, seemingly out of breath, and she searched his gaze as if she were seeing him for the first time—"expect it."

He didn't like the way she was looking at him. It made

his hands itch. Made him want to take her by the shoulders and pull her hard against him.

But she was the enemy. And he couldn't allow his determination to be dampened or clouded in any way.

"All of it is nonsense. Ridiculous," he hissed and turned toward the railing.

"Then, why all the fuss and bother? Why are you even chasing Lady Avalon in the first place?"

"Because that book is mine to protect." Elbows on the railing, he closed his hands into fists. "It is my duty, my responsibility, to keep it safe, and that is what I intend to do."

He refused to tell her the real reason or to open the raw wound that he'd been carrying with him all these years. Lady Avalon did not need to know what drove a man like him to obsession.

A frown pulled at the corners of her mouth. "Surely, there was a point in your life when your logical mind was open to the possibility that fables were true."

Lucien looked off toward the water as the boat paddled by one of the many castle ruins situated high on the hills along the river.

The answer was *yes*. There had been two instances. The last had been on the day he'd found her lurking in the corridor. But he'd soon discovered the predatory surge that had traversed through his blood had nothing to do with the recipe.

The first had come the day his parents were murdered. Two men had stolen into the keep, driven by their beliefs in the legend so much so that they were willing to kill for it. He might have been killed as well, if not for his sister.

From that moment on, Lucien had spent every day trying to unearth the proof that would make sense of it. He would never stop until he found it. And he would never let anyone or anything—like an unwanted attraction—stand in his way.

"I want you to know," he said, his voice hard and distant even to his own ears, "there isn't anything I wouldn't do to claim what belongs to me."

She surprised him by briefly covering his hand with hers. "I would expect nothing less. We are alike in that regard, Lucien. Once a person finally realizes what they truly want, they should do whatever it takes to have the life they desire."

"Good. Then, we understand each other."

As MEG stood at the starboard rail, she wasn't certain that she understood at all.

Something wholly unexpected had just happened.

During the heated defense of her own legend, she'd felt something stirring inside of her. And as she heard herself speak of believing in chance, fate and wonderment, that *something* had struck like an earthquake, sudden and startling, cracking her open in soul-deep fissures.

It was like eons of hardened clay and sand had been excavated in a thunderous jolt, revealing the burial chamber where her heart lay. This discovery left her exposed and vulnerable. But what surprised her most of all was that the entombed heart was still beating. True, it was raw and tender after Daniel's betrayal. But it was also filled with new hope.

In that moment she knew, beyond a shadow of a doubt, that everything had changed.

At least, for her.

Standing beside Lucien, she wondered what it would take to convince him that there was more than a book between them. Though, considering his profile was as stony and obstinate as the castle ruins jutting from the hilltops along the river's edge, she knew that changing his mind was going to be a hard-fought battle.

But she could be just as stubborn and dogged in her own pursuits when it mattered. And this definitely mattered. She was sure of it.

"Is there a reason you are staring so intently at me?" he asked, his glower so forbidding she was shocked when fish didn't rise from the river and flop onto the deck in surrender.

Twirling her parasol, she smiled up at him. "Just waiting for the arsenic to take effect and deciding what to do with your corpse."

His mouth twitched. "Come to any conclusions?"

"Not yet. But in the meantime, would you care for another scone? I do hate waiting."

She was rewarded with a flash of that solitary dimple and took that as a good sign. A very good sign, indeed.

Chapter 13

Forbidden fruit

Their journey along the Rhine filled Meg with promise. After a morning fraught with tension, they left cool spring behind, and warm summer stealthily crept in, blooming in a beautiful spectacle of nature and new life.

She spent the majority of the day at Lucien's side. And as the hours passed, she was glad to discover that he wasn't the typically condescending man she was used to encountering. Even though he was rather arrogant at times, there was something humble in his nature, too. It was in the way he always asked questions as if driven more by a need to understand than to judge or to be right.

She admired that about him. Which was rather convenient. After all, one would prefer to like the company of the person who'd reawakened one's heart.

Of course, the book was still a bone of contention. However, she was hoping to convince him that there was more between them.

She knew how peculiar the *Stredwick certainty* sounded to those who had not been raised on tales of it. The notion of fate and certainty and finding your soul's counterpart was too far-fetched for most. But she'd thought that if anyone would understand her fanciful family legend, it would have been a man with his own.

He hadn't.

That didn't mean she was giving up, however. In fact, she was now on a mission to prove it existed.

As evening washed over them in hues of orange and violet, she still hadn't come up with a plan. So she asked herself, *What would Lady Avalon do?*

The answer was simple: *Lady Avalon would do whatever she wanted to do.*

So when the boat neared the dock, Meg boldly slipped her arm through his and leaned close. She heard his intake of breath, felt his arm tense as he secured her closer still. For all she knew, he might have been ticklish and she had triggered a reflexive response, and taking possession of her arm was only a matter of protecting himself from a spirited attack. Either that or he simply wanted to feel her against him.

Whatever the reason, she liked the way he was looking down at her, his eyes intensely dark, his mouth curled in a quizzical grin.

"Fireflies," she said and pointed over the railing to the tiny flickering lights that winked drowsily from the shore. "When I was young, I called them fairies and pretended that they were gathering for a merry ball in the tall grasses." Then, remembering their previous conversation about butterflies, she gave him a playfully arched look. "Though, I suppose you're about to tell me that their flashing lights are not indicative of happiness at all."

"It is true that the purpose of the glow is merely to attract a mate. The male flies overhead, flashing the luciferin compound in his abdomen while the flightless female decides whether she's interested in his companionship. If she is, then she'll light up, too. In that regard," he said with a teasing lift of his brows, "I would imagine that at least a few of them are quite content, if not happy."

His audaciousness startled a laugh out of her. He could be so grim and intellectual at times, but there was also a roguish side to him. And when he lifted his hand, his knuckles curled to brush her blushing cheek, she hoped there was enough mischief in him to steal a kiss. Or two.

But then their captain started shouting out orders to the crew as they neared the dock, and the moment was lost.

They arrived at their hotel in Mainz late in the evening. And after spending the entire day in his company and coming to know him better, it was almost impossible to bid adieu.

"We had a lovely time, Your Grace," Maeve said as he handed her down from the carriage onto the courtyard flagstones.

Following close behind, Myrtle waggled her finger and winked at him. "It will be difficult for you to improve upon such a day. If you cannot, I fear we'll have to venture somewhere thrilling without you on the morrow."

"And just so you know, cousin, I will abandon you and go with them in a trice. After all, they keep me well fed," Lord Holladay interjected, patting his flat abdomen beneath the buttons of his paisley waistcoat.

"I would say they could have you, but I wouldn't wish you on anyone," Lucien replied, and when Pell stepped up to hand Meg down, he nudged him out of the way. Taking possession of her outstretched fingers and drawing her down, he said to her in a low voice, "As for you, I believe I've already promised not to let you out of my sight."

She knew that he was actually referring to Lady Avalon, and she would settle that matter sooner or later. But for the moment, she decided to take the warm glow in his gaze as a promising sign.

THE FOLLOWING morning, she dressed and went down to join the aunts at breakfast. Her steps were light and quick, but they faltered with pleased surprise when she saw Lucien at the bottom of the stairs.

"Good morning, Merleton," she said with a smile. "Waiting for someone in particular?"

"You," he said without hesitation, and a thrilling effervescence filled her veins. And he looked quite dashing in his green riding coat and fitted buckskin breeches.

As she neared, his thorough gaze swept from her head to hem and back up again, darkening behind his lenses with something that looked like hunger. Her stomach performed a queer little flip, and a warm flush traveled over her skin.

She tried to catch her breath before responding. "Oh?"

"I thought I might escort you to your aunts' table in the common dining room, and we could discuss our itinerary."

He proffered his arm, and she casually curled her hand over his sleeve as if the words *our itinerary* didn't make her feel a bit giddy with promise.

"I'm afraid I have regretful news," he continued grimly. "The captain is unwilling to negotiate another private tour. Today is his usual day of business, you see. And there are other passengers who've purchased tickets for their voyage." He hesitated and his eyes met hers, his brows lifting in an uncertain query. "Then again, you might be looking forward to the conversation of others."

"Conversing with the others holds little appeal for me. I should have preferred a private tour with you, I think," she admitted honestly. "Along with the aunts, of course, and your cousin."

"Of course."

Bemused, she watched as his expression softened. He even smiled. Well, almost. There was a slight shift at the corner of his mouth. But it was just enough for her heart to flutter with the hope that something had altered in him as well. That, perhaps, he realized there was something more between them than just a book.

"It will be late again when we arrive at our next lodgings," he continued. "However, the day after, I wonder if you would like to join me on a tour of the village. Through research, I've learned that they have an exceptional market, as well as many architecturally pleasing churches and estates that you might enjoy sketching."

A rush of warmth filled her chest, his suggestion indicating that he recalled her penchant for drawing. "I would have to speak with the aunts."

"I've already invited your companions, and they are amenable."

Oh, the aunts were likely more than just amenable. No doubt they were bursting with wedding-breakfast plans. Meg would have to remind them, again, that this was a holiday flirtation.

And yet, even to her, it was starting to feel like more.

"I look forward to it, then," she said.

He inclined his head. "In the meantime, I've asked the kitchens to prepare a wide variety of scones for our picnic on the boat this afternoon."

"Heavy on the arsenic?"

His elusive dimple flashed. "But of course."

OVER THE next few days, their peace treaty continued. They drifted along the river, picnicked and visited markets, all the while enjoying each other's company.

There were no more tense discussions about the book or their family legends. Their exchanges usually revolved around their current likes and dislikes, scientific observations and questions about each other's childhoods and daily life.

However, Meg's responses were carefully edited, leaving out the details that would reveal her family name. And Lucien's were brief, as though it pained him to speak of his past. So she tended to keep far afield of those topics. Her primary desire was to be with the man he was in that moment. Nothing more.

While they were usually in view of her chaperones, there were times when Maeve and Myrtle needed to pilfer a new recipe. The aunts would make their excuses, citing old age and a need to rest, while they encouraged the duke and the viscount to escort their charge to the next shop. And sometimes Pell would wander off, too, leaving her alone with Lucien.

Meg liked being alone with him. It felt so natural. She didn't even mind his pet name for her any longer. There was something fond in the way he called her *ma petite louve*.

Her designs had altered, as well. Instead of putting on a pretense of employing the three *F*s, she was flirting in earnest and hoping to gain every possible foothold into the duke's affections.

Yet, for some reason, the more she flirted, the more he began keeping his distance. It was thoroughly disconcerting. Not only that, but her inner Lady Avalon didn't utter a single syllable of advice.

Meg's outings with Lucien always began with ease and playfulness. But the more time they spent together, especially alone, the grumpier he would become.

Countless times, she'd caught him looking at her in a way that made her breath quicken, his eyes dark and hungry. She'd been almost certain that he wanted to kiss her . . . but he never did.

Meg decided to take matters into her own hands.

However, when she attempted an embrace—by way of polishing his spectacles and replacing them on his countenance—he'd remained perfectly still, as if he'd turned to stone. He hadn't even reached out to steady her as she'd teetered forward and *accidentally* pressed her torso against his. Instead, as the heated rush of his breath tangled with hers, he slowly drew her hands away from the nape of his neck. Then he stepped apart, cleared his throat and growled a good-night.

Clearly, she was doing something wrong.

"I do not believe the three *F*s are working for me," she'd complained to the aunts on the morning of their final day in Germany. "Just when I think the day has been absolutely perfect, he turns quite unexpectedly surly. Is there another *F* I should be employing?"

The sisters exchanged a look, a dusting of color saturating their powder-soft cheeks. The question seemed to render Maeve mute.

"I'm sure you're doing everything splendidly," Myrtle said with a conciliatory pat on her shoulder. "The only advice I can offer is this. When I was a girl, the vicar's son took a fancy to me and I to him. On Sundays, when the congregation gathered to picnic on the village green, we would slip away to take a turn around the park. I remember when he became particularly cross, and the only thing that would set his mood to rights was to"—she hesitated with a faraway look in her eyes and drew a breath as if to hold onto the memory— "press my hand to his. Without any gloves between us. It was quite thrilling." She expelled a wistful sigh, then smiled. "Perhaps that would set matters aright with your duke."

Now it was Meg's turn to blush.

Since she had already kissed him and, in retaliation, he'd done more than simply hold her bare hand, she wasn't certain that was the answer. But she was willing to try anything to be in his arms again.

🦋

THAT AFTERNOON, Lucien and Pell escorted her to a local carnival. The aunts decided to remain at the hotel and assist the maids with packing their trunks.

The village square was host to circus performers in brightly colored garb, juggling, spinning plates and performing acrobatics on the cobblestones. Merrymakers visited the half-timbered shops and the clock-tower tavern, along with huts and tents filled with various foods and games.

Beyond the fountain, Meg saw a stall where a burly, bearded man was challenging others to prove their skill by knocking the cuckoo from its perch.

"Let's try that one next," she said, tugging on Lucien's arm.

Thus far, he'd proven that there was *no such thing as chance* in the games of chance, his sense of logic besting the puzzles set before him. He'd received angry glowers from the carnival men, but proud and beaming smiles from her.

"Your aunts are correct—you *are* far too exuberant today. No wonder they begged Pell and myself to escort you here. You're a veritable Volta battery."

He looked down at her with a falsely disapproving expression. But he couldn't fool her. She knew the exact dimension of his true frown, and this was only a paltry imitation.

She stopped and shrugged. "Very well. Take me back to the inn if you cannot handle my enthusiasm. I'm sure to find a younger man who'll escort me and prove his manliness in these tests of skill."

His brows rose dubiously above the brass rims. "Knocking a tiny wooden cuckoo from a perch with a little wooden ball is your notion of proving manliness?"

"Oh, it most definitely is," she said with unquestionable sincerity. "I would likely reward him with a kiss, as well. Therefore, you may deliver me back to the inn without delay so that I can find this masculine specimen."

When she turned and took a step, he held fast to the arm curled around his, cinching her to his side.

He growled, "I accept your challenge."

She had to bite the inside of her cheek to keep from smiling as he hauled her to the game.

After three attempts, however, Lucien was unsuccessful. Even though the ball had struck the cuckoo, the bird never fell from its perch.

"The density of the ball is obviously insufficient to unseat the bird. I have struck it three times, and thrice it has remained. I conclude that it is clearly fastened to the perch," he accused, shoving his spectacles up the bridge of his nose.

The bearded man grinned as if being called a cheat was the highlight of his day. With a supercilious lift of his hand, he flicked the cuckoo from the perch with the tip of his finger to show how easily it could be done. Then he put the bird back in place, set the ball on the rail in front of Lucien and crossed his arms over his chest, daring his customer to try again.

Beside her, Lucien seethed through his teeth and reached into his pocket.

Meg put her hand on Lucien's arm, staying him. "There's no need to spend any more coin on this bit of foolishness. This man has likely made a fortune on the game when there isn't any possible way to"—dismissively, she swiped up the ball and sent it sailing through the air—"best it."

Just as the last syllable left her lips, the ball connected with the cuckoo.

The bird fell.

Meg instantly squealed with delight, clapping and bouncing on the balls of her feet. "Did you see that, Lucien? Did you . . ."

Her words trailed off when she saw the muscle along his jaw twitch.

He set the coin down crisply on the rail, then took her hand and started to walk across the cobblestones.

"I'm certain it was just luck," she said, trying not to laugh. But really, this was too amusing.

"There is no such thing as luck."

She quickened her step to keep pace with him, not bothering to hide her grin. "Then, it was likely the arc I was able to achieve from my height. If I've said it once, I've said it a thousand times, you are simply too tall."

"My height had nothing to do with it."

"Then, it must have been the size of your hands. They are simply too large." She thought she saw the corner of his mouth twitch, but she had to turn her attention away as he took her up the steps of the church and through the wide oaken doors. "Of course, it couldn't have anything to do with my skill."

The door swung closed behind them just as she giggled, the sound reverberating through the cathedral. The few villagers who were there admiring the stained-glass windows and the vaulted ceilings turned to glare at them. One even shushed her.

Meg barely had time to paste on a contrite expression before Lucien abruptly pivoted and stalked toward the archway on the far side of the vestibule, hauling her with him.

There, he led her through a narrow door. Inside was a steep set of stairs, the walls of the tower curving around every side. She looked up and up and up and saw the bell hanging overhead.

"Lucien," she whispered as he closed the door behind them, "why are we in the bell tow—"

She didn't have the chance to finish.

In an instant, he had turned her in his arms and lowered his mouth to hers.

Her eyes widened. Then she smiled as understanding dawned. She hadn't been wrong about those heated looks, after all. And this was so much better than holding hands.

But she barely had time to slide hers to his shoulders before he lifted his head and looked down at her. Lips parted, he panted, "Is this . . . acceptable?"

"Yes, yes." She nodded and tried to pull him closer to her once more. But he solved that problem by gripping her waist and setting her on the first step. "Even better."

He captured those syllables with a burning kiss. His body was so close that she could feel the heat of it through layers of linen, wool, muslin and cambric. Feel the last vestiges of his carefully controlled desire go up in flames as he held her face and took complete possession of her mouth.

This was different from the first time. That had been all stillness—a shock, a breath, a press and release. And, truth be told, she'd known little else about kissing. But this was so much more. All movement—lips parting, hungry sips, tongues sliding in delicious wet friction. And he didn't even seem to mind her untutored enthusiasm, like the way she raked her teeth over his bottom lip or suckled his tongue deeper into her mouth in an attempt to satisfy this new craving for the taste of him.

He growled, pulling her flush. But his glasses slid down the length of his nose. Frustrated, he shoved them back in place, then wrapped his arms around her, nudging her lips apart with his own . . . only to growl again when the saddle slipped.

"Take them off. Take them off," she said urgently, helping to dislodge the earpieces as her fingers threaded in his hair. A mewl of impatience escaped her when his mouth strayed from hers, but he quickly returned as if they were two magnets drawn together.

Dimly, she heard the faint clatter of something falling to the floor. But it didn't matter. Nothing mattered in this moment as he held her tighter, and she twined her arms around his neck.

"Why didn't you start with this?"

"What? This?" he asked, kissing her again until her toes curled.

She nodded, their chests rising and falling in a tandem crush, stomachs pressed. "You should have started right here."

"You expected me to bypass the carnival, march across the cobblestone and drag you into the bell tower?"

His mouth opened over her throat, sucking gently on the

vulnerable pulse, his splayed hand descending lower on her back, drawing her closer.

"Yes, yes and yes." She arched her neck, eyes closed, lost in pleasure. "You wasted far too much time being surly these past few days."

He smiled against her skin. "All was going to plan until that bloody cuckoo tipped me over the edge."

Then he took her mouth again. Gripping her bottom, he lifted her higher against him until her slippers were balanced on the edge of the step.

The solid feel of him distracted her thoughts, and she wasn't sure she'd heard him correctly. "Hmm?"

He answered with a hungry sound as he nudged her lips apart with tiny sips that beckoned her to do the same. It was like they were feasting on each other, licking and tasting until the kiss transformed into something new and urgent. His grip brought the apex of her thighs against a thick shape. Reflexively, her hips tilted against the imposing hardness, gauging, testing, until something of a purr vibrated in her throat. A guttural grunt left his, the sound tunneling deep into the pit of her stomach.

"This is madness," he rasped, pausing to gaze wonderingly down into her face, his eyes blazing and dark. "You're positively irresistible and clever and witty. I never stood a chance, did I?"

She shook her head, grazing her lips across his as her heart rejoiced. "There's something between us. I've known it from the beginning. I didn't want to accept it then, but now there's no way to turn my back on it."

"I know." He closed his eyes and kissed her softly as he lifted a hand to cradle her face. "With that book standing between us, it complicates everything. But it doesn't have to be that way."

"What we have is greater than any book. Something deep and lasting. We were brought together for a reason."

During these past few days, Meg knew that her Stredwick certainty had finally found her soul's counterpart. She'd thought the Fates had given her Daniel, but he'd never made her feel this way. Her tender feelings for him were nothing compared to this burning passion.

Lucien smiled as he smoothed the tendrils from her temple. "Yes, I know, and the reason was thievery. But I'm not angry about it any longer. I just want it returned to me, and then we can explore more of this. And I must confess, I've quickly become completely obsessed with your mouth," he said, nibbling at the corner.

She closed her eyes, absorbed in the pleasure of the moment. Yet, something niggled at the back of her mind, and she slid her hands to his chest.

"You said 'all was going to plan' a moment ago. What did you mean by that?"

"Precisely what it sounded like. I had everything under control in this game of ours. I was going to hold firm and not give in to your clever seduction. But when you picked up that little ball and knocked the cuckoo from its perch, all the while gazing at me with those fathomless eyes, madness took over. I couldn't stand it a moment longer. I had to surrender." He grinned at her, that damnable dimple winking. "Just tell me what I have to do to reclaim it. Name your price. I'll give you anything."

"Are you still talking about the book?"

"Of course," he said, his tone fondly teasing. "You were absolutely right when you left that note telling me that I'd met my match. I have, indeed. And I'm eager to put aside what is between us."

"And I wasn't referring to the book just now, but to fate," she clarified, as his smile fell and his brow furrowed.

He shook his head in confusion and lowered her to the step. Putting space between them, he raked a hand through his hair. "That's ludicrous. This is nothing more than passion. Desire. We both feel it. We both want to give in to it. I thought we were ready to bargain like two sensible adults. Apparently, I was mistaken."

"*Like two sensible—*" She stiffened, seething. "I should like to return to the inn now, if you don't mind."

He issued a curt nod and pulled on the hem of his coat.

Smoothing her hands over wrinkled muslin, she stepped down . . . and heard a crunch beneath her shoe.

His spectacles.

LORD HOLLADAY stayed behind to enjoy the clock-tower tavern, leaving Meg and Lucien alone in the carriage. With every jarring bump in the road, the silence and tension grew into a splintering wall, as if they were dropping stacks of firewood between the benches.

By the time they reached the inn, she had built her ire into a flaming conflagration surrounded by sharped-tipped spears. If he dared utter a single syllable more about that book, she was going to unleash every one of them on him.

And yet, she knew the anger was only protecting the vulnerable opening of her newfound feelings for him.

It wasn't love. Or at least she didn't think so. But she knew that she couldn't feel this way, this constant need to be with him, the ache when she wasn't, if there was nothing between them.

Dismally, as they neared the inn, she realized things would have turned out differently if she'd remembered to act like Lady Avalon. An adventuress. A woman who seduced men for her own gain . . . And a shield for someone who'd merely wanted to experience one grand flirtation.

Meg drew in a deep breath. "I am glad that you'll never know how it might have been between us."

"I'm certain I can imagine," he said, but she saw the way his throat tightened as he swallowed. Behind the rims of his broken, single-lens spectacles, his eyes were heated and hungry, the way they had been in the bell tower when he reluctantly admitted that he found her irresistible.

A surge of feminine power filled her.

Embracing her role as infamous book thief and vixen—at least as far as she could manage whilst knowing virtually nothing about either practice—she slowly removed her gloves. Then she crossed one leg over the other and leaned forward to adjust a twisted stocking, lifting her hem a few inches above her trim ankle. She peered up at him through her lashes and saw him follow every movement. *Excellent.*

Finished with the task, she situated her skirts and eased back against the squabs on a satisfied hum. A muscle ticked along his jaw, his hands flexing over the edge of the bench. Then, when he darted a glance to her lips, she wet them with the tip of her tongue and heard his quick intake of breath.

Her pulse thrummed hotly, triumphantly. "Whatever you've imagined isn't even close to the truth. I have a certain, shall we say, aptitude for pleasure."

"Aptitude?" His voice cracked. A slash of red painted the crests of his cheeks and across the bridge of his nose. "As in—"

"Talents. Skills. Surely, a scholar such as yourself does not require the definition." She lifted her shoulders in a delicate shrug that drew his attention to her breasts as the carriage rocked to a slow stop in front of the inn. "Needless to say, I can do things that no ordinary woman would even think of, let alone be bold enough to try. And it pains me to think of what might have been. And I've no doubt you'd have wanted to research all the ways that I can—"

As expected, the efficient porter opened the door and lowered the step. And she didn't bother to finish, because it was obvious by Lucien's one fogged lens that she'd already made her point exceptionally well.

Chapter 14

By the skin of his teeth

Lucien took a walk in the early morning fog, needing to clear his head. Yesterday's impulsive excursion to the bell tower had left him rattled. And now he wasn't certain how to proceed.

He never should have lost control. Yet, after days spent at her side, drinking in her smiles, laughs and light touches, he'd been going mad with desire. He'd even told himself, while marching across those cobblestones toward the church, that all he needed was one taste. Just one small sample would be enough to sate him. Then he could return his focus to the matter that had brought him halfway across the Continent.

But he'd been wrong. So very, very wrong.

At some point between the time that her intoxicating lips met his and her last sigh rushed sweetly over his tongue, he'd come to understand why men had reputedly lost their treasures to her. They'd likely just handed them over, willing to pay any price to have her. And he had been on the verge of making that same error.

The knowledge had shaken him. She'd done this to him, turning him wild with desire. Clearly, she was a master of her craft, which was all the more reason to steel himself against her charms.

So he'd forced himself to stop and remember his own purpose. This quest was about retrieving his family legacy. Not learning the precise dimension of her form pressed against him so that it would be impossible to stop craving her.

But she hadn't liked being reminded of their cat-and-mouse game. And to be honest, he wasn't entirely certain why she was still playing it when she'd already taken his most prized possession.

What else could she possibly want?

He was afraid of the answer. Afraid that his mind would begin to calculate all the ways he could give her whatever she asked.

Lucien returned to the inn just as the fog began to dissipate, the vapor stirred by a procession of porters bearing trunks, band boxes, portmanteaus and tapestry satchels. As he stood outside the door, they filed past him toward a rather familiar hired coach.

At once, his brow flattened, and his irritation spiked. Apparently, the Parrish women were leaving early. And since their party and his were supposedly traveling together, this change in the plan was news to him.

He knew the reason, of course. Meg was still vexed. Oh, but not nearly as much as he was in that moment.

"There you are, Your Grace," Myrtle Parrish said with a smile as she walked out with her sister. "We were afraid we were going to miss bidding you farewell."

"Farewell?" he asked with casual remoteness.

Then his gaze flicked to the open doorway to rest on a pair of icy-blue irises. The remaining fog gathered at her hem in filmy strands of mist. If someone were to tell him that she possessed meteorological wiles as well, at this point he would have believed them.

"Why, yes," Myrtle continued. "We're off to Italy now. Though, we were most forlorn when Meg mentioned last night that our parties will no longer be traveling together."

"Did she, indeed? Well, it just so happens that my cousin and I are still on our way to Italy. As planned."

Maeve Parrish smiled, a knowing gleam in her eyes. "Splendid news!"

"Simply splendid," Meg muttered under her breath.

"Perhaps we'll even happen to stay at the same hotels," Maeve continued.

"There is a high degree of certainty that we shall frequent the same places," he promised and saw Meg's eyelashes cluster together as she hurled icy daggers in his direction. With a bow, he added, "I would welcome any further acquaintance with you and your party, ma'am."

Then Lucien escorted them to their waiting carriage. Maeve and Myrtle filed in, chatting about their eagerness to meet again. Which left the she-wolf.

She said nothing as she stood off to the side. Her indigo traveling costume made the rim around her irises seem darker, giving the pale centers an almost bleached appearance. His gaze met with a hard, unapproachable glare as if she were considering chewing off his hand, should he dare to offer one.

But he presented his hand, nonetheless. And she waited five and three-quarter seconds before accepting.

The instant her fingers slid unerringly into the valley of his palm, a jolt rifled through him. Every blistering moment they'd spent locked in a fervent embrace teemed through his blood like a pack of howling wolves on the hunt. Reflexively, his fingers closed. Hers answered in kind.

Confusion marked her brow in delicate furrows as she glanced down. And when their eyes met again, she looked altogether too vulnerable. In that instant, he could almost hear her whispered declaration, *There's something more between us.*

But he shook his head, refusing to give any credence to her ridiculous notions of chance and happenstance. And the unspoken exchange fell between them like a frosted windowpane, splintering with ice crystals that would not be quick to thaw.

She pulled free and slipped inside the carriage, issuing one curt "Good-bye, Your Grace," before the door closed.

As the carriage rolled away, Pell staggered up beside him, shielding his eyes from the bleary morning light. "Lady Avalon seemed quite piqued this morning when I saw her inside and mentioned the carnival. Whatever did you do to her?"

"It's what I didn't do."

He didn't lose himself completely. Didn't allow her to steal his sanity by forgetting what was between them.

"Mmm," Pell hummed with intrigue. "It seems as though the lady is living up to her reputation. She'll have you in leading strings by the time we reach Italy."

"You're mistaken. It will be the other way around."

He was in control once more. And as long as he stayed away from her kisses and sly touches, he would remain that way.

"Are you sure about that? Because when you look at her, it seems as though—" Pell chuckled when he heard Lucien's growl. "Right. I'll say no more. Silent as the grave, I am. My lips are sealed. I'm turning the lock and throwing away the key. You won't hear another syllable pass these lips. Not the susurration of a whisper, or even the . . ."

Merlin's teeth, Lucien thought as his cousin rambled on, it was going to be a long way to Italy.

LUCIEN HAD been right.

Even though the days still contained the same number of minutes and hours, this past week had seemed like a month. A very cold month.

Some people claimed that hell was filled with fire and

brimstone, but he believed it was full of glaciers and . . . waterfalls.

He discovered this when they reached the Rhine Falls in Schaffhausen, Switzerland, and Meg decided to take a tour of the river, paddling toward the thunderous cataract. Myrtle Parrish accompanied her. Maeve Parrish was far too sensible. And Lucien was not consulted.

He'd only learned of this insanity after he'd finished his correspondence and saw Pell—who was supposed to be keeping an eye on her—in the gaming salon instead.

Lucien found her just when she was getting into the canoe. Then she refused to answer when he'd asked, quite sensibly, "What the devil are you doing?"

So he directed his next queries to the infant captain of their vessel—if one could even call that casket seaworthy—who could not even provide documents regarding his qualifications or experience.

The boy knew nothing about Archimedes's principle of buoyancy or even the flow velocity vector! And yet, she remained in that boat regardless.

Lucien had no doubt that she was doing it just to retaliate by means of torture. And he knew this because every time he'd shout from shore above the din of rushing water—rational warnings about rapids, eddies, the estimated percentage of capsizing risk, and the temperature in which hypothermia sets in—she would throw back her head and laugh.

Though, why it should bother him, he didn't know. Nor did he know why there was a damnable gnawing sensation in his gut that nearly rooted him to the spot.

He pressed a fist into the center of his stomach. It aggravated him when he couldn't make sense of something, when questions didn't have substantiated answers. He was the type of man who required a firm understanding of the things around him or else he felt trapped and unable to move forward. That was the reason he'd always kept such detailed notes of every experiment.

But he didn't have any notes on her.

Nonetheless, he forced himself to move, following their progress from the towpath. And every step of the way, he muttered curses beneath his breath.

His mood did not improve when the captain steered the canoe into a little cove a good distance from the edge of the falls. As the captain assisted Myrtle Parrish, Lucien hauled Meg out and set her on her feet.

"What do you have to say for yourself?" he asked through gritted teeth.

"Worried about me, Herzog?" Her eyes and teeth flashed in challenge as she leaned closer and laid her hand over his heart. "Admit it. You know there's something more between us. Even when we're angry, we cannot deny it."

Beneath her hand, a conflagration burned inside his chest. Then the blistering air seethed through his nostrils as he fought the urge to either shake her or toss her over his shoulder and—

He didn't allow himself to finish the thought. "Nothing could be further from the truth. My only concern was that you might have dashed your head on the rocks, and I'd never learn the location of my book."

On a sigh, she lowered her hand. And as he watched her walk away, he dismissed that gnawing sensation in his gut, believing it was nothing more than a strong aversion to idiocy.

UNFORTUNATELY, THAT acidic churning feeling returned during the last leg of their journey through the Alps.

At first, they traveled through the mountains by boat, on clear, sparkling waters with the view of snowcapped peaks all around them. The air was so pure, clean and cool that it seemed to dowse the last remnants of his irritation.

He stopped glowering at her. She began joining him at the rail more often than not. And there they goaded each other into conversation, talking of inconsequential things.

He made a comment about the formation of the mountains.

She replied that they reminded her of his unending stubbornness.

Then he remarked on the beauty of the water and how the blue made him think of—he hesitated on purpose as she batted her lashes before he concluded with—*fish*.

And she responded with a swat on his arm.

Lucien thought they'd returned to their initial understanding of each other. That they both knew where the other stood.

But realized he was only fooling himself when their caravan was forced to take the mountain road. It was the only way to reach their destination. But the spring-thaw erosion created a perilously narrow passageway of sheer walls that dropped down to a river which, from this height, appeared no wider than the width of a single thread.

Aided by copious amounts of whisky, Pell slept through all of the creaking, swaying and rocks tumbling down the cliff face. Hence, there was no one to distract him from his own thoughts of the carriage that traveled behind theirs and of the passenger that had somehow climbed beneath his skin, regardless of every logical inner argument he posed to the contrary.

When they finally reached the summit, their carriages stopped for inspection. Lucien clambered out and stretched his legs. As he briefly spoke with the border guards, he saw Meg emerge.

She was greeted by a breeze, kicking up in a sudden flurry of snow that glittered like diamonds around her. Her surprised laugh sounded like the chiming bells of a monastery, bringing brightness to the soul after their perilous climb.

Meg even opened her mouth to capture the flakes on her tongue and spun around in a circle, her arms wide. But then she slipped on the icy ground.

Lucien was there at once, his hand at her waist, pulling her safely into the frame of his body.

"Careful," he said, looking down at her flushed cheeks and snowflake-tipped lashes.

As she found her footing, she laid her hand against his waistcoat in the same manner she had done when he'd hauled her from the canoe. And there, in her flashing eyes, was the same challenge. "Can you admit it now?"

"Very well." He sighed, resigned. "There might possibly be a small percentage of misguided affection from my quarter."

She beamed, her smile warm as a ray of sunlight. "Though, surely more than five percent."

"Perhaps."

"Most definitely more than fifteen."

He pursed his lips and shook his head. "Certainly not."

"Poor you," she said with a tsk as she patted his chest. "The thin air has clearly affected your brain, because I'm almost positive that it has to be more than seventy-five percent."

Unfortunately, he had no opportunity to continue their banter. With a glance over Meg's shoulder, he saw that the elder Parrish women were gradually emerging from their carriage. Resting her hand on his sleeve, he walked over to assist them.

When the contents of a satchel spilled a tumble of yarn followed by several scraps of paper, Meg hurried over and dropped to her knees, her hands shaking in their haste to gather all wayward items.

"Here," he said, bending down beside her. "Let me."

But she snatched the last of it—a folded missive by the looks of it—and stuffed it inside before he could help.

"No need. I've got it." Then she stood, clutching the satchel with both hands.

The peculiarity of her actions, as well as her apparent nervousness, sparked his suspicion. "What is it that you're hiding?"

"It's nothing, Lucien. Just letters and whatnot." Then her chin notched higher. "Surely, you've already searched our trunks back in Paris and found nothing of importance. Then again, if you need to behave like a border guard and rifle through our belongings at every stop, then here."

She held out the satchel for him to take, her mouth set in a grim line.

And he was tempted to do just that. He even reached out . . .

But then he stopped, conflicted. Seeing those laughing eyes turn so cold and guarded did something to him. He felt an overwhelming urge to shield and protect her, even though she was the enemy. Logic told him that whatever she was hiding, she was hiding from him. And yet he could not bring himself to search the private contents.

It occurred to him in a sudden bracing shock—like a plunge in the moat through January ice—that he trusted her. Or at least, he wanted to.

So instead, he nudged the bag back toward her. "No need."

"Truly?" she asked, searching his gaze.

He nodded and earned a glowing smile in response that made him feel as though he'd made the right choice. And yet, by the time they were on their way down the mountain, he wondered if he wasn't fooling himself.

Chapter 15

A watched pot never boils

Lucien was still wondering if he'd made the right decision when they arrived at their hotel in Bellagio, Italy.

Since the incident on the mountaintop, whenever they'd stopped to change horses, Meg had seemed somewhat remote. Had she been hiding something from him in her satchel, such as letters from the man she was working for, perhaps? Or had she simply wanted him to trust her?

Whether or not it was unspeakably disloyal to his family, he had chosen the latter.

But he didn't yet know the weight of guilt he would carry for that decision until the concierge informed him that Lady Morgan Ambrose had checked in.

His half sister was here? The news not only surprised him but immediately made him question his own motives. Why had he chosen Meg over his legacy? It made no logical sense. And his self-recrimination only worsened when his gaze unerringly found her walking with her aunts as they followed a liveried porter toward their own apartments.

"Bollocks," he muttered beneath his breath. He should have done more. Should have coerced Lady Avalon, found her weakness, used it to pressure her into revealing the name of the man she worked for . . .

Instead, his only true accomplishment had been to catalog and obsess over the precise dimension of her mouth and how it fit perfectly beneath his.

"Cheer up, old chap," Pell said as they walked to their rooms. "It isn't the end of the world. It just feels that way when Morgan appears."

Their rooms were located on the opposite side of the hotel from the Parrish women. Opening the door, he was instantly greeted by the sight of gauzy curtains billowing in the breeze, framing a view of the blue lake and jagged mountains just beyond the balcony.

Morgan then entered from an adjoining room, looking perfectly at ease, as if this hotel were her home and they were her guests. "I thought I would join in on all the fun. By the by, how is the hunt going?"

Pell wasted no time in sinking onto the nearest uphol-stered surface, sprawling out with exhaustion as though he'd been the one to pull the carriage instead of the horses. "The prey has him tied in knots and chasing his own tail."

"Sounds dreadfully uncomfortable." She tsked and pressed a kiss to Lucien's cheek.

You have no idea, he thought, his mood fractious.

"I have matters well in hand," he lied. "Mr. Richards has supplied a good deal of information on Lady Avalon."

Morgan patted his sleeve before venturing to the side-board. "I told you he was the best man for the job."

Lucien had wanted to hire an investigator that his ac-quaintance, Lord Savage, had brought to his attention on his last trip to London. But Morgan had been rather insistent and claimed that she was feeling excluded. So he'd given in and contacted Richards on her recommendation, much to his current regret and frustration.

"I'm still waiting to hear more about the women she's traveling with. But I'll leave no stone unturned. Hell, I've even resorted to taking Pell's advice on the matter."

"Which reeks of desperation," Pell said flippantly.

Morgan smirked as she brought her cousin a glass of Madeira. "That's precisely what I was going to say."

"I know. You've become predictable in your old age," he said before he took a sip.

"Oh, cousin. Your humor is the reason why you should never trust a drink I give you. I know far too much about poisons." A flash of alarm crossed Pell's face, just before he spit the Madeira back into the glass and she chuckled. "Don't keep me in suspense, brother. Tell me, what was our cousin's advice? Was it as clever as your decision to open the gates?"

"Not now," Lucien growled.

He didn't need a reminder that it had been his duty to protect the book, to keep it from falling into the wrong hands, and that he had failed.

Throughout the ages, there had been men who'd wanted to claim the recipes for themselves. Power-hungry men driven to crush their enemies and elevate their own place in history. Decades had gone by without a single attempt. One would think that, in the age of reason, learned men would no longer believe in myths and legends. But his grandfather had warned him that history would always repeat itself. And he'd been right.

"What?" she asked, all innocence. "All I'm saying is that we should consider ourselves fortunate that the second attempt to steal the book in our lifetimes didn't end up like the first. Then again, we have no idea what your Lady Avalon might have done if her efforts had been thwarted at all."

"She isn't a cold blooded criminal."

"Are you sure, brother?"

Restless, he paced between the door and open window. He needed an occupation. If he were at Caliburn Keep he could go into the old buttery and try a new experiment. Not that it would matter without the book, he reminded himself.

But he was having difficulty imagining Meg guilty of

villainous compulsions. Or perhaps, the part of him that was inexorably drawn to her had simply murdered the part of him that was capable of rational thought.

Scrubbing his chin, he stared through the window, unseeing.

There had been moments when he'd felt so close to deciphering the mechanics of her mind that he could almost anticipate her next words just from a look. Then there were also moments that left him with more questions than answers. He was thinking, again, of the satchel, of the choice he'd made.

Pell stalked across the room to pour a fresh drink. "Wouldn't blame you if you weren't sure about her. Women are fickle creatures, the whole lot of them."

"Not this one," Lucien said, his mind made up about Meg. "She knows precisely what she wants and will stay her course. It is up to me to anticipate her next move and be there to intercept her."

A haughty laugh rang from Morgan's lips. "You make it seem as though you're hunting *her* instead of the book."

Could he have explored other avenues from the start? Perhaps. But he had made a purposeful decision to stay close to her and it was in his nature to continue on one course until every possibility was examined in depth. He would see this through, no matter how long it took.

"If a wolf steals a rabbit from your trap," he said, "then a man hunts the wolf to find its den, and there, he'll find the other wolves."

"But will he get the rabbit back?"

That was the question of the hour. And he hated to admit it, but he did not know the answer.

His sister came up beside him, her reflection smiling in the window glass. "Why don't you introduce me? Perhaps I can learn more about her—woman to woman—as you continue your hunt."

MEG AND the aunts were shown to a suite of rooms that were bright and airy with a view of the vivid rhododendrons blooming in the garden below. It was so lovely here that it was impossible to imagine that anyone could have a single trouble in the world. But Meg had plenty.

Lucien had given her his trust, and in return, she was still deceiving him about who she really was.

She was a horrible, horrible person!

Mentally, she gave that tail-twirling devil on her shoulder a firm talking to. But in midcastigation, a knock fell on their door.

It was a porter, bearing a handwritten invitation to the ladies from the Duke of Merleton, wanting their immediate response.

Maeve and Myrtle greedily skimmed the missive then said in unison, "We'd be delighted to accept."

The porter bowed and left. When the door closed, the aunts began chirruping excitedly.

"Already an invitation to dinner, and he wishes for us to meet his sister," Maeve said with a grin as she began pulling out the pins in her hair. Crossing the tiled parlor, she stepped through the open door of her bedchamber and onto a millefleur carpet that muffled her footfalls.

Myrtle practically skipped in the same direction. "And he hasn't been away from us for more than an hour at most. It seems that he cannot bear to be parted from a certain someone, hmm?"

"It certainly does," Maeve agreed, appearing in the doorway as she ran a brush through the thick strands of her gray hair. "If you'll recall, I had a feeling about this from the very beginning."

"No, indeed, sister. I believe that I had the feeling."

"And I believe," Meg interjected on a sudden rise of

throat-tightening nervousness, "that neither of you can have any sort of *feeling* at all, for two reasons. The first being that this is only a holiday flirtation, nothing more," she said and paid no attention to the fact that her words lacked conviction. "The second and most important is that the duke still believes I'm Lady Avalon. Remember her—the woman who stole his family's book?"

Myrtle shrugged. "Oh, higgledy-piggledy. None of that makes a bit of difference when romance is in the air."

"*What's in a name?* as Shakespeare wrote. The important part is that Merleton has come to know you, my dear," Myrtle said.

Meg sighed and stared sightlessly into her own wardrobe. They might not think it mattered, but she knew better.

He'd been different with her, more watchful ever since the day the satchel spilled. She supposed she couldn't blame him after the way she'd frantically tried to keep him from seeing all the letters from Wiltshire, from her brother, Ellie and Aunt Sylvia. Every one of them addressed to *Margaret Stredwick*.

But Meg couldn't risk him finding out the truth that way. Not in that moment. Not when everything seemed so promising. She couldn't let this feeling end. And she feared it would the moment he knew who she really was—not an exciting adventuress and agent provocateur—just a dried-up debutante, one step away from the shelf.

She planned to tell him everything, of course. But in her own time and in her own way.

They would be leaving for England in a month. Surely that should give her long enough to find the right words.

And when she did, she hoped she wouldn't lose him.

🦋

THE FIRST thing Meg noticed about Lady Morgan Ambrose was her stunning beauty. She possessed a wealth of dark auburn hair, swept up in a sophisticated twist, and she carried herself with a surfeit of confidence that was enviable. Her manner was neither stiff nor formal, her smile easy as she stepped forward and extended her hand.

"A pleasure," she said that evening, lightly clasping Meg's fingertips. "Miss *Parrish*, isn't it? I'm simply dreadful with names."

Meg swallowed, disliking the deception that had seemed so harmless in the beginning.

"Please, call me Meg," she said and saw the other woman's smile broaden. "What brings you to Italy?"

"A simple need to check up on my little brother. Wouldn't want him lost down any stray rabbit holes, after all." Lady Morgan flitted her fingers in nonchalance, but her eyes seemed serious. Though they were a different hue than her brother's, they both possessed that same calculating intensity. And if she was Lucien's older sister, then their age difference couldn't have been much.

They dined on the terrace with a cool breeze blowing in from the surrounding mountains and rushing over the calm waters of the crystal blue lake. It was a lovely meal, but the air grew too cold for the aunts, so the gentlemen escorted them inside.

Lady Morgan lingered, nibbling on an olive as she gazed at Meg from across the table. "I've seen the way you look at my brother. The way you pretend not to follow his every move and glance away the moment he turns to you. I'd almost suspect you're in love with him."

A startled laugh escaped Meg as she was caught doing that very thing through the open doorway. She felt her cheeks heat. "In love? Of course I'm not in love. I'm just on holiday."

"But you felt something that first time you met, did you not? I know because my brother felt it, too."

"He . . . he told you that?" Meg asked, her voice shaking as a hopeful tremor stumbled through her. Could it be true that he'd felt the same bone-deep certainty from the beginning, only he'd been much better at hiding it?

Then again, he was so logical that he likely required seventeen kinds of proof before he surrendered to any school of thought.

Lady Morgan nodded. "Oh, yes. We're family. We don't keep secrets from each other. Of course, he was far from elated that he should have been so affected by the woman who stole our family legacy. The very book"—she paused and looked pointedly across the table—"that our parents died protecting."

Meg gasped, her hand flying to her mouth. "I had no idea. How awful."

The guilt that had been pressing on her before increased tenfold.

"But don't mention it to anyone, hmm? It's a painful topic, and not even he likes to talk about it."

Meg nodded in agreement. Then her gaze found him again as he was handing the aunts a glass of sherry. When he stood, he turned toward the terrace, and she quickly looked back to his sister. "I'm so sorry that this has happened, and for my part in it. But I must confess, I honestly don't know where the book is. I did not take it."

Morgan studied her for a moment, torchlight flickering in her eyes. "Do you want to know something? I think I believe you."

A breath fell out of Meg. "You do? I'm so relieved."

"Then I'm glad. My brother is quite sure of you. And it isn't like him to hold someone in such high esteem," she said with a grin. "I've never seen him in such a state."

If that were true, then perhaps Meg wasn't wrong about their connection, after all.

A new hope fluttered beneath her breast.

She slid a glance through the doorway again, and her pulse quickened when she saw that he was still watching her. Tentatively, she lifted her hand in a small wave. His stiff shoulders relaxed at once, then he inclined his head.

Lady Morgan swirled the ruby wine in her goblet. "Be a dear and put him out of his misery. Talk to him. Spend time with him."

"But what about the book? Shouldn't I tell him—"

"Not yet," she said. "Let him come to know you better. Trust will surely follow. I know how my brother's mind works, after all. And besides, he has hired an investigator, and soon this book nonsense will sort itself out. Then, you'll both be free to explore whatever might come next."

Her words were still lingering on the fragrant breeze when Lucien appeared in the open doorway.

"I have been sent on an errand by the elder two Misses Parrish," he said to her. "They wish me to tell you that they are eager to retire after their day of travel, and if you would like, I could escort you to your door later."

As their gazes held, every ounce of uncertainty she'd felt since the Alps evaporated like smoke. She nodded. "I should like that."

She saw that elusive dimple of his, and her breath caught. This was most definitely a promising new stage of her grand flirtation. Or perhaps . . . something even more.

LUCIEN RETURNED after walking Meg to her door and strode into the small parlor where his sister was sitting, reading a novel by lamplight.

She looked up and lowered her book. "If I didn't know better, I'd say that was almost a grin on your lips. Did your evening end on a high note?"

"There was no singing involved," he said for the sole purpose of irritating his sister. She always hated it when he was overly literal. Standing at the sideboard, he heard her snarl of disdain, then grinned in earnest.

"You know very well what I mean. Are you any closer to knowing Lady Avalon's secrets?"

He turned with two drinks in hand and crossed the room to present one to her. "I do not know what you said to her, but she did mention a desire to tell me something important on the morrow. Which, I can only deduce, has to do with the book."

Morgan sipped her claret thoughtfully. "I wouldn't be too hasty in my assumptions if I were you. Because, earlier, I told her that you seemed to be affected by her. And before you grouse at me, think of the results. She was instantly elated by the news, which clearly means that you affect her as well. You can use this to your advantage."

Ah. So that explained the noticeable tenderness in her gaze when the two of them had lingered at her door. And, in the moment, the sight of it had sent a pleasing frisson of warmth through him. But now . . .

"She is exceedingly clever and needs no encouragement to spin webs around her victims. You should have told me of your plans. We had developed a certain rapport, an understanding of each other's characters. You may have undermined all of that with your interference," he said, feeling suddenly cross and cold to the marrow.

He didn't like knowing that everything between them might be a lie. There was nothing he could trust, not a word, a gesture or a single look. He would be a fool to forget that.

What he needed was to remain logical and grounded. This was not, after all, a mere holiday but a quest, and he mustn't allow himself to become distracted.

Well, not again.

"No, brother. One woman can tell when another is in over her head and she has allowed her more tender feelings to get the better of her. What may have started out as a mere game has turned into something more, at least for her.

Knowing this, however, my advice is to withhold any mention of the book for the time being."

He felt his brow pucker. "But she and I both know that is the reason we are here in the first place. Why would either of us need to pretend otherwise?"

"Because when I brought up the book to her, she became instantly defensive, making excuses that she didn't know where it was. So I pretended to believe her. And that was precisely when she became unguarded and revealed herself." She stood and laid her hand on his sleeve. "This book means a great deal to our family. After all that we have suffered to protect it, we cannot afford to let it slip through our fingers again."

Lucien knew she was right. And he felt guilty for the wayward thrill of anticipation that trampled through him at the very thought of spending the coming days with the woman who'd taken it.

Chapter 16

Falling like a soufflé

Meg wanted to trust Lady Morgan's advice, but waiting for the book theft to simply "sort itself out" seemed like it could take far too long. And there wasn't much time left of her holiday. Besides, holding fast to the secret that had been weighing on her heart might do more harm than good. So, when Lucien had escorted her to her rooms, she'd decided to take a chance and tell him the truth the following day.

Unfortunately, during their tour of the vineyard with the aunts, her nerves—and the wine—got the better of her. In the end, she'd fallen asleep in the carriage on the way back to the hotel and then slept in her rooms through dinner as well.

The day after that, she garnered her courage once more.

They took a rowboat on the lake while the aunts watched from beneath their parasols on the shore. Drifting along, alone with Lucien, would have been the perfect time to tell him everything. But when they were nearly halfway across the vast lake, a boy sailing a small skiff was caught unawares by a gust of wind. He toppled into the cold water, flailing and crying out.

Meg and Lucien were still a distance away. Yet, without hesitation, he stripped off his coat and spectacles and plunged over the side. Taking up the oars, she paddled behind as he quickly closed the distance with precise, powerful strokes. When they reached the capsized boat, however, the boy was nowhere in sight.

Lucien dove under the water.

Then everything went eerily calm. There were no more shouts from the shore, no gulls screeching overhead. It was as though they were all holding their collective breaths as the seconds ticked by, turning into minutes. And still . . . nothing.

Her lungs burned with the need to breathe, and she took in a raw gulp of air. But it only filled her with panic because she knew he wasn't breathing.

Gripping the sides of the hull, her fingertips dug into splinters of dried white paint as she searched for any sign of them. They had to break the surface soon or else . . .

No. She couldn't finish that thought. It was unbearable.

Nevertheless, her mind conjured a vision of her life without him, of the years passing without his hand to help her down from the carriage. Without his dark eyes to stare at her through smeared lenses that she would clean. Without the thunderous feel of his heart beating against her own. Without that disapproving mouth she so liked to kiss. Without . . .

The overwhelming emptiness of such a future brought her to the undeniable realization that she had fallen in love with him. Not the butterfly-tender, innocent love she had felt for Daniel. That had been a child's fancy. She knew that now.

But this? This was everything. An entire universe of feeling—burning comets, imploding stars, the crush of continents colliding, rising, breaking apart to form something new.

The notion that the Fates might have put him in her path had been one thing, but knowing it with soul-deep certainty was another altogether. *He* was her soul's counterpart.

And she was still in the boat, staring at the calm surface of the lake? No! She could not—*would not*—lose him.

Frantically, she began to unbutton her spencer, fully

intending to go into the water. She'd swum the river at Crossmoor Abbey, after all, so she knew she was a strong—

Just then, she heard a great splash. A heaving intake of air. A rough cough. And there, beyond the hull of the sinking skiff, Lucien breached the water. The boy, hacking and sputtering, was tucked securely against his chest.

She cried out in happy relief, her cheeks wet with tears as she fumbled for the oars and rowed over to where they were treading.

Taking fistfuls of the boy's sodden coat, she helped drag him into the rowboat. Then she leaned to one side as Lucien levered himself over the other, chest laboring beneath his plastered waistcoat. His shirtsleeves were transparent over the sculpted definition of his shoulders and arms, and a thick hank of dripping hair fell in a tapered rope down the center of his forehead.

After catching his breath and scrubbing the water from his face, he grabbed the offered spectacles. Then he took in Meg's appearance—her hat torn from her head, hair tumbling from its pins, her spencer wrapped around the boy's shoulders.

He gave her a hard look. "Do not tell me that you were planning to go in."

"Fine," she said with an offhand shrug as she swiped her fingertips over her damp cheeks. "I won't tell you."

Slipping a handkerchief from her sleeve, she held it out for him. And he took hold of it, seizing her hand as well.

Something fierce and tender passed between them as his gaze held hers. She could feel the moment her heart started beating again. It happened the instant that the pulse at his wrist thumped, strong and steady, beneath the pads of her fingertips.

He gripped her in return, his fingers like an iron shackle around her wrist. "Meg, you realize that the weight of your skirts would have taken you—"

She laughed. She couldn't seem to help it. A sudden dizzying swell of giddiness overcame her at the sight of his stern frown that tried ever so hard to mask the concern and warmth in his gaze. He'd worn a similar look when they'd stood on the mountaintop and she'd goaded him into revealing how he felt about her. "If I didn't know better, I might begin to think that your wayward affection has now surpassed seventy-five percent and is still climbing."

He released her, but only after his hand gently squeezed hers and the corner of his mouth twitched. "Surely not."

Then he took up the oars and rowed them to shore.

Meg should have told him the truth then. However, after enduring such a harrowing experience, she couldn't bring herself to tell him about her deception.

She'd had a taste of what losing him would feel like, and she couldn't risk it.

As THE days passed, however, she became conflicted.

At first, the sweetness of hot afternoon strolls along the lake—the air ripe with budding fruits, and evening walks beneath shadowed hillsides of olive trees, among gardens bursting with a fragrant bouquet of acacia, lupine and vining clematis—seemed to last forever.

But before she knew it, a handful of days had turned into a sennight.

Her holiday was nearing an end. They would depart for Venice tomorrow, and far too soon they would begin their trek back to England, where she would become the adventure*less* Margaret Stredwick once again.

Meg knew she had to tell him the truth. He deserved to know. After all, a woman didn't keep secrets from the man she loved.

He likely wouldn't believe her, just as he hadn't believed

her from the beginning. But she was going to explain why she'd pretended in the first place and knew that his logical mind would put the rest of the pieces together.

Doubtless, he would be cross with her. Perhaps even angry for leading him astray. But she hoped he would forgive her when she told him that she loved him.

Her heart squeezed with uncertainty as she lifted her gaze to the man on her arm as they walked the narrow, winding streets. Behind his lenses, those river-stone eyes crinkled at the corners as he smiled, reaching out to tuck a wayward lock of hair behind her ear.

"I imagine that Pell will become quite querulous when he learns that he missed the festivities. I've never seen so much wine."

She laughed softly, knowing it was the truth. "Perhaps you should purchase a few bottles to soften the blow when you tell him."

The viscount and Lady Morgan had gone to stay with a distant cousin at a villa across the lake a few days ago. But Meg hadn't minded because, instead of spending time with Lucien's sister, cousin *and* the aunts, a smaller party was far more intimate.

They had dined together every evening and lingered over sweet Italian wines and robust coffees until it was nearly dawn. She found it harder and harder to say good-night and wondered if he felt the same.

"I shall do precisely that as I gloat endlessly," he said, that solitary dimple flashing.

When he stepped away to head into one of the shops, the aunts exchanged a look and then crowded close to Meg. From their beaming countenances, she was afraid they were going to hint at marriage, remarking on the duke's attentiveness and obvious enjoyment of her company as they had been doing for the past sennight.

But Maeve surprised her when she leaned in to whisper,

"Be a dear and make an excuse to have the duke escort you away for a short time. My sister and I must retrieve something of vital importance."

"Yes, my dear," Myrtle interjected with a muffled clap of her gloved hands. "The cannoli were simply too divine. And we cannot leave Italy without that recipe."

"Regrettably, we have encountered an exceeding degree of protectiveness over recipes in this country. It is quite irksome," Maeve added. "But we are determined to take this one home with us."

Meg blushed. Earlier this evening, she'd overheard a conversation about the scandalous history of the decadent cream-filled dessert. Apparently, the pastry had first been created as a concubine's tribute to her emir's manhood and was said to give brides a better chance of conceiving.

On any other day, she would have found the information both amusing and interesting. From what she'd seen of statues and paintings, a man's member didn't resemble the sweet confection at all.

But the reason it still made her blush was because she'd been standing with the duke at the time . . . And he'd chosen that precise moment to look at her while she was in the middle of taking her first—not altogether delicate—bite, her mouth full of flaky pastry and decadent cream.

He'd looked away at once, seemingly embarrassed for her, because swift color climbed to his cheeks, and his throat tightened when he swallowed.

Recalling the moment, Meg decided not to share the history with the aunts. Besides, she'd been looking for a chance to spend a few moments alone with him.

"I'll mention that shop on the corner," she said, glancing down the lane.

There was a nervous churning in her stomach as she hoped to find the courage to tell him the truth and face whatever his response would be.

"Splendid," Myrtle said, and then she gasped and covered her mouth with her hand.

There was a sound of glass breaking, and Maeve's brows lifted. "Oh, dear."

Meg turned and saw the duke. He'd been splashed with wine by an apologetic, though inebriated, man who was enjoying the festivities to the fullest.

As the man tottered on by, Meg and the aunts went to Lucien at once, each of them with handkerchief in hand.

Chagrined, he shook his head. "It would be best if I returned to my rooms for a fresh set of clothes. But I won't be long."

"Of course," Myrtle offered with an understanding nod. Then her eyes brightened with animation. "But if it wouldn't be too much trouble, would you mind escorting Meg with you? Maeve was just complaining about having forgotten her shawl, and she suffers from such chills in these gray years."

Maeve cleared her throat. The glance she slid to her sister promised retribution at a later date. "Indeed. It is quite a cool evening."

"Then, perhaps we should all return," Lucien offered.

"No, no. That won't be necessary. We'll simply sit at that table over there and warm ourselves with a nice cup of tea. You two young people can do all the walking for us."

He inclined his head, then proffered his arm to Meg.

During the stroll back to the hotel, she was quiet, musing over the perfect way to explain everything to Lucien.

By the time they reached the lobby and the soles of her slippers met with the terra-cotta tiles of the floor, she decided that she would begin by returning the recipe that she'd stolen that first day. It was important that he knew she hadn't meant to deceive him in the beginning. It just sort of . . . happened.

She hoped he would understand.

At the top of the stairs, they parted ways to sort out their own errands.

When she entered her room, she began searching through the trunks that were already packed for their journey. But as she delved to the bottom of her own, she found an unfamiliar green shawl. Believing that it belonged to one of the aunts, she decided to take it with her when she and Lucien returned to the village. Yet, when she went to lift it from the bottom, she discovered it was wrapped around something rather heavy.

Curious, Meg picked up the large, rectangular object and set it on her lap, unwrapping the layers of woven emerald silk that surrounded it. Then she gasped when she saw what was inside.

A bejeweled book, weathered and timeworn, with gilt-edged pages.

She stared at it in disbelief. The book! It had to be Lucien's book. But how . . . ?

Surely, the aunts wouldn't have taken it. Surely, they knew how important it was to Lucien. And yet there it was.

This wasn't just a book of recipes that belonged in his family. It was his history and the very thing his parents had died protecting.

What had she done? By pretending to be Lady Avalon and asking the aunts to play a part in the charade, they'd had no idea what it meant to him, or that this wasn't all a lark. A mere holiday flirtation.

Oh, this was all her fault. She shook her head in despair, her vision blurring as tears collected in her eyes. Now that the book was in her possession, she knew that he would never believe she hadn't played an integral part in this grand scheme from the beginning.

She buried her face in her hands. If she revealed the whole truth, then Lucien would hate her. Yet, if she didn't, she would hate herself.

Chapter 17

A recipe for love

Lucien expected the knock to be the manservant he'd wrung for, so he didn't bother to don a banyan before opening the door, clad only in his trousers and boots.

But instead of a manservant, he found Meg, her face streaked with tears.

Before he could say a word, she rushed into his arms, her cheek damp against his bare chest.

"Oh, Lucien, I don't know how it happened . . . One minute I was looking for that slip of paper and the next there it was. I was stunned because I never suspected a thing. I had no idea. But I take full blame. It's my fault—only my fault—and I know you'll never forgive me, but I just couldn't live with myself if I kept it a secret from you," she said in a garbled rush, sniffing wetly.

Concerned, and only understanding half of the words, he closed the door and drew her into the room. "Has something happened? Whatever it is, I'll help you through it."

She started to cry again in earnest, and he wrapped his arms tightly around her, pressing his lips to the top of her head. As her body shuddered with sobs, his own heart was breaking.

He didn't know how it had happened, but at some point,

he'd grown to admire her, and that admiration had turned into affection.

No, actually, that wasn't correct. He realized his regard for her had changed twelve days ago when they'd toured the vineyard. The evening prior to that, she had mentioned a desire to tell him something important—which he believed was regarding the book—but when she'd fallen asleep after becoming a bit worse for the wine, he hadn't minded. And when the day after that passed by without any mention of the book, he discovered that he'd been enjoying her company too much to care.

There was something about the way that Meg looked at him. It was as though he were the only man in the world. She made him feel alive. He'd focused so much of his life on that book that he'd forgotten what it was like to live. With her, the world was new again, waiting to be discovered. Even the taste of summer fruit had become sweeter, colors brighter, scents bolder. And he didn't want it to end.

But he knew it would, once she gave him the book. It was only logical, after all, that they would each go their separate ways. So he hadn't pursued that course.

Bored with Italy, Morgan had grown impatient from waiting for Lady Avalon to reveal the location of their legacy and wanted him to demand its return, to threaten her, if need be. He'd vehemently declined.

She'd called him a fool for pushing his familial obligations aside for a woman who planned to leave him without a backward glance. They had argued, which had been the reason she'd left the hotel.

Though, to be honest, he hated that the book was between them. Hated that he hadn't met Meg under different circumstances. Because then he could be sure that he wasn't being played for a fool.

However, none of that mattered in this moment, as he held Meg in his arms. What had happened to leave her so devastated?

Before he could ask again, there was another knock on the door.

"That will be the manservant," he crooned softly, guiding her toward the chair facing the unlit hearth. "Just rest here for a moment, and I'll be right back, hmm?"

She wobbled her head in a nod.

Reluctant to leave her side, he took care of matters and quickly returned to her. Then, kneeling down, he took her face in his hands and smoothed the wetness away. "What is it, *ma petite louve?*"

A fresh deluge flooded over the rims of her startlingly clear eyes, her dark lashes clumping together in spikes. "I'll never hear that name again for as long as I live. Never see your face gazing at me with such tender concern"—she reached up and touched his cheek and mouth—"never kiss these lips."

"Damn it all! Will you tell me what has happened?"

Her lips parted on a staggered breath as her hand fell to her lap. "This."

He glanced down at the folded shawl, which he didn't realize she'd been carrying, then back up to her face without understanding. She looked so desolate that it sent a spear of alarm through him. "Just tell me."

"I have your book."

He heard the words, and yet comprehension didn't dawn until he watched her shaking hands slowly unwrap the scarf. Then . . . there it was. The book. *His* book.

He reached out to touch it as if uncertain if this were real or a dream. But it felt real to him. And as he thought back to everything she'd said in the last few minutes, the finality of her declarations, he put the pieces together. "So you're simply giving it to me?"

She nodded and sniffed, her nose red, cheeks blotchy. "Consider it a parting gift, if you must."

"And that's it? After taunting me all these weeks, you're going to hand over the book and then just leave?"

Looking down at her knitted hands, she nodded again.

He hated seeing her like this, so lost and humbled. She should be crowing at him instead. She was the one woman capable of challenging him at every turn, intriguing him, enticing him to the point of madness.

"Why?" he demanded.

"Because I've had this all along. I found it buried in the bottom of my trunk. And if it weren't for my own deception, you would have had it in your possession. I would have ensured it. Then, you wouldn't have needlessly suffered the pain of wondering if you might never see it again."

"So you think I'm just going to let you walk away? To let you slip out of my life for good? Not bloody likely."

Her gaze flew to his. "What was that?"

"I think you heard me correctly. However, if you require clarity, very well." He expelled a deep breath and said firmly, "I'm keeping you."

Her head tilted to the side as she blinked. Then a smile bloomed on her face. "As your prisoner?"

"It seems only fair, considering that I am apparently yours."

Only a fool would ever let her go. And the Duke of Merleton was no fool.

MEG WATCHED as Lucien took the book and set it aside. An instant later, she launched herself at him, arms wrapping tightly around his neck, mouths meeting in a fervent, wet kiss.

She knew that she couldn't have been the only one to feel this way. It just wasn't possible.

Without disconnecting, he gathered her in his arms and sat in the chair. This left her free to explore his broad back and shoulders. The powerfully sculpted muscles she'd only glimpsed when he'd been soaked to the skin that day in the boat were hard as granite.

"It's a wonder you didn't sink to the bottom of the lake,"

she said against his lips. "You feel as though you're made of stone. I hope you don't mind that I'm unabashedly fondling you."

He chuckled, his lips grazing along her jaw and nipping the plump lobe of her ear playfully with his teeth. "Fondle until your heart's content."

Now, that was an invitation she did not intend to ignore. His skin was warm and smooth beneath her touch. She couldn't resist running her hands all over him. Encountering the short, crisp hair on his bare chest, she eased back to take a better look than the one she'd had when she first knocked on his door.

She splayed her hands over him, fascinated by the dark furring over the defined mounds of his chest. The disks of his nipples were flat but pebbled beneath the light graze of her fingertip, the sight of which caused her own pulse to quicken. Her nostrils flared, drinking in the balmy scent rising from his wine-stained skin, tempting her to lower her open mouth and taste him.

He sucked in a breath, his hand sliding into her hair, cupping her face. "The way you look at me—"

His words faltered on a rush of breath as her hand descended, following the dark trail of hair from his navel all the way to where it disappeared beneath his trousers. The muscles of his abdomen bunched.

She grinned at him. "Are you ticklish?"

"Not usually, but when you do *that*"—he sucked in another breath when she did it again—"it feels like your fingers release tiny bolts of lightning."

He shifted beneath her, situating her on his lap, his hands lingering on her hips and thigh.

"Why is your front fall unbuttoned if you only had to remove your shirtsleeves?"

"Men's shirts are tucked in and under and . . ."

"And?" she asked distractedly, intrigued by a substantial

shape outlined beneath the placket. She boldly traced her fingertips along the length, discovering that it was impossibly hard and thick.

A choked sound left him. "I cannot think when you touch me there."

"Not at all?"

"Afraid not."

"Completely insensible?"

"Mmm-hmm."

"Then, should I stop?" Encouraged by his momentary speechlessness, she tentatively peeled back the flap to see a thatch of tight, dark curls through the opening, their texture coarse to the touch as she slid her hand inside.

He cursed, his head falling back. "Aye . . . actually, no. Yes. I mean . . . don't stop. Not ever."

Meg didn't have a single clue what she was doing. All she knew was that it thrilled her to watch him like this, eyes closed, throat tight as he swallowed. To touch him and to see him fall apart . . . because of her.

If this was even close to what Lady Avalon felt when she'd reputedly seduced dozens of men, Meg suddenly understood why.

But for her, Lucien was the only man she would ever want.

She was captivated by the feel of him, the flesh scalding hot and taut over the impossible hardness. Her fingers had to stretch to span the circumference to grip him. But when he issued a gruff grunt, her eyes flew to his. "Acceptable?"

In response, he nodded wordlessly and she took that as a good sign. And he was patient, too, which she appreciated. He would make an excellent model for one of her sketches.

Wanting to see him, she maneuvered his girth through the opening. The flesh was dark and dusky, the shape . . . well, it was rather intimidating . . . large and rearing. She would definitely require a sizeable canvas.

Exploring, she slid her hand down and then up again. Her

tentative stroke earned a fluttering surge beneath her palm. Then she saw a glistening bead of dew resting on the mushroomed head. Rolling the pad of her thumb up the underside, she touched the liquid, surprised to discover that it was warm and sticky, like honey.

Curious, she lifted her thumb to her lips and sucked on the tip. The flavor wasn't at all sweet, but salty and briny and . . . *him*.

Their eyes met, his blazing, hungry and dark.

Then he moved suddenly, kissing her, lifting her. And before she knew it, he was carrying her across the parlor and to his bed.

Meg wasn't a simpleton. She knew what would happen next. Well, vaguely. There would be mounting involved. And even though what she'd witnessed in the paddock all those years ago had been rather alarming, she wanted to . . . do *that* . . . as long as it was with him.

When he lowered her to her feet, she turned around, ready to present her hindquarters.

But before she could bend at the waist, he slid his arms around her and pulled her back against him, his mouth hot on her nape as he undressed her. His fingers must have been terribly deft on her buttons and laces, because she was standing in only her stockings in a matter of seconds.

Her breath came out in an astonished whoosh, her arms reflexively moving to cover her nakedness. "You're very quick."

"Not when it matters," he said, gently lifting her hands away to cup her breasts, her nipples instantly pebbling against his palms. His voice was husky and deep when he murmured, "I knew I had calculated your dimensions correctly."

Spoken by any other man, it wouldn't have been nearly as romantic or thrilling. But with him . . . *yes*. As he grazed the tender peaks with the pads of his thumbs, her head fell back against his shoulder, her arms lifting to twine in his hair, spine bowing, drawing her derriere against the hot, imposing shape of him.

He grunted in response, hips flexing against her. "You are diabolical. The way you move, the way you tease and touch"—he kissed the curve of her throat, then nipped her shoulder in a playful reprimand—"it makes me insensible. But I won't allow you to unman me. Not yet. I want to take my time with you."

His fingertips plucked at her nipples, sensations tunneling low inside her body, shifting, tilting. A warm, liquid ache throbbed at the juncture of her thighs, and she pressed her knees together as if to hold it in. "How much time?"

His hand skirted lower, splaying over her abdomen, pressing in a slow circle that seemed to rub a place inside and draw it tight.

"Just enough," he said, gliding farther downward to the thatch of dark curls guarding her sex.

She inched back again in reflexive modesty as he cupped her. Then he groaned, telling her how wet she was, how warm and perfect as his fingers deftly navigated along the swollen folds, making her gasp and arch as he circled the tender throbbing bud, her fingers gripping his hair.

Meg squeezed her eyes shut, the pleasure too intense, swiftly bringing her to an unbearable peak. She thought about their first kiss in the market, the shock and wonder. And she thought about the way he'd practically dragged her into the bell tower because he couldn't stand another moment without having his mouth on her, touching her, gripping her . . . And she felt herself tumble over the edge of something wonderful.

Then suddenly, her hips hitched, jolting on a shudder. She heard the catch in his breath as rapture broke over her, flooding her in molten waves that rippled outward, tingling all the way to the tips of her fingers and strands of her hair.

He turned her in his arms and kissed her deeply, intimately, her body still quaking as she melted against him. And then they tumbled together onto the bed.

"You're very quick," he teased, but there was an urgency in his gaze as he looked down at her, his body tense.

She could feel the heat of him between her thighs, and it caused another sweet clench inside her, sending out another ripple of pleasure. "I don't think so. I've been waiting my whole life for you to do that."

Apparently, that was the right thing to say, because he kissed her, deeply, hungrily. His thick arousal was poised, nudging against her opening. Her arms wrapped around him, her back rising, arching, wanting to be closer. She reveled in the feel of skin on skin and the tickling brush of his crisp hair against her breasts.

But when he barely pushed inside, they both hissed. Her body clamped around him tightly, stilling his progress, her damp flesh stinging from being stretched.

His breath fractured. "I've miscalculated."

Before she could ask what he meant, he moved, turning them, lifting her so that she straddled him as he sat with his back against the bolster.

Hands braced against his broad chest, she looked down at their position, at her dark curls tangled with his, and his engorged flesh rearing, the dusky head taut and glossy.

"So *I'm* mounting you, instead?" It was less a question and more an intrigued observation. She quickly surmised his intention, and she was curious enough to make an attempt. But that didn't mean she knew what to do.

He swallowed and adjusted his spectacles, apparently not willing to take them off and miss something vital, even though the lenses were foggy around the edges. "This position will allow the juncture of your hips to splay wide enough to accommodate—"

She silenced him with a kiss, fusing her mouth to his. It drove her positively wild when he talked like that.

Wrapping her arms around him, she tilted toward him, hips rocking, arching. He grunted, his breaths shallow and quick as he endured the tentative slides of her slick cleft along the length of him. She liked this. A great deal, in fact. Her body was humming, breasts tingling. Her lips ate at his, nipping, nuzzling, tasting.

She could do this forever.

"You're making me insensible," he rasped, the words threaded with tension. His fingertips gripped into the supple flesh of her backside, pulling her closer, lifting, urging her to take him inside her body.

And she did. Or, at least, she tried.

With her hands braced on his shoulders, she took him by inches, her body stretching taut, burning, stinging, as the heat of him gradually impaled her until she couldn't bear any more. She wondered if she was doing something wrong. Because this wasn't necessarily inspiring the euphoria that her sister-in-law had mentioned. "Are you sure that . . ."

"Aye," he rasped, lifting her, guiding her up to the tip to start all over again. His eyes were hooded and dark as he watched where they were joined. "It's just that you're so . . . But the laws of probability dictate . . . something . . . Ah, you feel so . . . I'm not sure that I can—"

He hissed as she swiveled her hips, his head falling back. She opened her mouth over his throat, her nipples taut against the tickling brush of his chest hair. *Mmm* . . . perhaps this wasn't so terrible after all.

She sank down on him a bit more, her passage slick, flesh gripping flesh in a way that tugged on the pulsing bundle of nerves that he'd stroked before. And oh . . . *Oh, my.*

"There's something positively divine . . . about friction," she panted as she repeated the process, a warm ache coiling low inside her body.

His throat bobbed in response but he offered no opinion. Perhaps he was assessing the merits of friction. Or perhaps, somewhere behind those black glazed eyes and tight jaw, he wasn't thinking at all. He did look rather primitive as she made several more attempts.

Then she was finally seated over him, her knees shaking, walls snug around the impossible fullness. And he groaned against her mouth, one hand tangled in her hair, the other on her breast. Claiming. Possessing.

She surrendered her lips to him and took his in return. He was hers now, body and soul. Nothing else mattered but this.

Responding to the instinctive urgings of her body, she began to move over him. Her efforts were clumsy and hurried, but he didn't seem to notice.

He met her thrust for thrust, telling her all the ways she was driving him insane, wicked, scandalous words that put her in a frenzy of need, body trembling as her neck arched and her fingernails bit into his shoulders. *Yes, yes* . . .

He placed his hands on her hips. "Wait. I need to—"

"I know. I need you, too. I love you, Lucien."

She kissed him again and felt him jerk beneath her, thrusting mindlessly as she clamped around his flesh, milking him deep as a guttural shout tore from his throat, and he filled her with endless spasms of hot honey.

Collapsing against him, she pressed her lips to the curve of his throat, opening her mouth to taste the salty beads of sweat. She felt his flesh jolt inside her. Her body clenched in response, and she closed her eyes on the sweet sensation.

After a moment to catch their collective breaths, he gazed up at her in wonder, smoothing the wild tumble of her inky hair away from her face. "What have you done to me?"

"Bewitched you," she said with a smile. "You're under my spell now."

He kissed her again and whispered, "Irrefutably."

Chapter 18

Leave the duke. Take the cannoli.

When Meg left Lucien asleep in his bed, the sun was just setting on the horizon in blissful strands of violets, pinks and apricots.

He'd fallen asleep shortly after tucking her against his side, his breathing heavy and even. She'd watched him for a time, marveling at this newfound love and letting it fill her with every steady beat of his heart beneath her palm.

It wasn't until she shifted beneath the coverlet and felt the rush of fluid between her thighs that she understood the history of the cannoli.

And then she remembered the aunts.

She startled, her eyes opening wide. Beside her, Lucien stirred murmuring nonsensical syllables in his sleep as he cinched an arm tightly around her, his big warm body enticing her to linger. But she couldn't. The aunts were expecting her to return with their shawl, and she had been gone far longer than anticipated.

Carefully slipping out of bed, she went to the washbasin to clean up, then dressed as well as she could. He was sleeping so soundly that he didn't stir when she pressed a kiss to his cheek and whispered again that she loved him.

Stepping out of his room and rushing down the corridors to her own, she was still trying to think up an excuse to tell the aunts when she intercepted them in the hall, their strides quick, their faces drawn with tension.

She started guiltily. "I apologize for taking so long. It's just that—"

"I'm afraid we're in a bit of a rush, my dear," Maeve said, taking her by the arm as they hurried by on the way to their apartment.

Meg was instantly alarmed, her heart thudding. "What has happened? Are you ill? Have you received news of some sort? Is it my brother? Ellie? My nephew?"

"No, no. Do not fret. It is nothing like that." Maeve opened the door, ushered them inside and then closed it soundly.

"It may actually be worse," Myrtle said lightly, keeping a smile fixed in place as she bustled through the room, gathering discarded gloves and whatnot. "You see, we've made an error in judgment. But how were we to know that when someone claims it's a *secret family recipe* that they aren't simply being braggarts?" She huffed, tossing her handful of various belongings into the open trunk. "Well, anyway, to make a long story short, we were caught."

"And the brother of the cannoli master just happens to be the owner of this fine hotel," Maeve supplied. "In short, we've been asked to leave. Immediately. Before he summons the constable."

Meg was still trying to absorb the shock of it.

"We are leaving *tonight*? But what about *Luc*—the duke?" she corrected, coloring. "Surely we would want to explain and bid farewell."

"Where is Merleton, by the by? We thought he would be with you."

Her throat went dry at Maeve's question, and she issued a tight shrug. "I had just come from knocking on his door when I saw the two of you. There was no answer."

"Oh, but he's likely still seeing to his attire. Wine stains are a nuisance. I can only imagine the trial he suffers without a proper valet traveling with him. No cause to worry, dear," Myrtle said as she squeezed her hand. "We'll be seeing him soon enough, I imagine."

A hard knock fell on the door, and a gruff Italian voice told them that their carriage was ready. Then four attendants came in and began to carry down their trunks with utmost haste.

"But what about Bryony and Mrs. Pendergast?" Meg asked, falling into a state of panic and wondering what to do about Lucien.

Maeve touched her shoulder and directed her to the writing desk. "They are already gathering their things and will meet us by the carriage. As for your duke, I'm afraid we only have time for you to leave a missive."

Heart in her throat, Meg nodded. Taking a piece of paper, she scribbled a hasty note, telling him where they'd gone and asking him—if they should happen to miss each other at the next inn or at any point on the journey back to England—to come and find her at her address in Wiltshire. Then she signed it with all her love and her real name.

She wished she could see him and tell him in person, but all she had time to do was slip the note beneath his door.

"Don't worry, my dear," Maeve said as they sat in the carriage lantern light. "Any man who looks at a woman the way your duke does will surely cross mountains to find you."

LUCIEN AWOKE to a fist pounding on his door. His primary concern was for Meg. But when he turned reflexively to shield her, he was confused to find the space beside him empty.

Scrubbing a hand over his face, he reached toward the bedside table for his spectacles. The first thing he saw was that her clothes were gone from the floor and his banyan—he noticed, with a grin—was carefully draped over him. She had tucked him in, apparently.

The thought warmed him, and he logically concluded that she had gone to find her aunts.

Shrugging into the banyan, he opened the door to find his cousin. "Pell, you have absolutely dreadful timing."

"It's Morgan," he said, his tone raspy and stark.

Only then did Lucien notice his drawn and pallid face. "What's happened?"

Pell informed him that Morgan had fallen suddenly and gravely ill, and that the physician didn't expect her to make it through the night.

A wash of dread fell over Lucien, agonizingly cold. She was more than a sister to him. They shared a bond that was unlike any other. She had been the one to save his life, and the one to encourage his pursuits for the majority of his life. Losing her, after all they'd been through and after that terrible row they'd had, would be unfathomable.

Alarmed, Lucien dressed at once. He stopped by Meg's rooms, but there was no response to his knock. She was likely in the village with her aunts. So he scribbled a note and slipped it beneath the door, asking her not to go onward to Venice without him.

LATER THAT week, he returned to the hotel, eager to see Meg and tell her of his sister's remarkable recovery from the malady that they still did not understand. But, for the first time in Lucien's life, making sense of something didn't matter. All he cared about was that his family—such as it was—was still intact.

Upon entering the terra-cotta-tiled lobby, however, the concierge delayed this reunion by stopping to deliver his correspondence. One was a letter from his investigator in England, and the other . . . was the missive he'd slipped beneath Meg's door.

Seeing the confusion on his face, the concierge crisply informed him that the Parrish women had left in haste the same evening that Morgan had taken ill.

An icy shiver of foreboding washed over him. He thought back to that night and wondered how long he'd been asleep before Pell had knocked on the door. An hour? Two? He wasn't certain. But it was possible that the reason the letter was now in his hand was due to the simple fact that Meg had never read it . . . because she'd already been gone.

Then again, as an intellectual, he knew that a folded scrap of paper and the word of a concierge wasn't proof of any sort of subterfuge. And Lucien required proof.

He started toward his rooms. Numbly, he opened the missive from his investigator and skimmed the contents as he strode down the hall.

It was the news he feared.

According to Mr. Richards, a groundskeeper by the name of Bagdemus—once employed by Maeve and Myrtle—said that as far as he knew, the Parrish women were deceased.

Lucien crumpled the page in his fist.

So he'd been right. The name *Parrish* was just another alias. But did that mean everything that followed was a lie as well?

He didn't have the answer. Not yet. But he was almost afraid to open the door of his room. Afraid of what he'd find.

Drawing in a deep breath, he steeled himself and turned the key.

The apartment was still and eerily quiet as he stepped inside. He searched the parlor . . . the bedchambers . . . the terrace. Nothing. No note. And no book either.

On a shout of frustration, he began ransacking the rooms, looking for any small thing she might have left behind. He turned over cushions, upended chairs and tables as the sound of his own idiocy crashed around him.

He had been a fool, after all.

She had taken the book, but hell would freeze over before he'd let her get away with it again.

🦋

IT WAS nearing the end of September at Crossmoor Abbey, the morning grim and rainy, and Meg staggered groggily from her bedchamber. Just as she opened the door, the scent of coddled eggs seemed to rise from the breakfast room two floors below and smack her across the face.

She instantly dashed back inside, grabbed the glazed chamber pot and cast up her accounts. Over and over, even when there was nothing left.

"Again, miss?" her maid said with concern as she rubbed a hand in circles over her back. "It's been nearly a fortnight now. Perhaps it's time to tell your brother or Lady Hullworth."

Huddled over the pot, Meg shook her head vehemently and squeezed her eyes shut tight. "They mustn't know. Especially not Ellie. She would surely imagine the worst."

Then again, the truth was likely just as bad as anything her favorite worrywart of a sister-in-law could conjure. And more to the point, it had actually been a month now since the sickness had first begun. Meg had just been better at hiding it in the beginning.

Taking a deep breath, she sat up and sagged against the side of her bed. "Besides, this cannot last forever. So there's no need to bother anyone about it."

"I think, perhaps, there is a need." Beneath a ruffled cap, Bryony looked at her with concern and handed her a square of damp flannel. "After all, you haven't had your courses for two months. Ever since you returned from your holiday."

Meg swallowed.

Her holiday—when she'd decided on the brilliant notion of having one grand flirtation before she put herself on the shelf. She had been determined to have one scandalous secret to keep with her as she grew old, just like the aunts had done once upon a time.

But somewhere between France and Italy, she'd accidentally fallen in love.

She'd thought Lucien had, too. But he'd never come for her. Not once during the month of travel back to England or in the weeks that followed. And by the time autumn fell around them, it had become all too clear that she'd been a fool to believe in fate again.

Because all the Duke of Merleton had ever wanted from her was the book.

She settled a hand over her midriff and sighed, finally coming to terms with the fact that she wouldn't be able to keep her scandalous secret for long. "I think I might have brought home an unexpected souvenir from my travels."

Chapter 19

You can't handle the proof

Two years later

Lucien arrived at Caliburn Keep just as the post was being delivered. Knowing that Mr. Gudgeon was occupied with ordering the groomsmen to see to his trunks, he paid the postman himself and riffled through the letters as he walked inside, travelworn and weary.

He'd been searching these past twenty-four months and seventeen days for Lady Avalon. But she had disappeared without a trace.

There had been a few reports of her whereabouts and each one of them a dead end that had kept him running around the Continent like a madman.

For a short time, he'd even been fool enough to worry about her, wondering if she'd been injured during her flight from him, or if, perhaps, the man she worked for had done something despicable to her.

After worry came renewed anger. It burned inside his veins every time he thought of her laughter and smiles, and those eyes that had gazed at him with such tenderness that he'd believed every lie she'd told him.

Though, primarily, he'd been angry at himself for being a fool.

After Morgan's illness, she had been too frail to leave Italy. So they'd stayed for the remainder of the month. During that time, Lucien had traveled to Venice, holding on to the very last percentage of hope that Meg hadn't been deceiving him about everything.

But it was all for naught.

It was still hard for him to believe that two elderly women and a cunning adventuress could disappear without a trace. Though, according to every hotel and coaching inn between Italy and France, they had done just that. He had even checked all the harbors to see if they had sailed from Italy. They hadn't. So they were either still in Italy or—he thought wryly—they'd constructed Icarus wings of wax and flown out.

Merlin's teeth, he was tired of beating his head against a brick wall. For these past two years, he'd been riding himself ragged, fueled by fury and the need for retribution. But perhaps he should just come to terms with the fact that she was gone—that the book was gone—forever.

And yet, it was simply impossible that she had left no trail. Had completely disappeared off the face of the earth.

Well, not unless she were . . . dead.

He shook his head at once. In fact, every time his logical mind suggested that possibility, he instantly rejected it.

Peculiarly, no matter how incensed he'd been about her betrayal, the very idea that the woman with the laughing eyes, the one who'd beleaguered and challenged him at every turn, was no longer on this mortal plane always caused a heaviness to fall over him.

He kept moving onward, one step in front of the other. Seeing that none of the letters were from his investigators, he laid the stack on his steward's desk in the anteroom just outside Lucien's study.

Mr. Collins looked up and instantly stood. "Your Grace. I trust you had a pleasant journey."

Lucien grunted in a noncommittal fashion as he walked

through the door of his paneled study but called over his shoulder, "Any news to report?"

"Nothing out of the ordinary since our last correspondence, sir . . ."

As his steward rattled off the list of tenants who'd paid their rent, the repairs to the ramparts in the south quadrant and other minutiae, Lucien sorted through ledgers and maps, meticulously charting the ground he'd covered in search of her.

"Collins, have you seen the post? Mr. Gudgeon wasn't in the foyer, and there was nothing on the salver," Morgan said, her voice drifting in from the outer office as Lucien bent over a map, marking it with cartographic precision.

"Good day, Lady Morgan," Collins said with a panting, puppylike adoration. "I do enjoy your routine of bringing the post to my desk. It is the highlight of my every day." He cleared his throat. "However, His Grace, brought in the post just a moment ago. In fact, I was actually—"

"Lucien?" she called and soon swept into his study. "I didn't know you were back. Ah, I see that your focus remains on finding our legacy."

She sighed and stepped around his desk to press a kiss to his cheek before walking toward the window to unlock the hinge and let in a warm breeze that chased away the staleness. The corner of his map fluttered before he set the inkwell down on it.

Another familiar face joined the party as Pell sauntered in, a glass of amber liquid carelessly dangling from his fingertips. "Could the rumors be true? Surely not. This cannot be my estimable cousin covered in road dust and rags. You're looking a bit long in the tooth, old chap." Pell chucked him on the shoulder and smiled affectionately in greeting, and Lucien nodded in kind. "Three months gone on this last stretch. Thought we'd lost you this time."

"Nonsense." Morgan laughed dryly as she thumbed

through his travel ledger. "Lucien will never be lost to us. We'll always find him dutifully looking for our book."

"Until he decides to give up this dogged hunt and settle down, of course," Pell said as he collapsed into one of a pair of leather wingback chairs, limbs splayed like a limp starfish.

Mr. Collins strolled in, still recounting his list. "There have also been invitations from society families with marriageable daughters, requesting your attendance at their house parties, along with the usual weekly letter from your great-aunt reminding you of your familial duties and that you are—and I merely provide a direct quote—*growing older by the day*." He cleared his throat nervously. "My apologies, sir."

Lucien gestured with an absent wave of his hand as he marked the map. "Think nothing of it. I feel every bit as old as my age today."

This entire business had been taxing, wearing him down by degree. There were some days when he swore that the scenery through the carriage window was the same as the days and weeks before, as if he'd been going around in circles.

"And a letter from a woman who claims to be the mother of your daughter. Your usual reply, milord?"

Pell scoffed over the rim of his glass. "Apparently, this one isn't quite as sharp in the old noggin as all the others. At least they had the sense to claim to have birthed you an illegitimate *son* as they tried to trap you into their scheme."

It was true. There were always the futile attempts to ensnare a duke or ensure a sizable income via blackmail. But he'd always possessed far too much control over himself to ever make the mistake of an indiscreet affair, especially one that might result in a child. In fact, in his entire life he'd never lost—

His heart stopped for an instant, and a shiver rolled down his spine.

There had been one time. One time that he'd been so utterly enthralled that the world could have burned to ash and he never would have cared or known, until it was too late.

He shrugged off the chill. Whoever had sent this letter, it was not Lady Avalon. She was far too clever to resort to a debutante's scheme. So clever that he wondered if he would ever see her again.

"Aye, Collins. Send the usual reply." Which was, actually, no reply at all. He did not deem these manipulations worthy of paper and ink.

"Oh, Mr. Collins," Morgan said with an uncharacteristically warm smile. "Might I see that letter? They are always so amusing."

Lucien put the pen in the inkwell and exhaled in exhaustion as he looked down at two years of work. Two years, and all for nothing.

He stalked to the window. Looking out toward the drawbridge gate, he remembered his decision to open the grounds to tours years ago. At the time, he'd imagined families picnicking here. No harm in that, he'd thought.

Oh, what a fool he'd been. "I see little humor in the games and deceptions. It puts me in mind to take a wife and just be done with all of it."

"All of it?" his sister asked, her voice barely heard above the crumpled page in her grasp. "What do you mean?"

Pell stood and pushed a whisky into Lucien's hand. "It means the old chap is finally done with all this madness. It's about bloody time, too. Let's be off to London and find you a bride."

Lucien tossed back the drink, then nodded.

"Well, that's wonderful news, brother. I'm glad to hear it. Because now I know that I can tell you of a rumor I heard regarding a certain lady of your acquaintance." When he whipped around to look at her, she merely shrugged. "I was only trying to protect you from another wild-goose chase. As impossible as it might seem, I do worry about you."

Lucien knew he should just let it go. He knew that it was the right decision to put all this behind him and finally live his life. These pursuits were driving him to madness.

Just one more time, a voice whispered in the back of his mind. *This will be the last, I promise . . .*

He steeled himself against it. If he used past experience as a rubric, there was a one hundred percent chance of failure.

And yet, he couldn't explain it, but a fresh surge of adrenaline sprinted through him at the thought of another chance to find Lady Avalon and take back everything she'd stolen from him.

"Tell me the rumor," he said.

Chapter 20

Revenge is a dish best served cold

Lucien usually avoided Wiltshire. The last time he'd traveled this way, he'd had a series of unfortunate events that had been so confounding that he'd vowed to travel by any other route from that point on, no matter how long the detour might take.

He wasn't a superstitious man by any means, but he preferred not to dally in places where he'd encountered such tremendous stupidity that it had boggled his mind.

"Never thought to find us in Wiltshire again, Your Grace," his driver said.

"Neither did I, Kay. And I am eternally grateful that you are perfectly hale. I should not wish to see you in such a state as last time, and the two of us at the mercy of a backwater driver who could not navigate himself through an open door."

"Had us turned upside down, he did. Traveling north instead of south to Somerset. Then there was that strange storm that took us farther off course. And that stone in the road that broke the wheel." He shook his head. "Thought we'd never get home."

"Rest assured, this compulsory visit will be quite brief," Lucien said, ninety-nine percent certain that he wouldn't find a trace of Lady Avalon here either.

Unlike his other hunting expeditions, this time Pell and Morgan would join him in a few days. Since his sister still suffered bouts of fatigue after her illness in Italy, he hadn't wanted her to risk the jaunt across the countryside. But she'd insisted and told him to go on ahead of them.

So now here he was in an idyllic village, filled with flower boxes beneath shopfront windows, neatly swept pavements beside the narrow, winding cobblestoned high street and townspeople who greeted one another with a smile and a tip of the hat.

In other words, it was hardly the place where he might find an adventuress like Lady Avalon.

Over the course of the past two years, he'd heard rumors of her living in large cities, teeming with crowds to conceal her and with excitement enough to satisfy her nature. But his quests had been fruitless.

Standing in the shadow of the clapboard inn, he surveyed the cluster of honey-colored stone buildings, calculating where best to begin making discreet inquiries. The butcher, the baker and the haberdasher were most likely to know the local gossip.

As he took a step, a sudden gust swept down the lane, strong enough that he lifted a hand to the brim of his hat. But instead of securing it, he went still, heedless to the black beaver topper tumbling off his head and onto the ground.

"Something amiss, sir?" Kay asked, unstrapping the portmanteau.

A familiar scent invaded Lucien's nostrils, and a shiver rolled down his spine, his flesh prickling beneath his starched linen. Out of the corner of his eye, he caught a glimpse of raven-black hair, porcelain skin and lips as red as candied cherries.

His pulse quickened, and he turned swiftly.

But the morning sun glanced across his spectacles, blinding him for an instant. By the time he removed them, the figure was gone.

"Did you see a woman with dark hair and a fair complexion walk by just now?"

Brushing off the hat against the side of his long coat, his driver handed it to him. "No, sir. But are you feeling quite well? If you don't mind my saying, you've gone a bit pale."

Lucien shook his head. "Too much traveling of late. I'll be glad to be home after this."

And he would stay there for a time, vowing to ignore whatever rumors might come his way. He would have to put Lady Avalon and the book from his mind. This pursuit—this obsession—was killing him. If he didn't stop, he would likely find his way to an early grave without having anything to show for his life.

He was just putting on his top hat when he heard something that sparked his interest.

"Good day, Mrs. Arthur," a man said. "We have more of that cherry jam you fancy."

"Thank you, Mr. Osborne. But I'm afraid I lingered too long over ribbons at Mrs. Baxter's shop, and I must make haste back to the house. Tomorrow?" a voice called out, growing fainter on the breeze.

"Until tomorrow, then."

Somewhere between the first syllable and the last, Lucien's heart had stopped beating. He knew that voice, the way it lilted musically as if forever on the precipice of a laugh.

She'd likely laughed all the way out of Italy where she'd left him more than two years ago.

His heart started again in hard, angry beats. This time he was certain.

He fell into stealthy pursuit of the figure in a lavender pelisse and straw bonnet. As she scuttled along the pavement, he peevishly wondered why she was in such a hurry. Behind schedule for her latest conquest? Another duke waiting to be hoodwinked?

Turning the corner at the end of the lane, she bumped her basket against the lamppost, and the contents spilled. She paused, lowering to collect her scattered assortment of brightly colored ribbons.

"How clumsy of me," she said with a self-deprecating laugh as his boots appeared in her line of vision, and he bent down. "I'm grateful for your assist—"

The instant the brim of her bonnet lifted and their eyes met, she stopped. Her face drained of all color. Even her eyes seemed a bleached blue, and more startling than he remembered.

Her lips formed the syllables of his name, but no sound came forth.

"Surprised?" he asked coldly.

Even so, he felt a brief, unanticipated swell of relief at seeing her alive. It lodged in his throat and he had a sudden urge to haul her into his arms, to hold her, to—

No. He refused to acknowledge any misplaced mawkish sentiment. It had no place here. But anger, outrage and resentment? Aye. Those were his bedfellows and he would hold fast to them.

"What . . ." she rasped, then swallowed. "What are you doing here?"

"To take back what's mine."

She stiffened and stood, watching him warily as he did the same. "I do not have anything that is *yours*."

"I beg to differ. Surely, you know by now what my legacy means to me, and I will not leave here without it."

"Over my dead body." Instant ferocity flared to life in those eyes, and she bared her teeth like a wolf guarding her pup. "You've shown absolutely no interest in me or your *legacy*. So whatever reason you think you've come here for . . . Well, you can think again. Because you're not going to lay a single hand on her."

"We shall see about that."

"We will, indeed."

She stalked off, head high. And he let her go for the moment.

It was clear that she was comfortable here and had set down roots long enough to become familiar with the towns-people, at least. Perhaps he'd finally found the wolf's lair. It would be difficult for her to flit off in a hurry, which gave him ample time to ask a few questions in the village.

Then, once armed with information, he would pay a call on her. After all, what kind of a gentleman would he be if he didn't return the basket and spilled ribbons she'd so thoughtlessly left behind?

🦋

MEG RETURNED to Crossmoor Abbey without remembering the steps she'd taken to arrive at her home. Even though she'd lived here for the majority of her life, the three sto-ries of smooth ashlar stones and crenellated towers on either side seemed foreign to her.

All the workings of her mind had stopped on one thought: *Lucien is here.*

"Anything amiss, Mistress Stredwick?" the butler asked as he opened the recessed front door. "Shall I summon your aunt or Lady Hullworth?"

She shook her head, catching her ghostly white reflection in the foyer's filigree-framed looking glass. "I am fine, Mr. Tidwell. Just a bit winded from the walk, I suppose."

Numbly, she climbed the stairs with the intention of checking on Guinevere in the nursery but only made it to the first floor, where she sank onto one of the benches that lined the wainscoted hallway.

Lucien was here. It was almost impossible to believe. She might have convinced herself he was an aberration if not for the heavy thudding of her heart and the soul-deep ache that reminded her how little she had meant to him.

For the first month after her return from her holiday, she'd been worried and frantic. She'd paced the floor at nights, sleepless and imagining all sorts of calamities that might have befallen him.

By the second month, she'd been furious when she'd read in the society papers that he'd returned to Somerset. She'd even been tempted to travel there, pound on his door and demand answers. Did he think their night together meant nothing?

By the third month . . . she'd had other things on her mind, like how to tell her brother about her night of indiscretion and the child that had resulted from it.

The conversation had been humbling, humiliating. She'd let everyone down. Her family believed in love matches, not reckless nights of abandon. They waited for the Stredwick certainty, for fate, to guide them. And she thought she had as well.

But she'd been wrong about Lucien. Just like she'd been wrong about believing she'd loved Daniel Prescott.

Over that summer, she'd come to realize that what she'd felt for Daniel was a childish infatuation. What she had felt for Lucien was genuine, but only on her part, apparently. To him, she meant nothing. And it was with equal sadness when she realized that there would be no love match for her. Not ever. Because she couldn't trust her own heart.

When Brandon had demanded to know the name of the blackguard, she'd refused to give it. She'd also sworn the aunts to secrecy, which they'd agreed to because they hadn't wanted it known that they'd been chased out of Italy for stealing.

However, she had told them that she'd written countless letters to the gentleman in question and received no response. That had been the only reason Brandon hadn't overruled her. That *and* because of Ellie.

Meg's sister-in-law had looked into her husband's eyes

and simply asked him if he would truly force Meg to marry an obviously thoughtless and self-serving man. And since he'd nearly lost Ellie to such a man—until she'd seen the truth for herself—Brandon had accepted Meg's decision. Albeit with gritted teeth and immense reluctance.

Her Aunt Sylvia, who lived with them at Crossmoor Abbey, had smiled softly when Meg had told her. She'd taken her hand and said that love was precious, that one should cherish all the gifts that came from it and that everything would work out as it was meant to.

Bryony knew the truth, of course. The other servants and the rest of society, however, would never understand a highborn woman choosing to have a child with no husband. So Aunt Sylvia had *accidentally* mentioned to her own abigail that Meg had fallen in love and married in Italy in a whirlwind romance. But her new husband, a gentleman of a fine family, had been called away on a matter of business and would return to her once he secured their fortune and future.

And just what was the surname of this mysterious gentleman who'd stolen the heart of their mistress?

Arthur, of course.

Meg could think of none other than the legendary king who'd started it all. After pretending to be Lady Avalon and Miss Parrish for a few months, it wasn't terribly difficult to answer to the name Mrs. Arthur for a time.

After Guinevere was born and Mr. Arthur never presented himself, however, the servants started gossiping about the lack of letters coming from his quarter. They saw her send many out, but none—other than from her friends—came in.

She wasn't entirely sure how Mr. Arthur had ostensibly died. All she knew was that Brandon had mentioned to his manservant that her supposed husband had befallen an accident—one too gruesome and scandalous for feminine

ears—which had likely reflected his own desires to in-
flict retribution on the true culprit. But it was apparently
so terrible that the servants wanted to erase his memory
altogether.

So they called her Mistress Stredwick, while those in the
village referred to her as either Mrs. Arthur or, with a pitying expression, the *Widow Arthur.*

But now that Lucien was here, the truth would be revealed, and she would bring humiliation on her family.

Meg had to leave Crossmoor Abbey. There was no other
way. He was here to take Guinevere—his legacy—from her,
and she refused to let that happen.

That thought brought her to her feet, the sudden fire in her
blood driving away her residual shock at having seen him.

He'd been just as impossibly tall, perhaps taller, and one
of his lenses had been smudged. His face was familiar to her
and yet so much colder than she remembered. In fact, the
last time she had seen him he was—

Don't, she told herself. Thinking of what they'd been to
each other, or what she'd thought they'd been, only made
her heart break.

It was all too clear that she'd been wrong and that the
Fates had never brought them together at all.

When she appeared in the nursery doorway, she saw that
Guinevere was down for her nap, her wispy pale blonde hair
fanning out over the pillow.

It had been a surprise when her hair had grown in blonde,
considering that both of her parents were dark. But perhaps
the Stredwick lineage that had given her brother nut-brown
hair had something to do with that.

A healthy child, Guinevere had her mother's roundness
of face, and when she smiled, she flashed a dimple. But only
on the left side of her cheek, just like her father. Her eyes
were a changeable blue that seemed to grow darker each
day, as if on the cusp of turning a rich river-stone brown,

and there was no mistaking the flecks of gold that were undeniably like Lucien's.

Since her daughter was not a sound sleeper, Meg quietly tiptoed away and went down to her own bedchamber.

She rang for Bryony immediately and informed her of the news.

"Then, we'll be gone for a long while, I should expect," Bryony said without hesitation. "We'll manage just fine. I'll start packing your things straightaway."

Meg squeezed her hand with affection. "I don't know what I would do without you. I'll go to the attic with you to fetch as many valises as we can carry. We cannot tell the other servants. Not yet, at least. I'll have to speak with Aunt Sylvia first."

"Don't you fret. It'll all turn out right in the end."

Meg tried to smile, but she remembered thinking that same thing when she'd left Italy. And as far as she could tell, nothing was turning out the way it was supposed to at all.

Chapter 21

In a pickle

Two hours later and with her bags packed, Meg went in search of her aunt. But she was informed that Lady Hullworth was tending to a matter with the master gardener.

This did not come as a surprise. Aunt Sylvia practically lived in the gardens that she had designed and cared for during the years that her husband had been the Marquess of Hullworth. Crossmoor Abbey had been his estate until an outbreak of typhus had taken Sylvia's husband and eldest son, along with Meg's father.

This family knew too much about loss, but also a great deal about love. And that was the very reason Meg knew her aunt would understand her need to leave.

She refused to lose her daughter to a man who hadn't shown an inkling of interest since her birth.

Resolved in her decision, she returned to the nursery to prepare Guinevere for their journey. Instead, she found the nurse in the hallway, looking frantic, her face pale with concern.

Meg stopped at once. "She's done it again, hasn't she?"

"I only turned away for a second to retrieve the doll she wanted from the top shelf," the nurse said, fretfully chewing on her thumbnail. "By the time I stepped down from the stool . . ."

Meg nodded and quickly scanned the surroundings for her little escape artist.

It wasn't the nurse's fault. Ever since Guinevere could walk, she'd dart off without anyone the wiser. It had happened to Aunt Sylvia, to Maeve and Myrtle and Ellie, even to Brandon when he was watching both his son and his niece.

Usually, Guinevere would take her cousin with her, and locating the pair of them was much simpler as there was often giggling involved.

But Brandon and Ellie had taken Johnathon with them to visit the north estate and then to close up Maeve and Myrtle's house for the winter. Since Guinevere was without her favorite cohort, there was no telling where she'd run off to this time.

Unless . . .

"Yesterday, we'd had a picnic in the garden, and there were fuzzy caterpillars munching on the leaves. Then last night, I tucked her in with a story of a caterpillar who became a butterfly named Guinevere," Meg said, already turning on her heel. "I'll look there. You check all the rooms with butterfly collections."

The nurse nodded, and Meg dashed downstairs.

Once outside, Meg could hear her daughter's giggle rising from the walled garden, and she sighed with relief.

Stepping beneath the ivy-shrouded archway, she called, "Sweetheart? Are you in here—"

She stopped in her tracks.

Lucien was there, sitting on the stone bench beside her daughter.

"After your less than cordial greeting to me earlier, your term of endearment comes as quite the surprise. But you were always rather changeable, were you not, *ma petite louve*?"

Her heart lurched painfully. "Don't call me that."

"I should hardly know what to call you, then. Lady Avalon, Miss Parrish, Mrs. Arthur or . . . Margaret Stredwick?"

Meg felt cold, frozen in place. She wanted to get her daughter away from here as quickly as possible, but she couldn't seem to move or make her feet cooperate. How many different ways could he ruin her life, if he chose to?

"More, more," her daughter said, the words sounding rather like *mo, mo* because her rosebud mouth refused to form certain letters like *R*s and *L*s. But that didn't stop her from pointing excitedly to the butterflies as she tugged on Lucien's coat and repeated her favorite word.

Lucien chuckled when she climbed up to stand on the bench so that she could put her hands on his cheeks and direct his attention to the cerulean butterfly. He obliged her with a grin, listing the Latin name and scientific classification. "That is the Adonis Blue, *Lysandra bellargus*."

If Meg weren't a pillar of fear, she'd almost think the sight of them together was sweet, with their heads close, her daughter's blonde ringlets brushing Lucien's cheek. He was patient with her, too, obeying her every rude command.

He glanced over his shoulder. "She's quite an inquisitive child. Your brother's, I presume?"

"My brother's?"

"Brandon Stredwick, the Marquess of Hullworth, married to the former Elodie *Parrish*," he supplied with that knowing look. "It is astonishing what one can discover in a small country village in a matter of minutes. And it seems that you weren't lying about having an older brother, after all. Though, I never would have guessed he would be so well-esteemed in society. That *you* could have a brother with such an unblemished reputation. It must be difficult being the black sheep of the family, all the secrecy involved in hiding who you really are."

She'd told him exactly who she was in the note she'd

left. And she was mortified to recall the beseeching, almost pleading, words she'd written.

Come to me, Lucien. I will be waiting for you. With all my heart . . .

But never once, in the last two years, had he bothered to find her.

Not that it mattered any longer. "What are you doing here?"

"As I said, you stole the book that is my legacy, and I will not leave here without it."

The book?

She blinked. As she started to put the pieces together, a great rush of relief flooded her. He wasn't here to take Guinevere?

He was only here for the book.

Apparently, Lucien's spectacles had never corrected his myopic vision in his quest for those recipes. He either didn't care that he'd sired a child with her or didn't realize this was the daughter she'd written to him about.

Whatever the reason, she was relieved.

Her limbs thawed, and she stepped into the garden and picked up her daughter. "Then you've come to the wrong place. I left that book with you when we were last . . . together."

He stood. Something hot flared in his gaze, and suddenly the memory was so potent between them that she felt flushed from head to toe.

Her body's uncontrolled reaction irritated her, and she forced herself to take a step back. "Whatever you've done with that book since then is no concern of mine, I'm sure. Now, please leave."

"I will. But not until you've given me the name of the man you're working for—the one you *actually* gave the book to."

"I've told you this a dozen times. There is no man. When are you going to start believing me, Lucien?" At the irritation in her voice, Guinevere started to fuss, her cherub cheeks puckering sourly. Before she started to cry, Meg held her close, rubbing a soothing hand down her small back. Over the top of her head, she whispered, "I am going now, and I expect you to leave here and never return. As I recall, you're good at disappearing."

He frowned as she turned on her heel, and she thought she heard him mutter, "I would say the same of you."

Stepping into the house, she pressed her back against the door and released the breath she'd been holding for, it seemed like, forever.

"Out," her daughter said on a heavy sigh, resting her cheek against Meg's shoulder as if she'd been through an ordeal as well.

She kissed the top of her head. "Yes, Mummy knows you like to play outside, but you mustn't run off like that again."

Her daughter grumbled her disagreement, and Meg started to walk through the house to find the nurse. And then Bryony.

If Lucien was only here for the book—which she still didn't understand, since she'd left it with him—then it stood to reason that her sudden flight would only cause him to give chase. And quite possibly alert his suspicions. Because, at the moment, he assumed that Guinevere was Brandon's child.

But how could that be after all the tear-filled and, eventually, hate-filled letters she'd sent to Caliburn Keep?

They must have been misdirected. Which meant that she would have to tell him, face-to-face. It was the right thing to do. And yet . . .

If she told him while he was still convinced that she had his book, wasn't it possible that a man who was so focused and driven on a singular pursuit would use anything he could against her?

Meg held her daughter close as she climbed the stairs.

She knew in that moment that the best course of action would be for her to stay here, where she would have the support and security of her family around her, while she tried to figure out what to do next.

Until then, she would have to keep her family from knowing the truth. They couldn't find out that Lucien was the father. At least, not yet. And in order to keep her secret, he would need to stay far away from Crossmoor Abbey.

But what were the odds that she'd gotten rid of him so easily?

Chapter 22

Guess who's coming to dinner?

Standing by the white marble mantel, Lucien flashed a triumphant grin when the little wolf appeared in the parlor doorway of Crossmoor Abbey early that evening.

"Aunt Sylvia, I—" Meg stopped with a noticeable jolt, her eyes widening.

"Ah, Meg, there you are," the Dowager Lady Hullworth said with a fond smile. She had a soft spray of wrinkles beside her temples, where moon-silver strands were pulled back into a pair of combs. "You've been so busy with whatever you were doing in the attic today, I didn't have a chance to tell you that we were having a guest for dinner. I should like to introduce you to the Duke of Merleton. Your Grace, this is my niece, Margaret Stredwick."

He bowed but made no move to cross the room to her. For some unknown reason, he wanted her to come to him. "A pleasure to see you again, Miss Stredwick."

"Oh, yes, I forgot," Sylvia said. "Lucien mentioned he'd met you in the garden this afternoon."

"Lucien?" Meg's brow knitted in confusion at the familiarity, her hand falling to the doorknob as if she needed the support.

Sylvia nodded. "We are old friends, you might say. I've known him since he was at Eton with your cousin. So many years ago." Her smile turned wistful as she spoke of her late son, who had been a good man, a brilliant man, that Lucien had admired. "But Meg, shame on you for not saying anything earlier."

"I . . ." She swallowed. But when she glanced at him, something in his countenance must have revealed his enjoyment of her discomfiture, because she squared her shoulders at once. "The encounter completely slipped my mind. My apologies."

His mouth twitched as she slid an unapologetically icy glance his way.

But Lucien had already anticipated this cold reception, calculating that it would take a certain degree of charm to keep his name on the guest list while he remained to search for the book. "Understandable, considering you had your hands full at the time. Delightful child, by the by. Your brother must be proud."

The women exchanged a glance before Meg quickly interjected. "Yes. He is undeniably fond of her."

Draped in a gown of dark indigo satin, she stepped farther into the parlor, moving with poise and grace. As the fabric shifted and caught the candlelight, he noticed the changes in her. In the two years since they'd last met, her face and figure had altered somewhat. Where her cheeks were once rounded, they were now more refined, sculpted in a way that drew even more attention to her startlingly clear blue eyes and those lush red lips. And it seemed that any plumpness in her mien had drifted down in subtle degrees to her fuller breasts and to the enticing curve of her hips.

Somehow during their time apart, she'd become even more stunningly beautiful than before.

"I believe you referred to her as *Guinevere*. Not a very common name, is it?" he asked pointedly, needing to keep his thoughts directed on his purpose. Allowing himself to be distracted by her was far too costly an error, he recalled.

"No, it is not."

"I believe it derives from Arthurian legend," he said, watching her closely. "I was well acquainted with your brother years ago, but he never mentioned an interest in the old stories. Perhaps it is a great family secret."

Her throat tightened infinitesimally on a swallow. "Or perhaps it is merely a coincidence."

The instant she said the last word, her brows knitted as if she knew her mistake. As if she knew he was thinking that there was no such thing as a coincidence.

"It is a pity that Brandon could not be here," Sylvia offered from an upholstered armchair, her gaze flitting from Meg, who eased down onto the cream-colored sofa on one side of the low oval table, to Lucien, who sat in a chair directly opposite. "He is away with his wife, her two aunts and their son, Johnathon."

Thinking about the little girl who'd wandered alone into the garden, Lucien was confused. If Hullworth had taken his wife and son, then why would he leave his daughter behind? Then again, perhaps he thought she was too young to travel.

But he pushed the question aside and continued his cat-and-mouse game.

"Would those aunts be the Parrish sisters?" he inquired and felt Meg's nervous glance on his profile. He wondered how much her family actually knew of her exploits.

Sylvia tilted her head. "Are you acquainted?"

"I was fortunate enough to make their acquaintance on my travels, years ago."

"Is that so?" she answered and smiled softly, her gaze shifting to her niece and back to him again as if she were watching a badminton match on the lawn. "Well, then, I shall have to do my utmost to implore you to stay in Wiltshire until they return."

"I'm sure His Grace has other affairs that require his attention," Meg interjected. "Let us not force him to feel obligated."

"As it would happen," he said, "I have no fixed engagements at present. My sister and cousin will be joining me in a day or two at the village inn."

"Oh, but you must stay here. Brandon would surely enjoy seeing you on his return and would be quite cross with me if he learned you were staying anywhere else," Sylvia insisted.

Meg opened her mouth to respond, but Lucien spoke first. "I would be delighted."

"Then, it's all settled. You'll stay at Stredwick Lodge, where our bachelor guests reside."

A separate house for unmarried men was certainly something he would expect from a man like Hullworth, who'd always valued his family name and reputation. It was just one more piece of the puzzle that Lucien added to the pile with all the others.

When the butler appeared in the doorway, Sylvia stood. "Lucien, would you be so kind as to escort Meg to dinner? And I'll just send a footman to the village for your things, if you are amenable."

"I am, indeed."

No. No. No! Absolutely not, Meg thought all throughout dinner.

This couldn't be happening. Just when she was hoping to be rid of him, Aunt Sylvia invited him here? And worse, she knew that look in her aunt's eyes. Even though she usually saw that conspiratorial glee brightening Maeve's and Myrtle's gazes, there was no mistaking when a relative's thoughts turned to matchmaking.

Drat! Now what was Meg going to do? Doubtless her aunt was already contemplating ways to throw the two of them together.

As if reading her thoughts, Aunt Sylvia brushed the napkin across her lips and smiled. "My nephew is so very content in his marriage. Have you given the state of matrimony any thought, Lucien?"

Meg nearly groaned. She was playing right into his hand and didn't know that he had an ulterior motive. If the past had proven anything, he wasn't going to leave until he had the book. That was the only reason he was exhibiting so much charm, deceiving her aunt like he'd deceived her with the same ploy.

His not-so-rare-anymore dimple winked with triumph across the table. "I have never declared myself against it. After all, a man must think of the future and the legacy he leaves behind."

"Then, you must plan to have children one day."

He inclined his head. "I would be able to think more clearly on that topic once I have a few things settled. You see, someone stole something from me—a book, an heirloom, actually. It is part of that legacy I mentioned, and I must do whatever I can to reclaim it."

"How awful for you," Sylvia said, and Meg rolled her eyes. "I do hope that it is returned to you posthaste. If there is any way that we can assist you, we would be more than glad to be of service."

He claimed it was stolen, and yet Meg knew better. It was clear to her that, at some point, he must have lost it. Either that or someone else had taken it—the real Lady Avalon, perhaps? But once again he had the ludicrous notion that *she* was responsible. Well, if he had bothered to read any of her letters, then he would have realized she'd been far too busy.

"That is very kind of you, ma'am," he said. "If only I had the assistance of one who not only had a cunning mind but also knew of the old Arthurian legends, then I could find a way to reveal the culprit sooner."

"Oh, but Meg is exceedingly sharp and knows those stories by heart. The two of you must work together. In fact, we have all manner of old manuscripts throughout the manor that pertain to that legend. She could show you where they are, and you could peruse them at your leisure."

Meg growled into her wine goblet.

"I would hate to impose," he said smoothly, his eyes glinting behind his spectacles as he looked across the table.

If they had been playing chess, she believed he would have said *Check.*

"I'm certain it would be no bother. Would it, Meg, dear?"

Resigned for the moment, she set down her glass. "No bother at all."

He grinned again. *Check and mate.*

"In the meantime," Aunt Sylvia said, "perhaps the two of you could tour the side garden, where there is a hill that overlooks the bachelor's lodge. I'm sure your things have already arrived. Meg, you wouldn't mind, would you? I think it's time for me to retire for the evening."

The sound of the slow grating of her molars filled her ears as she fixed a smile in place. "I'd be delighted."

Chapter 23

Simmer down

Begrudgingly, Meg led their guest along the path toward the park that overlooked Stredwick Lodge. It was a cool night, the moon hanging overhead like a sugar-dusted biscuit that had been cut perfectly in half. *The other half had likely been discarded and left forgotten for two years*, she thought peevishly as Lucien kept pace beside her.

If it weren't for him, she would be enjoying this lovely stroll. The air was sweetly scented with dew and damp earth and filled with the chirruping songs of frogs and crickets as they approached the creek.

This used to be her favorite spot, sitting on the walking bridge and feeling the cool, silken caress of stone-tumbled water over her toes. But he'd ruined that for her, too.

When she'd returned from her holiday, her heart shattered anew each time she saw the dark rocks flecked with gold that reminded her of his eyes. And now he was here, threatening to destroy the life she'd tried so hard to create after she'd been broken and had carefully put herself back together.

Irritated once more, she sent him a withering glare. "Whatever you intend to accomplish by this charade of yours—this charming facade you've adopted for the evening—I tell you there is nothing to gain. I do not have your book. And you are only leading my aunt to believe there could be something between us."

"At one point, I thought there could have been," he said with that disapproving frown of his, as if he were in earnest, and that just vexed her all the more.

She huffed and held up two fingers. "Says the man who made no attempt to contact me in two years."

"Says the woman who disappeared without a trace."

"I. Left. You. A. Note!"

"So you claim, but when I returned to my room, there was no note. *And* no book."

She growled. It was so futile trying to prove her point, like beating her head against a—"Wait a minute. What do you mean when you *returned*?"

"I had to leave that night," he said on a heavy breath, his gaze distant as he looked toward the dark tree line on the horizon. "Morgan had taken ill. The doctors weren't certain she would live."

Meg covered her mouth with her fingertips. "Oh, no. I'm sorry. I had no idea."

"It was a month before she was well enough to travel, and I am thankful that her health is greatly improved. But the episode only cemented the fact that my family's welfare and legacy rests on my shoulders." He turned to her, his gaze searching. "Meg, my half sister, is nearly the only family I have left, and I almost lost her. I have a great-aunt in Cheshire who is ninety-seven years old, and I suspect the only reason she is still alive is to write to me with constant reminders to produce an heir. And every time I visit or read her letters, I am forced to come to the conclusion that Pell will likely marry before I do, and he has vowed to wait until he is a septuagenarian."

He shook his head and raked a hand through his hair. "The point I am attempting to make, however, is that I cannot even consider the possibility of a different pursuit until the book is returned to me. Not only do I have experiments yet to prove, but it is my duty to preserve the Merleton legacy. Can you not understand that?"

His speech was so adamant, so vulnerable. So unlike the logical and calculated man she'd come to know that she suddenly saw his quest in a new light.

It wasn't simply an obsession. There was deep sentiment and heartfelt need behind his driven nature. And that knowledge tugged at her heart, whether she wanted it to or not.

"Lucien, I promise you that I do not have, or know who might have, your book. I want you to find it. I want you to have whatever brings you fulfillment." She stepped toward him and almost took his hand in hers. Almost.

Thankfully, her sense returned, and she thought of Guinevere.

Crossing her arms to ward off the chill, she added, "But you'll not find it here. And I need you to go before my aunt suspects that you and I are much better acquainted than she knows."

He studied her carefully for a moment, an erudite gleam in his eyes as his brows arched. "It seems the bold Lady Avalon has a weakness, after all."

She stiffened at the thinly veiled threat and pointed her finger at him. "This is not a coy game. I'm no longer on holiday, pretending to be someone I'm not. Don't you see? You were only supposed to be my one grand flirtation, and instead—"

"We became lovers," he said in a voice so low that it spiraled directly into the pit of her stomach.

Then he took her off guard when he reached out and grasped her wrist. He towed her toward him. On a squeak of surprise, she lost her firm footing, staggering forward, and he caught her against him in a shock of breathless sensations and, before she knew it, she felt the tug. The giddiness. All the things that had kept drawing her to him again and again from the moment they'd met.

Much to her dismay, she couldn't seem to stop touching him. Her hands were on his broad chest, fingers fanned out and tingling with the memory of the crisp, dark furring that she knew was beneath his waistcoat and shirt. The warmth of him. The feel of his heart beating against her own.

It was happening all over again.

"We did," she admitted on a rasp, making a feeble attempt to put space between them. "And if my family realizes what we were, they would force us to marry."

She meant it as a threat to scare him off. To compel him to release her like a hot coal.

Instead, he pulled her closer. Her betraying body softened against him as if she belonged there. And oh, it felt so good. Too good.

He leaned closer, his cheek against hers as he breathed her in. "As my wife, you would be in my bed every night, neck arched, body flushed with desire, my name on your lips." His heated whisper brushed the sensitive inner whorls of her ear, sending shivers spiraling inside her. "You're already thinking about it."

"I'm not," she lied and realized that doing so still made her nose itch. Ignoring the sensation, she flexed her fingers on his shoulders.

He arched a dubious brow. "Your eyes tell a different tale. The pupils are full-blown with desire."

She hiked her chin, which—she happened to notice—brought their mouths closer. If she were to rise on her toes . . .

But no, she didn't want to think about that. Or acknowledge that he still smelled just as good as she remembered. Better. "It is nighttime. Pupils naturally expand in dark places in order to let in more light."

"Your lips are plump and your cheeks are flushed. Proof of increased blood flow toward the surface of your skin."

"I have a similar reaction to eating too many strawberries before my skin begins to itch," she said, grasping at straws, her pulse thudding.

"You can lie to yourself. But I'll be damned if I'll let you lie to me again." His fingers gripped her hips, drawing her flush. "Your nostrils flare as if to catch my scent, and your breaths are shallow and quick."

"So are yours," she accused as she felt herself molding against him, her body cradling that enticing hardness and clenching on emptiness. "Drat, you horrible man! I hate you for doing these things to me."

"Not as much as I hate you, *ma petite louve*," he said as he curled his hand around the nape of her neck.

Meg felt her spine bow toward him, head tilting. Blast it all! She couldn't seem to stop herself.

Was she actually going to let him kiss her?

Kissing him went against every vow she'd made to herself in the past few hours.

But a few hours ago, she had been a different woman. Her willpower was her friend—an angry, bitter friend that would rather have seen him drawn and quartered than here in the moonlight.

Now that same willpower friend was fanning herself, lounging on a chaise and hoping to be thoroughly ravished.

Lucien lowered his head, an errant ray of moonlight creating shadows beneath his spectacles, his eyes smoky with promise—

Then a cry broke through the night air, shattering the spell at once.

Meg shoved out of his embrace. She stepped apart, her hands trembling as she smoothed them over her skirts.

With as cold a voice as she could manage, she said, "I must go. I trust you will find your own way to Stredwick Lodge."

LUCIEN WATCHED her flee the garden, a puzzled frown furrowing his brow.

He hadn't intended for that to happen. But once again, he'd been suddenly overwhelmed by a primitive need for her. As if she belonged to him, with him, over him, under . . .

He let out a heavy breath, confounded by his own behavior, staggered by this need that left him shaken.

It made no logical sense. But with Meg, it never did.

He'd had trouble thinking straight when it came to her before. He couldn't allow that to happen again.

He didn't know what game they were playing this time around. But he didn't like this feeling. His hands felt empty. His body coiled tight. He passed the side of his closed fist over the surface of his lips to ease the peculiar ache. Then he pressed it to the center of his chest where his heart thudded flatly as if it had been dropped from a great height.

No, he did not like this feeling at all.

Chapter 24

When life gives you lemons . . .

"That man is like a bad penny," Meg grumbled to herself as she stood in the upper gallery, looking down on the foyer as the duke crossed the threshold.

"Oh?" Aunt Sylvia said, startling her as she sauntered up to the railing. "I thought for certain there was something between the two of you. The air fairly crackled when you entered the parlor last evening."

"How odd. I didn't notice a thing."

"And I've never heard anyone challenge Lucien the way you did. Many people find his keen intellect and brooding austerity intimidating. Coupled with the fact that he rarely mingles in society, it prevents him from being at ease enough to reveal the more agreeable aspects of his nature."

"Are you certain he has any?"

Aunt Sylvia smiled and offered a wave when the duke glanced up and spotted them, inclining his head in turn. "He seemed to last night. I think he was quite taken by you."

Meg felt the uncontrolled quickening of her pulse when his gaze fixed on her. But remembering the sole reason he was here, she turned away.

"I pray you are not hopeful on that account. He has made it amply clear that his interest is in finding his lost book and nothing more. And for that, I am glad," she said, needing to put a stop to any matchmaking ideas. "Once he realizes that what he came to find isn't here, he will think nothing of walking away without a backward glance. As for me, he could leave this very day and never return, and I would be grateful."

"Is that truly how you feel?" her aunt asked with a puzzled frown.

Meg swallowed, then nodded. She'd lain awake most of the night, thinking about their encounter and everything he'd said, every impassioned reason behind his search for the book. And she'd felt her heart soften a little more.

She was afraid that the foolish organ had not learned its hard lesson well enough and was at risk of breaking all over again if she let him get too close.

"The sooner he leaves Crossmoor Abbey," she said, "the better."

Sylvia sighed. "Then, I wish I hadn't already written to your brother to tell him of our esteemed guest, along with Lady Morgan and Lord Holladay, who will be joining us in a few days. Especially if the duke will likely be gone before Brandon, Ellie and little Johnathon return."

Meg hid the alarm that sprinted through her. Brandon and Lucien beneath the same roof? No. Sometimes her brother could be too perceptive for his own good.

"And, of course, Lucien would wish to pay his respects to Maeve and Myrtle, too," her aunt continued. "Though, I have to wonder when he might have met them, as he'd mentioned last night. As we are all aware, the Parrish sisters take great pride in knowing about every bachelor in England. And to share an acquaintance with a duke? Well, I'm rather shocked that they never attempted to introduce you to him."

Then again, Aunt Sylvia could be a bit too perceptive, too.

Meg carefully schooled her features.

All it would take was one random slipup to reveal that

she or the aunts had met him on holiday. Then her family would know that he was Guinevere's father. Brandon would say something to Lucien. And there was no telling what he would do.

He hated Meg. No matter what she told him to the contrary, he believed that she'd stolen his book, fleeing with it that night in Italy. Once he learned that he was Guinevere's father, he would have the means to truly hurt her—either by taking Guinevere away or by forcing a union between himself and the woman he despised.

Then she would be the first Stredwick in a loveless marriage, and she refused to do that to *her* family legacy. No, she would rather not marry at all and raise Guinevere alone, if she had to, than marry without love.

"Perhaps they know that I cannot tolerate brooding and condescending men who are far too tall and wear a constant disapproving frown," Meg offered with a shrug. Then she clasped Sylvia's hand with warm affection. "But that is neither here nor there because the duke will be gone soon. Therefore, I shall write to Brandon myself and inform him that there is no need to shorten his stay on this account. I have the matter well in hand."

🦋

LUCIEN STEPPED into the library, surprised to find Meg at a writing desk in front of one of the windows that overlooked the gardens.

She lifted her head at the sound of his footfall but did not look over her shoulder. She simply said, "I suspected you'd wish to start in here, Your Grace. And I'll be happy to direct you to my father's collection in a moment. I'm just finishing a letter to my brother."

"Telling him to stay away from the abbey for as long as possible?"

The curve of her cheek lifted. "How did you guess?"

"I know how you think."

Her cheek fell, and she expelled a hard breath. "Clearly not, or we wouldn't be here, would we?"

As he walked farther into the room, he watched as the morning light fell across her face, the line of her throat, the graceful sweep of her arm beneath a willow-green flounced sleeve. And he wondered where they might be if he did know all her secret thoughts. With her in irons and him at Caliburn Keep, the recipes still locked in the vault? Or perhaps still together in that room in Italy, where he would have known her plan to run away and decided to lock the door and hide the key instead?

A hard fist clenched in his gut as that idea took shape.

But musing over impossible things would only drive a man to madness. He'd been on the precipice before because of her; he wasn't going down that path again.

After sanding her letter, she folded it carefully and dripped the wax to press the seal. Then she surprised him by showing him the neatly penned address. "Just in case you don't believe I'm actually writing to my brother."

His mouth twitched as she sauntered toward the bellpull. A long line of pearl buttons down her back undulated with the sway of her hips, as if the wolf were playfully wagging her tail.

"I think I'll like this new arrangement," he said, "where I know precisely what you are doing every minute of the day."

"Shall I tell you what I ate for breakfast?"

Seeing her bat her lashes, then roll her eyes, he felt compelled to accept her challenge. "Tell me."

"A scandalous amount of coddled eggs and a jam tart."

"Cherry?"

She gave him an arched look, then coolly said, "Lemon."

"Liar," he said. "The lodge had tarts this morning, too. Cherry. I had one myself. The cook even told me they were your favorite."

Her nose twitched, and she huffed. "Fine. It was a cherry tart. Does that please you?"

He considered the question for a moment. Knowing that she lied because the mention of cherries likely reminded her of their first kiss in the German market, he decided, "Indeed, it does."

He hadn't been able to look at a cherry for the past two years without thinking about her. It only seemed fair that she endured the same torment.

When the maid appeared in the doorway, Meg handed her the letter. "And if you could also send a tea tray, filled with every available cherry tart. I should like to throw them all at the duke."

Lucien coughed a laugh in surprise, and she grinned peevishly at him, wrinkling her nose.

But when the freckled maid looked at her blankly, she amended with, "Just the tea tray will be fine, Becca."

"Are you going to pour the pot over my head?" he asked when they were left alone.

Standing beside a bank of shelves near the corner of the room, she shook her head. "Tempting. But I wouldn't want to risk my father's collection, which is here." She gestured to the rows of books bound in leather and buckram. "You'll find the older books on the top shelves. Their bindings are fragile so—"

"I'll be careful," he promised.

The books were well cared for, though some showed their years in the fraying edges and tea-colored pages. A few of the tomes were even dated before the fifteenth century, their flat spines worn thin to show wood slats and the ligaments that bound the parchment and vellum beneath.

He was honored to be permitted to handle them at all. Were these in his collection, he would likely keep them in the vault. Though little good that might have done him with Lady Avalon on the loose.

They studied the volumes in companionable silence, occasionally sharing a glimpse of an exceptionally artistic illumination, the vibrant reds and blues, gold and silver shimmering on the page as if they'd been inked that very day.

Her father had an extensive variety of old manuscripts. Lucien had seen many of these same titles during his years of study. Some were in his own collection. Then there were others that he was exploring for the first time, and he lost himself in the joy of discovery, forgetting his purpose far too often.

Whenever that happened, he would carefully replace the book and then look over to Meg. It felt as though she'd become his mooring line, always drawing him back to a fixed anchor before he set off again.

They paused briefly for tea—sans cherry tarts. He watched her with some curiosity when she moved the tray from the low table between the settee and the hearth and laid it on the writing desk instead.

Noticing his scrutiny, she issued a nonchalant shrug. "This seems a more efficient location for our current task. This way, you can continue your search without interruption."

That much was true. However, he surmised that she likely didn't want either of them relaxing in each other's company, even if only long enough for tea.

He'd been thinking the same thing. Being too at ease with her never ended well for him.

But it didn't seem to matter where they were in the room, because they always ended up beside each other, riffling through the pages.

She slid a book onto one of the shelves and cast an appraising glance in his direction. "You mentioned last night that you need the book because you have experiments to prove. What kind of experiments?"

"On the recipes, testing their validity." He absently

turned the pages of a more recent printing of *Le Morte d'Arthur* by Thomas Malory, finding pressed flowers and fern fronds, and with an inscription in the front that read:

> *For my daughter, Margaret the Fair,*
> *keeper of stories and of her father's heart*

Lucien closed the book with care and placed it back on the shelf as an image of little Meg, with her dark ringlets bouncing as she skipped through a meadow picking flowers, drifted across his mind.

"So you cook, then?"

"I experiment," he clarified.

"Where? In the dungeons of Caliburn Keep?"

His mouth twitched at the teasing edge in her tone. "In the old buttery. And the former great hall beside it has an inglenook hearth that most closely resembles the kitchen depicted in one of the book's illuminations."

"Ah. So you are trying to preserve the integrity and authenticity of the recipes."

"Always."

"And, as I recall, you wear an apron, too."

He straightened. "A blacksmith's apron."

"In other words, a man's apron," she said, her tone mockingly severe. "And you likely use a large hammer to roll out pastry dough for the pies."

When she pantomimed swinging her fist in a downward arc onto an imaginary table, he crossed his arms. "Are you enjoying yourself?"

"Immensely." She flashed her teeth in a smile. "So tell me, was that the reason you were covered in soot that day? Because you were baking, and everything went up in smoke?"

He took a step toward her. "One more word out of you and I'm going to toss you over my shoulder and—"

"And?" she challenged saucily with her hands already on her hips.

"Put you on the roasting spit as my next experiment."

She laughed gaily. "Try it and you'll find yourself knocked over the head with a fire poker."

"It might be worth it," he said with a grin of his own before he turned and resumed his search.

Beside him, she leaned her back against the shelves. "Have you had any success with your attempts?"

"Do you mean, have they proven beyond a shadow of a doubt that they can imbue a man with the strength of a great beast? Make his enemy's heart falter? Compel him to reveal his deepest, darkest secrets?"

When she nodded, he considered just shaking his head and leaving it at that. But for some reason, he decided to tell her the truth.

"I'd thought so," he said. "It was actually on the day we met. I had just eaten a sample of the latest experiment, and then I saw you in the corridor. I felt a surge, something predatory, rise inside me."

"I remember when I was putting on your glasses that your breath tasted like spices—cinnamon and clove." She inhaled deeply as if she were there in the corridor, with him, once more.

He nodded, transfixed by her rapt attention, her pupils expanding, her face tilted up to his. "Aware of these changes in my physiology, I left you so that I could describe the sensations in detail in my ledger."

"So you *did* believe in the legend."

"For a few days," he admitted. "Until I met you in Calais."

She frowned. "Are you now accusing me of ruining your experiment *and* your faith in your family legend, in addition to stealing your book?"

"Nothing like that," he said with a playful tug on her fingertips. "I knew it wasn't the recipe because, the instant you launched yourself at me and broke my spectacles, my physiological reaction was the same. Which led me to the conclusion that it was you all along. Just you."

A breath slowly slipped from her parted lips, and she searched his gaze for a long moment. "That might be the most romantic thing that any man has ever said to the woman he hates."

"I have my moments." He shrugged. Realizing that he was still holding her fingers in the clasp of his palm, he released her and cleared his throat. He needed to remember that it was far too easy to become distracted by her. Turning back toward the shelves, he said, "Now, where is my book hiding?"

She grumbled under her breath. "Fleeting moments, apparently."

After that, they resumed their search in tense silence. Nothing could be heard between them but the whisper of her skirts shifting as she moved, and the crisp rasp of the pages sliding against each other.

Then, after a while, he simply broke.

Lucien wasn't certain what drove him over the edge— whether it was her nearness, her scent filling his every breath or the accidental brush of their fingertips as they reached for the same spine—but he snapped.

"No more games, Meg. Just tell me where it is."

She sighed. "Believe me, I understand what this book means to you. It's your legacy. Your heritage—"

"No, you don't understand. You cannot. My parents died protecting this book."

She sobered at once, her exhaustion over the topic replaced by sympathy as she nodded. "Your sister told me."

"Did she also tell you that they died because of me?"

She flinched at the sound of his raised voice, her expression stricken as she moved a step closer to lay her hand on his arm.

He shrugged her off. "It was the middle of the night. I don't even know why I decided to go to the vault. Obsession? Mere curiosity? The desire to study the pages without anyone looking over my shoulder? I don't know." He raked a hand through his hair. "But I thought it was strange when I couldn't locate my key. I'd kept it safe in my room where no one could find it, just like my father had told me to do. And yet, it wasn't there. So I went downstairs to see if, perhaps, I'd left it behind."

He could remember every step he'd taken. The cold draft that blew through the corridors. The flickering shadows cast by the light from his chamberstick. The scent of someone's sweat, sharp and pungent as it hit the back of his tongue—the way an unbroken horse smelled before it was tamed for the bridle.

"And there was the key. It was hanging in the lock of the vault door, and I just stared at it, dumbfounded because I knew I hadn't been that foolish," he said, his voice sounding far away to his own ears. "Then everything happened at once. A suit of armor crashed to the floor. Two figures darted out of the shadows, pistols glinting. My parents shouted and—" He drew in a quick breath as the memory of the shot ringing out reverberated inside his mind. "It was over in the space of three heartbeats. I'd counted them. And then they were both on the floor."

The images faded, slinking back to the shadowy corners of his mind. He blinked and exhaled.

When the library came into focus, the morning light was almost too bright. "Don't you see, Meg? They were protecting the book. And I cannot live my life knowing that they died for nothing. I have to prove its validity."

She stared at him, her face stark and white, eyes filling with unshed tears. "Oh, Lucien. I didn't realize. I'm so sorry."

"How can you stand there and believe the words you're speaking when you are the one keeping that book from me?"

"But I'm not. I promise you, I'm not," she said, reaching for him yet again. He shrugged out of her grasp. She took in a shuddered breath, then turned to leave. But she paused to say, "They weren't protecting the book. They were protecting *you*. That's what a parent does for their child. They did that because they loved you. Not because they wanted you to be tied to the book instead of living your life."

She was wrong. He knew she was wrong.

But when she stepped away, he also knew he couldn't let her go. Not like this.

So he moved in front of her and took her hand, staying her. She lifted those liquid, questioning eyes as he cupped her face, wiping the dampness from beneath her lashes.

He swallowed, feeling like an arse. "I apologize. I don't usually lose my temper, and I won't make excuses. I just ask that you consider forgiving me for that outburst."

"You have every right to be angry . . . just not at me. No matter what you may think, I wouldn't keep it from you if I had it. Especially not after what you just told me. Surely, you don't think I'm that callous."

Damn it all. He knew she wasn't that cruel. She was playful and cunning, but never cruel. And yet, he knew that she was the last one to see the book. He'd been asleep when she'd left. Therefore, it had to have been her. There was no other logical explanation.

So then why was he suddenly filled with doubt?

He shook his head. "Don't go. It's better if you're here."

"What is?"

Everything was the immediate answer that an errant, misguided portion of his brain conjured. It irritated him that he couldn't rely on his own pia mater around her.

He left the word unspoken. Instead, he dropped his hands and lifted his shoulders in an offhanded shrug. "If you leave, I'll just have to follow to see what you're up to, and then it will take me twice as long to finish searching the library. And neither of us wants to delay my departure for longer than necessary."

Though, even as he made the final declaration, he wasn't altogether sure he believed it.

Chapter 25

A hard nut to crack

The following two days commenced much like the first.

Under duress, Meg escorted Lucien through the house to ensure the book was not there. The only problem was she was starting to enjoy his company again. In other words, she was sort of *over* her duress.

That worried her. The last thing she wanted was to open her heart to the Duke of Merleton once more.

She tried to distance herself, keeping to one side of the room while he occupied the other. But that invisible rope tied through her middle kept drawing her closer and closer until she'd often find herself gazing up into his smoky eyes and standing within arm's reach.

It was only a matter of time before one of them took the final step.

However, she was determined that *someone* would not be her.

She had given herself over to him before only because she'd been certain of her heart and his. But she'd lost her certainty, among other things, along the way, and she couldn't afford to make the same mistake without losing so much more.

Therefore, after dinner that evening, she excused herself. And she'd made a point of leaving before Sylvia could, which her aunt had done the past two evenings, leaving Meg and Lucien alone to linger over claret and conversation. Those evenings had become far too cozy.

On her own, she climbed the stairs to the nursery to check on Guinevere.

Peering into the room, she expected to see a little blonde head resting on a pillow. Instead, her daughter was wide awake and playing with her doll in the moonlight shining in through the window.

Meg tsked as she stepped inside, and her daughter giggled. "You are supposed to be asleep."

"No sweep." She shook her head, adamant. But her argument was somewhat diminished when she yawned and scrubbed a tiny fist against her eye.

"What about a story, then, my sweet?" she asked, and her daughter instantly dropped her head onto the pillow and hugged her doll close.

And Meg began. "Once upon a time . . ." Guinevere giggled again, kicking her feet happily beneath the coverlet ". . . there was a fair princess who lived in a grand house surrounded by beautiful gardens as far as the eye could see. She was loved by everyone who knew her. And the princess grew to be a strong, independent woman who lived a happy life without ever needing a charming prince at her side."

Meg tucked her daughter in with a kiss on the forehead. Yet, as she continued the story, she caught herself gazing wistfully out the window toward the moonlight, remembering another night with such a moon.

"But there were times," she said softly, "when the wind brought her the scents of fig trees and of grapes on a summer vine, or when the stars winked on a cloudless night, a small ache entered her heart. And in those moments, she caught herself yearning for a certain someone and wishing that . . ."

Meg couldn't finish that thought. Instead, she took a

slow, shuddering breath. "But, in the mornings, she always arose with new determination to live a happy life. The princess had her family, and they were all she truly needed."

Glancing down, she saw that Guinevere was fast asleep. So she pressed one more kiss to her forehead. But when she turned to leave, she found Lucien instead.

She startled, heart beating in a panic. And he was just standing there, shoulder propped casually against the doorframe.

Crossing the room at an agitated pace, she shooed him out of her way and he followed her into the corridor.

"What are you doing here?" she whispered, closing the door with a soft click.

"You're good with her," he said quietly, ignoring her question. "Ever thought about having one of your own? Not all princesses need to be strong, independent women, after all."

Seeing his smirk, she leveled him with a perturbed glare and started walking down the corridor. "Shouldn't you be at the bachelor's lodge by now?"

"I was given leave by your aunt to tour the gallery."

"Then, why aren't you there?"

His mouth twitched as if he enjoyed this testy side of her. "I must have taken a wrong turn."

"And two flights of stairs," she muttered, trying to outpace him, but it was futile. His legs were much longer than hers. Strong, too . . . with defined, lean muscles and dusted with crisp dark hair that had sent tingles over her skin when their legs had been intertwined . . .

She shook herself away from the memory, her hand splaying over that terrible tug in her midriff.

It was getting worse all the time.

His nearness was driving her mad, his scent invading her nostrils, his shoulders looking annoyingly fine in his coat. *Beneath it as well*, she remembered all too vividly. She caught herself looking at his hands—those strong, dexterous hands—throughout the day, half of her wary and half of her filled with anticipation, wondering when they might touch her again. He often did as if by accident, brushing against her just long enough to send shivers of need trampling through her. And there were times when she just wanted him to drag her into the nearest closet, lock the door and—

"*This* is the gallery," she said, interrupting her own dangerous thoughts. Stopping in the doorway, she gestured for him to proceed, then turned to leave.

But then his hand touched her wrist, fingers curling around her flesh just enough to halt her. Just enough to send her pulse skittering.

He looked down as if the contact surprised him as well, but he did not release her. His gentle clasp lingered, his fingertips brushing the harried pulse. When their eyes met, she saw his pupils expand, and the devil on her shoulder whispered the location of the nearest closet.

"Would you be willing to endure my company a few moments longer? After all, I should like to know about those who are in the portraits."

"Why?" she asked crossly, pulling free. "Trying to discover if I come from a long line of blackguards, knaves and swindlers?"

He raised his hands, palms facing her in surrender. "Nothing of the sort, I promise. I'm merely curious about your family. And I am a man who prefers to have a concrete picture in my mind when I hear you speak of them."

That much was true. Lucien preferred proof in all things.

Absently, she rubbed that place on her wrist and decided there wasn't any harm in such a request. So she relented and took him through the long, paneled room, introducing him to her family.

Stopping by a portrait of her great-great-great-grandmother, she told him of her eight children and wry sense of humor.

He looked at her curiously. "You speak as if you knew her."

"I feel as though I did," she admitted. "You see, she planted the orchard—plums, peaches, apples and pears. But through the diary she left, she confessed to being an abysmal gardener and was surprised every day when she didn't see a bunch of twigs standing in a row. She was also something of a scientist and cooked up batches of her experimental jams in the kitchens. One of her diary entries speaks of the Great Jam Disaster of 1682."

Glancing at the portrait again, his mouth curved into a grin. "I should have liked to meet her, too."

Meg nodded knowingly. "My father often said that the best way to honor those we've loved and lost is to speak of them as if they'd merely stepped out of the room for a moment, remembering the things that brought us smiles and laughter. Through the stories he told, I came to know my mother and grandparents, and their parents before them." She gestured to the portraits lining the wall. "Surely, even you can understand how important stories are."

"Is that a smirk, Miss Stredwick?"

Her brows lifted in an ambiguous arch, and they moved to the far end of the room, where there was a door leading onto the arched stone loggia. In the moonlight, the orchards in the distance looked like a small forest that had been planted in orderly rows.

When he was silent, she glanced at him to see that his expression softened. "We used to have troubadours at the festivals held at Caliburn Keep. They would play their citterns and sing songs of the old legends. The groomsmen would dress in armor and give out small wooden swords to the children. We even had a Lady of the Lake," he said with a wry laugh. "And a sword set in a stone to test a man's strength."

"You should host them again," she said, seeing his obvious fondness for those memories.

He slid her a look. "Difficult to do, considering I no longer have the one piece of history that links my family to any of it."

"And for the last time, I do not have your recipes," she said on a sigh.

He lifted his shoulders in an offhand shrug, their argument diminishing before there was any ire to ignite it.

Then they walked on, stopping at the portrait of Brandon, Ellie and their son.

Lucien's countenance formed that disapproving frown again. "Why isn't Guinevere in this portrait? And for that matter, why didn't your brother take her on his trip? I had thought, perhaps, that he might have deemed her to be too young and rambunctious. But from what I have seen, she's well-behaved. Never once in these days that you've brought her into the room with us has she had a tantrum or been anything other than inquisitive, which is the best quality any child could have."

There were two reasons that Meg had brought Guinevere along. One was simply because she desired to spend time with her daughter. And the other was that she was in desperate need of a chaperone—even a pint-sized one—to keep her from making the mistake of being too comfortable with Lucien.

But it only worked against her better intentions to see the two of them together and how patient he was with her.

Just today, while Meg and Lucien were perusing the shelves in Brandon's study, Guinevere had played on the floor with her doll. Tugging on Lucien's pantleg, she'd wanted to see the books, too. And so had her doll.

Instead of telling her *no,* or even explaining that none of them were filled with pictures, he'd simply asked which book she'd like to see. Then, after she'd pointed to one, he'd sat down in the chair with her and her doll propped on his lap, then began to read the very boring history of horticulture. But he'd spoken in a manner that had made every word sound like a fantastic story, filled with adventure.

He'd had Guinevere's rapt attention. And Meg's, too.

She'd found herself drawing closer, her hand resting over the back of the chair, her fingertips tingling with the need to smooth back the hank of hair that had fallen carelessly over his forehead.

Thankfully, the nurse had arrived just in time to put Guinevere down for her nap, saving Meg from accidentally giving in to temptation.

But before her daughter had left, she'd held up her doll for Lucien to kiss. And he had, without a moment's hesitation, bussing loudly enough to make Guinevere giggle.

And now, in addition to remembering how good it had felt to be with him in the past, Meg was starting to have visions of what a future might be like. And that, she knew, would never happen because she refused to risk her heart again.

If only that organ would cooperate.

"My brother isn't taking a holiday. He is helping the aunts ready their house to be let. Even though Crossmoor Abbey has been their primary residence since before my nephew was born, they hadn't officially decided to move in until this summer, and much to the dismay of their caretaker. The crotchety Mr. Bagdemus did not take the news well. In fact, rumor has it that he began telling people that they *up and died*. Isn't that simply dreadful? Well, I suppose he felt abandoned, the old dear. And it's clear that he'd grown quite fond of them . . ."

She realized she was rambling when Lucien's expression turned focused and assessing, in the way that it did when something just occurred to him. Not knowing what that might have been, she glanced at the portrait again.

But when her eyes drifted to the bronze placard on the wall, engraved with Brandon, Ellie and Johnathon's names and titles—*along with a very telling date!*—she jolted with alarm. And just in case Lucien hadn't noticed it, she stepped in front of the placard.

"As for Guinevere, I don't think she was born yet," she lied, quickly scratching her nose before she gestured to the waiting corridor. "And that was the gallery. I imagine you are eager to return to the lodge and prepare for the arrival of your cousin and sister tomorrow."

"Hullworth should have a new portrait painted with his *entire* family," Lucien said, pausing in the doorway, his brow notched with three vertical lines. "And your portrait should be beside his, along with your future husband and child, of course."

Her heart pinched. "I've told you before, my family only marries for the deepest, most enduring love. Every person in these portraits was certain beyond a shadow of a doubt that they were spending their lives with their soul's counterparts. And I will settle for nothing less."

"In other words, because your *Daniel Prescott*," he emphasized with a noticeable sneer, "was an idiot, you're choosing to spend the rest of your life alone?"

The ire, which had failed to ignite just a moment ago, suddenly flared.

"I don't see that it's any concern of yours."

He took a step toward her, his large form eclipsing the sconcelight. His eyes were volcanic, all simmering pupils behind those lenses. "Then, tell me, *ma petite louve*, who does the princess think of when she looks up at the stars and smells ripe figs and wine grapes in the air?"

"Not you, that's for certain." Her nose itched.

"Liar," he said, his breath brushing her lips as he lifted a hand and tenderly tucked a stray tendril behind her ear.

She made a strangled sound, curling her fingers into her

palms to keep herself from reaching out for him. Drat that man for having a slight smudge on his glasses, compelling her to rise on her toes, lean against him to take them off and . . .

The effort to keep still made her tremble. But she held firm. "Would the truth change anything between us?"

He studied her intently for a moment—eyes, lips, flushed cheeks—and she could see him calculating every possibility, every outcome.

"No," he said at last. "There would still be something between us. I fear that fact will always remain unchanged."

She had a sense that he was talking about something far more intimate than the book, and the way he looked at her caused her womb to clench, her knees quaking with longing.

But in the end, he dropped his hand, turned and walked away. And she told herself that it was the best outcome for both of them.

Chapter 26

Just desserts

The following morning, Lucien was in a foul temper, unable to resolve the conflicts warring within him.

Trust her—don't trust her.

Leave—don't leave.

Search for the book elsewhere—stay here with her.

These opposing schools of thought were threatening to rip him in half.

If that wasn't bad enough, there was something else wrong with him, too. He felt sluggish and muddled whenever he was in the bachelor's quarters. But as soon as his steps crossed the threshold of the main house, his senses became alert and keen. Almost painfully so. Colors were too bright. Aromas too potent. And when he was alone in one of the rooms he was searching, he would swear that he could hear Meg moving around in the nursery, even when there were several floors between them.

It was utter madness.

After all, why should he have cared that Meg's portrait wasn't hanging in the gallery? Why should he have felt a sudden flare of anger at the mention of Daniel Prescott?

Lucien knew Prescott was no longer in her life. He'd investigated the man two years ago and discovered that he was cousin to the Earl of Edgemont, a peer who'd never indicated a desire for power or political gain or whatever else the person who'd stolen the recipes might have wanted. Then Lucien's investigator tracked Mr. Prescott to Upper Canada, where Meg had said he'd gone. By all appearances, their relationship had been just as she'd said, and it had nothing to do with the book.

So then why did Lucien want to murder the man for breaking her heart? Or was it the fact that he'd stolen her heart in the first place that bothered him more?

He growled as he strode up the lane, his hessians kicking up dust along the way. He hated this constant battle. It was far worse than a failed experiment. At least then he had detailed notes to decipher what had gone wrong.

His path led him to the stables where he came each morning. In his current mood, he decided that a much longer ride for exercise was in order. He was always plagued by the sensation that something was familiar to him. Logically, he knew that couldn't be the case so he shrugged it off.

Today, however, he suddenly understood why. He looked at the stablemaster and recognized him, though he couldn't recall from where or when. It could have been any number of places over the years. Even at Caliburn Keep.

Lucien's suspicions sparked, and he decided to have his driver make a few discreet inquiries into this man's history.

In the meantime, he needed to expend as much tension as possible. He and Meg were performing a search of the attic later, and he knew from previous experience that resisting her in a confined space was nearly impossible.

IT WAS stifling in the attic that afternoon, and Meg was having a difficult time keeping on task.

Her chemise and pink muslin were constantly clinging, much like his shirtsleeves. She tried not to stare at him without his coat. But with his sleeves rolled up to the elbow, it was impossible not to watch the movement of those corded forearms that had first taken her fancy.

Lucien had a restless aggressive manner about him today. He was very physical, always shifting crates, stacking boxes, lifting heavy portmanteaus, his muscles undulating, straining, rippling . . .

She suspected he was the one making it hotter up here. So hot she could hardly think.

These days spent with him were leaving her frayed, like a shawl only one stitch away from unraveling completely. The air was forever charged, prickling with heat—either from their mutual animosity or mutual desire, she didn't know which.

What she did know, however, was that her own animosity wasn't what propelled her into dreams of him every night.

Such wicked, scandalous dreams.

Throat dry as parchment, she took another glass of the lemonade that the maid had brought earlier, drinking it down in thirsty gulps. Over the rim, she saw him watching her and the way his biceps flexed when he wiped the back of his hand against his brow.

When some of the tart juice dribbled on her chin, she caught it with her fingertips, pressing them to her lips to sip the droplets from her skin.

He growled at her for no reason at all. "Are you trying to torment me?"

"I don't know what you could mean. I was merely thirsty," she said primly as she set the glass back on the tray and smoothed her damp palms over the clinging waist of her skirts.

His gaze missed nothing. "And you drank the last of it, I see."

"I could fetch more. It would only take a moment."

He arched a dubious brow. "I've come to discover that *a moment* for you is an indefinite amount of time."

She set her hands on her hips, the air between them crackling with swift-igniting tension. "And just what is that supposed to mean?"

"Only that you're very good at leaving." He closed the lid of a trunk with decided force. The hollow thunk reverberated along the low, arched ceiling.

"Is this about Italy?"

"Of course this is about Italy," he said as if she were a simpleton and made a sweeping gesture to encompass everything around them.

She growled and marched across the attic floor, finger pointed. "I left a note and you bloody well know it! Not to mention the numerous letters I sent to you in Somerset."

"*Letters*," he scoffed.

"It's true. I wrote to you for two years—two whole years—until I decided to hate you instead. Now I'm tired of your accusations, your incessant poking and prodding, and I demand that you leave here at—"

She tripped over a blue hatbox. And the lid jarred loose, snagging the toe of her slipper. She stumbled. Momentum propelled her forward, one-footed and tilting, her arms flailing for balance, graceful as a dodo.

He caught her full-on, chest to chest.

His hands settled on her waist, his gaze on her lips. "If you think that I'm foolish enough to be pulled into your web of seduction a second time, think again."

"I wouldn't allow you into my . . . web even if you begged me!"

Her declaration might have held more weight if she didn't immediately rise onto her toes, take his head in her hands and crush her mouth to his.

He responded instantly. Taking hold of her nape, he slanted his mouth over hers on a greedy, satisfied grunt.

That instant flame of desire sparked to life again as if it had been waiting beneath a curfew all this time and only needed one hot breath to ignite it. His form was so firm and lean, and she fit against him perfectly.

They consumed each other, with lips and teeth and groping hands. Like ravenous animals, they licked into each other's mouths, fists curled in each other's hair and clothes.

Picking her up with one arm around her waist, he carried her to a narrow trestle table against the wall. He sent boxes crashing to the floor, then set her on the edge and stepped between her ruckled skirts, his mouth never leaving hers. When his hips bumped hers and a sound—something between a sigh and exultant cry—rose up inside her, he swallowed it down on a guttural growl.

She clung to him, hips arching, desperate to ease the burning ache thudding in heavy liquid pulses between them. He pressed against her, a slow, thick grind that made her shudder.

"I still think about that night." His tongue dipped into the shallow valley at the base of her throat. "The way we fit together, moved together. Do you remember?"

"Yes," she rasped, her head falling back, neck arching. She felt a rough tug at the cap sleeves of her dress, the sudden relief of seams rending, and then his mouth closing over her breast. *Yes.*

Her fingers threaded into his hair, molding over his scalp to hold him close as he drew the ripe peak into his mouth. He suckled her flesh in deep pulls, her body clenching, warm and wet.

He looked up at her as he licked the perspiration from between her breasts. "I'm going to take you. But it's going to be hard and fast the first time. Slow later."

She nodded, shifting restlessly as he stood between her thighs and lifted her hem higher, his fingertips on the bare skin above her stockings. That heavy pulse thrummed hotter, more insistent.

It was taking forever for him to touch her.

"Hurry," she said, fumbling with the fastenings of his trousers, her hands shaking.

He stilled her efforts.

"Let me touch you. I need to please you first because"—he cursed under his breath as he cupped her sex, the linen drawers damp between them—"I'm not going to last. I'm almost over the edge."

She agreed. This was no time to argue, after all.

He found the slit in her drawers and her eyes closed on the sweet ache as a ragged breath fell from her parted lips. Oh, how she wanted this. And so did he. His desire was so potent, she felt the tremor of his fingertips as he sifted through her curls and heard it in his rough murmur of approval at finding her drenched for him. And it only took his deft slide along the swollen cleft to circle the tender bud once—*twice*—before his name came out on a sigh. *Lucien.*

"Not *too* quick," she begged as he circumnavigated again.

He nudged her entrance with the blunt tip of his middle finger, then sucked in a breath as he pushed inside the tight constriction. "*Damn.* I cannot . . . promise anything . . ."

She completely understood. Blindly, she took hold of his wrist, feeling tendons and muscles shifting beneath her grip as he edged inside. Garbled sounds left her with every thrust. And when he added a second finger, wordless pleas were followed by ecstatic exclamations as he drove deeper, his palm rotating against that frenzied pulse.

"Shh . . ." he whispered in her ear, going still. "I think I hear someone on the stairs."

No sooner had he spoken than Aunt Sylvia called out, "Meg? Are you up here?"

Her eyes flew open. And she felt him stiffen, still inside her, with her body clamped tightly around his fingers. He looked over his shoulder to the mountain of crates between them and the stairs before he spoke.

"It's Lucien, my lady," he said. "I believe Miss Stredwick went down to the kitchen for more lemonade."

The footsteps fell silent on the stairs. Every movement paused—even their own. Though, it was clear that neither of them wanted to stop. He hadn't moved away from the welcome of her hips, and she was still holding on to his wrist.

What if they were caught like this. What would she say to her aunt?

Lucien was just handing me down from the table. This is how it's done on the Continent.

Um . . . no. She'd never believe that.

Then, perhaps, if Meg incorporated a bit of truth: *You see, there was this hatbox, and I stumbled toward the table, and at the very last moment, Lucien was kind enough to . . . slip his hand beneath my skirts to ensure that I was unharmed . . .*

No. That wouldn't do either.

He was saving me from a spider?

Erection? What erection?

Nervous, Meg licked her lips and saw his gaze darken. His hand twitched, fingers shifting, flexing inside her. Her breath fractured in response, and he silently quieted her with a kiss against her lips.

But the contact only made her body more eager, her walls issuing an encouraging squeeze. And even though she couldn't think of a single excuse to prepare for the possibility of discovery, she still couldn't force herself to stop.

"Very well. I shall look for her there," Sylvia replied, and Meg's shoulders sagged with relief. "However, if you should see her first, please inform her that she has a guest. A Mr. Daniel Prescott. I'm sure she'll wish to be forewarned."

As the footsteps retreated, so did Lucien. And from his suddenly stony gaze, she felt as if she'd been doused in cold water.

Slipping down from the table on unsteady legs, she attempted to put her clothes in order. Of course, there was nothing she could do with the torn sleeve. Her hair was in complete disarray, her skin flushed. Disheveled as she was, she likely looked like she'd been in a battle with a wild animal.

She noted that he hadn't bothered to turn away but faced her with his arms crossed, his expression unfoundedly suspicious.

"What?" she asked, seating a hairpin in place. "It isn't as if I've invited him."

"I thought he lived in Upper Canada."

"Well, apparently, he's back in England," she rifled back with equal terseness. After all, he wasn't the only one leaving this room unfulfilled.

In response, he growled and snatched his coat in his fist before he tromped down the stairs.

Well, if he wanted to be in a snit, perhaps she would have to give him a reason.

With one last shake of her wrinkled skirts and hopeless flick of her floppy sleeve, she stormed downstairs, too.

Drat you, Daniel Prescott, she thought on a huff. *Why were you never around when I needed you, but suddenly here when I do not?*

Chapter 27

A bitter pill to swallow

Lucien wasn't about to walk all the way to Stredwick Lodge for a fresh change of clothes before meeting the infamous Daniel Prescott. The man was a veritable legend, according to Meg. So he donned his coat, straightened his sleeves, jerked at the hem of his waistcoat, then went directly to introduce himself to this *paragon* who'd first captured Meg's fancy.

"How good of you to come down to meet our guest," Sylvia said when he stepped into the parlor. "Lucien, this is Mr. Prescott, an old family friend of Brandon and Meg's. And Daniel, this is the Duke of Merleton, who is staying at Stredwick Lodge for a time."

That was his introduction? Lucien thought he deserved more than being essentially labeled a tenant. A squatter. Considering his activities a few minutes ago, he should be addressed as an intimate family friend at the very least.

Nevertheless, he inclined his head to the younger man. Prescott sketched a bow in return, offering a prolonged view of the top of his head, his hair the color of camel dung, seemingly tousled with pomade to resemble a bird's nest.

At a glance, he knew this man was the dramatic type who likely spent hours every day waxing poetic and filling the room with pretty words without ever really having anything to say.

And Meg had lost her heart to *him*?

"By the by, Lucien," Sylvia said, sidling up to him, "did you happen to see my niece, after all? She wasn't in the kitchens. One of the scullery maids was sure she'd gone to the attic."

Ah, the attic. The mere mention of it made his pulse quicken. "I believe she is in her rooms, freshening up for her unexpected guest."

Sylvia stared at him for a moment as if bemused by his crisp articulation of the last five syllables. Briefly, he wondered if he should repeat himself. Perhaps add the word *unwelcome* to the mix?

But then she smiled. "Yes, of course. I'll just run and see if she requires my assistance. Gentlemen, I'll leave you to become better acquainted."

Lucien moved deeper into the room but remained standing near the settee, which had a closer proximity to the door.

Prescott also remained on his feet, the nest listing with curiosity. "Lady Hullworth didn't mention how you know the family."

"I went to school with her son. And I've known Hullworth for a number of years as well."

"Then, you are not acquainted with Miss Stredwick."

"I am, actually," he said simply. Quite well, in fact.

"Strange, I never heard her mention you. Must be a recent acquaintance, then."

Lucien offered a patient smile. "She mentioned you, however."

Prescott's eyes brightened. "Did she?"

"Weren't you the man who jilted her?" He watched with a degree of satisfaction as those eyes dimmed.

"I suppose you could say that. But her brother and I were of the same opinion—that she was simply too young to know her own mind. We thought it best that she should have a Season or two to understand more of the world."

"And what were her thoughts on the matter?"

Prescott blinked. "I'm afraid I don't catch your meaning."

"Correct me if I'm wrong"—which, of course, he wasn't—"but wasn't it *her* future the two of you were deciding?"

"I suppose it might be misconstrued in such a way. But we had her best interests in mind. And she hadn't yet lived. Not really. Nearly her entire life had been spent beneath this roof, and before that in a small parish up north at her father's estate, which was near my own. You might say we've always been part of the same family."

Lucien pursed his lips thoughtfully. "Hmm . . . I don't believe that *one who lives on a neighboring estate* is the correct definition for *family*. One must be related either by blood or marriage. And I believe you married someone else, didn't you?"

"Well, yes. However, my intention had always been to wait for her."

Lucien knew a good deal about waiting *and* craving.

Yet, as far as he was concerned, running off to marry the first woman to come along was neither of those things. If Meg had meant anything to this man, he would have been too consumed with desire for her to want anyone else.

"Intentions, I find, are a man's greatest weakness if he cannot rise to the challenge of fulfilling them," Lucien said.

Prescott didn't seem to know how to respond to that. He opened his mouth, then closed it several times. But then his eyes cleared, brightening again as he looked toward the archway and smiled broadly.

Lucien didn't need to follow the gaze to know that it was Meg. He felt his skin react, covering in gooseflesh, tightening over his skeleton.

He turned to greet her . . . only to have her sweep right

by him as she bustled into the room with a happy "Daniel!" on her lips.

Lucien bristled. As he raked a hand through his hair, he caught a faint fragrance—a combination of salt and the earthy sweetness of musk—and knew at once what it was. *Her scent.* It lingered on his hand, on his skin. Utterly intoxicating. And it filled him with a surge of primitive pleasure to recall that it hadn't been *Daniel* on her lips a few moments ago.

No, indeed. It had been *Lucien.*

Even if their brief encounter had been due to the heat of the moment, it was clear that there was still something palpable between them. Something that required further study. *Without* any unwanted interference.

"I'm so glad to see you again," she said, coming forward to take both of his hands in hers for a moment as she smiled. When Lucien growled, she cast an arched look over her shoulder and then back to *Daniel.* "You were introduced to Merleton, were you not?"

"Indeed," Prescott said sitting in one of the armchairs. "We've been having a nice chat between gentlemen."

"Have you?" she asked and lowered to the settee cushion. She looked to Lucien and wordlessly indicated that he should sit as well, her pointed gaze directing him to the chair at the far end of the grouping.

Seeing this for the challenge it was, he took the other cushion of the settee, then rested his arm along the curved, filigreed back. Her spine stiffened, and she primly rested her folded hands on her lap, as if pretending that those very hands hadn't just been fumbling with the fastenings of his trousers.

He smiled and nodded in response to her query. "In fact, we were just coming to the subject of Mr. Prescott's marriage to another woman."

"Well, it wasn't precisely on that topic," Prescott hemmed, sitting opposite Meg.

"No? Then, what were we discussing? Ah, yes, I remember. You intended to wait for Miss Stredwick but were unable, due to reasons beyond your control."

Meg shot him a warning look. "I'm sure Mr. Prescott can speak for himself."

Lucien lifted his shoulders in a shrug of innocence.

"Merleton is more correct than he likely realizes," Prescott said. "There were circumstances beyond my control. Or so I believed. But oh, how I wish I'd listened to you, my darling Meg—forgive me, Miss Stredwick. You were always so certain that we were meant to be, you and I." He flicked a petulant sneer to Lucien before he continued. "But in my efforts to ensure that you had all the experiences that you deserved before marrying, I found myself in a position to help another young woman out of the jaws of destitution. It was a chance meeting, or so I thought. And you know enough of my regrets for past selfishness—and my subsequent wishes to make amends for the errors of my ways—to understand that I could not have lived with myself if I'd knowingly allowed her to suffer such agony when I had the power to help."

"Such a paragon," Lucien muttered under his breath.

Though, Meg must have heard him, because her shoulders bunched, hackles rising, and she expelled a taut sigh. "Let's not talk about it. Besides, all that truly matters is that you are happy."

Prescott suddenly stood, then took the chair closest to her, sitting forward with his forearms braced on his knees. "That is why I came here to talk to you. I am ashamed to admit that I was duped by Dolores. I thought she loved me. I truly did. Otherwise, I never would have . . ." He gazed at her beseechingly. "I'd have waited for you. But I recently discovered that she was already married. Her husband came and together, they left . . . along with every farthing I put in a separate account for her."

"Daniel, I'm so sorry." She leaned forward to take his hand in comfort.

Lucien stared, incredulous. After all this man had put her through—breaking her heart, leaving her to turn to a life of subterfuge and seduction, causing her to doubt her own beliefs—and she was still compelled to soothe him? The man was nothing more than an infantile idiot!

"Didn't you know anything about your wife before you married her?"

Meg shot a glare over her shoulder. "Not everyone needs to compile research, Merleton. Some are led by their hearts."

"Instead of their minds, apparently," he muttered.

Then, too agitated to listen to any more of this sitting down, he stood and skulked to the window.

"But if Dolores was already married, then your union could not be legally binding," she said, and Lucien's shoulders stiffened.

"You are quite right," Prescott said. "My solicitor is doing all he can. Then, I will be free to move on . . . hopefully to a happier and brighter future. This was all just a bit of bad luck."

Lucien gritted his teeth. The man believed in fate, chance *and* luck. No wonder Meg had been drawn to him. It was as though she'd molded him out of clay to be her ideal husband.

But Lucien would never be that man. He needed proof, certainty and trust. Things only attained after careful consideration, investigation and research. He'd already put aside his doubts and leapt into the unknown once, and he'd been burned because of it. He'd be a fool if he did that again.

So then, why was he so tempted to be that fool?

Just a bit of bad luck . . .

Meg's intention, in coming in here all smiles and warmth, was to dust off her inner Lady Avalon and show a certain duke that he wasn't the only man in her life. No, indeed. She had Daniel. And she had hoped to paint a portrait of enviable options.

Unfortunately, Daniel was making it all rather difficult by droning on and on about his wife.

"And now you've been to Upper Canada," she said cheerfully, trying to alter the topic. "You know, I've never crossed the Atlantic, but I've always imagined it would be quite thrilling."

Daniel released her hands to pull on his neckcloth, his expression turning a bit green. "Not for me. Seasick the whole way. Both times."

She repressed a desire to roll her eyes. "What a shame."

"On the bright side, I'm here to stay."

He held her gaze in a way that used to make her heart flutter. Now it did nothing more than make her aware of the utilitarian qualities of the blood-pumping organ beneath her breast. It tha-thumped as expected. And she was still alive. *Thank you, unfluttering heart.*

But she wanted more.

"Once everything is settled," Daniel continued, "I'll be ready to begin a new life."

She heard a growl from Lucien's quarter, and her heart responded instantly, pattering away like a herd of eager puppies all begging to have their bellies rubbed. It meant nothing, of course. But then a brief vision of herself, panting and rolling onto her back for him, flashed in her mind, and her pulse thudded hard and fast, calling her a liar. *Down, girl!*

It was best not to entertain those thoughts.

Thankfully, Aunt Sylvia arrived just then with a maid in tow. They both carried a tray, one with tea and the other with lemonade. And Meg took one glance at the latter beverage and blushed. Would she ever see lemonade without being reminded of those sweltering few moments with Lucien?

He seemed to share her thoughts because, when Sylvia

asked which one he would prefer, he looked directly at Meg and said, "I have a partiality for lemonade. There never seems to be enough to quench my thirst."

Meg swallowed, feeling rather parched herself.

But no! It was best to put that out of her mind. The episode in the attic had been a moment of insanity. She hadn't even been thinking of the consequences. And if she knew Lucien as well as she thought she did, then he wouldn't think twice about her when it was time to leave after he finally realized she didn't have the book, after all.

Fortunately for her, this time Daniel came to her wayward mind's rescue when he began relaying his sad tale once more for Aunt Sylvia's sake.

And Meg did feel sorry for him. She could see the pain in his eyes, and the humiliation. The Daniel she knew wouldn't have rushed into marriage unless he'd been head over heels in love. And she understood, firsthand, how much agony he must have suffered by Dolores's betrayal.

Not because of the heartache that he'd put her through but from the despair she'd experienced after losing Lucien.

She knew that she had truly loved Lucien, but not Daniel.

She'd been fond of him, of course, but more as a friend. Nothing compared to the overwhelming and all eclipsing love she'd felt for Lucien. Those feelings, unfortunately, had left an indelible mark upon her soul. They still lingered inside her, whether she wanted them to or not.

But Daniel's sudden hindsight revelation brought her to an epiphany of her own.

She wanted a love that could stand the test of time. To be the one woman whom a man would wait for, no matter who came along to tempt him. She wanted him to look at her with the same soul-deep certainty that she felt and to know that they were meant to be together. Not because he was heartbroken and she seemed like a convenient option, but because she was inconvenient and confounding and no matter how hard he tried to fight it, he couldn't stop himself from loving her.

Yes! That was precisely what she wanted.

When she looked at Lucien, she noticed that he was already gazing back at her, his expression unreadable. Then, setting down his empty glass on a pie-crust table, he stepped forward and adjusted his spectacles as if he were about to say something.

Before he could speak, however, the sound of a carriage's approach drew their attention to the open window.

"Do you think it could be Brandon, Ellie and little Johnathon?" Aunt Sylvia asked, rising from her chair.

Lucien parted the curtains to allow Meg a glimpse as she came up beside him. "I believe that is my cousin's carriage."

Peering out the window, she felt a twinge of alarm rising inside her as the landau approached. His cousin and half sister were here? She'd been so distracted of late that their potential arrival had slipped her mind. And now she was left to wonder if they would mention meeting her on holiday.

Oh, but they would. There was no way around it. Then her secret would come out, and her entire family would soon know the truth. All of it.

No sooner had the thought formed before she felt the light, reassuring clasp of Lucien's hand. Wordlessly, she looked up at him, and he nodded, promising in his unspoken communication to take care of everything.

She squeezed his hand in return and regretted the moment she had to let go.

🦋

Lord Holladay smiled the instant he clapped eyes on Meg. Ignoring Lucien's summons, he handed his hat and gloves to Mr. Tidwell and strode across the foyer to bow to her. "Well, aren't you a sight for sore eyes. And I must say that mine are aching. Cousin Medusa over there has been trying to turn me to stone since we left Somerset."

Morgan, who was engaged in a hushed conversation with her maid, did not hear the teasing remark or likely would have sent a jab in return.

"It is good to see you again, Lord Holladay," Meg said with genuine warmth.

"That's Pell to you. We're old friends, after all. Though it's been an age, to be sure. Haven't seen you since—"

"London," Lucien interjected, setting a hand on his shoulder. "We haven't met *Miss Stredwick* since we were all in London, years ago."

The viscount tilted his head at first, but after following his cousin's pointed glance up to where Sylvia stood at the top of the stairs, his eyes widened in swift understanding.

Seeing that her aunt had been delayed by Daniel, Meg wondered what they were talking about. And yet, at present, she didn't want to think about it.

"Ah, yes," Pell offered. "I remember it well. You were there and so was I, along with a monkey in a feathered turban and—*No*?" he asked when Meg shook her head on a reluctant laugh. He hadn't changed a bit. "Oh, wait. That might have been another year. Hmm. Perhaps my cousin would be so good as to refresh my memory?"

Lucien offered a succinct nod. "Later. For now, I must have a private word with my sister."

Before he could step away, Meg reached out and touched his sleeve. "Thank you, for everything."

"Everything?"

She took one look at the dark brow arching over the rim of his spectacles, at the heat simmering in his gaze, and suddenly her thoughts were transported back to the attic. Her cheeks heated. And she was just about to clarify before he interjected with "My pleasure."

Then he had the audacity to walk away before she could take it back. How dare he!

"I see you and my cousin are still getting along as usual."

She heaved out a frustrated sigh. "Yes. We are a pair of feral cats tied in a bag. At least, until he realizes that I don't have the book and decides to leave."

"Well, between you and me, I'd prefer it if he stayed a bit longer. This is the most relaxed I've seen him in eons. Do you know that he hasn't been home for more than a day or two in the past two years? He's always off, chasing one rumor after another, searching for the book. Searching for you."

Meg glanced to where Lucien was talking with his sister and felt her heart pinch. All those days spent away from a home that he loved so much must have been unbearable at times.

She thought again about all the letters she'd sent. "Who sees to Caliburn Keep when he's away?"

"Morgan enjoys her position as reigning queen of the castle. However, his steward sees to minutiae of maintaining the accounts, upkeep, correspondence . . . all those trivial matters," he said with a shrug. Then he leaned in and, with his teasing voice, asked, "Do I detect a note of concern on his behalf?"

She forced out a papery laugh. "That would be quite silly, wouldn't it?"

"Wouldn't it, indeed?" Pell's astute gaze glinted in the sunlight streaming in through the windows.

Meg made no comment.

Chapter 28

Bubbling over

Lucien didn't want to leave Meg in the company of Daniel Prescott the following day.

Clearly, he was up to something. What other reason could he have had for privately conferring with Sylvia yesterday?

Given his history for deciding Meg's future for her, he was likely attempting to do the same. Not only that but exactly nine times during dinner last night he had mentioned his plans to return for another visit in a month.

Of course, none of it mattered to Lucien. Meg could look after herself, as she was so fond of reminding him. And yet, after hearing Mr. Prescott drone on and on this morning about receiving an invitation to breakfast at the main house, it took every ounce of Lucien's control not to do something that would wipe the smug grin off his face.

In the span of a single second, he'd calculated seventeen delay tactics, nine methods of imprisonment and three accidental deaths that Prescott might encounter on the way up the lane to the abbey.

Instead of deploying any of those, however, Lucien had merely grunted a sound of indifference and set off for the stables with Pell.

A short while later, they stopped their mounts on a hill overlooking the countryside. A cooling breeze drifted over the dew-dappled grasses, but the air was already thick and humid. It was going to be another scorching day.

The promise of rain had been lingering for the past few days, with a heaviness in the air and red bands of clouds streaking across the horizon. But instead of lifting, the pressure only seemed to build, much like his foul mood.

"'Tis a fine prospect, I suppose," Pell said from atop a sorrel mare beside him, "if your course runs to quaint country cottages in honey-colored stone. A trifle too bucolic for my tastes. Fairly screams of leg shackles and a wife, a dozen children and chickens in the stable yard."

Distracted, Lucien frowned in confusion at the mention of chickens. "What are you talking about?"

"I thought we were searching for a property for you and your lady? One close to her family, since you seem quite protective of them all of a sudden."

"Simply because I asked you and Morgan not to mention meeting Meg on the Continent is no indication that I am trying to shield her or her family. There are many logical reasons for keeping our previous acquaintance a secret."

Pell's tawny brows inched higher. "And those are?"

"First of all—" Lucien stopped. "Any idiot could parse out all the benefits of remaining in good standing as a guest."

He had pulled them aside shortly after their arrival to mention the need for discretion and pretending that they had met in London years ago, instead. At the time, neither his cousin nor his sister had questioned this decision. He'd thought they simply understood that it was the only way to continue searching for the book. And that, by being cordial, there was a greater likelihood of discovering the information he needed to uncover the identity of the other persons involved in the theft.

The only problem was Lucien wasn't sure that there was anyone else involved. Not only that, but he was starting to have his doubts that she had anything to do with it either.

There were just little things here and there, snippets of conversations, mentions of her family and upbringing, as well as his own recollections of their tour of the Continent. Nothing that provided irrefutable proof. And yet, compiled, it all made her seem rather . . . innocent.

This altered perspective meant nothing, of course, he told himself. An intelligent man was able to weigh both sides of an argument and entertain many schools of thought without being persuaded one way or the other. Therefore, any misgivings he had about her culpability were merely part of the analytical process.

"So it's *Meg* now, is it?" Pell asked. "I'm not certain Mr. Prescott would like to hear that."

"Mr. Prescott is welcome to apply the fixed, corded braiding of hemp fibers to his cervical vertebrae and descend from a platform at a rapid rate of speed."

Pell blinked in confusion. Then after a moment, he threw back his head and laughed. "Did you just say that Prescott could go hang himself?"

Lucien wiped his spectacles on his sleeve and carefully resituated them. "I did, indeed."

"You're jealous, old chap! Bloody hell, it's finally happened."

His cousin's endless amusement was exhausting, and he rolled his eyes as he waited for it to end. "Are you quite finished? There is no cause for your jocular barking. I am not jealous of Mr. Prescott. I knew of her regard for him from the beginning. You've misconstrued my reaction. I'm merely dumbfounded by the fact that she could hold such an idiot in high esteem."

"You're in love with her."

Lucien startled. The horse whickered, shifting restlessly beneath him.

Looking away from his cousin, he leaned forward and rubbed a soothing hand down the stallion's sleek black neck. "I am not predisposed to unquantifiable romantic sentiment. You should know that by now."

"Ah. Then, I don't suppose it would bother you that I overheard him talking to Lady Hullworth about taking a property nearby." When Lucien's mount shifted again and pawed the ground, Pell gave him a sideways glance, his mouth curved in a smirk. "Looks like your horse needs a bit more exercise. Care for a race?"

"To the victor, the spoils," Lucien answered. "First one back to the house wins."

Then without hesitation, he spurred the stallion, tearing up the earth beneath them.

And during the return ride, he came to one conclusion: he would sooner buy every property in Wiltshire before he would permit Mr. Prescott within a hundred miles of Meg.

🦋

NEEDING TO clear her head after her talk with Daniel, Meg went to the morning room to catch up on her correspondence. She had a heap of letters from friends and family to answer.

Ever since Brandon had married Ellie, Meg had not only gained a sister-in-law but had also been generously welcomed into the fold of *her* dearest friends. Among those were Winn, Viscountess Hunt; Jane, Viscountess Northcott; and Prue, the Marchioness of Savage, each of them strong, capable women who knew their own minds and precisely what they wanted out of life.

Meg envied that. At one time, she had also shared that sense of certainty but learned that it was pointless if only one party desired a future together.

And now? Well, she was more conflicted than ever.

Woolgathering over a blank page, she heard the heavy thundering of hooves, fast approaching. Looking out the window toward the stable yard, she saw that it was Lucien, apparently returning from a morning ride.

The black stallion's barreled lungs expanded, his coat glossy from sweat, and he shook his mane in a way that Meg knew he was content after a good ride. Dismounting, Lucien patted him fondly.

Then Viscount Holladay rode up. Stopping his mare, he pointed crossly and said something that made Lucien laugh. She felt her own cheeks lift in a smile.

Somewhere along the way, he'd lost his hat, his hair tousled. The sight of it made her fingers tingle and curl around the pen in her grasp. She entertained the brief fantasy of what it would be like to ride with him, racing hard and fast across the countryside, and return to the stables, disheveled and perspiring, her hands reaching up to set him back to rights . . .

"Have you seen my brother, Miss Parrish?"

Meg startled away from her ruminations and glanced over her shoulder. "Oh, good morning, Lady Morgan."

"Forgive me, I meant to say Miss Stredwick, of course," she said, misunderstanding the reason for Meg's guilty surprise. "Such a fun little charade we're having."

Her green eyes glinted like a cat who'd spotted an opening in the aviary and planned to eat every finch in sight.

"I appreciate that you didn't mention where we'd actually met," Meg said.

"Think nothing of it." She flitted her fingers as she sauntered into the room, giving the bric-a-brac on the tables a cursory perusal. "Although, I do wonder at the reason for such secrecy. Surely, the Dowager Lady Hullworth knew that you were bound to make acquaintances abroad. One might even think she would be thrilled to have a niece who'd spent so much time in the company of a duke. Unless, of course, it was because of all those days and weeks spent with my brother . . ."

As the words hung in the air, Meg's heart lurched. Her stomach churned as she thought about Guinevere and how her own gargantuan secret seemed to be teetering on the head of a pin.

". . . that you now regret the association," Morgan continued after a weighted pause. Then she pursed her lips. "And here I was so looking forward to becoming your friend."

Meg expelled a sigh of relief, her fear of discovery abated for the moment. But she knew it was only a matter of time. She would have to tell Lucien soon, whatever the consequences might be.

"There is nothing to prevent us from becoming friends. I do not regret the association at all. It's only that"—she swallowed, hating all these lies upon lies—"I don't want my aunt to have any grand notions that there is anything between the duke and me."

Lady Morgan nodded. "Ah. Likely for the best. My brother has other interests that keep him far too absorbed to even consider marriage. It's reassuring to know that you have such a good head on your shoulders for one so young."

"Thank you, my lady. You are too kind." Meg smiled politely or hoped she was smiling and not sneering from that verbal pat on the head. "I believe you'll find your brother in the stable yard."

Morgan hesitated at the door as if she planned to say something else, and Meg held her breath. But then Bryony came in.

"Beg pardon, my lady," she said with a curtsy. "Your maid sent me, asking me to remind you that it's time for your tonic."

Lady Morgan did not glance to the clock but merely smiled in that way she had, with her lips curling slightly at the corners. Without a word to Bryony, she turned back to

Meg. "I'm so looking forward to knowing more about you. Much more."

As Meg watched her leave, she felt a chill slither down her spine. That sounded almost like a threat, rather than a promise of friendship. But she pushed the notion aside.

Morgan's footsteps receded down the hall, and Bryony came closer. "Forgive me for saying so, miss, but I don't like her one bit. And I don't trust that maid of hers either. Caught her coming out of the housekeeper's office last night. But she said she'd gotten turned around and thought that was the way to the stairs."

"The duke mentioned that his sister had been gravely ill. Perhaps she was merely looking through our medicines to see what would make her mistress more comfortable," Meg offered, trying to put aside her own misgivings.

"No guest should go poking about whenever it strikes their fancy," Bryony grumbled. "I just don't like it."

Meg laid a hand on her maid's shoulder, admiring her fierce loyalty. "I'll speak to the housekeeper to ensure that everything is in order. In the meantime, we'll simply have to make the best of it. I suspect they'll be gone soon enough. After all, there aren't many rooms of the house left to search."

The thought brought an ache to her breast.

Bryony seemed to read it in her expression and gently asked, "And how will you fare when your duke is gone?"

She was about to correct her maid and tell her that Lucien wasn't hers. But instead, she merely shrugged. "Just like I did before."

Left alone with her thoughts, Meg sat at the desk and tried to finish her letters, but she couldn't concentrate.

It had happened again. All those old feelings she'd once had were returning, multiplying by ten and flooding inside her like a dam about to break.

And, just like before, she was keeping a monumental secret from him.

She had to tell him about Guinevere. She *wanted* to tell him. After coming to know him better and seeing the way he was with his daughter, she was no longer afraid that he would try to take her away. He was not a cruel man.

But what Meg feared most was that he would come to hate her again.

She couldn't risk it. Not now. Not when everything was still too new and raw between them.

Oh, if only he'd read all those letters she'd sent, then she wouldn't be in this current predicament.

With a troubled growl, she gave up her writing and locked the unfinished letters in the desk.

Thinking of her daughter—the wonderfully unanticipated consequence of falling in love on holiday—she went up to the nursery.

But Guinevere wasn't having a good morning either. In fact, she was behaving rather rambunctiously when her mother arrived.

The petulant cherub sat at the little table in the corner, with a cup of milky tea, a bowl of porridge, a piece of toast and a pot of jam. Or rather, what was left of the pot of jam. The rest of it was everywhere—on her face, in her hair, on her pinafore, across the floor and on the nurse.

"Guinevere," Meg tsked, shaking her head. "What have you done?"

The nurse stood up from the floor, where she was wiping up one of the sticky splatters. "My apologies, mistress. I don't know what's gotten into her today. She keeps asking for something called a *wooshan*, but I don't know what that is."

"No. Woo-shan," Guinevere clarified testily, her brow puckering above the bridge of her nose.

Understanding, Meg felt her cheeks heat. Clearly, she'd been speaking too familiarly with Lucien, and now her daughter was using his given name, too.

Reaching for the bellpull, she said, "I think I might. We'll just send down to the kitchens for some hot water. In the meantime, you may freshen up. I have her."

As the nurse left, Meg gathered her sticky daughter in her arms. "Sweetheart, you cannot go about throwing jam every time you don't get your own way. That isn't how a lady behaves. Especially not over a man."

Holding her on her hip, she walked to the window where there was a clear view of the bachelor's lodge. Her daughter took her face in her little jammy hands and pointed out the window. "Wooshan."

Meg kissed her upturned nose and smoothed away the wisps of pale hair from her forehead. "After your bath and your nap, we'll put on your best dress and visit Lucien. Would you like that?"

Guinevere nodded and yawned, supplying a clear view of the white protrusion just beneath her gums.

And when the nurse returned to take the child, Meg said, "I think that new tooth is ready to come in. She always becomes a little inconsolable when that happens."

"That must be it," the nurse agreed, and there was no more talk about Lucien. "I'll just get her cleaned up. And . . . you might wish to do the same, mistress. Or else you're going to have cherry-stained cheeks all day."

Meg touched her sticky face. "Good heavens. Well, at least it isn't porridge in my hair again. Who knew learning to use a spoon would turn into such a disaster?"

Smiling, she left the room, but as she descended the stairs her heart felt heavy again.

She wished there was something *she* could throw around the room until she had everything she wanted. And she wished things were different between her and Lucien. Wished that they could have had a life together because whenever she was with him . . . it just felt so right. So certain.

If only he felt the same.

Lost in her thoughts, she ended up at the gallery railing that overlooked the foyer instead of having turned toward her bedchamber. And she didn't pay any attention to the figure charging up the stairs until he was almost upon her.

She startled at Lucien, his face strained with concern. "Whatever is the matter?"

"Who hurt you?" he demanded as he bounded the last three treads to reach her.

Meg was so dumbfounded by the fierceness in his voice, his breathing short and erratic, eyes wild as if he were planning to rip her supposed assailant apart with his bare hands, that she didn't remember the episode in the nursery. Not until he cupped her face . . . and his brow furrowed in confusion.

"It's only jam," she said. "And it's your fault."

He peeled his hands away from her cheeks and sniffed the residue. "Why are you covered in cherry jam? And, more importantly, how is it my fault?"

"Guinevere was actually asking for you—or for *Wooshan*, rather. But the nurse didn't understand. So the little imp took out her frustrations on the table, the floor, the walls . . ."

She stopped when he smiled broadly at her.

Her heart stopped, too.

"*Wooshan*, is it?" He reached into his pocket, likely for a handkerchief, but came up empty-handed. The man never carried a handkerchief. Though, it didn't appear to alter his good humor. "And does she ever misbehave when she wants to see Mr. Prescott?"

Meg set her hands on her hips. "No. She didn't care a whit when Mr. Prescott left this morning to return to his estate up north."

Lucien's smile remained. And it was a little too arrogant as far as she was concerned.

"And why are you so happy, Merleton? Surely, you don't imagine it had something to do with your peevish display yesterday. You didn't scare him off, if that's what you're thinking. However, you did give him every indication that there was something between us, when you and I know better."

"*Do* we know better?"

"The book is not between us. I've told you before that I don't have it."

She huffed in exasperation and marched back across the hall, leaving him behind as she made for her bedchamber.

But he followed. He was at her side in a few strides, his hand reaching out to stay her. "I wasn't speaking of the book."

Then he turned her, his eyes smoky and dark.

She knew that look. It did terrible things to her. And right then, it sent a tug deep inside her and weakened her knees.

But she held firm and stood her ground. "Don't think you can simply kiss me again because of what happened in the attic."

"No?"

"No." Her gaze slipped to his mouth, and she swallowed. "I want more than that."

His lips curved. "How much more? Which way is your bedchamber?"

"There. At the end of the hall." She gestured, then lowered her hand and shook her head. "I wasn't talking about that when I said *more*."

"Don't you think about it, our night together?"

All the time, she thought. "Never crosses my mind."

He crowded closer, his smirk calling her a liar as he reached up to tuck a curl behind her ear. "I do. All. The. Time."

Her breath stuttered. She could feel her resolve weaken, feel her hands begin to lift, her lips grow plump and tingle with longing. But she stopped herself.

She wanted more than his kiss.

She needed to be the only one he thought of. She needed him to acknowledge that there was another reason he was there.

Putting her hands against his chest to keep him from getting any closer, she said, "Is that so? Tell me how long it was before you found yourself in another woman's bed? A week? A month?"

"I cannot answer that without being able to divine the future."

She was ready to shove away until she absorbed what he said. Then she blinked, staring at him blankly. "Are you saying that you haven't been with . . . anyone?" She shook her head at once. "I don't believe it. Unless . . . was it so terrible with me?"

Given the fact that she'd had no other experience in her life, she wasn't going to be too hard on herself, whatever his answer was. Although, as far as she could recall, they'd both enjoyed themselves immensely. Not half bad for a first time out of the gate.

"*Merlin's teeth.* What have you done to me? I just said *divine the future* as if such a thing were possible. I really am going mad. Ever since you entered my life, I've been plagued by this all-consuming, undefinable . . . *something*. It's relentless, hounding me, wearing me down until I've become a stranger to myself." His hand gripped her nape, his forehead against hers. "And to answer your question, I haven't been with another woman because . . . damn it all . . . because none of them were you."

Then he kissed her. There, in the hallway, in a wash of morning light, where anyone might happen upon them.

She wasn't sure which one of them came to this realization first, but when they broke apart, they both looked around. Thankfully, there were no servants about, and her aunt was likely in the garden.

"We cannot do that again. We're going to be *cau*—"

She broke off on a gasp as he suddenly swooped down, gathered her in the cradle of his arms, and began to stride to the end of the hall. It was on the tip of her tongue to ask him where he was taking her, but she knew the answer.

Instead of arguing or fighting against it, she slid her arms around his neck and said, "Hurry."

Chapter 29

~

The greatest thing since sliced bread

Meg simply couldn't wait or deny herself a moment longer. It wasn't possible. She needed this. Needed Lucien as much as he, by all accounts, needed her.

They weren't slow at all. Before the door closed, their mouths were fused, and she slid down the length of his body to drag him deeper inside the room. He turned the key in the lock while kissing her *and* while unbuttoning the back of her dress. The man was a wonder of efficiency. Then he shoved her dress and petticoat to the floor.

She tried to match his deftness and managed to strip off his cravat, but his waistcoat suffered a few button casualties.

Seeing the outline of a heavy shape beneath the fall of his trousers, her body responded in a low, liquid rush. The memory of how it had felt to have him fill her made her clench sharply as she moved the flat of her palm along his length.

A breath left him as he watched her. She didn't know why she'd always been so bold with him—even from that first meeting in the corridor at Caliburn Keep—but perhaps, some part of her had always known that he was hers.

Wanting more of him, she tugged at his fastenings. The fall flap was barely parted when she slipped her hand inside. And they both groaned in satisfaction as she gripped him.

She was fascinated by the shape and feel of him and loved seeing the way his throat constricted as he swallowed, head back, eyes closed.

"That thing . . . you're doing . . . with your thumb . . ."

"What, *this*?"

A low, guttural sound escaped him as she rolled her thumb up the underside, sliding to the tip. He swallowed again, his hands fisting in her laces. "It has a ninety-five percent guarantee of making this an intolerably brief interlude."

"We cannot have that," she said but didn't stop. And she even leaned in to open her mouth over the exposed skin at the base of his throat.

He growled, his hand tugging at her corset. Then he cursed. "I've tied a knot."

"It doesn't matter. Just take me like this," she said, pressing urgent kisses along the open V of his shirtsleeves and wrapping her arms around him. She was ready to climb him and impale herself on his erection to satisfy the gnawing ache at the juncture of her thighs.

He lowered his mouth to hers, taking her lips in a toe-curling kiss, his leg insinuated between her thighs. Lifting her to her toes, his mouth glided lower, his tongue laving the rapid pulse at her throat, descending to the ruffled edge of her bodice only to growl again in frustration. "I want you naked underneath me. I want to taste you and feel you melt on my tongue."

She shuddered, hips tilting.

Oh, she wanted that, too. Now. Right this instant.

"Then, cut the laces. Cut off all my clothes. I don't care," she said fervently, unabashedly arching against his leg.

"My dirk."

"Your *what*?"

His eyes blazed down at her, his color high, and all he said was "Boot. Knife."

Oh, *that* dirk.

She wasted no time. On trembling legs, she lowered and reached into his boot where she saw the clover shape of the dagger's hilt rising just above the cuff. Not wanting to accidentally maim him in the process, she took care in removing it, the blade flashing silver in the light through the parted drapes.

A humorous thought occurred to her, and she smiled up at him. "This seems rather like an Excalibur moment, as if destiny had a hand in all this."

"Then, it's your destiny to be naked," he said.

And in a matter of seconds that very destiny was realized.

After lowering her to the bed, he shucked his own clothes and gazed down at her. "You are the most captivating woman I've ever known. Everything about you is an enchantment, your laugh, your scent . . ."

He didn't finish. But she didn't mind because his body settled over hers.

She welcomed his weight on a satisfied sigh as he kissed her deeply. Then he nibbled beneath her jaw, moving down her throat, exciting her pulse along the way. Plumping her breast in his hand, he lowered his mouth over her and drew her sensitive flesh into his warm mouth, flicking his tongue over the tender peak until she was writhing beneath him, clutching his head.

When she cried out his name, he lifted away to blow a thin stream over the wet, pebbled skin. Then he tsked. "It seems I've gotten jam all over you, wherever my hands have touched."

"You can clean it up later," she said, tugging on his hips. "Just take me."

There was a positively wicked gleam in his eyes when he said, "Oh, but I like the idea of cleaning you up right now. Everywhere I've touched."

She gasped as his hand descended to her sex. Her back

arched as he cupped her fully, his fingers delving into her saturated curls. He kissed her body, lingering over her breasts with suckling flicks and deep pulls that sent quivering spears of sensation directly to her womb. And she was lost in the pleasure of his touch, her body thrumming, ready.

His tongue circumnavigated the rim of her navel as he looked up at her with heavily lidded eyes, his finger sinking into her slick swollen channel, and a desperate mewl tore from her throat.

"Shh," he crooned, blowing softly against her thatch of curls. "You're so wet for me. Let me, darling. Let me see if you melt."

She wasn't entirely sure what he meant. Not until he sealed his mouth over her . . . *there*.

She bucked against him. Surely, he wasn't going to. He didn't mean to kiss her there?

Oh, but he most definitely did. And then he groaned, his eyes closing as his mouth opened over her, the flat of his tongue rolling all the way up to the throbbing, sensitive bud, swirling with meticulous precision until she gasped and her head fell back.

Then she was no longer trying to budge him.

She threaded her fingers through his thick locks, feeling the heat of his scalp as he laved her endlessly. He made greedy guttural sounds as his tongue circled and suckled, his thrusting finger drawing out more of the warm honey that saturated her. And he made good on his promise.

She melted on a sudden liquid cry, back bowing, hips tilting jerkily as his tongue delved deep, drinking every last drop until she was limp and boneless.

When he settled over her, there was a smug grin on his lips. "This is no time for gloating."

"It cannot be helped. I've been thinking about that for longer than you can imagine, and tasting you was even better than every one of my calculations."

"There you go again, being all romantic and scientific," she said with a smile. "I love the things you say."

Something shifted in his gaze, his eyes warmer, tender. He lowered over her and kissed her softly. She tasted a faint briny essence, musky and sweet. *Her.* And she didn't shy away. It just seemed . . . natural.

Then he took her hands and set them over her head, first one and then the other, and twined their fingers. "I don't want any obstacle between us any longer. Not the book. Not anything. I just want to be with you."

A strangled, happy sound escaped her, and a tear slipped from the corner of her eye. "Truly?"

He nodded, pressing his lips to the damp trail. Then he kissed her eyelids, her nose, her mouth as he entered her body in a leisurely thrust, the hard heat of him filling her, stretching her, in a slow, thick slide until there was nothing between them.

A satisfied grunt left him, his heart beating against her own. Then he moved inside her, their hands held fast. Wanting to hold him, she wrapped her legs around his waist, undulating with him until it was almost too much pleasure.

He took his time, bringing her to another inexorable rise before she shattered again, her love for him bursting in a shower of colorful sparks behind her eyes. Then he followed her over the edge in a wash of molten heat.

After catching her breath, she kissed his shoulder. "I thought you said the first time would be hard and fast."

He nuzzled her nose with his. "I wanted to make it last longer."

"Then, stay here." She tightened her legs around his hips and felt his flesh twitch inside her.

He closed his eyes on a hiss. "You're clamped around me so tightly I don't think I could move if I wanted to. It's good that I don't. You've wrung me out, darling. However, you still have jam on your skin, and it makes me tremendously hungry."

When he started nibbling on her throat, she arched her neck. "If my maid comes to the door, I'll pretend I'm sick."

"Just don't cough," he said and when she looked up at him confused, he moved his hips and she understood. "At least not for ten minutes or so."

She pressed a kiss to his palm, murmuring her delight in tasting the cherry sweetness, warm on his skin. Then she licked him, from wrist to the tip of his middle finger. Seeing that he'd lifted his head to watch her and how dark his eyes had become, she sucked his finger into her mouth.

In the end, it didn't take ten more minutes, after all.

LATER THAT night, Lucien stole into the house and crept to her bedchamber. Before he rapped on her door, she flung it open and pulled him inside, wrapping her arms around him.

"What took you so long?" she chided, rising up on her bare toes to nip his chin.

Finally, the ache that had been with him since he'd left her bed subsided as he lifted her into his embrace. "It took Pell forever to go to bed so that I could slip away."

"Will you stay all night?"

"I'll leave at dawn."

She sighed but nodded reluctantly. "We both have obligations."

He laid her down and sat back against the side of the bed to remove his boots. His ruminations were turning in circles with her at the fulcrum. They were quiet as he began to undress, both lost in their thoughts of obligations and what would happen next.

It had seemed so simple—though agonizingly painful while he resisted—to get to this point, as if he were following the natural order of things. But he didn't know what the future held.

"Lucien," she said, biting into her bottom lip when he lifted the hem of her nightgown, "I'm a little . . ."

Even in the low firelight, he could see her blush. They had made love twice that afternoon, and doubtless, she was tender. Her nipples were still dark from being thoroughly kissed. "I just want to hold you, that's all."

Dubiously, she glanced down to his engorged penis.

"Can I help it if I'm noticeably excited by the prospect of holding you?" he asked.

She laughed, snuggling up to him, and not shyly at all. Every soft and supple part of her molded against him with sublime perfection. With their limbs entwined, it was almost impossible to discern the different parts of the single knot they made.

For a moment, he closed his eyes feeling as though he were swinging on a pendulum between bliss and agony.

She sighed contentedly. "Now there's nothing between us, just like it was meant to be."

He kissed the top of her head, and they both fell silent again. But it was the kind of silence where he knew that her thoughts and his were woven together. As if she were inside his head, tidying up and putting everything in place so that he could relax into the future that was unfolding. And yet . . .

He was used to plotting his own course, methodically detailing every moment spent so that it would have a purpose, leading to a desired end result. He lived his life like one of his experiments, a carefully controlled environment with a set expectation. He didn't allow things to unfold gradually without direction, without careful observation.

He didn't believe in *meant to be*.

"You're thinking about the book, aren't you?" she asked on a resigned breath, her hand splayed over his heart and likely noticing the troubled beats beneath her palm. "It's understandable. I know it's important to you and that you'll have to continue your search. But I'll help you, if you'll let me."

He held her tighter, breathing in the scent of her hair. "I would welcome your assistance."

As he caressed her soft skin and her fingertips sifted through the hair on his chest, he thought about a life like she suggested—searching together for the book during the days, holding each other every night.

But the vision didn't bring him the peace he sought. The frustration, the failures, the dead ends and starting all over again . . . He didn't want that for her.

He wanted more than that, both for her and for himself.

"What if . . ." he began as if merely hypothesizing a random thought, instead of a problem that had been weighing on his mind a great deal of late, "I stopped searching?"

Distractedly, she traced the outline of his flat nipple with her fingertip. "Just for now or altogether?"

"The latter, perhaps. But then"—he took a breath—"what would I have to show for all the years I've spent?"

"You have your notes, do you not?" When he issued an affirmative grunt, she nodded. "Then, you can continue to experiment with the recipes and find the proof you need."

Detecting the emphasis on the last two words, he arched a brow and placed his hand over hers, stilling her tickling ministrations over his sternum. "I'm not the only one interested in affirming the potential findings in a book of historical significance."

"I'm sure you're right," she said. "However, there are two kinds of people in the world. There are those who enjoy experiencing the wonder of everyday occurrences—a flower blooming, a butterfly emerging from its chrysalis, rainbows arcing through the sky after a storm." She smiled against his rib cage. "Then, there are those who dissect every com-

ponent down to the very basic elements. But they don't realize that just because you can *prove* how something grows or
appears doesn't mean that it isn't still magic."

"Actually, that is precisely what *proof* means."

"We shall agree to disagree, Herzog," she teased and
nipped him lightly with her teeth.

He grinned, but after a moment, his thoughts got the better of him. "But if I did stop, what would I do? I cannot simply exist without direction. What would be my purpose?"

She knew the answer without hesitation, as if she'd found
it written on a note that he'd left on the desk inside his mind.

"This," she said and pressed her lips to his chest, directly
over his heart. Then she moved over him, her raven hair
falling around him like a midnight veil, her eyes like blue
stars in a constellation. "And this."

She kissed him, softly, slowly. Then she moved down his
body in a silken exploration of hands and lips, enveloping
him deeply, hotly, in a dream from which he never wanted
to awaken.

Chapter 30

Your goose is cooked

Over the next few days, Meg and Lucien couldn't get enough of each other. Every moment apart was agony. And each night, it always felt like they'd been separated for years, eons, the rapture of coming together almost too overwhelming to endure.

Thankfully, they survived it again and again.

At least, until her brother returned.

It was a Thursday afternoon when the carriages pulled up the drive. Brandon swooped her up in a fond embrace and pecked her on the cheek. Then he did the same to Aunt Sylvia, who swatted him affectionately and told him that she was far too old for such things. Ellie smiled broadly and hugged her, whispering that she couldn't wait to tell her some happy news over tea.

If Brandon's exuberance and Ellie's bright eyes were any indication, Meg could guess what the happy news might be. A new child on the way, their family and their love for each other growing every day.

She was thrilled for them, but a touch wistful, too, wishing to have a husband of her own who was so overjoyed to spend his life with her that he couldn't contain it.

But Lucien had made no indication that he wanted to marry or have a family. In fact, aside from that first time they were together, he'd taken special care to spill outside her body. Not that she minded. With nothing settled between them, it was better that way. She was content, for now, simply to be with him.

Lucien had stepped out a short while ago. Morgan had wanted to visit the village shops and so he'd taken her and her maid, Nina, along with his cousin on an outing.

Aunt Sylvia explained this in passing, which told Meg that she'd been keeping Brandon well-informed in her letters. Her own letters to him had been, well, a little . . . less informative. Brothers and sisters were bound to have their secrets, after all.

But hers seemed to be growing bigger and bigger every day, like air filling a Montgolfier balloon. The problem was the balloon could only hold so much before it burst.

She knew she would have to tell Brandon the truth. Tonight. Not everything, of course. But enough for him to know what was at stake for her. And perhaps, he might even help her figure out a way to tell Lucien the truth without losing him in the process.

Knitting her fingers together, she watched as Brandon gathered her sleeping nephew in his arms and carried him up to the nursery, while Ellie followed to greet Guinevere.

Maeve and Myrtle stepped out of their carriage next, along with Mrs. Pendergast, who looked a bit green as she shuffled into the house.

Myrtle expelled a long-winded sigh. "Gracious, we thought we'd never arrive. Poor Mrs. Pendergast suffered a bout of carriage-sickness, and we had to stop a dozen times at least."

"We'll be sure to pack ginger tea for next time," Maeve said, her face drawn with exhaustion. But she offered a smile, nonetheless. "It's good to see you, my dear."

"And you," she said to both of them. Knowing that Aunt Sylvia was nearby directing the servants with the trunks, Meg continued in a whisper. "I'm sure you've heard that we have guests. A party whom you may recall meeting in London"—she stressed—"during my last Season. The Duke of Merleton, his sister, and cousin, Viscount Holladay."

They exchanged a look. Then Maeve squeezed her hand. "When we read your letter, we quickly understood the need to alter certain truths. We felt it most imperative to hasten our journey. But it has been days since, and we need to know—"

"Did he propose? Is he here to ask your brother for permission?" Myrtle's voice chirruped, and she had to clap a hand over her mouth to stifle her excitement.

Meg shook her head. "He doesn't know the truth. Apparently, he never read the letters. So when he came here, he still thought I was Lady Avalon. But that's changed now. I think. Nevertheless, it's still rather complicated between us. So . . ."

They both nodded in unison.

"If he needs a little shove in the right direction," Maeve said, and Myrtle finished with, "We'll be right behind him with a fire poker."

Meg giggled, and then she threw her arms around both of them. "Oh, I've missed you."

❧

AFTER DINNER, everyone retired early except for Meg.

Ellie and her aunts were exhausted from the days of travel, and Morgan from her shopping excursion.

Lucien looked thoughtful all evening, distracted. Then, without lingering over port in the dining room, he and his cousin departed for the lodge. So apparently, he had no desire to speak with her brother on any certain topic that might have been weighing on his mind.

As she stepped onto the terrace into the cool night air, she wondered if he would return later and steal into her bedchamber. If he did, she could ask him what they were to each other. What she meant to him and whether he had any intentions at all.

In their time together, she'd already learned that he revealed more of himself and his inner musings when they were in bed, with nothing between them. And yet, even as her own questions spun circles in her mind, she knew they would be unfair to ask when she kept her secrets from him.

She needed to tell him. But every day seemed to be bringing them closer, and she couldn't bear the thought of revealing the one thing that might drive them apart.

However, now that Brandon was home, Lucien would soon realize that Guinevere didn't belong to her brother. It would take him but a second to put the rest of the pieces together. *And* for the rest of her life to fall apart.

Brandon stepped out onto the terrace and joined her by the balustrade. He lifted his gaze toward the crescent moon. "So the Duke of Merleton is here at last."

She didn't pretend to misunderstand.

Earlier that evening in the parlor, Morgan had let it slip that she and her brother had been in Italy two years ago when she'd taken ill. Meg had gone still, expecting a sudden knowing exchange of looks between her aunt or brother or Ellie. But none had come. And in that moment, Meg realized that she hadn't been the only one keeping secrets.

"How long have you known?"

"Since you first returned from holiday, with your eyes red-rimmed as you stepped out of the carriage. You said you were merely tired, and I pretended to accept that. Then I went directly to my study and sent off some inquiries." When she stared agape, he shrugged. "Surely, during your Seasons, you didn't imagine that I possessed a preternatural ability of knowing which man you could dance with and which men you needed to avoid like the plague?"

"No, I thought you were overbearing and trying to keep me from experiencing life."

"Well, you're partly right," he admitted with a trace of chagrin. "I might be a trifle overbearing at times."

She scoffed.

"But I've always wanted your happiness." He looked down at his hands gripping the stone rail, his knuckles white around the edges, a muscle twitching in his jaw. "Ellie warned me not to interfere unless you asked me to. But, let me tell you, it was killing me not to take that man by the throat and squeeze some sense into him. How dare he take advantage of you, then leave you to bear the consequences all on your own."

"He doesn't know," she said quickly, laying her hand on his. "For much of the past two years, he hasn't been at his home. So his steward handled all the post. What I've gathered from our conversations, is that Lucien—*Merleton*," she corrected at the sound of her brother's growl, "has been beleaguered by so many invitations, and even proposals, over the years that his steward sorts through what is important and what is not. Though I cannot be certain, the man might have assumed my letters were some sort of false claim in a scheme of entrapment and summarily disposed of them." She shrugged. "All I know is that when Lu—*the duke* arrived, he thought I was someone else, a certain Lady Avalon who'd stolen his priceless heirloom."

"The book?"

She nodded. Then she explained how it had all begun with the stolen recipe at Caliburn Keep and gradually turned into her ruse of being Lady Avalon and how, before she knew it, she'd fallen in love and returned home from her holiday with an unexpected souvenir.

"You do intend to tell him," Brandon said after it was all out in the open.

"Of course I do. I just . . . don't know how without losing him."

"If he dared to walk away from you after he realizes—"

"Brandon," she interrupted with a shake of her head, "I don't want him to marry me out of obligation."

"He should, at the very least. Neither you nor Guinevere

can have a life without someone questioning the existence of *Mr. Arthur.*" He rolled his eyes. "You've simply been surrounded by those who would rather choose to pretend to be oblivious because they are too fond of you to lay such a stigma on your shoulders."

She supposed she'd known that all along. After all, one would have to be blind not to see the sideways glances when she visited the village.

"Daniel was here the other day," she said after a while, changing the topic.

Her brother nodded. "I know."

"Of course you do." She sighed.

"I also heard about his wife. I am sad for him. He hasn't had much luck with the fairer sex, and he's a good man."

"I think he came here to see if I would marry him," she said, looking out on the horizon. "For a minute or two, I thought I could. For Guinevere's sake. Daniel is kind enough to have me and likely to accept her, too. But being with him when he was here, it just felt . . . wrong. Uncomfortable, like a favorite dress I've outgrown. It's hard to explain."

A soft smile touched his lips. "That's almost the way it felt when I first met Ellie. Nothing made sense. The world suddenly dimmed, and the only light was glowing from her. And when she wasn't near, I was edgy and out of sorts."

"I remember those days," Meg grumbled. "You were impossible."

He laughed ruefully. "Perhaps. But when she was near, every sense suddenly came to life. Food tasted better. Colors were—*are*—more vibrant." Smiling, he shook his head. "I was reluctant to accept it at first. But from the moment we kissed, I knew. Something inside of me clicked like a lock tumbling into place. It was the same for Father and Mother, too. For all of the Stredwicks. It's inescapable. Once you find that one person, being with another would be nearly impossible. Life would be tasteless. Colorless."

"So . . . if Daniel had truly been my soul's counterpart, then he wouldn't have been able to marry someone else."

"No," Brandon said with sympathy. "I wanted him to be yours because you had been so certain. But when he came to tell me that he was leaving until you were old enough to know your own mind, I knew he wasn't yours. If he had been, there wasn't any way he could have left your side."

She mulled over this, thinking back to the past two years. "What if your soul's counterpart doesn't believe in the Stredwick certainty or in anything that cannot be proven?"

"Then, he would have to be the most stubborn, mule-headed man in existence. I don't see how it would be possible. It would be like choosing to go through life in a constant fog." He cupped her shoulder and met her gaze. "Would you like me to talk to him?"

"No. It boils down to the fact that I want what our family legacy has created. And I want the same for Guinevere when she's older. She deserves nothing less. And unless he changes his mind . . ."

"Or someone changes it for him," her brother muttered under his breath.

She shook her head. "I need him to choose me out of love. And that is going to be impossible enough when he learns the truth, *without* my brother's interference. So no matter what happens, promise me that you'll let him decide."

He growled again and expelled a hard breath through his teeth. Yet, in the end, he agreed. "I suppose I'll have to invite him hunting."

"As long as you bring him back," she said with alarm.

"I shall do my best." He pressed a brotherly kiss to her forehead, then turned to go back inside. However, before he was out of earshot, she was sure she heard him say, "But accidents do happen."

Chapter 31

~

When the fat hits the fire

I t was just after dawn when Lucien stepped onto the lane between the main house and the lodge. The faint golden glow on the horizon cast eerie shadows against the trees on either side.

He'd gone to Meg's room last night, regardless of the countless reasons he knew he shouldn't—first and foremost of those being that her brother was home.

But no matter how hard he'd tried, he hadn't been able to stay away.

He experienced an actual physical ache when he wasn't near her. Any logical man would assume that it would begin to subside after all the nights they'd spent in each other's arms. He had thought so, at least.

Instead, the feeling, the craving, the outright *need* for her intensified until nothing would quiet the restlessness inside him except for the welcome of her warm embrace.

They had both been frantic lovers last night, tumbling onto her bed, clutching each other, rising and arching together as if they were caught in the sand of a giant hourglass, knowing that their time was running out.

There had been so many things he'd wanted to say. And she, too, had looked at him with unspoken emotion in her eyes. But every time it seemed as if the words would simply

spill out, she would kiss him, and he would kiss her, and all
the words remained locked on their tongues until they were
both spent and exhausted and claimed by slumber.

Even after losing himself again and again, it had been
impossible to leave her side. But he knew he had to before
anyone awakened, especially her *bro*—

"Merleton!" Hullworth's voice called out.

Lucien froze. The lodge was in sight. He could make a
run for it. But that might appear a trifle too guilty. So instead, after quickly calculating the likelihood that he'd just
been caught—ninety-nine and nine-tenths of a percent—he
turned around and faced the consequences.

"I was in my study when I saw you pass by my window,"
Hullworth said, surprisingly not holding a pistol.

"My apologies," he said, his throat dry. "I didn't mean to
disturb you."

"Not at all. I've had my share of restless nights wandering the gardens. Sometimes it's the best thing to clear one's
head. Then again, sometimes a man needs a bit more."

Lucien swallowed at the way the marquess's eyes narrowed and his jaw tightened. There was a sixty percent
chance he was carrying a dirk in his boot. In a rage, it
would take him approximately four, perhaps five, seconds to retrieve said dagger and plunge it into Lucien's
chest.

Hullworth continued. "Like a day of hunting, for example.
What say you? Are you game?"

Lucien wondered if he deliberately intended his question to have a double meaning, as if the duke himself
would be the game being hunted. And if Hullworth knew
all the wicked things Lucien had done to his little sister
last night, well . . .

He shifted slightly. "I'd be glad to go out hunting. Regrettably, I didn't bring any weapons with me."

"I'll take care of all that," Hullworth said and clapped

him on the shoulder. Hard. "Your cousin is welcome to join us. Unless you'd rather it was just the two of us."

Lucien had a brief vision of Hullworth holding a rifling flintlock and *accidentally* aiming it between his eyes when the groomsmen were distracted by the dogs and fallen waterfowl. Seventy-eight percent chance.

He shook his head. "No. I'll ensure that Pell joins us. The more the merrier."

"Excellent. An hour, shall we say? I trust that will give you time enough for you to change out of your evening attire." He raked a hard gaze down his form, that muscle twitching in his jaw again. "We'll break our fasts, then ride out."

Without another word, Hullworth turned on his heel and marched back to the house. And Lucien wasn't entirely certain if he'd just been caught or if he'd managed to evade detection by one-tenth of a percent.

🦋

BY THE time he arrived at the main house, Lucien had donned proper attire, dragged his cousin out of bed and reminded himself that he was the Duke of Merleton, a man known to intimidate others by his stare alone.

He would talk to Hullworth, man to man, about his intentions. But first he would need to speak with Meg. She was a grown woman and didn't need to have decisions made for her.

So with his head held high, he crossed the threshold, even though he still wasn't sure if he would survive the day. Thankfully, Pell would be along soon, either to bear witness to his murder or become victim number two.

Hullworth was just coming down the main stairs with his son on his hip. So proud, he looked like a man who'd been crowned king. But where was his daughter?

Lucien frowned. He'd noticed last night at dinner, and in

the parlor before, that Hullworth only talked about his son. It was as if Guinevere didn't exist for him.

He'd always thought Hullworth was a good sort. He even admired him. And yet, this was unacceptable.

"Where is Guinevere?"

Hullworth looked perplexed by the question. "In the nursery, last I saw. Why do you ask?"

"Do you not think that she would wish to come down and bid you farewell?"

Lucien's jaw was tight, shoulders tense. It occurred to him that it wasn't his place to interfere with family matters, but perhaps someone needed to tell Hullworth that he was being a right solid prig by abandoning that sweet little girl.

The boy wiggled in Hullworth's arms. "I'll fetch Gwenny, Papa."

But no sooner had the boy dropped neatly to the tiled floor than a familiar, mischievous giggle floated down from the top of the stairs.

"The little escape artist has appeared," Lucien said with a grin, more to himself than to Hullworth.

The marquess laughed. "That's what Meg calls her, too."

In the distance, he could hear the nurse calling for her. It only made her scramble down the stairs faster, scooting on her bottom with alarming speed. Lucien crossed the foyer and climbed halfway up before he realized what he'd done: he'd stepped between a father seeing to his own child's safety.

However, Hullworth hadn't moved. He was merely watching the proceedings with interest.

Reaching Guinevere, Lucien was prepared to scold her gently for not being careful. But then she smiled at him, her cheeks smeared with some unknown yellowish-orange substance.

"Wooshan!" she called out, lifting her arms, and his breath caught.

He took the remaining stairs on peculiarly unsteady legs and then picked her up.

Below, he heard the boy ask, "What's a *wooshan*, Papa?"

"The duke is," Hullworth answered darkly, and Lucien grinned.

Holding her, he quickly discovered that the mysterious substance was on her hands as well, and now on his lapels. It smelled of apricots, sunshine and little girl.

"What are you doing out of the nursery?" he mock-scolded.

She giggled and then she placed her sticky hands on his cheeks and looked him directly in the eye and whispered, "Papa."

His heart stopped midbeat, and he felt a sharp pang that he'd never experienced before. He told himself that children likely use words without knowing the meaning. It was up to him to correct her.

But before he could, she bounced forward and pressed her wet apricot mouth to his with a resounding smack and said "Wooshan" again, as if the other word had never been uttered.

Looking up to the landing, he saw Meg standing there. Her hand was splayed over her heart as if she had been stricken by the same peculiar ailment he was suffering. And he realized in that moment what it was.

He wanted one of these little creatures. A dozen of them. And he wanted them with her.

❦

WHEN MEG saw the look in Lucien's eyes as he held his daughter, the tender fondness caused such a wealth of yearning in her heart that she almost couldn't bear it.

She had to tell him. Too much time had elapsed already.

But just when she was going to ask to have a private audience with him, Brandon called up the stairs.

"We're going hunting, Meg. No need to look so alarmed. I'm sure I'll come back in one piece. Cannot be too certain about Merleton, though," he said with a dark chuckle. "Would you mind taking Johnathon back to the nursery with Guinevere?"

Her nephew was already tromping up the stairs as Lucien climbed the rest of the way and deposited Guinevere in her arms.

"She's a trifle sticky this morning," he said with the evidence glistening on his face.

She laughed. "Believe me, I'm familiar with this state."

Without thought, Meg withdrew a handkerchief from her sleeve and pressed it to his cheek before realizing how intimate the gesture was. She moved to withdraw, but he stilled her hand and gazed into her eyes.

"When I return—*if* I return," he added with a wry lift of his brows, "I should like to speak with you. In private."

"I should like to speak with you, as well," she said with a nod.

His gaze warmed as he took her hand in his and bowed over it. Then he stole her handkerchief from her grasp. "I accept this favor you've bestowed on me and will ensure its safe keeping while I am away at battle, my lady."

His teasing brought out a giggle from their daughter and a quiet gasp from Meg when he turned her wrist and pressed his lips to the pulse that always beat faster for him. Only for him.

"Until then," he said with a promise before his gaze flicked to a point over her shoulder. "Good morning, sister."

Meg turned and saw Morgan's hard stare. But in a blink, it was gone, replaced with a polite grin.

"I think my brother has taken a fancy to you."

Glancing back over her shoulder, she saw that Lucien was at the bottom of the stairs and out of earshot. "I feel the same about him."

"He has a bit of a blind spot when it comes to you, I think."

"What do you mean?" she asked, watching her nephew scamper past on his way back up to the nursery.

"Lucien hasn't done the math. But I have," Morgan said with a pointed glance to Guinevere. "And apparently, he doesn't remember that he had pale blond hair until the age of ten, a towheaded family trait. It was the most peculiar sight to see it change."

Meg went cold. "I'm going to tell him when he returns."

"Then, I wish you luck. Lucien isn't the most forgiving of men. He despised you for two years for stealing that book, remember?"

"But I didn't."

She shrugged. "The point I'm trying to make is that you need to tread carefully. If you simply blurt out this news, then it will be as if you've slapped him across the face with it."

Meg considered this. She'd actually been thinking that Lucien would prefer the direct approach. Simply tell him and then apologize for misleading him. After all, she'd seen the tenderness in his expression as he'd looked at Guinevere.

However, Morgan was right. He had hated Meg for two years, believing the worst. And he'd never read the letters, which had likely been destroyed by now. So she had no proof.

And he always needed proof.

"Perhaps you can ask the kitchen to prepare something he might like," Morgan suggested. "Something that might become his new favorite, and gradually ease into the conversation."

Until this moment, Meg hadn't been sure if Lucien's sister liked her. She was a cold person, but perhaps she'd warmed to her. And her advice sounded precisely like what the aunts might have said.

She smiled. "Thank you, Morgan."

"Think nothing of it." Then she flitted her fingers in the air and walked down the hall as Meg went upstairs to the nursery.

On the way there, she remembered the recipe she'd stolen from Caliburn Keep. And written across the top were the words *The Duke's Favorite*.

Suddenly, she knew precisely what recipe she would have the cook prepare . . . if Maeve and Myrtle would be able to find it in their collection.

🦋

AFTER CLEANING up Guinevere and leaving her with the nurse, Meg found Maeve and Myrtle in the sewing parlor that overlooked the fountain on the south lawn. Situated between their bedchambers, this combination of rooms was now considered their apartments at Crossmoor Abbey. They were family now.

In the future, she would likely have her own apartments when she returned with Lucien and their daughter. At least, once they became a family and moved to Caliburn Keep. Well, *if* they became a family. Even though her heart was certain of her desires for such a future with him, she still only wanted to marry for the deepest, most endurable love.

Her doubts that she might never have such a life were quickly dissolving away, like sticky jam in warm water.

Lucien loved her. She could think of no other explanation for the way he looked at her and touched her. She was almost sure of it. And that was precisely why she wanted everything to be perfect when he returned.

She entered the parlor, the cheerful room bursting with every color of a spring garden. The bright hues and eternally blooming wallpaper seemed like an extension of the ageless women who occupied this space. They were always in the spring of their lives.

At the moment, however, they were both staring down at a series of small caskets, the lids removed to reveal papers in various sizes and shapes, some folded or crumpled. These were the ill-gotten gains, the infamous pilfered recipes of the Parrish sisters.

Seeing their confused expressions, she asked, "Is something amiss?"

"Maeve asked me to retrieve the cannoli recipe." Myrtle glanced askance to the doorway and then continued in a whisper. "The one that had us excommunicated from Italy."

"That isn't the right word, sister."

She shrugged. "Nevertheless, when I went to fetch it from this box, it wasn't in there with all the others from Italy. It was in the Germany box. And some of the France recipes had found their way in there, too. Now they are all in a muddle."

"Perhaps someone knocked them over by accident and simply put them back to tidy up," Meg offered, not understanding the reason for their confusion.

"I had thought of that," Maeve added. "However, the caskets were kept in different drawers. Which means that someone would have been looking through all of them at the same time."

"But for what purpose? We are all family here." Even as Meg said the words, she felt a cold shiver down her spine. They were not *all* family here. "Perhaps the duke, then. He has been given leave to search the house for his book."

Although, she was under the assumption that he'd given up that pursuit for the most part.

"We had thought of that, too. And we surely wouldn't have minded admitting that handsome young man with those splendidly broad shoulders into our rooms." Myrtle waggled her brows.

Maeve shook her head in exasperation. "Then Mrs. Pendergast told us that she saw Lady Morgan's maid outside our apartments when we were down to breakfast this morning."

"But Mrs. Pendergast's eyesight isn't what it used to be. In fact, we were going to speak with Merleton about spectacles—"

"Which is neither here nor there at the moment," Maeve added impatiently. "The most puzzling thing of all is that nothing is missing."

"Just mislaid," Myrtle said and nodded.

Meg swept a glance around the room and to the disorder of the papers in the caskets. This wasn't the first she'd heard about that maid, Nina. "It is rather odd. However, a simple explanation is that she was likely looking for thread and thimble to repair one of her mistress's gowns and was directed to the sewing room."

The sisters looked at each other with relief.

"Of course, that must be the reason," Myrtle said.

Maeve nodded and gestured to the cabinet against the wall. "She looked through the drawers. The recipes spilled. And she simply put them back."

"Speaking of . . ." Hearing footsteps in the corridor, Meg moved closer to the aunts before she continued. "Do you happen to have the *England* recipes on hand? I'm searching for the one we pilfered from Caliburn Keep."

"The Duke's Favorite?" Myrtle said with an excited gasp. "We were hoping you'd come to ask. Are you planning to serve that for a special—"

She fell silent as a figure stepped inside. It was Morgan.

Her green eyes scanned the room. "Good morning. I hope I didn't interrupt. I was just looking for a thimble. My maid was unable to find one earlier."

"Of course not," Meg said with an easy smile. Their mystery was solved without any fuss. "You are welcome anywhere at Crossmoor Abbey. Think of it as your home."

A pair of dark auburn brows lifted. "That's quite a generous invitation. I thank you."

For an instant, a riffle of worry trampled through Meg, wondering if, perhaps, she had revealed too much of her own hopes too soon. But she quickly cast those doubts aside. She knew her own heart, and she knew Lucien's, too.

Surely, there was no need to worry.

Chapter 32

If you bake it, he will come

After hunting with Hullworth, Lucien returned to Stredwick Lodge—thankfully one hundred percent intact—early in the afternoon. Almost immediately, a missive arrived from Meg, inviting him to tea and demanding the safe return of her handkerchief. He grinned and readily gave his acceptance to the footman, then went to clean up.

Entering his chamber, he discovered that his finest clothes were already laid out, pressed and waiting. His borrowed valet, whom Sylvia had sent over that first day, stood at the washstand, sharpening a razor against a leather strop. Mr. Ector was quiet, discreet and efficient. So efficient, in fact, that he seemed to possess the uncanny ability to read his mind.

Even now as Lucien merely cast a quizzical glance in his direction, wondering how the stately older man could possibly have known he'd wish to look his best, the valet answered without hesitation. "Your Grace voiced a list of advantages and disadvantages earlier, before the hunt."

"Ah. That explains it." Lucien had been preoccupied and tended to mutter to himself when he was in a quandary. Sitting down in the chair and before Ector could drape a hot towel on his face, he asked, "Well, what do you think?"

He considered for a moment. "I'm afraid I can offer no impartial opinion. However, at last count, His Grace mentioned three hundred forty-seven advantages to a union with Miss Stredwick and one disadvantage."

The book, Lucien thought. That was the only thing keeping him from being completely certain. That missing piece of his legacy was tied to the deaths of his parents, his own purpose and his trust. If he just knew where it was, then . . .

But he didn't. And he may never find it. So was he willing to spend the rest of his life searching, while he let the woman he loved slip through his fingers?

The answer was simple.

When he came out of his rooms a short while later, he was not surprised to see Pell at the sideboard pouring a drink. However, he was surprised to see Morgan.

His sister studied Meg's note with a concerned frown, then dropped it onto the marble-topped side table. "This is precisely why I had to come. From the conversation I had with her earlier, I knew she was planning something. But then, I saw her whispering to Maeve and Myrtle Parrish, and they each went suspiciously quiet when I entered the room."

"And?" Pell said. "Surely, people do that all the time when you enter a room. You should be used to it by now."

"Well, it was obviously something they didn't want me to hear. And I needed my brother to know, just in case."

Pell delivered a whisky to Lucien. He was about to decline, but then he was suddenly distracted by the thought that Meg might have compiled a list of her own. And if so, what were the cons?

Suffering an unanticipated swell of nervousness, he tossed back his drink and felt the fortifying burn all the way down. "In case of . . . ?"

"In case you were about to make a mistake of monumental proportion. I saw the way you looked at her earlier, and it's obvious to me that you're in over your head. Again. Just like last time," she said. "I don't want to see you hurt by trusting her too readily. You need to pay attention to the things you've witnessed. Like the fact that you first met her sneaking around belowstairs at Caliburn Keep."

"Which was likely just as innocent as she claimed. She'd simply become turned around."

"On the very same day that the book went missing and you found the note in the vault? Come, now, little brother. If not her, then who else?"

He was already growing impatient with this conversation and wanting to be at the main house. However, his sister brought up a salient point. "I've been thinking about that a good deal of late, and about the initial report that Mr. Richards provided. In it, there isn't a description of Lady Avalon. Nothing detailed, at any rate."

"I'm sure you're mistaken."

"I'm not. The pages only stated that she was alluring. Captivating. The rest has all been hearsay and conjecture. In other words, we don't know with absolute certainty what she looks like. But one of the other men will." He turned his attention to Pell. "You might recall mention of Mr. Sudworth, who'd allegedly developed the formula for a youth serum that was stolen. Well, I believe he keeps a hunting box in Wiltshire. Would you be willing to look into that?"

His cousin sat up straighter and offered a sincere nod. "I'd be honored, old chap."

"This is ridiculous, Lucien," Morgan hissed. "You're turning into one of them, you know, letting Lady Avalon scramble your wits. I knew I was right to worry when you opened the gate."

He growled. "I don't want to hear another word about the bloody gate. I opened it because I was tired of keeping the rest of the world at arm's length. And yes, I acknowledge that it led to the theft of our family's legacy. But it also led me here, to a place where I've been able to simply breathe and be at ease. And after spending the past two years practically killing myself, I've come to realize that I'm exhausted. I want more, Morgan. I hope you can understand that."

"Of course, I understand. You're a man, after all," she offered in a placating manner. "And just so you know, I like Meg, too. She has a certain way about her that makes one forget how devious she can be. I can even respect her for that. She is a woman who knows what she wants, and she won't settle for anything less. But I wonder—"

"Tell us, o divine mistress of contempt," Pell intoned raising his glass. "What is it that you wonder?"

"If this might all be a clever ruse, like the last time." She lifted her hands in surrender. "I didn't want to say it, but no one else in this room seems to be thinking straight. I expected as much from Pell, who only has snails skulking about in his skull. But you, Lucien, I just hate to imagine that you're about to fall into another trap."

"I've heard enough," he said and moved toward the door.

But Morgan wasn't through.

"Think, brother. You cornered her at her family home. Then she was forced to do something drastic when you started searching the house, room by room. She knew it was only a matter of time before you found something. And she was likely willing to do anything—say anything—to distract you from your purpose."

He didn't realize he'd stopped, until she sidled up and patted him on the shoulder.

"Just remember what happened in Italy," she continued, "and be on your guard. That's all I'm asking."

He knew his sister meant well, but she didn't see the whole picture the way Lucien did.

Even so, he felt his brow pucker as he stepped outside. He didn't want to give her ramblings any credence. And yet, thinking back to Italy, to all the things that Meg had said that night, and then how she, and the book, were both gone in the morning . . .

No, he thought, refusing to let doubt creep in. He had no proof that she'd taken the book, no proof that she'd taken anything, other than his heart.

And that was all the proof he needed.

MEG STOOD in the parlor and smoothed her damp palms down her blue-striped skirts. The dress was tighter than it had been the last time she'd worn it, but she wanted everything to be perfect.

Even so, she was dreadfully nervous by the time Lucien arrived.

However, one heated glance from him and all her jitters faded away.

"You look"—his gaze traveled down her form, lingering here and there, and then back to her eyes—"beautiful."

She blushed. "I wanted to wear the same dress I wore—"

"On the day we met," he finished with a grin. "I remember it well. Only then, you had on a little coat."

"A spencer," she supplied. "It was too warm for that today."

And besides, she couldn't button the blasted thing over her breasts any longer.

He stepped forward and took her hand, her blood rushing warmly beneath the surface of her skin. "Before tea arrives, there's something I want to ask you . . ."

"And there's something I need to tell you . . ."

But before either of them could continue, the aunts bustled in with the tea tray on a rolling trolly, their happy hums accompanied by the clatter of the cups and saucers.

"Here we are," Myrtle chirruped. "And we have something very special."

Together, the aunts went to the round satinwood table

near the corner and set up the tea service, along with a pair of silver candlesticks in the center and two silver domes on either side.

"It's perfect," Meg whispered to them as they pressed their cheeks to hers before they slipped out of the room.

The duke grinned and stepped over to the table. "What's all this?"

"I had the cook prepare something special, and I think you'll like it." Meg was feeling shy all of a sudden, her fingers knitting together as she bit into her bottom lip. She gestured with a nod of her chin. "Go on, then."

He removed the domes with a flourish. A molded canelé sat in the center of each plate. The risen pudding was filled with cream and topped with a spear made of sculpted sugar and resembled a sword trapped inside a stone.

She almost laughed. What a perfectly fanciful dessert for the Duke of Merleton.

"Your favorite," she said, looking at him expectantly.

It was only then, that she saw the way he'd gone still, his hands remaining aloft with the silver domes in his grasp. His mien was expressionless.

He must have been delighted into speechlessness.

"This is not *my* favorite," he finally said after setting the domes on the table.

It wasn't until she saw those three vertical notches and the stony look in his eyes that she realized something was wrong. Very wrong. "I do not understand. Don't you like it?"

"This was my grandfather's favorite. The previous duke. Our cook kept a recipe card in the kitchen with the words *The Duke's Favorite* scrawled on the top. And you would only have assumed it was my favorite if you had taken it."

She felt the color drain from her face. "Lucien."

"You've been lying to me. Are *still* lying to me."

"I can explain."

"Oh, I'm sure you can," he said darkly.

"I planned to tell you everything today. I didn't want any more secrets between us. It all started with that recipe, and that's the only thing we took from Caliburn Keep. The aunts will tell you."

"The three of you were upstairs whispering about it earlier today. Doubtless, you were all formulating the same story."

She shook her head. "No. It isn't like that. It never was. I've been telling you the truth—well, most of the truth—from the beginning. The only things I lied about was that I was never Lady Avalon, and I've already told you why, and I did steal the recipe from your kitchens. I had it under my foot when we met."

"Anything else?"

She swallowed nervously, wringing her hands until they ached. Panic flooded her in icy torrents and settled inside her stomach like a rock. "I didn't want to tell you this way but . . . Guinevere is my daughter. *Our* daughter. She was born on May the tenth, last year. Which is nine months after—"

"Italy," he snapped. "I can bloody well count."

"I had never been with anyone else," she admitted quietly, daring to take a step toward him and lay her hand on his sleeve. "I thought for certain you'd noticed how awkward I was. That had been one of my fears—that you had abandoned me because I had disappointed you when you were expecting someone like Lady Avalon."

"You seemed adept enough."

His statement was like a slap. She stepped back, her hands falling to her sides as he crossed to the mantel on the far side of the room.

She tried not to take his anger to heart. Keeping all her foolish secrets had clearly hurt him, greatly. And she regretted that.

"When I was certain of my condition," she continued,

determined to have it all out, "I never attempted to keep it from you. I wrote to you. For two years, I wrote to you. That is no lie. And I left you a note in Italy with the book."

"So you've said. But if any of that is even remotely true, then—" He stopped and raked a hand through his hair, exhaling deeply as if fighting for control. But when he turned to face her again, his eyes were dark with fury. "Why didn't you tell me about my daughter before? You let me assume that she belonged to your brother."

"I was afraid, at first."

He scoffed. "Afraid of what?"

"That you'd take her away," she said and saw his expression turn incredulous. "You hated me when you first arrived."

"But that changed, didn't it?" he said on a growl. "We've been together every night. You've had ample opportunity. So why have you waited to tell me this, if not for the purpose of distracting me from your other lies"—he flung a hand toward the table—"like the fact that you *have* actually stolen from me?"

"I'm not trying to distract you," she explained. "Lucien, I love you."

"And you choose to prove it by ensuring that I'm trapped into marrying you?"

She flinched, her eyes prickling with incipient tears. "I have no proof to offer you that I'm not trying to *trap* you, other than to tell you that if you were to ask right this moment, I would refuse your proposal."

"I'm sure your brother will make that point moot before the day is over."

"No, he won't. Like I've said before, Stredwicks only marry for love—a love shared by both parties, not just one. And if you don't believe me, you can ask him. He has known the truth from the beginning, and he never approached you with any demand. Instead, he has shielded me as only the most excellent of brothers would have done."

"It doesn't matter. You'll simply have to put aside your childish dreams of *fate* and *destiny*. If Guinevere is mine, she is going to have my name, and you are going to marry me. Then, whatever is yours—or whatever you've confiscated—becomes mine. Problem solved."

He dusted his hands together in a gesture of finality as if he didn't need her agreement.

"You are still welcome to search every room, but that will be the last thing you'll ever do in this house," she promised.

Then, with her head held high, she stormed out.

🦋

LUCIEN LEFT Hullworth's study, slamming the door behind him. He'd never been so incensed in his entire life. How dare he refuse to give his consent!

Lucien wasn't some ne'er-do-well cub after her dowry. He was the bloody Duke of Merleton!

"Brother, I just heard." Morgan appeared, rushing alongside him as his agitated steps ate up the marble tiles.

He stopped and glared back in the direction of the study and gritted his teeth. "If Hullworth thinks I'm leaving here without his treacherous little sister and *my* daughter, then he can think again. They are coming home with me."

"What do you mean?" She issued a haughty laugh. "Surely, you don't intend to marry her now, after all she's done."

"Of course I do. Marrying her is the only solution to every single problem she's presented since we first met."

Lucien hadn't needed to do any lengthy calculations to make his decision. He knew it was the only way. And damned if he wasn't looking forward to seeing her face when he presented the special license he would obtain. Then nothing—not even Hullworth's lack of consent—could stop him.

"I see," Morgan said, her gaze distant and contemplative.

"And your pursuit of the book? I mean, it's likely beneath this very roof in a place you would least expect to find it."

He nodded, but his mind was on sending a missive to the archbishop of Canterbury. Distractedly, he said, "I'm in no hurry. The book has doubtlessly changed places several times. And if I know Meg, as I'm sure I do, she'll likely use it to barter with me for her freedom. Another attempt at distraction. But I'll not be dissuaded. No, indeed. I am too certain this is the right course of action."

"Perhaps. However, if you found the book first, then she would have nothing with which to barter. You would, at last, have the upper hand," she said, drawing his attention. "If the book has changed places, as you say, then you'll likely find it somewhere that you've already searched."

His gaze instinctively lifted as he recalled that the search of the attic had been cut short.

Why, that sly little wolf, he thought and almost smiled. She was about to find out that he would be a thorn in her side for the rest of their lives.

Chapter 33

The bitter truth

Everything was falling apart. The day had started out with so much promise.

Now Lucien was threatening to marry her, whether she accepted or not.

Brandon was telling her that he would do all he could, but that the duke was well within his rights.

Ellie understood Meg's desire to bolt and steadfastly vowed to assist her in any possible way—as long as it didn't involve ladders or standing in precariously high places—but she also advised her to give it time and to consider the proposal with a cooler head and a clearer heart.

Aunt Sylvia reminded her that love was forgiving.

Maeve and Myrtle were upset that no one had bothered to taste the *canelés*.

Guinevere was crying over her new tooth and wanting *Wooshan*.

And if that weren't enough, Meg also had a splitting headache.

The trying events of the day left her enervated and in need of respite and sustenance. It was nearly six o'clock in the evening and she couldn't remember the last time she'd eaten.

Sinking down on the settee in the library, she thanked

Becca for the overladen tea tray and told her that she would ring when she finished. The maid had brought an ample number of cups and saucers for anyone who might happen by, but—given Meg's popularity at the moment—she doubted she would require more than one.

"Ah. There you are," Morgan said from the doorway. "The house is in quite an uproar. I thought, perhaps, you could use a friend."

Looking over the scalloped back of the settee, Meg watched her saunter into the room, graceful as a cat on the prowl, the hems of her deep burgundy skirts fluid and soundless with each step. "I would appreciate a friend. Though, I should have thought that you would surely be cross with me, too."

"I have a different perspective on things, you might say." Morgan perched on the edge of one of the upholstered chairs. "Shall I pour?"

"That would be lovely, thank you. But I need to tell you that I did not take your family's book. I realize that we aren't well acquainted and there is no reason for you to trust—"

"I know," Morgan offered with an unconcerned flit of her fingers as she carefully arranged the cups. "If you had taken it, my investigator would have informed me."

Meg shook her head in bewilderment. "Both you and your brother employ investigators?"

"The same one, actually. It's only that I've known Mr. Richards much longer, and because of that his allegiance tends to favor me. So he'll often send my brother's reports to me first. That's how I know about the book."

"Oh." Meg supposed that cleared up matters. It did seem odd, though—keeping an investigator in the family as if they were always anticipating a deception of some kind.

She remembered that her father had often said, *If you expect to see butterflies wherever you turn, that's what you'll* find. But just remember, the same is true if you *expect to see* wilted flowers.

In other words, those who look for the worst will always find it.

Hearing the shush of steaming liquid fill the porcelain cup, she realized she was woolgathering, her gaze on the low flickering flames in the hearth.

"Milk and sugar?"

"Yes, please," Meg said, turning her attention back to Morgan as she stirred the tea with methodical clockwise precision, much like her brother might have done. "I wish Lucien was as convinced of my innocence as you are."

She hated the way they'd left things. If only he had listened.

"Once my brother settles his mind on something, he doesn't divert from his chosen path. Well, not until you came along. Before then, he spent his time studying the book, day after day, night after night."

"That doesn't seem like much of a life," Meg said, her heart bending a bit. But only by the smallest degree.

Accepting the cup, she sipped gratefully. The brew was strong, however. Bitter, too, but the sweetness from the sugar helped her take another swallow before she rested it on the saucer.

Morgan sat back and drummed her fingers against the arm of the chair. "Lucien is a lot like our father. He was also driven to the point of obsession. Oh, the hours—days, months and years—he spent poring over the pages, searching for a cure for my mother's illness, a wasting disease that weakened her blood. Father was forever locked away, trying new experiments. I thought his sacrifice was noble, heroic even. We both wanted the same thing, after all: for Mother to be well again. Alas, his efforts came to nothing."

"I'm so sorry," Meg said. She knew how devastating it was to lose one's mother.

Morgan shrugged in an offhand fashion. "After she died, I thought Father would stop. I thought he would sit with me in his study and talk about all sorts of things, the way he used to do . . . before." She expelled a sigh. "But his obsession never ceased. He stayed in that little cupboard of a room, searching tirelessly while I wept alone, missing my mother. Yet, even then, I saw his pain and thought him stalwart and brave. I looked up to him."

Meg recalled her own experiences. When her mother was gone, she'd had both her brother and father for a time. And yes, she saw her father's pain, but she was fortunate that he hadn't sequestered himself. Instead, he'd treasured his children all the more, spending as much time with them as he could, teaching them and telling them stories about their mother. And that was how they'd healed, through love.

She thought about Lucien and Guinevere. It would be unfair to keep them apart and she couldn't be that cruel to either of them. But that didn't mean she would marry him. She still needed to honor her own legacy and her own heart.

These musings were making her head ache again. So she picked up the cup and drank more, hoping it would help to clear her thoughts.

After another sip, Meg said, "It was only natural that you would look up to your father."

"And I did, for a time. Then, a few months later, he went away to find Tintagel—King Arthur's castle," she clarified, and Meg nodded, remembering the legend. "He went to find answers, but he came home with a new bride instead. My brother followed shortly thereafter. And with his birth something changed in my father. He seemed to forget all about the book and all about my mother. Those years he'd spent locked in that room poring over the pages meant nothing any longer. And I hated him for it. Oh, how I hated him and his new wife *and* Lucien."

At the noticeable bitterness in Morgan's voice, Meg

frowned. Her first inclination was to defend Lucien. None of it had been his fault. He deserved no hatred. And neither did his father and mother, for that matter. They had found love, and it was the most precious gift that anyone could hold.

However, she tried to think about those events from a child's perspective. "It's understandable that you would have felt hurt and even betrayed at that age."

"You're quite right," Morgan agreed. "And it might have faded in time. However, when Father told my little brother about our family legacy and also that protecting the book was up to him—*not me*—my hatred returned and festered."

There was something unsettling in her vehemence, in the way her green eyes flashed. Her mouth was drawn tight, white-edged and surrounded by a spray of wrinkles. It was the first time that Morgan actually looked like Lucien's older sister. Much older, in fact. And yet, as she sat with her hands balled into fists, she seemed almost petulant. Child-like. It was as if she was still trapped in that time of her life, refusing to move beyond it.

But even a child shouldn't have been filled with hate. Jealousy, perhaps, but not hatred for her own family. It was unthinkable to Meg.

A sudden wave of dizziness assailed her and her head spun.

Realizing she should have eaten something earlier, she closed her eyes briefly and rested against the back of the settee. She knew she would feel more like herself once the milk and tea were settled in her stomach.

"Are you unwell, Meg? You look rather pale."

"Just a bit tired, I think. It's been a rather long day. Perhaps I should go to my bedchamber."

"That isn't necessary. Just keep your eyes closed and rest for a spell. I don't mind," she said soothingly, and Meg felt the cup at her lips. "Here, drink some more."

How odd. *Motherly* was not a characteristic she would

have attributed to Morgan. But Meg swallowed nonetheless. She noticed that her tongue felt oddly thick.

Another chill stole through her. Even though there was a fire in the grate, she couldn't feel the warmth from it. She should add another log, but found that she was too fatigued to move. And when she felt her legs being lifted onto the other cushion of the settee, with her body naturally reclining and her head sinking to an embroidered pillow, she didn't object.

"I'm sure your father loved you. And the love you learned from him, you gave to your brother," Meg offered groggily, sensing that it needed to be acknowledged. "Lucien told me about that night and how you saved his life."

When only silence greeted her, Meg wondered if it was a mistake to bring up such a painful memory.

But then Morgan expelled a heavy sigh. "No one else was supposed to be in the vault that night. And I was livid when I saw what those two thieves had done. They were only supposed to take the book."

Meg felt the flesh of her brow pucker. She'd heard this story before, from Lucien. And yet, something wasn't right. The version she'd been told didn't match this one. According to him, they had died protecting the book from men who were obsessed with the old legend. But what if that wasn't the truth, after all?

"You hired the men who killed your parents?" she asked, her voice sounding far away to her own ears, a sick churning in the pit of her stomach.

"Not to kill them," Morgan said. "Just to take the book. I knew that if I could make it look as though Lucien was responsible for losing his key so that it found its way into the wrong hands, then Father would rely on me again. It was the perfect plan. But then those louts became greedy. They started rifling through the collection of ancient swords with bejeweled hilts. And it was likely the suit of armor crashing to the floor that had alerted Father." She clucked her tongue. "I'd heard it, too. By the time I arrived, it was too late. The report of the pistols was still echoing in the antechamber, and the acrid char of gunpowder floated like a haze. And do you want to know something?"

Meg felt a rise of bile, burning the tender lining of her throat, and couldn't answer.

However, Morgan didn't need her to. "You can never forget the sharp, coppery scent of blood. Once it's inside you, it stays there. And it lingers in places, seeping into the stones of the foundation. There are times when I stand in that room outside the vault and I can still smell it."

Lucien believed their deaths had been his fault. It haunted him to this day. He needed to know the truth.

She had to tell him. But when she tried to sit up, her head was too heavy, her limbs curiously weak. She was starting to wonder about the bitter taste at the back of her mouth. "Did you . . . did you put something in the tea?"

She tsked. "Meg, really. Would I do something like that? When my brother is so determined to have you, no matter the consequence?"

The acrimony dripping from every word did nothing to ease Meg's swiftly climbing fears. She tried again to get up, to move, to do something to escape the nightmarish images inside her head. But she couldn't. Morgan had done something to her. She was sure of it.

"Have to . . . tell . . . Lu . . . cien."

"He'd never believe you. I did save his life, after all. I'm the ideal elder sister." She snickered. "Those idiots would have likely tried to shoot him, too. But then the little tow-headed genius informed them that their flintlock pistols were only equipped to fire one shot without reloading. The men laughed. Then one of them had the audacity to stroll up to me and say, 'Couldn't help it, love,' as if that excused their stupidity. So I stabbed him with one of the swords.

"It wasn't as difficult as I thought it would be—killing a man," she continued with a flippant air. "The second man escaped with one of the bejeweled daggers before the servants rushed in. And that's when I first hired Mr. Richards. I had to find that thief and teach him a lesson. It took planning, but I had a natural aptitude for it. And I must say, watching Lucien's lifelong efforts to prove that his parents didn't die in vain has given me a strange sort of satisfaction."

In that instant, it all clicked into place at once.

"You stole the book," Meg slurred. "You are Lady Avalon."

"She was my invention. Pretty clever, hmm? I'd been planning it for years. Of course, I had to make a name for myself with a handful of affairs and acquisitions. All in good fun. After that, a few discreet rumors to the right people carried the stories onward. You might say I became my own legend." She laughed. "It worked out better than even I could have imagined. All I needed was a way to make her real enough to convince my ever-logical brother. And then you came along.

"For a time, you were the perfect distraction, and I made you the perfect criminal. Until Italy." She huffed. "Then you had to ruin everything by giving him the book that Nina had hidden in your trunk, instead of letting him discover it for himself. So I had to resort to other means."

This all seemed like a dream to Meg. A bizarre and gruesome dream. She kept fighting to stay awake so that she wouldn't be trapped in it. And she wished her eyes would open, but her lids were weighted down.

"In Italy," she rasped, her throat dry. "But you were gravely ill."

Morgan patted her cheek, leaning over her like an auburn-haired wraith. "A carefully administered poison did the trick. My own recipe. I gave you a bit more. Had to be thorough, you know. After all, I can't have Lucien giving up his pursuit to take a wife, like Father did. Then it would all have been for nothing."

Meg moaned. This couldn't be happening. She wasn't dying, surely. "No."

"Don't worry. Lucien will find your note of remorse along with the name of the mysterious man you've been working for. He'll be sure to hate you forever."

"Guinevere . . ."

"Oh, she'll stay here with your family. I certainly don't want her. And I doubt my brother would want any reminder of you."

A tear slipped from the corner of Meg's eye and drifted down into the whorls of her ear. Vaguely, she felt the weight of the cushion rise and surmised that Morgan had left her alone. And with the settee facing away from the door, no one would find her until it was too late.

If it wasn't already too late.

Chapter 34

The proof is in the pudding

Lucien stalked toward the attic, driven by the consuming need to have all the answers.

Soon, everything would be revealed, once and for all. He despised secrets and the vagueness of uncertainty. Without proof, he felt so powerless, anxious.

A similar feeling had plagued him since the night his parents had died. As a boy, he'd only stood there, frozen and terrified, while their lives had been draining out of their bodies. And the only thing he could do was try to make sense of it, albeit after the fact.

That very same quest had brought him here. And yet, as he reached the narrow stairway, he stopped.

The book was likely waiting in there. He could spend the next few hours searching for it. And when he found it, he would have the leverage he needed to force her hand.

Yet, as soon as the thought entered his mind, he knew he didn't want to coerce her. Oh, he wanted *her*, there was no question about that. One hundred percent certainty. But he was startled to realize that he needed more. Startled to realize that he'd already imagined their life together—her smiles, clever wit, the effervescence of her laughter brightening his days. He'd pictured her inside the rooms and corridors of Caliburn Keep, her presence bringing warmth and light to a place that had been dark for far too long. That was the life he wanted to share with her.

In fact, he needed that life. With her. She'd had it right all along. There should be nothing standing between them, all the barriers stripped away. Only then would she finally, truly, be his.

The book didn't matter to him. Not as much as she did.

As the words filtered into his consciousness, Lucien was hit by a sudden, dizzying tidal wave of certainty. It had been this way from the beginning, only he'd been too blind to see it.

The past two years hadn't been a search for the book, or for Lady Avalon. He had been looking for Meg!

It had all been about her. That was the real reason he'd stayed. Because for every question he'd ever had in his life, she was the answer.

A great weight seemed to lift from his shoulders. He felt buoyant as he turned away from the attic stairs, intending to seek Meg out. Then together they would go to the nursery for Guinevere. And his heart swelled at the knowledge that they had created a child together.

I have a daughter, he thought, thunderstruck. And he wanted a dozen more just like her with cherub cheeks and jammy fingers.

Rounding the corner, he saw the Parrish sisters marching toward him in the corridor. And by their stern expressions he could tell that this was not going to be one of their more pleasant conversations.

"I have a bone to pick with you, Merleton," Maeve said with an upraised index finger, confirming his suspicions.

Myrtle nodded, looking very much like an angry bird with a topknot of downy feathers and her brown shawl flapping at her sides. "And I, as well. How dare you not even taste those little puddings."

"Sister, now is not the time for that. We have more important matters to address." Maeve turned a steely glare on him. "You should be ashamed of yourself for thinking the worst of our Meg. She never stole a thing from you."

He grinned at them. "Without any desire to argue with, or to upset, either of you, I happen to know *otherwi*—"

"You only assume you do. But we have proof to the contrary. Come."

Lucien had been about to soothe their ruffled feathers by admitting that Meg had stolen his heart like a besotted fool. But now he was so intrigued by Maeve's suggestion that he held his tongue and readily agreed to accompany them to their rooms.

A few minutes later, as he was facing a scattered whirlwind of paper scraps, he felt his brow furrow. "And you've stolen *all* of these."

"Oh, these are only the ones from our holiday," Myrtle declared proudly. "We have heaps more in the garret. Three trunks full, to be sure."

He took it all in, remembering the times when they'd wandered off and left Meg alone. Now he knew *what* they'd been doing. "But why?"

"For the grandest wedding breakfast ever held. We have a reputation to uphold, after all. The feast was featured in the society pages. See?"

She thrust a newspaper into his grasp. And sure enough, there was the article remarking on *the vulgar display of fine dishes* and hailing it as a *triumph for Miss P— and Miss P— of Upper Wimpole Street*.

Lucien felt his brow pucker, remembering the entire ordeal of locating proof of these women's identities. And yet, here was a newspaper article practically drawing a map to the Parrish house?

He rarely read the society pages. Those were usually confiscated by his sister, who had more interest in the trivialities of the *ton*. But his hired investigator, on the other hand, should have found something, considering there was an address for these two in London. It didn't make any sense.

And yet, he recalled Meg mentioning an old cantankerous caretaker who'd begun telling everyone that the Parrish sisters had died. That could explain any discrepancies in the report he'd received. But not really.

It became quite clear that he was going to have to break the news to Morgan that Mr. Richards was an abysmal detective. This mystery could have been solved before he'd ever left Calais.

Now he wondered what other obvious clues Richards had missed.

He scrubbed a hand over the back of his neck and lowered the page. "How is it that you left Italy without a trace? I'd stopped at every single hotel and coaching inn searching for the three of you."

The sisters exchanged a speaking glance. Maeve cleared her throat and looked askance, plucking a thread from her sleeve. "That was our doing, as well. You see, there was a reason we needed to leave Italy, and we might have needed to employ certain measures to ensure that any potentially angry *panettiere* or brother of said baker wouldn't be able to follow us."

"So we flirted, in order to gain the silence of the proprietors," Myrtle said with an abashed shrug. "Rather shamelessly, I'm afraid. They were ever so kind. In fact, three of them still write letters—"

"Sister! Have you no shame?"

"At my age, what would be the point?"

Maeve sighed heavily, then looked at Lucien. "So now you know our sordid secrets. And our Meg had nothing to do with it."

"And we would do anything for that girl," Myrtle added. "Anything at all."

Even lie for her so that she could pretend to be Lady Avalon? Lucien wondered.

And yet, he already knew the answer. So he thanked them for clearing up some matters and went downstairs.

He needed to find Meg. But he also needed a moment to alter the proposal he'd practiced earlier that morning . . . before everything had gone to the devil.

Stepping outside, he began to walk the grounds.

It wasn't long before he found himself at the paddock fence just as the stablemaster was exercising one of the Arabians. And that damnable sense of familiarity was back again.

"Is there anything I can do for you, Your Grace?" the man asked when he brought his mount to heel near Lucien.

It wasn't until then that he realized he'd been staring quite fixedly. He was about to shake his head in dismissal, knowing that his investigator would soon send him the report on this man's history. However, having learned a good deal about Richards's capabilities, or lack thereof, Lucien decided on the straightforward approach.

"How long have you been in this trade?"

Beneath the broad brim of his brown felt hat, the man's brow furrowed. "I've worked in these stables my whole life. And my father before me."

"Impossible. I know I've met you before. London, perhaps?"

"Not in London, sir. But aye, we've met," he said with a rusty chuckle. "It was years ago. Can't remember the whole of it, but I think your driver took ill. Then your carriage hit a rut, and you were in a right foul temper. You asked to speak with the marquess, but he was too preoccupied to meet you. Even so, I took care of everything and sent you on your way."

He was starting to remember it now. That was the dreaded day he'd spent in Wiltshire . . .

The hair on the back of his neck lifted. "Why was Lord Hullworth preoccupied?"

"Well, that was nigh on ten years ago, I'd say . . ." He looked thoughtful for a moment and then nodded. "But, if I recall, that was the day Miss Stredwick fell from a tree."

Lucien could almost hear Meg telling him the story.

I remember, when I was young, climbing the wishing tree . . . I put a coin in the cradle of the highest branch and whispered my heart's fervent wish to have my future husband appear that very day . . . But then I fell.

No, it couldn't be, he thought as the breath dropped out of him. And yet, it all made a strange sort of sense now.

How had he not seen it before?

Fate, he thought dazedly. It had been fate all along.

A sudden clap of thunder rumbled in the distance as if the heavens were in agreement.

"MERLETON, HAVE you seen Meg?" Hullworth asked, stopping Lucien the instant he strode through the front doors.

He shook his head. "I was just coming to speak with her."

"Ah. Well, she's probably off looking for Guinevere, too," Hullworth said, frowning. "My niece has escaped again. Johnathon said they were playing hide and seek, and now the nurse is frantic."

"Guinevere likes the butterfly garden. But"—Lucien looked toward the tall windows flanking the doorway and at the bank of dark gray clouds looming over the tree line— "surely, she wouldn't go out in this."

Hullworth shook his head. "Storms frighten her. She would want to be with Meg. When we find one, we'll find the other." Then he put a hand on Lucien's arm. "I've already spoken with the servants, including her maid, and she hasn't tried to run away. So if that's what—"

"No," he said resolutely. "Meg is too brave for that. Besides, she likely wants to rub it in my face that she was right all along."

"Wait. I seem to recall that you were determined to prove that you were right only a couple of hours ago."

"That was before Maeve and Myrtle cornered me upstairs."

"Pestered you into submission, did they?" Hullworth chuckled.

"Very nearly," Lucien admitted. "They dragged me to see their recipe collection and told me why they'd had to leave Italy."

Hullworth's brows inched toward his hairline. "Oh? And why did they *have* to leave Italy?"

"Hmm . . . I realize by your reaction that I may have said too much."

"And you're loyal, too. I like that." The marquess clapped him on the shoulder before they split off in different directions.

At first, there didn't seem to be an alarming sense of urgency. Yet, as the distant calls for Guinevere drifted through the corridors and remained unanswered, Lucien's pulse escalated, and his footsteps quickened.

He stopped a maid in the hall. "Have you seen Miss Stredwick or Guinevere?"

"I took a tea tray to Miss Stredwick in the library a short while ago, Your Grace."

"Thank you." He walked on, his brow furrowing in perplexity.

Surely, Meg wouldn't still be in the library if their daughter was missing. She would have gone to the nursery.

None of this was making sense, and he felt himself pick up the pace as he headed toward the library.

He paused just inside the doorway, where his sister was standing at one of the windows, her back to him. "Morgan, have you seen Meg?"

"I just stepped in here a second ago to watch the storm," she said with a glance over her shoulder. "But I haven't seen her."

He passed a cursory glance toward the grouping of furniture on the far side of the room. From over the curved top of the scalloped settee, he could see the remnants of an afternoon tea on the table. But there was no one else in the room.

"If you see Meg, could you mention that I'm looking for her?"

"Have you forgiven her so soon? All for the best, I suppose. She seemed rather despondent after your argument."

Despondent? That didn't sound like the Meg who'd stormed out with her head held high.

"So you've seen her, then?"

Morgan shrugged, moving toward him. "A moment ago. She was upstairs."

"Where?"

"With those busybodies, the Parrish sisters," she said, sliding her hand into the crook of his elbow and ushering him toward the door.

Lucien's lips parted to explain that it wasn't possible. He had been with them not long ago, and if Meg had gone up after, he would have passed her on the stairs. Before he spoke, however, he thought he heard a sound from deep inside the library.

He paused to look over his shoulder. But with the storm outside and the fire little more than embers in the grate, the room was too dark for him to reveal whatever it might have been.

"Come, brother. I'm sure we'll find her upstairs."

His feet remained rooted to the spot. Something wasn't right. A peculiar cold chill slithered down his spine, sinking into the pit of his stomach. Normally, he would shrug it off. But after experiencing an overwhelming epiphany just a moment ago, he wasn't sure he should discount any sensation, even one of dread.

A low growl of thunder vibrated the windows, and he thought he saw a movement by the curtains in the far corner. He squinted.

Morgan tugged on his arm. "Lucien."

Then a blur darted out from behind one of the drapes.

"Wooshan!" Guinevere called out and ran directly to him, clinging to his legs.

Bending, he picked her up as she buried her tearstained cheeks against his chest. She was shaking.

"Where the devil did she—" Morgan stopped, bewildered.

Lucien held his daughter close, soothing her in passes with a hand along her back. "What's wrong, sweetheart?"

She lifted her face, her eyes flashing as she pointed to Morgan. "Bad."

"Children. How delightful," Morgan said dryly.

And then, there was that sound again. So faint, it was barely a whisper. But this time, it drew him deeper into the room . . . Then he saw Meg.

He jolted, rushing around the settee. Kneeling, he put Guinevere down and picked Meg up in his arms, the flat of his hand roving over her face. She was cold, alarmingly cold, her complexion ashen.

"Meg! Meg!" He tapped her cheek, trying to get her to respond. A breath left her, faint and stale.

Out of the corner of his eye, he saw Guinevere pick up the cup of tea.

Reflexively, he smacked it out of her hand, startling them both when it shattered against the hearth.

"No," he said and pointed to the broken cup. "Bad."

Her eyes filled with tears, but she nodded. "Bad."

"Oh, dear. What's happened?" Morgan gasped, her fingertips at her lips. "I knew she was dejected, but I never thought she would resort to this."

Lucien had had his suspicions over the years about his sister's darker side. But he had always pushed them aside, telling himself that she was hard and aloof because she'd had to be. She'd been the one to save his life, after all.

But there was something in her eyes from time to time that reminded him of that night and the coldly calculated way she'd stabbed that intruder. He saw that look right now, too.

"What have you given her?"

She smiled. "You're being silly. Think about it, brother. She was dismayed. All her schemes had been discovered. She couldn't face the humiliation."

As she spoke, he leaned in to smell Meg's breath, to look for any residue that might aid him. She moaned when he lifted her. "What did you give—"

He stopped when he heard her brother calling out for her in the hall, and shouted, "Hullworth! In here!"

The marquess appeared in the doorway.

"We need a physician," he said, gritting his teeth to hold on to the last shred of his control. Giving himself over to panic wouldn't solve anything.

Concerned, Hullworth moved into the room, just when Morgan turned to dash away.

"Stop her!" Lucien yelled. "Lady Morgan has poisoned your sister. She won't tell me what she gave her."

Hullworth, so horrified by the news, nearly let Morgan slip past him. But he shook himself and reached out to seize her arm. "What have you done?"

"Nothing," she said, all innocence.

"I'll send for a doctor and have a footman sequester her in her room." Hullworth began to pull Morgan to the door.

Lucien felt the faint pulse on Meg's neck. "No, wait! She will have the vials among her things. We cannot let her destroy them. It may be our only hope. Search her maid's rooms as well. Keep them separated."

"It's too late, brother. The poison has already served its purpose."

At that, Lucien saw the cold gleam in Morgan's eyes, and he feared that he was going to lose Meg. And there would be nothing he could do to save her.

Chapter 35

The bitter end

The storm finally broke. A sudden deluge washed over the countryside, powerful enough to prevent the physician from coming.

In Meg's bedchamber, Lucien hovered over her like a man possessed. He barked orders for charcoal and water and muslin, doing everything he could think of to counteract the substances in the vials they'd found sewn into a hidden placket in the maid's satchel.

He refused to stand by and do nothing. And whenever the dread of losing her threatened to overwhelm him, he reminded himself that he was no longer a helpless seven-year-old boy.

He would not let her die! Not when their life hadn't even begun.

So he stayed by her bedside all through the night, and even for the days after Dr. Bedivere arrived, ignoring everyone who told him to go and rest, that he'd done enough. But it wasn't enough. Not yet. Not until she opened her eyes.

Lucien didn't know what time it was when he heard the voices in the hall. All he knew was that there was a patch of pale light leeching in through the part in the drapes.

Through the partially opened door, he saw the gray-haired physician speaking to someone. "I'm not certain I would have thought to give Miss Stredwick doses of charcoal and water. But she likely would have been lost without it."

"'Would have been?'" Hullworth asked, his voice raw.

"It appears as though she has come through the worst of it," Bedivere said. "She's resting now, peacefully."

On the other side of the door, several soft sobs answered this statement.

Lucien wanted to feel relief, but he was still waiting for proof.

Sitting on a chair beside the bed, with Meg's hand in his own, he studied her face. She was still too pale, the flesh beneath her eyes tinged violet, her lips not even a tenth of their usual color.

Her sister-in-law touched him on the shoulder. "I believe you heard that, too. So I suggest you take a moment to eat and freshen up."

"I'm not leaving her, Ellie," he said stubbornly.

"I want to change her bedding and her clothes," she clarified with a blush. When he remained implacable, she added with an uncharacteristic huff, "This is not a request but an order."

Too exhausted to argue, Lucien allowed himself to be shooed from the room. But it was a long while before he stopped pacing in front of her door.

After the midnight chime of the clock in the main hall, Sylvia gave him a gentle shove and made him leave a second time. Touching his cheek with a fond pat, she told him not to come back until after dawn.

So he climbed the stairs to check on Guinevere.

The nursery had two occupants, and he was careful not to wake either one as he crept across the floor. Kneeling, he pressed a kiss to his daughter's wispy blonde hair, inhaling the sweet smell that was similar to her mother's but tinged with the fragrances of honeysuckle and ivy.

My daughter, he thought in wonder as he looked down at drowsy lashes resting on her sleep-pinkened cheeks. He was a father. It hardly seemed real. And yet, he recalled feeling an instant connection to her, a need to protect her that he hadn't experienced when he'd met her cousin, Johnathon.

Meg had told him that she'd written to him for two years, and he hadn't wanted to believe her because he hadn't had proof. Yet, here was the proof, sleeping beneath a blue coverlet, with a little cherub face.

Though, he should have guessed by her name alone. Only Meg would have thought to name their daughter Guinevere.

And he would have known sooner if not for Morgan.

Leaving his daughter's side, he went downstairs and into his sister's bedchamber.

Thinking back, he hadn't paid much attention to her peculiar eagerness to collect the mail at Caliburn Keep. He'd only thought she was toying with his steward's affections. She'd always liked little games like that. But now that he knew more, it was entirely possible that, for the past two years, she'd been hiding Meg's letters. In addition, it shed new suspicion on her insistence to use Mr. Richards. And Lucien had asked Pell to look into that.

The bedchamber was in disarray, the servants having been instructed to leave it untouched for the time being.

Lucien lit the lamp on the low bureau beneath an oval looking glass and sifted through the trunks that had been opened, contents spilled in a mad search to identify the poison. But he wasn't looking for anything in particular. Perhaps he was merely attempting to understand.

He spotted the fringe of a familiar green shawl sticking out from beneath her bed. Bending down, he carefully lifted it, remembering the night in Italy when Meg had used this to wrap the book. It was empty now, the woven cashmere folded flat. But it was proof that Meg had been telling him the truth.

She had not taken the book.

This realization didn't hit him with sudden enlightenment. He wasn't startled by it either.

Because, somewhere in the back of his mind, he'd always known. But perhaps he'd needed to give himself an excuse to chase her, to find her. Perhaps he'd needed to give himself permission to stop his quest for the book so that he could have a new purpose. A new life. And he wanted that life with Meg.

However, Hullworth was right, too. It had to be her decision. He wasn't going to force her to be his wife. She wanted magic, while his nature preferred facts.

He lifted the shawl and breathed it in, hoping that some remnants of her remained in the weave, but they were lost to the stale mustiness of time. He was about to drop it into the trunk, when he heard the rustle of paper. Then a folded sliver of foolscap drifted to the floor.

Seeing the neat scrawl, he bent to pick it up.

Dearest Lucien,

> *Circumstances have forced me away this very night, and I must bid you farewell in this note. From here, the aunts and I travel to Wiltshire and my home at Crossmoor Abbey.*
>
> *My love, as you know, I am a firm believer in fate. Our paths would only have crossed if it was preordained. If you feel the same—if you feel anything at all—then, come to me, Lucien. I will be waiting for you.*
>
> *With all my heart,*
> *Margaret Stredwick*

His fingers curled around the missive, and he closed his eyes. If he was the kind of man to believe in wishes, he would have made one just then.

Morgan had caused this.

Her hatred of him and need for revenge had driven her to commit despicable acts. Not wanting to leave Meg's side, he hadn't confronted his sister about what she'd done. But he'd heard her shouted rantings drift up the stairs as the constable had dragged her out of the house, and so he knew her reasons went back to their father.

Remembering bits and pieces of instances over the years, he was able to surmise how she'd accomplished her deception. And, even though he'd been young when his parents had died, he could recall every aspect of that night. Including the fact that Morgan was the only one who could have known how to take the key from where it was hidden in the hilt of his dagger. Only Morgan could have left the study window open for the intruders. Only Morgan could have hired them.

But Lucien had chosen to ignore those things as a child because she'd saved his life.

She was nearly the only family he had left. Family was something that his father and mother had taught him to treasure.

So he'd chosen to ignore years of petty remarks. Years of her sly comments that left him feeling guilty and ashamed for what he'd supposedly done to cause his parents' deaths. Years of her teaching him through her own deceptions that no one was to be trusted.

On a heavy sigh, he smoothed Meg's note, carefully folded the page, then tucked it in his pocket.

Leaving his sister's room, he was wrung out and listless, his gait slow and ambling, without purpose. It felt like his skin didn't fit him any longer. Like it had been singed to a crisp and was ready to slough off, revealing the raw flesh beneath.

Not paying attention to his footfalls, he went back to Meg's chamber, intent on being at her side.

But he stopped cold when he saw Hullworth speaking to Bedivere, a stark expression on his face. Beside him, Sylvia and Ellie were in tears. Distantly, he heard words like *worsen, deteriorate, lapse*.

Numbly, he started walking again, ignoring Hullworth's request to speak with him.

Inside, Lucien saw Meg in the flickering light of a single taper, her breaths shallow and slow, her skin ashen. There was an eerie stillness in the room that wanted to root him to the floor. But he staggered forward, counting each step, each heartbeat.

Her hand was shockingly cold in his own. Her warmth all but gone. And she looked so small, so frail, so unlike the vibrant woman who had thoroughly transformed his life.

She had made him want to live, to drink in each day, to taste the sweetness of every moment. And now she was just going to leave him? To spend endless years, utterly lost without her?

Agony broke over him, so great that it brought him to his knees. He couldn't breathe. He was choking, his eyes burning with tears. Then his heart fractured, splintering into trillions of shards, the detritus moving through his blood with painful slices, opening every vein.

This couldn't be happening. No, Bedivere had said that she was through the worst of it.

Refusing to believe this was anything more than a nightmare, he squeezed her hand. "Wake up, my little wolf. Come on, now. You've slept long enough."

He tried to sound severe, disapproving, but his throat was raw, shredded from holding on to his last hope.

He couldn't fathom a world without her in it.

Looking at her face, he wanted to see her eyes open to that startling blue and her teeth flash in the smile that he knew so well. But his spectacles were useless disks of glass, wet and smudged. So he tore them off.

He pressed a kiss to her cool cheek, her temple, her hair. He breathed in her scent, needing to hold it inside him forever. Then he whispered a plea to the heavens, to her, to whoever would listen.

"It was fate that brought us together, my love. I know that now. Fate that put you in my path. And fate that tethers us, that will *always* tether us. You are my soul's counterpart, and I cannot live"—his breath stuttered—"without you."

Then the sob he'd been holding at bay finally broke free. "Please, *please*, don't make me live without you."

Chapter 36

The icing on the cake

Meg awoke with a start.

She'd been having the strangest dream. A nightmare of blood and pain and encroaching shadows that smothered her, slowly paralyzing her until she was unable to move or scream or draw a breath. Until the darkness fully claimed her.

She lingered, buried under heaps of cold earth, for what seemed like an eternity. But then she felt herself drifting, light as a downy feather on a breeze to a different place. A void. A nothingness. A world of dark gray skies and a vast, unending plane covered in ash.

Behind her there was darkness, and up ahead, the smallest, barely perceptible glow of light. As she moved toward it, the empty skies altered to dove gray, then gradually slate gray, and finally to a pale cloudy blue.

She liked it there. It was peaceful, the nightmare behind her. She thought she would stay there for a long while and simply rest.

But then she heard a sound from far, far away. Barely a whisper, the voice was hollow and pained and talking about fate.

It made her heart ache to hear those words, and she felt a weight pressing down on her chest. Beneath it, her heart thudded heavily, and it was hard to catch her breath.

Afraid that the suffocating nightmare had returned, her eyes flew open on a strangled gasp.

Her throat felt raw, and her tongue tasted like she'd licked the bottom of the ash bin.

She rolled it around in her dry mouth, behind a wall of chapped lips. Lifting her hand, it felt like it weighed ten stone and she dropped it halfway to her face. That was when she discovered the reason it was so hard to breathe. Someone's head was on her chest.

Recognizing the efficiently layered hair beneath her fingertips, she whispered, "Lucien?"

The bed jolted. She heard a startled inhale. She felt a squeeze of her hand, her face touched, cradled and then kissed.

"You're alive," he breathed against her forehead. "And awake."

She was about to make a quip about how strange a greeting that was, but opening her pasty mouth proved too difficult. *Had* she licked the bottom of an ash bin?

She heard the scrape of chair legs, followed by the sound of items clattering to the floor as he groped for something on the table. He cursed. And then a light flared to life, the solitary flame blindingly bright.

She squinted as he brought it near, while he clumsily hooked his spectacles over his ears. Then he hovered over her, scrutinizing. As he did, the flame wavered, light flickering in stark shadows over his face, making him look thin and drawn as if he hadn't slept in days.

"Your color has returned." A sigh left him, and he wavered on unsteady legs. So he set the chamberstick down, took her hand again and brought it to his cheek. Then he smiled. "And you're warm, too. Are you thirsty? Do you think you can drink?"

She opened her mouth, but nothing came out except for a dry rasp. So she nodded.

He moved swiftly, nearly overturning the highbacked chair, the legs scraping across the floor. Gripping the porcelain ewer by the handle, he stumbled around the room in disoriented haste. She'd never seen him like this before—bumbling around as he searched for the glass, muttering under his breath, only to realize it had been on the bedside table all along.

Gently, he propped her head up on the pillows and brought the glass to her lips. "There, now."

The first sip was painful, as if her throat was lined with corn husks. But the coolness felt too refreshing to stop. After several grateful gulps, he lifted it away for her to catch her breath.

"Much better," she whispered hoarsely, her tongue clumsy. Then she nudged upward in a wordless demand for more.

After she drank her fill, he set the glass down and slumped into the chair. Leaning forward, he took her hand and laid his cheek in her palm, gazing at her. "Am I dreaming this?"

It was only then that she noticed that his eyes were red-rimmed, his voice as shredded as her own. And the memory of the library came back to her.

"Your sister," she said, and he nodded, answering the unspoken query in her eyes. "Did she . . . hurt anyone else?"

He shook his head. "No one else drank the poison. Our daughter is safe and sound asleep. If it wasn't for our little escape artist, I might not have found you in time." His breath hitched as he turned his head and pressed a lingering kiss into her palm. "And I couldn't bear it if you were gone. I love you too much to lose you."

Her throat constricted on a sudden rush of joy, and all she could do was whisper his name. "Lucien."

"Surely, that doesn't surprise you," he said. And then, in a smug, scholarly way, he added, "I've hypothesized the likelihood of such an occurrence since the day we met."

She rolled her eyes. "You have not. The only thing you hypothesized that day was how I managed to steal your book, which I did not do."

"Which I knew all along as well."

"What a liar you are," she said with a papery laugh that left her winded.

A concerned frown notched his brow for an instant before he schooled his features. Then he reached for the glass and held it to her lips once more. She drank dutifully before a wave of exhaustion crashed over her and she yawned.

Tucking the coverlet around her, he pressed a kiss to her forehead and temple. "We'll simply have to agree to disagree. After we marry, we'll have many years to argue over it. But for now, you need your rest."

"Was that a proposal or a command?" she asked, her brows lifting. Her heart fluttered, too, but she tried to ignore it.

This was about the rest of her life and her own legacy. If she had learned anything over the course of these last two years, it was to look before she leapt.

"Darling, you know we'll be married. We have a child together."

"It seems to be all wrapped up in a conveniently tidy package, doesn't it? I imagine it even looks good on paper—husband plus wife plus child equals marriage. But what if I want more?"

"More than my promise to love you with every beat of my heart for the rest of my life?"

She swallowed. And even though it pained her to do so, she nodded.

He studied her for a moment, puzzled. Then a flame seemed to ignite behind his eyes, and gold flecks shone bright behind the lenses of his spectacles.

"I understand," he stated simply. "You require proof. And you shall have it, because I'm not going anywhere."

Every day of the next month, Lucien asked her to marry him. And every day, she refused.

Meg's reasons began with solid concerns. Such as the fact that his proposal came from the shock of her near death or even misplaced guilt over his sister's involvement. However, as the month progressed, her reasons started to sound like . . . well . . . precisely what they were. *Excuses*. And her heart broke every time she said no.

But what else could she do? She couldn't very well pass on the legend of the Stredwick certainty to Guinevere when both of her parents hadn't been struck by it. Only one of them had.

Then again, perhaps she was being foolish. All that truly mattered was that they loved each other. Right? She knew it was impossible to expect her completely logical duke to suddenly accept the fact that they were meant to be.

She sighed. These musings had been her bosom companion for over a month now.

After the first three weeks, her strength had improved enough for her to join the family at dinner. By the fourth week, she could climb the stairs without needing to rest to catch her breath. And by the fifth week, she was walking in the garden, hand in hand with Guinevere.

It was on such a day, with the cool autumn breeze sending cyclones of fallen leaves skittering along the path, that mother and daughter spotted Lucien dropping down from the bowed branch of a tree.

And not just any tree, but *the* tree.

The same one that she'd slipped a coin into and fervently whispered the words *I wish to meet my soul's counterpart. Bring him to me. Please, oh, please.*

"Papa!" Guinevere called out, releasing Meg's hand to scamper down the lane in her pink pelisse. She still called him *Wooshan* on occasion, but it was mostly *Papa* now.

The three of them spent hours together each day, having tea and reading books, with Lucien dramatically recounting the tales of King Arthur, Excalibur and the Knights of the Round Table. Not surprisingly, Guinevere loved to hear about her namesake, and both she and her cousin, Johnathon, had developed a fondness for swinging wooden swords.

There were great battles waged in the nursery these days, Meg thought with a smile.

Up ahead, Guinevere giggled as Lucien lifted her impossibly high in the air. Then he spun her around, gave her a kiss and said, "You are a wonder of creation."

Meg's heart stopped and seemed to swell. She splayed her hand over that susceptible organ to keep it from bursting as tears gathered in her eyes. Oh, how she loved that man.

Lucien turned then, and his gaze alighted on her. Concern glanced across his features for an instant before she offered a smile to let him know that all was well. Or at least, it would be soon. Because when he asked her to marry him today, she was going to say *yes*.

She turned to discreetly blot her tears and saw the nurse coming out of the house. Then Lucien set Guinevere on her feet. "Give your mother a kiss and then go with Miss Elaine. Then later, I'll tell you a story about a king named Pellinore."

With a squeal of delight, Guinevere scampered back to Meg, pausing just long enough to press a wet kiss to her lips before dashing off.

Lucien was by Meg's side at once, the brush of his fingertips tender on her cheek. "Are you up for a longer walk today?"

"I'm perfectly hale, as I've been telling you all week," she said, a teensy bit crossly, too. But she couldn't help it. He was treating her as if she were fragile.

Well, except for when he kissed her. And oh, how he kissed her.

Every night, he was like a man starved, a knight returning from battle, leaving her trembling and weak-kneed at the door to her bedchamber. Then he would stop and gaze down at her hungrily . . . and ask her to marry him.

He wasn't playing fair.

She slid him a sideways look, and his mouth twitched as if her petulant mood amused him.

Covering her hand with his, he strolled along the winding path toward the walled garden. "Have I ever told you about the first day I came here?"

"I believe I already know this story. I found you sitting in the butterfly garden with Guinevere."

"True. But that wasn't the first time."

Her head tilted. "You'd been to Crossmoor Abbey before?"

"Years ago, in fact," he said with a nod, surprising her. "The experience was so confounding that I spent the past decade avoiding Wiltshire altogether."

She laughed as he told her about the directionless driver who had taken him north instead of south, how a storm blew in without the slightest atmospheric forewarning, which exposed a colossal stone in the middle of the road, which broke the carriage wheel.

"What an utter disaster," she said with a laugh. "After suffering all of that, I'm surprised you weren't stranded."

"I would have been, if not for your stablemaster. Mr. Weston set everything to rights, and I was able to depart without further incident."

She shook her head. "How odd that you should have been here, and yet my brother never mentioned it to me, and neither did Aunt Sylvia."

"I made an attempt to pay a call on your brother, to thank him for his hospitality, but he was preoccupied, as was your aunt, I imagine. There had been an accident."

"What kind of . . . accident?" The hair on her nape suddenly lifted. And even before he answered, she knew.

Lucien casually guided her beneath the ivy-covered arch and into the garden. "Apparently, his little sister had fallen from a tree."

"You were here that day?"

"The most perplexing day of my life. I could not make sense of it."

And yet, it all made perfect sense to her. No wonder she hadn't felt as strongly for Daniel in all the years she'd known him as she had for Lucien from the very first moment they'd met.

As she gazed up at him, the gold flecks in his dark eyes sparkled, and there was an arrogant curl at one corner of his mouth. She stopped in her tracks and faced him. "How long have you known?"

He shrugged. "A while."

"All these weeks that you've been asking me to marry you?" When he nodded, she squinted at him, and he chuckled. She jabbed the center of his waistcoat with an accusatory finger. "And do you finally accept the fact that fate played a hand in our meeting?"

"I do," he said without appearing the least bit contrite for having kept this from her. Lifting her fingers, he pressed a kiss to the tips, then gathered her close, his hands slipping beneath the fringe of her shawl to splay over her lower back.

She tilted her face up to his. "Then, why did you wait to tell me?"

"I wanted you to be ready to hear it. Because the instant you say *yes*"—he brushed his lips across hers with enticing promise—"I'm going to take you."

The man truly wasn't playing fair.

Weak-kneed though she might be, she managed to put space between them. "Well, if you think I'm going to accept the proposal of a man who claims to have no choice in the matter—"

He kissed her into silence, hard and ravenous, until she melted against him.

"A wise person once said that there are two kinds of people in the world—those who enjoy experiencing the wonder of everyday occurrences, and those who dissect every component down to the very basic elements. I am one of the few scholars in the former category," he said smugly. "After all, in order to truly appreciate the miracles in one's life, one must first accept that not everything can be proven beyond a shadow of a doubt. Some things simply *are*. There is no explanation."

She felt the dubious lift of her brows. "Are you telling me that you didn't calculate every single coincidence between us in search of proof?"

"I filled an entire ledger," he said with a trace of chagrin. "Then I left it on the bough of your wishing tree."

She laughed brightly, throwing her arms around him. "And what did you whisper to the wishing tree?"

He held her gaze, his expression solemn, earnest. "I said, *Let her know that I am here . . . waiting.*"

Her heart bloomed, blossoming in a sudden burst of joy that she couldn't contain. She smiled as tears spilled from her eyes. "Marry me, Lucien."

Epilogue

Six weeks later

The portrait artist expelled a huff of impatience. The progeny of the Duke and future Duchess of Merleton refused to stand still for a single instant.

"Itchy," Guinevere groused, tugging on the ruffled collar of her dress as she stood in front of Lucien.

"I know, sweetheart," Meg said from beside him, breathtaking and regal in a brocaded gown of silvery blue and a long train that swept around her feet, which their daughter had tried to wear as a cape just a moment ago. "But a lady never fidgets."

Their little lady grumbled her disagreement, likely scowling for the painter.

She lasted thirteen seconds before she wriggled again. And then, apparently fed up with it all, she dashed off and darted out the door.

The nurse followed in pursuit. The artist groaned but continued his brushstrokes.

"Perhaps," Meg whispered without moving from her pose, "we could do this another time, darling."

Lucien spoke through clenched teeth. "I'm determined to see this through. Our family portrait will hang in the gallery of Crossmoor Abbey before we leave, directly after the ceremony on Wednesday."

"After the wedding breakfast, you mean."

"I still don't understand why we agreed to wait for the banns when I'd already obtained a special license."

The artist issued a disapproving throat-clearing. "Your Grace is glowering."

"This is not a glower," Lucien muttered for Meg's ears only. "If it were, that man would be quaking in his spattered, buckled shoes."

Meg stifled a laugh. "We are waiting because the aunts have been preparing for weeks. And they were over the moon when you jotted down a few of your family's recipes from memory and then chose to share them."

"Had I known that my actions would have caused this endless series of days to commence, I would have remained selfish."

For the past month and a half, Hullworth had turned into a bloody overlord, intercepting nearly every one of Lucien's attempts to be alone with Meg. And it was driving him mad not to sleep beside her.

She nudged him subtly with her hip. "Surely, they haven't all been endless. In fact, I can recall several rather satisfying stolen moments."

"I want you all to myself, for hours, days, weeks," he murmured, fighting the urge to slip his arms around her, portrait be damned.

"Well, all we must do is be patient for a little while long—"

Her words broke off as a sudden peal of giggles erupted from the doorway, just as Guinevere streaked into the parlor without wearing a stitch of clothing.

The nurse gave chase. And Meg's shoulders began to shake.

"Don't laugh," he said but felt his own lips curve into a grin.

Then their daughter scurried beneath the gown's train, her exposed feet kicking as she squealed in delight.

The artist tossed down his brush, threw up his hands and then stormed out. "I give up!"

The absolute insanity of the past few hours suddenly broke over Lucien. His head fell back on a hearty laugh as he pulled Meg close. *Merlin's teeth*, but he loved his family.

"Beg pardon, Your Grace," the nurse said as she held their daughter's dress. "The little miss rushed into the breakfast room and stole a handful of—"

"Coddled eggs," Meg concluded on a thick swallow. Her smile faded, and she turned a bit green.

Lucien didn't even have a chance to ask what was wrong before she hefted up her skirts and made a mad dash for the door. But she didn't make it farther than the demilune table before she bent over, gripped the two handles on either side of a gilded Warwick vase and cast up her accounts.

Worried, he went to her side, soothing her with gentle passes along her back, and smoothing the hair from her face. "My darling, you're ill. This is all too much for you. It's too soon."

She shook her head as she dabbed a handkerchief to the side of her mouth and then discreetly draped it over the opening of the vase.

"I'm perfectly hale." When she looked up at him, her color was swiftly returning, her eyes bright, a secret smile on her lips. "This has been happening for a few days now."

Alarm sprinted through him. "That's it, then. I'm postponing the wedding."

"I don't believe that would be a wise decision. Or else my brother will be quite angry at you when he discovers that all his efforts were for naught," she whispered and splayed a hand over her midriff. Then she stepped closer and reached up to adjust his spectacles. "You're looking a bit stunned, *Herzog*."

He blinked, then tightened his arms around her, grinning.

"I imagine I'll wear that expression quite often for the rest of my life. Because I am surprised every time I look into your eyes and fall in love all over again."

🦋

"HAVE ANY of you seen Lucien?" Meg asked as she entered the drawing room the following afternoon.

She found Ellie standing with her friends, Lady Northcott and Lady Holt, at the bank of mullioned windows lining the far wall. Jane and Winn had arrived earlier with their husbands and children in tow, bringing an abundance of joy and warmth to the wedding festivities.

"I don't see Merleton, but it's possible that he's assisting with the crate," Winn offered, absently sweeping a stray strawberry blonde curl from her cheek without turning away from the view.

Curious about what could be holding their rapt attention, Meg stepped farther into the room. "Crate?"

She went to the window to look toward the courtyard. But when she peered through the diamond paned glass, she didn't find Lucien with the others. However, what she did see made the flesh of her brow pucker in confusion. "Is that . . . chainmail?"

"Lord Holladay arrived a short while ago with the suit of armor that Merleton is giving to Brandon," Ellie explained. "Apparently, he brought a few other things from Caliburn Keep."

"And the gentlemen have decided to hold a tournament of sorts," Jane concluded.

Sure enough, the men were engaging in mock-battles, sparring against each other. Their exertions caused their breaths to crystallize in the crisp November air. And, as one might expect, Maeve and Myrtle were standing nearby in their pelisses, pink-cheeked and grinning as they waved colorful ribbons, as if to bestow their favors on knights errant.

"What is it with men and their swords?" Ellie asked with a shake of her head, attempting to sound disapproving. But she wasn't fooling Meg.

Winn agreed and tsked. "They are nothing more than fully grown boys."

And yet, none of them turned away from the spectacle.

"Raven does look rather exceptional in that jerkin. His biceps should be sculpted in bronze," Jane said with an appreciative hum.

"The sight of Asher in tights and a codpiece is not something I'll ever want to forget," Winn practically purred. "In fact, I wonder why those ever fell out of fashion."

"And just look at the way Brandon wields that heavy halberd," Ellie added breathlessly. "Good heavens!"

Then the three of them looked at each other and started to giggle like schoolgirls.

"I think my aunts have the right idea. Perhaps we should go out and join them."

Jane grinned. "Now that is a flawless plan."

"But wait," Winn said, hesitating. "Haven't we forgotten something?"

Their collective gazes fell on Meg an instant before she was taken by the hand and led to the rosewood table in the corner. And in its center sat a bandbox tied with string.

Ellie slid it toward her. "It's from all of us."

Meg wasn't one to feign a disinterest in presents. There was no pretense of *Oh, you shouldn't have* or *For me? Really?* that fell from her lips. Instead, she dove right in with a quick tug on the string and a lift of the lid, tossing it aside. Inside the box was a sheaf of paper, a bottle of ink, and a pen fashioned with an ornate steel nib. She picked it up, testing the pleasing weight of it in her hand. "It's absolutely perfect. I'll be able to write so many letters with this."

Not for the first time, her heart ached at the thought of leaving Crossmoor Abbey. Even though she wanted to start a life with Lucien more than anything, she would still miss her home.

"True," Ellie said, squeezing her hand. "And I expect several from you each week. However, we did have something else in mind."

Jane nodded. "As you know, we started to write a book a few years ago on the *Marriage Habits of the Native Aristocrat.*"

"But it turned out that we learned more about the *Mating Habits of Scoundrels,*" Winn added with a playful lift of her brows.

"And now we invite you to write your story."

Meg felt the sting of happy tears along the rims of her eyes. "I'm honored. But Lucien isn't a scoundrel. In fact, I was the one who pursued him without ever intending to marry—" She stopped when it suddenly occurred to her. "Wait a minute. I'm the scoundrel of my own story!"

A burst of bright laughter abruptly spilled down her cheeks and they joined in her merriment.

"We've come to realize that we all have a bit of scoundrel in us," Jane said with an erudite gleam in her eyes.

Winn winked. "Our husbands bring it out of us."

"In the best possible ways," Ellie added. "Now, let's go down to shamelessly ogle our gentlemen."

Yet, as they entered the courtyard, Meg still didn't see Lucien. Where could he have gone?

Before she went back inside to look for him again, she asked the aunts.

"I believe Merleton is in the kitchens, dear," Myrtle chirruped as she tied a ribbon to the pommel of Pell's sword.

Maeve tutted. "We weren't supposed to say anything, sister. It is a secret, remember?"

"Rather more of a surprise than anything," Lucien said from behind them, descending the terrace steps. On his way to her side, he raked a hand through his hair and adjusted

the cuffs of his coat. But there was a spray of powder—
flour, perhaps?—on his waistcoat and, as usual, his lenses
were smudged.

She tilted her head in question. "What have you been up to?"

Dutifully, he put his glasses into her waiting palm and
she cleaned them. Then he lowered his head as she lifted up
on her toes to set him to rights, their simple routine almost
like the steps of a dance. And with her face close to his, he
grinned and whispered, "All in good time."

Before she could pester him for more information, a
sleek black carriage arrived, the door emblazoned with the
crest of the Marquess of Savage. Her heart lifted at once.
Prue was here! Even though they corresponded every week,
they hadn't seen each other since shortly after Guinevere
was born and Prue's own daughter was just over a year old.
Meg couldn't wait for their two little girls to meet again.

As they waited for the occupants to emerge, Lucien
spoke for her ears alone. "I stopped by the parlor and noticed that our portrait is underway again. Without us."

"Would you rather be standing there, dressed in all your
finery?"

"Certainly not. I'm just wondering what methods of co-
ercion you used on our temperamental painter, and whyever
didn't you employ them before?"

"I merely gave him several sketches of us for a frame of
reference. Then I warned him that, if he couldn't work with
those, I would commission him to paint a dozen portraits of
Guinevere."

Lucien laughed. "Have I told you that you're absolutely
brilliant?"

"Not today," she beamed up at him, batting her lashes before she slipped from his side.

She went to greet Prue and they whispered in secret
before Lucien came close enough to hear. "Any news to
report?"

"Only the very best," Prue whispered and handed over a heavy leather satchel.

Meg was brimming with excitement, but she refused to take the credit. "It's all because of you. So I think you should tell him."

"Oh, but I couldn't. The last time I met the duke . . . well, let's just say, he was a little suspicious of my motives."

"Fear not, moonflower," Lord Savage said fondly, turning from the open carriage with his daughter on his hip. Her pale head rested on his shoulder as she yawned and opened a pair of sleepy green eyes. "I'll be glad to take the credit. I've been wanting to tell Merleton *I told you so* for ages." He flashed a grin.

Meg knew that look. He'd been her brother's schoolmate and there was nothing Savage liked better than a friendly competition. "Be nice, Leo."

"What?" he asked, all innocence. "I'm *Saint Savage*, remember?"

Lucien joined them, those intense river-stone eyes bearing down on the marquess. "And what's all this?"

"I was just about to tell your betrothed about the time when you came to London and I mentioned knowing an exceptional investigator, but you refused my assistance." He pursed his lips thoughtfully. "Then I heard a rumor about a certain duke losing a certain book and . . ."

Ever-perceptive, Lucien glanced down to the leather satchel and back to the marquess. And his voice was barely audible when he asked, "Did you find it, then?"

"No," he said, a smirk remaining on his lips. "My exceptional investigator, Mr. Devaney, found this tucked behind a loose stone in the ruins of St. Michael's Tower on the Isle of Avalon."

Lucien appeared dumbfounded and it was up to Meg to put the leather strap in his grip. That seemed to jolt him out of his stupor. He opened the satchel and reached inside to take the cloth-wrapped tome. And as he trailed his fingers reverently over the bejeweled cover, Meg felt her heart pinch. She knew how much this meant to him.

He shook his head. "I cannot believe it was in Glastonbury Tor all this time. That's just a stone's throw from Caliburn Keep." He reached out to clasp Leo's shoulder. "Thank you, Savage. And if you need to hear it, you were right."

The marquess grinned. "I always need to hear it. Now, what do you say to a little sword fight between friends?"

"Men," Prue said to Meg, rolling her eyes.

Lord Holladay stepped up, his eyes widening as his gaze fell on the book. "Cousin, is that . . . the book? You know, I haven't actually seen it since we were children."

"*Our* book, Pell," Lucien corrected, putting the treasure into his cousin's arms. "Our legacy. We are the faithful stewards who will guard and protect it."

"Do you mean it?" Pell blinked at him, his expression falling somewhere between awe and disbelief.

"Well, you couldn't do any worse than Merleton's done," Savage said with a chuckle.

Lucien gave him a dark look, but laughed, too.

Then he turned to face the rest of their party, who were all gathering close for a peek at the legendary book.

Standing at Meg's side, he settled a hand against her lower back. "It was a long-standing tradition at Caliburn Keep that we celebrated family and friends with a festival, merriment and food. I intend to restore that very tradition and I hope that each of you will join us in the coming years. In the meantime, however, Hullworth has been good enough to lend me the use of his kitchens and, with the help of his staff, we've prepared a small pre-wedding feast. So, without further ado, I invite you and the children to join us in the ballroom for some revelry."

"You planned all this?" Meg asked as they walked inside behind the others, except for Pell who lingered nearby, slowly carrying the book as if it were made of glass. "But I thought you couldn't wait to leave Crossmoor Abbey."

Lucien shook his head as he led them away from the main party. "While it is true that I am impatient to have you to myself, I also want to share our lives, not separate them. So I intended to bring a certain percentage of Caliburn Keep to Crossmoor Abbey."

She sighed adoringly. "That is a lovely thought. Have I told you how absolutely wonderful you are?"

"Not today," he said. "But I cannot take all the credit. The servants agreed to keep you away from the ballroom for the past week while we decorated it in true Arthurian style. Not only that, but my cook, Mrs. Philpot, arrived yesterday with boxes of iced buns. And, make no mistake, we will all be ready to depart after the wedding breakfast. However, there's one more surprise I have for you."

"Well, don't keep me waiting," she said with an eager squeeze of his arm.

"I've made you a pie."

Pell groaned from behind them. "Here we go again."

"What's in it?"

"Trust me," Pell interjected. "It's better if you don't ask."

They entered a small room that faced the walled garden. This was referred to as the butterfly parlor. A round table sat at its center, a glass dome shielding a deep pie with a glossy fluted crust. And when he lifted the dome with a flourish, the air was filled with sweet scents of cinnamon and clove.

"Mmm," she hummed appreciatively. He cut it precisely down the center, the interior was essentially comprised of a layer of mincemeat, topped with a surfeit of . . .

"Cherries," she said with a broad grin. He had made her a pie. He had planned a festival. He had brought Caliburn Keep to Crossmoor Abbey and all of it made her heart swell with so much love she couldn't contain it. And she wouldn't want to, even if she could.

Just as she was about to wrap her arms around him, Pell squeezed in beside her and gave the pie a cursory sniff. "Well, it smells better than those frog brains, or whatever you had me eat last time."

"It looks quite scrumptious, doesn't it?" she asked, wafting the plate under Pell's nose. "And do you know what? I think you should be the first one to try it."

He blinked at her. "Really?"

"Indeed," Lucien said, already cutting a thick wedge. He seemed to know exactly what Meg had in mind, for he put the tapered end against Pell's lips, encouraging him to take hold of it with his teeth. "Now, don't get any on the book."

Then, without a by-your-leave, he was nudged backward over the threshold and the door closed in his face.

Meg giggled and wrapped her arms around Lucien's neck. "Lock the door, Herzog. We're going to need privacy for this."

"What do you have in mind?" he asked, smiling as he nibbled the corner of her mouth.

"Something guaranteed to make your lenses foggy."

Vivienne Lorret launches a brand-new series in late 2023 with a story about a debutante who makes up a fake fiancé . . .

THE LIARS CLUB

Next month, don't miss these exciting new love stories only from Avon Books

Max Wilde's Cowboy Heart by Jennifer Ryan

When a horrible misunderstanding drove Max Wilde and Kenna Baker apart, Max thought his chance to find love was gone forever. Now, their lives have collided once again, as Kenna is the only witness to a murder and needs a place to hide. Max is determined to keep her safe on his ranch, and also maintain an emotional distance. But as they spend more time together, the closer they get.

A Kiss in the Moonlight by Cathy Maxwell

Dara hatches a daring plan: she and her two sisters gamble what little they own to finance a London Season. It seems her crazy plot might work . . . but then Dara's plans are challenged by the likes of Michael Brogan, who provokes Dara as much as he attracts her. The handsome, clever, and rising politician is definitely not a duke, but tempting all the same.

The Portrait of a Duchess by Scarlett Peckham

Cornelia Ludgate dismisses love and marriage as threats to freedom. But when an inheritance gives her the chance to fund the cause of women's rights—on the condition she must wed—she is forced to reveal a secret: she's already married. To a man she hasn't seen for twenty years. Although determined not to sacrifice her principles for passion, Cornelia is still drawn to the man whose very being threatens her independence.

REL 0223